Praise for

JUDY BAER

and her novels

Norah's Ark

"Fans of Baer's *The Whitney Chronicles* will enjoy this
lighthearted Christian romance."
—*Publishers Weekly*

Million Dollar Dilemma

"*Million Dollar Dilemma* is a million-dollar treasure you
must read! And give a wonderful gift to a friend."
—*Armchair Interviews*

"From laughter to tears to wonderment,
readers will feel like such a part of the story and
definitely be inspired. First-time readers of Ms. Baer
are bound to rush out in search of her backlist after
finishing *Million Dollar Dilemma*."
—*CataRomance Reviews*

"Baer's reputation—bolstered by the popular novel
The Whitney Chronicles—means that this new novel
is likely to sell briskly, especially since the eponymous
Whitney makes an appearance among its cast of
supporting characters."
—*Publishers Weekly*

The Whitney Chronicles

"This debut novel in Steeple Hill's new Christian chick lit line is absolutely fantastic. Baer has created fascinating characters with real-life problems and triumphs that show readers the details of living out faith daily. A side story featuring breast cancer and depression gives complexity to the plot. Full of humor and infused with God's truths, this book will allow readers to come away with a happy heart and increased faith."
—*Romantic Times BOOKreviews*

"Whitney Blake...becomes not just a fictional character, but a 'girlfriend'—so much so that readers might have to remember they can't meet her for a cup of coffee. This is...real life, good and bad...subtle nuggets of wisdom...experiencing life with Whitney does offer a sense of camaraderie...fun twists and witty lines... Baer's writing is fresh and imaginative as she seamlessly weaves diary entries into a story many will relate to and enjoy."
—*Christian Retailing*

"With sixty-five books to her credit, Baer knows how to spin a good tale...the results are genuinely enjoyable."
—*Publishers Weekly*

JUDY BAER

THE BABY
CHRONICLES

Steeple
Hill®

Published by Steeple Hill Books™

STEEPLE HILL BOOKS

Steeple
Hill®

ISBN-13: 978-0-373-78587-2
ISBN-10:   0-373-78587-9

THE BABY CHRONICLES

www.SteepleHill.com

Printed in U.S.A.

For Tom, who is patient beyond measure.
I love you.

People were bringing little children to him in order that he might touch them; and the disciples spoke sternly to them. But when Jesus saw this, he was indignant and said to them, "Let the little children come to me: do not stop them; for it is to such as these that the kingdom of God belongs. Truly I tell you, whoever does not receive the kingdom of God as a little child will never enter it." And he took them up in his arms, laid his hands on them, and blessed them.

—*Mark* 10:13–16

Chapter One

Monday, March 1

My assistant, Mitzi, cancelled the office waiting room subscriptions to *Vogue* and *Elle* and replaced them with *Fit Pregnancy* and *American Baby.* I realize now that I should have appreciated it when she was only giving me fashion advice.

Frankly, the one magazine Mitzi should be allowed to read is her signature publication, *Harper's Bizarre* (sic).

My name is Whitney Blake Andrews, and today I'm starting a new volume of my personal journal. It's been quite a ride since that first day two years ago when I began keeping what I fondly call *The Whitney Chronicles.* My best friend, Kim Easton, has overcome breast cancer, and her son Wesley has turned three. I've been made vice president of Innova Software, located in downtown Minneapolis, and been married for almost two years to Dr. Chase Andrews, the most incredible husband in the universe. That's my personal bias, of course.

And Mitzi Fraiser is still the most aggravating person on this planet, but she's *my* aggravating person, so I love her anyway. Most of the time…at least some of the time…in brief spurts… Hmm… I *do* remember having a pleasant thought about her sometime between last Christmas and New Year's Eve. I think.

Kim stopped over after work tonight so that we could debrief each other on our day at the office. She likes to come to my house for three reasons. There is no LEGO embedded in the carpet, Ernie and Elmo are not the anchormen during the evening news, and there is always chocolate.

I've been sacrificing myself in the name of medical science, researching the curative uses for chocolate. It has the same health-promoting chemicals as fruits and veggies. It's the least I can do for the good of mankind. How often did I dream Mom would tell me to eat my chocolate cake instead of my Brussels sprouts?

Oh, yes, that's another thing I don't understand about Mitzi. She hates chocolate. This is another indication that she is an extraterrestrial—something Kim and I have suspected all along.

"What's up with Mitzi these days?" Kim curled her feet beneath her on my overstuffed couch, looking all of fifteen, instead of her actual thirty-three years. "She's been acting weird lately."

"More than usual? How can you tell?"

Kim grinned and took a piece of milk chocolate with almonds. "The magazines, for one thing. I got a copy of *Pregnancy* in my mailbox this morning. And the fact that she's turned into the food police. Did you see her whip that Twinkies out of Bryan's hand yesterday? You'd have thought he was having a toxic-waste sandwich."

Bryan Kellund was my assistant before Mitzi was assigned to me. He's the only person I've ever known who can disappear in plain sight. He fades into the background as though he's wearing wallpaper camouflage. That's why I'm so amazed that he found a girlfriend who's even more inconspicuous and retiring than he. They cook tapioca pudding to spice up their dessert menu.

Bryan's current idea of subterfuge is sneaking into the office break room and substituting decaffeinated coffee for the fully leaded stuff and then patiently watching and waiting for Harry's and Mitzi's energy to wane. I've caught him a time or two, but I never say anything about it because I've done it myself. Anything that makes Mitzi and Harry a little less hyperactive is fine with me.

"I've learned not to attempt to figure out what Mitzi is up to," I said. "Frankly, I'm more curious about Harry."

My boss, Harry Harrison, is a software genius and our office mascot. Okay, *Harry's* not our mascot, exactly, but his *hair* is. Two or three years ago he discovered the curly perm and he's resembled a Chia Pet ever since.

"I think he's depressed," I murmured, more to myself than to Kim.

"Harry? Don't you think *I'd* recognize it if Harry were depressed?"

Kim has battled depression much of her life. She now has it under control with medication and lots of exercise to get those endorphins moving.

"Wouldn't you be depressed if your claim to fame

was being washed down the shower drain?" I persisted. "Have you looked, really looked, at Harry's head lately?"

Understanding dawned on Kim's pixielike features. "His *thinning* hair, you mean?"

"Thinning? Kim, he's only six strands away from a comb-over."

"Shades of Rudy Giuliani—you're right. No wonder he skulks into the office wearing that wool felt hat that makes him look like an Indiana Jones wannabe."

"We need to be nice to Harry. My own dad's hair is starting to thin, and he's very sensitive about it. Mother caught him wearing a baseball cap in the shower last week. She says he can't stand to see the reflection of his head in the mirror."

And that's only one of the many weird aging games my parents play. Dad now insists he's in male menopause. What it really is is revenge for what my mother put him through when she was "of a certain age."

"'…vanity of vanities! All is vanity,'" Kim intoned.

"You can say that again. Harry and Dad may be prime examples, but look at all the silly, pointless things we've done…."

"The grapefruit diet?"

I never did get into that. I was in love with a cabbage soup diet that produced enough gas to replace fossil fuels.

"Remember the Approved Veggie Diet? The only 'approved' vegetables were arugula, chicory, bok choy, kohlrabi, leeks and dandelion greens."

We waxed nostalgic about the smoothie diet—best made with ice cream; the metabolism-revving diet—

basically seasoning everything with cayenne pepper; and "EEAT"—Ecclesiastical Eaters Anonymous Training, a diet group at church that actually worked.

Kim rubbed her brow. "What does my weight matter when Wesley is etching new creases here every day? No one cares about my figure when they see the Grand Canyon on my forehead."

"'Can any of you by worrying add a single day to your life span?'" I quoted, knowing just how crazy she is about that naughty little buzz saw of a boy. "But back to Harry. If food is the way to a man's heart, then good hair is the way to his ego. If Harry actually goes bald, he'll have to start therapy."

"Men are definitely wired differently from women," Kim agreed. "I see it in Wesley already. He and his dad spend hours piling blocks into pyramids and knocking them down. They laugh and high-five each other like they've just invented football. Yet when I ask Kurt to vacuum the floor, he says 'Didn't I just do that *last* month?' as if he detests repetition in any form."

"Knocking things down and picking things up are two entirely different concepts. One is male, the other, female. Even Chase says so."

Chase. Two years of marriage, and I love him more than ever. God really knew what He was doing when He put us together. It doesn't hurt that his sandy hair is shot with gold, his eyes are an inky Crayola blue, and his physique… There's only one way to describe it—hunky. Oh, yes, and he's crazy about me, and a doctor besides. This morning he sent me yellow roses for no reason at all except that he loves me.

"Now you're thinking about *him*," Kim observed

grumpily. "You've got that moonstruck look on your face again."

"And you don't feel that way about Kurt anymore?" I teased.

"Of course I do." Kim's attention drifted from me to some private thought of her own. "I wish…"

"Wish what?" I held the candy dish under her nose to refocus her with the scent of chocolate.

"Kurt and I have been talking lately—" Kim reached in and took a piece of Dove dark chocolate, fortifying herself for a heavy-duty conversation "—about having another baby."

My stomach took a roller-coaster ride from peak to valley and up again.

"Wesley will love a baby brother or sister! That's wonderful…."

Frankly, Wesley has become a bit of a tyrant, having control as he does of two entire households—Kim's and mine. It wouldn't hurt a bit to have a new baby around, someone who instinctively knows how to establish a dictatorship. It may seem absurd to think of a baby as a despot, but I can't think of an autocrat more qualified to put Wes in his place.

My excitement evaporated when I saw the expression on Kim's face. "Isn't it?"

"Of course it is!" she blurted, and burst into tears.

At that moment, a flurry of activity erupted as my cats, Mr. Tibble and Scram, growling and hissing, rolled together past our feet in a single absurd kitty ball.

"Ignore them," I advised.

"Won't they hurt themselves doing that?" Kim snuffled.

As she spoke, Mr. Tibble tired of the game and went limp, as if his bones had liquefied. Scram tumbled halfway across the room by himself before he realized he'd been abandoned, then stood up and marched off huffily, his tail straight in the air in a gesture of disdain.

I'd insulted Mr. Tibble deeply when I introduced Scram into his peaceful kingdom, but he'd taken on the kitten with aplomb, taught him who was boss and generally made Scram a being subservient to his own royalty. Just like what Mitzi tries to do with us at work.

"So tell me about this new-baby conversation," I urged, "and why it makes you cry."

"If we don't hurry up, Wesley will be grown-up. I don't want a large age gap between him and a baby brother or sister."

There's not much danger of being all grown-up when one still sucks his thumb, refuses to sleep without his blankie and demands Cheerios in church, but when Kim is emotional, logic flies out the window.

"What's stopping you?"

Kim looked pained. "Kurt is worried about my health. He's been on the Internet trying to find out if getting pregnant with my personal history of breast cancer will increase the risk of the cancer recurring."

"And…?"

"If the cancer returns while I'm pregnant, treatment options are limited. Chemotherapy can be given without hurting the baby, but it is not given in the first trimester, when the major organs are forming. He knows I'd never do anything to harm the baby, even it if were risky for me. Kurt is afraid of my having a recurrence. He doesn't want me putting my own life on the line." She rolled her eyes helplessly. "He's been spouting information about hormones like they were football statistics."

"Is the danger real?"

"It is definitely real in Kurt's mind."

"'Accept the authority of your husband,'" I murmured. "There's the rub."

"That might be a thorny issue for some, but to me that means voluntary compromise and teamwork with someone I love and respect. Kurt and I have discussed it. Whatever we decide will be mutual." She looked troubled. "But he has even stronger feelings than I. He's convinced I would be inviting problems if I had another baby right now. He's also afraid that being pregnant might exacerbate my depression."

Not a minor concern, considering Kim's history.

"He wants to have another child, but not at the expense of my health. He's adamant about that." Tears welled up in her eyes. "The idea of not giving birth again breaks my heart! I desperately want to have a brother or sister for Wesley."

"Aren't you putting the cart before the horse? Who says you won't? Besides, is this about giving birth or about being a parent? There are other ways to…"

But she didn't seem to hear me.

After she left, I put some lasagna into the oven, tore up lettuce for salad and still had over an hour before Chase was due to arrive home from work. I couldn't get Kim out of my mind. How would it be like to be caught in the place in which Kim found herself? Another child, or her health. What would it serve if having another child deprived Wesley of his mother?

To distract myself, I picked up our wedding photo

album. Looking at those pictures always turns me into a slobbering romantic. When Chase arrived for dinner, I met him at the door holding his slippers and a newspaper and doing my most seductive siren imitation. Unfortunately, his cousin's dog, Winslow, had made a hash of his slippers last weekend, and to find them I'd had to dig through the garbage can. Fortunately, they didn't smell *too* bad. Since we both read the paper at work, I'd also had to substitute an *O* magazine for the *Tribune*.

Clever man. He knew immediately that something was up.

"Now what have you and Kim been doing?" he asked as he put his arms around my waist and gathered me to him. "Last time you tried the newspaper-and-slippers routine on me, you'd agreed to foster a potential seeing-eye puppy without talking to me first."

"Did you even consider that it might be because I love you and I want to show it?"

"No." He grinned, and his dimples deepening. "I know you love me. You show it every day and in every way. Something else is going on."

I ran my finger along the chiseled line of his jaw and was supremely thankful to have this man is in my life. *Blessed. I am so blessed.*

I stared into the inky blueness of his eyes and watched them grow round with surprise as I whispered, "Chase, how do you feel about having a baby?"

Chapter Two

Though I'd caught him off guard, radiant warmth spread across Chase's features.

He took me in his arms and kissed me until I totally forgot our topic of conversation. When he finally set me away from himself, he held me at arm's length to ask, "Do you really mean it?"

"Huh?" My lips were deliciously swollen and rosy, my cheeks were flushed, and a little mechanical monkey in a red suit was riding a bicycle around in my head where my brain had been. Over two years together, and the impossible just keeps happening—I fall more and more deeply in love. If this is the way God's will feels, then never let me out of it.

"A baby? You're ready?"

I tipped my head and stared at him. "It's not as if we haven't talked about having children before, Chase."

"True, but I've never heard you say you're *ready* for them, either."

I have to admit that several things have been standing

in my way—the thought of having my blissful relationship with Chase change when a little third party arrives, what I would do about my job at Innova, and the enormous responsibility of bringing a brand-new soul into the world for eternity.

There's also that little issue of my mother. Even though she desperately wants grandchildren, she's recently begun telling people I'm her younger sister. She says she's not old enough to have a daughter my age. It's problematic to have my mother stop aging while I continue to grow older. When I surpass her in age, she'll have to start introducing me as her *big* sister.

Becoming a grandmother might send her over the edge. Then again, why worry? She's been dancing pretty close to the edge for some time now.

The baby conversation feels right this time. Maybe it's because Kim's been harboring the same thoughts, or that Mitzi keeps leaving baby magazines and maternity clothing catalogs on my desk at work. It was Mitzi who decided I needed to get married and registered unwilling me for an evening of speed dating with Hasty-Date. She'd had high hopes that someone would take pity on me and ask me out. Hasty-Date turned into a Hasty-Dud, but I ultimately met Chase, who is Kim's doctor and Kurt's good friend.

I'd also humored Mitzi when she told me I had to get rid of all my out-of-date clothes and found me a personal shopper. And the time she said my hair would look great in cornrows. When Mitzi decides it's time for something to happen, there's no stopping her. Could I put up with Mitzi's pride if she thought she'd convinced me to have a baby? The idea gives me cold chills. I can already imagine her volunteering to be my conception coach, carrying a megaphone and a stopwatch and cheering me on.

"How do *you* feel, Chase? This isn't something you can agree to, just to make me happy. When we make this decision, we both have to be ready."

Chase is far too indulgent with me. He lets me eat saltines and drink hot chocolate in bed and wear his new T-shirts as pajamas. He shares his toothbrush with me when we're traveling and I've forgotten my own—the definitive sign of true love. The only thing he really holds the line on with me is football. I can snuggle with him, blow in his ear, rub his back or sleep on his shoulder. But I cannot turn the television off during an interception thingy, walk in front of him during a touchdown or keep asking him why they have "downs" instead of "ups." It's a small sacrifice on my part, I think, since I really love taking naps in his football jersey on Sunday afternoons.

"I can't imagine anything I'd love more than having a beautiful little mini-Whitney around the house."

"It could turn out to be a mini-Chase."

"As long as you're involved, he or she will be perfect."

"Besides, there's no way we can duplicate me. Dad says I'm one of a kind."

"He's correct there."

"He also says I wasn't spoiled as a child but that I just smelled that way." I learned humility from Dad.

"Life will imitate art." Chase pulled me close and cradled me in his arms. "And you, my dear, are the highest art form I know."

As I closed my eyes and let him kiss me again, I reminded myself *never* to let Mitzi know that those baby magazines she left on my desk had had any effect on me whatsoever.

Tuesday, March 2

The idealistic baby fantasy lasted almost twenty-four hours. Then Kim asked us if we'd watch Wesley while they went out for dinner and discussed the "you-know-what" issue.

I know why they didn't want Wesley along while they were trying to decide if they should have another child. Wesley—precocious, beautiful, intelligent, gifted, *spoiled* Wesley—is the finest form of birth control ever invented.

He marched into our house on chubby BabyGap jean-clad legs, pulling a little wheeled suitcase. He shrugged off his denim jean jacket, ruffled his pale blond curls, opened his big baby blues in an expression of vast innocence and said authoritatively, "Disney-dot-com."

"Wes, you know Aunt Whitney doesn't let you play on her computer," Kim chided.

"Sorry, buddy. The dot-com era bit the dust. Didn't you hear? According to the *Wall Street Journal*, it's still in recovery mode."

He stared at me, his lower lip wobbling tremulously, a single perfect tear forming on the center of each of his lower eyelids, giving me an opportunity to relent and stop the floodgates of misery and mayhem about to erupt.

I, like a fool, didn't bite.

In slow motion, Wesley's world, and even Wesley himself, crumbled. He fell to the ground, opened his mouth and let out a wail that shattered all my crystal in the dining-room buffet, scared Scram and Mr. Tibble off the couch and into the bedroom and put a slight crack in the picture tube of my television.

Okay, I'm exaggerating a little. The television was not damaged.

"What's this about?" I yelled to Kim over the din.

"He's in a phase. Just ignore him."

"It would be quieter in here if my house were sitting in the middle of an airport landing strip."

"He's had separation anxiety lately. His supper is in his little suitcase. You know what a fussy eater he is." Kim smiled weakly. "If we do have another baby, I don't think we'll indulge him or her quite so much."

"Good idea." I picked Wesley up by the armpits and made a wet, noisy raspberry sound on his bare belly. He quit crying out of sheer surprise, waved goodbye to his mother and demanded ice cream. So much for separation issues.

Chase walked upstairs from the basement. "Who's being murdered up here?"

"Say hi to our houseguest."

"Hey, buddy." He and Wesley high-fived. "How about some smoked oysters and a little football?"

Wesley chortled and lunged out of my arms toward Chase.

And so much for the fussy-eater thing.

Tonight was different from the other times Wes has stayed with us. I kept imagining him as my own little boy, with us not for a few hours, but for a lifetime.

As the evening progressed, I tallied in my head all the wonderful—and not-so-wonderful—aspects of being a parent. Clearly there are glorious things about having a child.

1) The way a baby smells after a bath—soap, lotion, powder and that natural fragrance of sweet breath and fresh skin.

2) Baby toes.

3) Baby kisses.

4) Watching him suck his thumb as he soothes himself to sleep.

5) The kittenlike snore that reminds me of a purr and signals he's no longer messing with my mind and is really, truly, asleep.

6) Pink, full lips relaxed in an innocent smile.

7) The comical way Wesley holds my face in his and turns it toward his own when he wants my attention.

8) Long, fine eyelashes that delicately fringe sleepy eyes.

There are, however, some not-so-blissful things about having a little one around, too.

1) The way a baby smells after depositing a large treasure in his training pants.

2) Baby toes—when they are uncovered because said baby has flushed his shoes down the toilet.

3) Baby kisses—when they are open-mouthed and that same mouth has recently been eating smoked oysters and crackers.

4) Watching him suck his thumb, biding his time, waiting for me to turn my back on him so he can wreak more havoc in my household.

5) The strange sounds children make in their

sleep—the snuffles and grunts that make me leap to my feet to check on said child every few minutes.

6) Full, rosy lips screwed up into a pout.

7) The way a child can manage a vise grip on your face so tight that it feels like he might screw your head off to get your attention.

8) Long, fine lashes through which he can turn a glare into a full-scale emotional assault. With a look, Wesley can make me feel guilty for everything I've ever done to him, including administering vitamins, combing his hair, stopping him from putting his finger in a light socket and preventing him from pulling off my cat's tail without anesthetic.

9) Potty training—and little boys with very bad aim.

10) Stubborn refusal to wear "big boy" pull-ups to bed. Changing bedding. Twice. In three hours…

Sometimes it's best not to record everything in one's journal. It makes reality too clear and, well, too much of a reality.

Chase, of course, loved every minute of the evening— me getting soaked when Wesley splashed in the bathtub; me standing on my head trying to get him to eat green peas; me setting off a crying jag by suggesting that Wesley might sleep better if his pajamas weren't on backward.

It appears that as long as I serve smoked oysters with crackers to them as they sit on the couch watching men in ridiculous outfits try to injure each other over a bit of pigskin and a pumpful of air, everything will be fine. Maybe it's a guy thing, but Chase came down on Wesley's side of every issue.

About toilet training: "Little boys need the practice. Don't worry, the floor can be washed." *By who, I wonder?*

About flushing: "I'm sure Kim and Kurt have lots of other shoes he can wear."

About pet care: "Don't worry, Scram will grow another tail."

"Chase, are you going to be one of those indulgent fathers who thinks everything his son does is cute?"

"It will be, won't it?"

"What if your daughter decides it's okay to pee on the floor, flush her shoes down the toilet, eat oysters and burp?"

He thought about it for a moment before answering. Then he glanced at me hopefully. "Then I won't have to worry about guys flocking to our door asking her out on dates before she's ready."

Before she's thirty, you mean.

Chapter Three

Wednesday, March 3

To whom it may concern:
To the owner of the leaking Ziploc bag that at one time may have contained a sandwich and some baby carrots that now houses fuzzy mold and oozing liquid, please remove your biological warfare project from our refrigerator. There are some in this office who want to keep their lunches cold and do not want vomitous yellow gunk dripping onto our yogurt cups. If this is not done immediately, fingerprints will be lifted from the plastic bag and the guilty party will be fined large amounts of money and forced to eat the contents of the baggie.
The Management

War has broken out in the Innova lunchroom, and it isn't pretty. We've been eyeing each other with suspicion, covertly watching our once-trusted friends and

coworkers stash their lunches in the break-room refrigerator to identify consistent patterns of behavior.
Betty is my top suspect, for leaving a Tupperware
container of cottage cheese and pineapple on the
counter until the cheese aged into a yellowed slime the
texture of yak milk.

Harry usually picks up something at the deli, so I
assume the half-eaten pastrami on rye that's fossilizing
on the bottom shelf is his. Bryan is hard to pin down
because he brings his lunch in everything from old bread
bags to cast-off foam containers. Mitzi carries her meal
in a tidy Gucci purse she's turned into a lunch box. I
suspect that beneath that designer exterior lurks a
plebian plastic bag carrying the hard-boiled eggs that
she intentionally leaves in the fridge for weeks at a time
to torment the rest of us. Old eggs give off a distinctive
rotten, sulfurous smell that is easily recognized but
requires a full-scale refrigerator cleaning to eradicate.

And that's part of the problem. Nobody wants to be in
charge of cleanup, so we've allowed a zoo of microscopic
bacteria, fuzz, mold and moss to build and flourish. Our
lunchroom is not called the Bacteria Buffet for nothing.

I've ordered Mitzi to do the dirty deed, but she says
it isn't in her job description, that removing toxic waste
is the task of a professional. Her only concession to
helping out with this office problem was to send her
cleaning lady in one day to do the job—and then sub-
mitting her bill to me for payment.

Mitzi breezed into the break room on strappy sandals
that matched her pink designer suit, put her Gucci lunch
box on the table, opened it and took out a delicate tray
of sushi. She batted her fake eyelashes at me and put the

sushi in the refrigerator. Then she took a bottle of designer water out of the bag and tripped off to her desk to file her nails, read the paper and make sure she and her husband had secured tickets for the symphony—all of which, she insists, are somewhere in the "unwritten" agreement concerning her job description.

Mitzi missed her calling. I could see her as an executive for a company run by Barbie and her stiff-legged dolly friends. Barbie has a Dream House. If she ever develops a Dream Office, Mitzi is the one for her. Work would involve picking out professional-looking suits in all shades of pink, refurnishing rooms with expensive furniture and groaning over long days at the office when one should really be at the beach.

"There you are, Whitney. I've been looking for you. Where have you been?" Harry had a stack of contracts in his arm and a frazzled look on his face.

"Standing here. You've gone by the door three times and looked in."

"Nonsense. You must have been hiding."

I didn't bother to point out that hiding from the boss during office hours is frowned upon, even here at Innova where the expression "running a loose ship" was probably invented. Besides, I know from experience that around here, you can run but you can't hide.

"Take a look at these, decide what we should do about them, report back to me and we'll determine our next step." He thrust the papers at me as if they were the proverbial hot potato. All Harry really wants to do is design software. Things written on paper bore him, even contracts that bring in paying customers.

He spun on his heel to leave, then paused and turned

back. He's very graceful for a short man who's carrying more weight that he should around his middle.

"Whitney, I don't say it much, but I really do appreciate what you do around here. Bringing you into the Innova family was the smartest thing I ever did."

I blinked, dumbfounded. "Why, Harry, thank you…"

"And get those things back to me ASAP and tell Mitzi to get the lipstick off her teeth on her own time." The touchy-feely moment was over, and he was gone.

The Innova family. I like the sound of that. Dysfunctional as it is, I'm glad I'm part of it, too. Then the word *family* brought me back to the conversation Chase and I had had last night, the one about starting our own little family.

How much, really, had the idea of having a child right now been sparked by the thought of sharing those special months with Kim? We shop together, we eat together, we pray together. Maybe being queasy and nauseous together would be fun, too.

After work I stopped at Norah's Ark, my favorite pet shop, to get food for Mr. Tibble and Scram. Norah was behind the counter, having a deep conversation with a turtle. Her dark, curly hair was fastened into a ponytail that erupted from the top of her head. She has remarkable gray-green eyes, full of humor and compassion and a ready grin.

"Hi, Whitney, how's Mr. Tibble? What's Scram up to? Oh, yes, and Chase?" Norah always asks about the pets first.

After leaving the pet store, I picked up a pizza and arrived at home by six-fifteen. Chase was already there. Odd. He usually doesn't arrive until seven or after.

At least I thought he was home. His car was in the garage, but the house was dark. I found him in the darkened living room, lying on the couch with a pillow over his eyes. Mr. Tibble was sleeping on his chest, his head nuzzled beneath my husband's chin. Scram, who's learned his place in Mr. Tibble's pecking order—below the bottom—was sleeping across one of Chase's ankles.

When Mr. Tibble heard me come in, he turned his head and sleepily kneaded his claws into Chase's chest. That started a chain reaction. Chase jumped at the needle-sharp nail pricks, Mr. Tibble yowled and hung on by his claws to Chase's shirt. Scram, jettisoned off Chase's leg and sure he must be somehow the cause of all this commotion, headed for the hills, or, in this case, the back of my favorite chair.

"I usually don't see this much excitement when I walk into a room," I commented, first prying Mr. Tibble off Chase and then rubbing the broad part of Chase's chest where the cat had been hanging.

"So much for a nap. I think I may be going into cardiac arrest. Could you do CPR on me, please?" Smile lines crinkled around his beautiful blue eyes, and I felt my own heart do a little lurch.

"Oh, I'll bet you say that to all the girls." I put my arms around him and kissed his lips. "What are you doing home? I didn't expect you until seven."

"Tired, that's all. I got done early today and decided to sneak out." He brushed a strand of hair from my eyes. "Maybe I'm getting old and can't keep up the pace."

I searched his face, unable to tell if he was joking or serious, but he smiled at me and, as usual, banished every sensible thought from my brain.

After dinner, as we sat together on the sofa, Mr. Tibble and Scram once again snoozing next to us, Chase asked. "What's Mitzi been up to today?"

The Mitzi saga is Chase's idea of a soap opera, and I'm his verbal TiVo. I replay my day with Mitzi every evening so he can have a few laughs.

"That podiatrist husband of hers is clamping down on shoes with pointed toes. She says he's seen a rash of bunions lately and wants her to wear flats. As you can imagine, Mitzi is fit to be tied. She's been wearing sensible shoes out of the house and hiding high-heeled shoes in a briefcase and bringing them to work but has begun to feel that's being 'unfaithful' to her husband. Recently she forced Betty Noble to stay late and teach her how to sell her shoes on eBay."

"At least she didn't waste work hours on it," Chase commented.

"She didn't have time. She was too busy researching cellulite cures during the day."

"How is Kim?"

I waved my hand. "Up and down. Chase, do you think Kurt is right to be so worried about her having another child?"

"Kurt's cautious. The man is going to be a certified public accountant. Those types don't make their money taking risks. It's in his nature to be cautious. There was a time that it was assumed that the hormone surges of pregnancy fueled breast cancer. That's not so black-and-white today, especially in women like Kim whose cancers were caught early. Kurt and Kim need to get all the facts from their specialist and then make the decision.

"It can go either way," Chase added matter-of-factly.

"For women whose cancers are caught early, a subsequent pregnancy may not be nearly as dangerous as was once assumed. Still, Kurt can find information out there that says a woman's survival is affected negatively, as well. They need to be talking to their doctors, not scaring themselves on the Internet."

"It's so hard for them."

"They'll be okay, Whitney. They're a praying pair."

Of course. I felt my mood lighten. "You're right. They have the God factor on their side."

Chase pulled me close. "Did you think anymore about *our* conversation last night?"

"I didn't think about much else. Poor Harry didn't get much bang for his buck from any of his employees today. I prayed about it, too."

"I know. I did—"

The phone rang, interrupting what Chase was about to say.

"Whitney, this is Kim. What are you doing?"

"Having a romantic tête-à-tête with my husband."

"Oh, good, I didn't interrupt anything important, then."

Chase overheard her comment, rolled his eyes and went to make coffee, leaving me alone with the conversation.

"Very funny."

"What are you guys doing tonight?"

"Nothing. Especially since you interrupted our *romantic* talk."

Kim didn't take the hint.

"Then you wouldn't mind if I came over? I'm feeling a little stir-crazy here. Today Wesley developed a fascination for fishing in our saltwater aquarium. He spent the morning turning light switches on and off until I thought I was either living with a strobe light or having a stroke. Then he picked up a terrible word from the neighbor child, which he's finally tired of saying. And about two minutes ago I discovered that he'd been tinkering with the knobs on our stereo. I thought I would turn on some nice, soothing rain forest music and nearly blew out my eardrums."

So it had been a day just like any other with Wesley.

"Does Kurt have class?" He's finishing up his degree in accounting and preparing to sit for the CPA exam while driving a truck during the day to pay the bills.

"He does. It's me who needs the diversion. Wesley discovered he can make the entire house tremble if he sets the tuner knobs just right. Until Kurt arrives to put a lock on the cabinet door, I'll be peeling Wesley off the entertainment center. If I go deaf before Kurt gets home, I won't be able to hear what Wes is doing next."

My experience with Wesley is that when I can hear him, it's okay. It's when things are silent that I begin to worry. Entire rooms can be colored with crayons up to a height of two feet from the floor in virtually no time at all. Uncleaned litter boxes can be emptied onto many square feet of flooring. Kitchen cupboards can be cleared of their contents and many cereal boxes opened. Oh, no, noise isn't the problem with Wesley. Silence is. Of course, it's not my house that's trembling.

"Can we come over?" Kim was as determined as a bulldog. I knew that even if I did say no, it probably wouldn't stop her.

"I suppose…"

"Good. We'll be there in twenty minutes." The line went dead.

"What was that about?" Chase returned from the kitchen carrying a huge butterscotch walnut sundae and two spoons.

"Kim's sanity is slipping. Wesley has discovered he's mechanical." I told him about the stereo.

Chase shuddered and then sighed. "I guess I'd better start making more sundaes."

When in doubt, eat. It's one of my coping mechanisms, too.

When they arrived, Wesley marched into the house first and flung himself at Chase's leg, where he stood with both his little Nike-shod feet on Chase's shoe. He refused to let go of Chase's leg, forcing him to walk stiff-legged down the hall to greet Kim, dragging Wesley with him.

"Too bad he doesn't like you," I muttered to Chase. "The child is like a barnacle attaching itself to the hull of a ship. How are you going to scrape him off?"

Chase winked at me. "You're just jealous that it's not bedtime yet."

Chase is Wesley's favorite playmate, but I am queen of the bedtime story and back-scratching professional extraordinaire. I come into my own with Wesley the moment he starts rubbing his eyes and wanting to cuddle.

The color was high in Kim's cheeks, and from the glint in her eye, I could tell that she and her son had come to an impasse and leaving the house was their only logical recourse. With Kim and Wesley, as with Kim and Kurt, when stubborn meets stubborn, it's like two mountain sheep ramming horns. Nobody wins, and everybody gets a really bad headache.

They didn't even have time for the normal niceties.

Wesley bounced off Chase's shoe and went straight for the huge plastic box that harbors his toys, dumped them onto the floor and then started chasing the cats. Mr. Tibble, wise to Wesley's ways, dodged him by leaping onto the just-out-of-reach-for-Wesley back of the wing chair. With an intelligence born of experience, he also tucked his long black tail beneath him so that there were no handholds for Wesley to swing on. Scram—not the brightest bulb in the package—was rescued by Kim, who scooped him out of Wes's grabby little mitts.

I, as silently as I could, breathed a sigh of relief. Kim is always saying, "He'll grow out of it." That's true, but he always grows *into* something else.

"Okay, you two," Chase demanded. "What's up?"

Kim took the sundae he offered her and sank onto the couch with a relieved sigh. "I'm half-deaf from that sound system Kurt insisted was everything we'd ever need and more, I'm exhausted from running after a three-year-old with boundless energy and limited common sense and I'm smart enough to know that Uncle Chase and Aunt Whitney can make me sane again. Do you have any cherries for this sundae?"

This is the woman who wants another child? If the baby is anything like Wes, there isn't enough ice cream in the world to keep any of us sane—and the biggest nut may turn out to be Kim herself.

Chapter Four

"What stage is he in now?" I inquired sweetly. "Heat-seeking missile, search-and-destroy mission or kamikaze LEGO airplane pilot?" I could hear Chase and Wesley roaring with laughter about something hysterical in the kitchen. My recent attempt at a chocolate layer cake, probably.

"Maybe Kurt *is* right," Kim said glumly as she plunged her spoon into the melting mound of vanilla bean ice cream. "Maybe it *is* a bad idea. Not for the reasons he brings up, of course, but there are some grounds for calling it quits."

Perhaps Wesley really has driven Kim off the deep end. "What are you talking about?"

"Having another baby, of course." She stared at me accusingly. "Didn't you hear a word I said?"

"Surely you won't let a three-year-old determine whether or not you have more children."

"That's not it. Like I told you before, we both *want* more children, but Kurt is being difficult—no, *impos-*

sible—about my getting pregnant again. Today he announced that the pregnancy shouldn't happen because he's been reading up on my condition on the Internet and he's not willing to put me through anymore stress. Whatever happened to deciding this together?"

Kim crossed her arms over her chest. "You'd think he'd consult me before putting his foot down. That's what we agreed to do. I'm the one taking all the risks. I deserve a vote in this."

"It seems only right. Why didn't he?"

"Because he says I'm letting my emotions overrule my common sense and that I'm not being rational."

"And *are* you irrational?" At the moment, she appeared suspiciously so.

"Of course not! Well, maybe…just a little… No!" She waved her spoon in the air. "Whitney, you have to help me convince Kurt that having another baby is a great idea. You're practically my sister. He listens to you."

I rolled my eyes and sank deeper into my recliner. I may believe I am my brother's—or sister's—keeper, but this is ridiculous.

After Kim left, I discussed the twists and turns of Kim and Kurt's lives and logic with Chase. As always, he is cautious not to make judgments without having the full picture. With Kurt and Kim taking opposite sides on the issue, the last place either of us wants to be is in the middle.

He leaned back in his chair and laced his hands behind his head. I love it when he does that, because I get a great view of those pectorals he works on at the gym and a peek at his washboard abs when his shirt pulls tightly across his torso. I love watching Chase, feeling his chest rise and fall as we sit together on the couch watching football or hearing him humming to himself in the other room while he reads the paper. I delight in him just because he exists. Miraculously, that's just the merest hint of the pleasure that God gets from being in a relationship with me.

I'd almost forgotten I'd asked Chase a question—too occupied with my happy little visual feast—when he finally spoke. "This may be a matter of ethics."

"'Ethics?' People have babies all the time and don't think about the moral principles behind it."

"Maybe they should. It's not a frivolous thing to bring a child into the world. In Kim and Kurt's case, there's more to consider than for some."

His expression was intense. "*If* Kim's cancer were to recur—and I don't believe it will—there's always the risk that she won't be around to raise either Wesley or the new baby."

"You can't think…" But the thought had crossed my mind, as well.

"No. I don't think it will happen. I know Kim's case. I believe she's fine, but I'm a doctor, not a visionary. I respect Kurt for not only being concerned for Kim's safety, but also for Wesley's well-being. Granted, he's gone a little overboard…."

"Kim's very frustrated right now."

Chase looked at me oddly. "Is she depressed?"

"No. Not that I've noticed." A dim lightbulb finally flickered faintly in my brain. "You mean because of the hormones?"

"Kim *is* depression-prone. Kurt's not only worried about Kim's physical state but her mental state, as well."

We'd all walked with Kim through a very bad time that none of us—least of all Kim—wanted to repeat. "Do you think that a pregnancy will affect her in that way?"

"I can't blame Kurt for being wary."

For all the heedlessness and lack of consideration with which some babies are conceived, one thing is still true. Every time parents bring a new child into the world, it is here for eternity. Another soul who exists not only in the present but in infinity. Now and forever.

No wonder Kurt is thinking this through so carefully. The enormity of the responsibility, once one begins to think of it, is mind-boggling.

Friday, March 5

The next morning, Bryan, showing more energy and enthusiasm than he has in months, collared me as I entered the Innova office. His eyes were narrow and his pupils, angry pinpoints. "Are you the one who took my pierogis out of the refrigerator last night?"

Pierogis? I've never tasted one, and from the look of them, they are definitely not something anyone would want to steal. In fact, they'd probably be pretty hard to give away. Bryan, whose Polish grandmother has made them for every holiday since he was a child, has an unnatural attachment to these lumps of dough filled with mashed potatoes or sauerkraut. More peculiar yet, she makes dozens of them and gives them to him as a Christmas present. Bryan freezes them and metes them out slowly between Christmas and Easter so he doesn't run out until his grandmother refills his stash on his birthday. He guards them like gold nuggets and brings them to work boiled or fried in butter. At noon, he heats them, slathers them with sour cream and eats them at his desk

"Bryan, you know I'd never steal anything, especially your Christmas present."

He sagged and looked woeful. "I suppose it's my own fault, leaving them there overnight. They were just too tempting, and someone just couldn't resist."

"Tempting?" I put a knuckle between my teeth to keep from laughing. Bryan took it as a signal of my upset and sympathy.

"Who could pass up my grandmother's pierogis? I should have known better than to leave them in the refrigerator to entice people. If you discover who might have taken them, will you let me know?"

Move over, Nancy Drew. Now I'm on *The Case of the Purloined Pierogi.*

Mitzi entered the office in a cloud of Chanel N° 5 and the aroma of chocolate. "Treats, everyone!" She set a bakery box on my desk and opened it to reveal chocolate éclairs and chocolate doughnuts frosted in chocolate and covered with sprinkles.

"Why do you do this to me, Mitzi?" I take Mitzi's treats as a direct attack on my waistline. Because Mitzi doesn't like chocolate, she can ignore it completely. She knows that I, an admitted chocoholic, will succumb repeatedly before the day is done.

"Self-preservation," Mitzi said with her characteristic straightforwardness. "I like people around me who are heavier than me. It's good for my self-esteem."

"What about *my* self-esteem?"

"Oh, you're in charge of that," she retorted airily. "I can't take care of yours and mine, too. Éclair?"

No wonder I leave the office with a headache.

"Have you seen the pierogis Bryan left in the refrigerator?" I asked, hoping to catch Mitzi in a petty crime.

"Those white lumps he eats for lunch? They look like brains and boiled cauliflower."

Now *that's* a visual.

"His lunch is missing today."

"He can have an éclair. I'll put them in the break room." And Mitzi tripped off happily, acting as if she'd solved every problem but world peace.

Then Kim slouched in wearing a baggy sweater and jeans even though it wasn't casual Friday. When I greeted her, she walked by me as if I wasn't there.

Now, I'm accustomed to that kind of treatment from Mitzi, who is usually too involved in her own little world to notice mine. But Kim? That's another story.

I caught up with her in the back room. "What's going on?"

"Nothing. Absolutely nothing." She flung a peanut butter and jelly sandwich into the refrigerator and slammed the door. "Nada. Zip. Nil. Zilch. Nothing."

Before I could point out that there seemed to be a whole lot of "nothing" going on, she burst into tears and flung herself into my arms, toppling us into a file cabinet. "The doctor said no, Whitney. What am I going to do?"

It took me a moment to recall that yesterday was the day Kim and Kurt were to visit her oncologist.

"'No?'" I snapped my fingers. "Just like that?"

"Not exactly," she snuffled. "He said 'not yet.' My oncologist is very conservative, and he recommended that I wait. Since my cancer was caught very early, it's not likely another pregnancy would be dangerous, but he wants to follow me medically for a while longer before I try to have a second child. Of course, Kurt picked that up and ran with it, reminding the doctor about my issues with chronic depression."

This didn't sound good. "And?"

"The doctor called to consult with a specialist, who said that women with a history of depression before pregnancy are almost twice as likely as other women to show signs of it while they are pregnant. It has to do with hormone imbalances." Her face crumpled. "My doctor started talking about my susceptibility to postpartum depression, and Kurt put his hands in the air and said, 'That's it. There's no way I'd ask my wife to go through that again.'"

"The doctor tried to assure Kurt that babies exposed to antidepressants in utero don't seem to be set back by it, but you know how stubborn Kurt can be. He never heard another word the doctor said."

"He's trying to take care of you, Kim. You can't fault him for that."

Kim scrubbed away her tears with the back of her hand. "I know it. And I know we have to be in agreement about this before we try again. But I don't think he'll change his mind. He says he loves me too much to jeopardize my health."

"It's hard to argue with that. He loves you, Kim. He's seen you in both physical and emotional pain."

"Not having another child will hurt me, too!"

That was something I wasn't going to touch. Only God was smart enough for that one.

Friday March 19

Today, I was innocently minding my own business as I put treats out for afternoon coffee. My plan was to infuse the staff with pure sucrose, to give them a sugar high that would last until the end of the day, so we could get some work done around here.

"Ahah!"

The door to the office coat closet flew open and crashed against the wall behind it, revealing Byran standing there, piles of extra toilet paper at his feet, his head in a tangle of wire coat hangers.

I dropped the Tupperware container of divinity I was carrying and grabbed my chest with both hands. "CPR! Call an ambulance! Someone, start CPR!"

"Sorry, Whitney, I thought you were the Pierogi Bandit." Bryan slunk out of the storage closet where he'd been hiding and began to pick up the white globs of divinity candy that were now on the break room floor. "You had white lumps in your hands. I thought…"

"Give it up, Bryan. Ask your grandmother to make you some more pierogi. Give me her number and *I'll* ask her. You can't continue to leap out of cupboards and shuffle through our desks looking for food."

"It's just wrong," Bryan insisted. "There's a thief on the premises, and I'm going to find her."

"'Her?'"

"There are four women in this office and two men. It's got to be a woman. The odds are in favor of a female."

Talk about allegiance to your gender. I wish some of that loyalty would rub off on Mitzi. For the past two weeks, while Kim has been utterly distracted by her debate with Kurt over another child, Mitzi has turned into Lady Godiva—Godiva chocolate, that is. She's even had her housekeeper bake goodies for the office— German chocolate cake, cookies, fudge and seven-layer bars. I might as well just slather them directly onto my hips as process them through my mouth. Betty the office dragon is beginning to mutter about banning treats from the lunchroom entirely, but Harry, who has to consume a lot of calories to maintain his waistline, wouldn't be happy. And if Harry isn't happy, nobody is happy.

Otherwise, life has been fairly routine. Chase is covering for another doctor who's on a mission trip, and he hasn't been home enough to even discuss the baby issue. The main man in my life has been Mr. Tibble.

The problem with Mr. Tibble is that no matter where he is, according to him, he is on the wrong side of the door. If I'm in the bathroom with the door closed, Mr. Tibble wants in. If he's stuck with me while I'm in the tub, he wants out.

He finds it amusing to go into the laundry room and bat the door shut behind him, barricading himself in with the food, water dishes and litter box. Poor Scram is so traumatized that he refuses to leave the laundry room for fear he'll never be able to return. I've had to keep the litter box in the living room, where Mr. Tibble cannot seal it off from Scram. This does not provide enjoyable evening entertainment.

Scram has learned to be resourceful and now drinks out of the toilet off my bedroom. This does not make for pleasant daily ablutions.

Until Mr. Tibble learns something useful, like behaving himself, he's going to put a crimp in both our television watching and our bathing. On top of all this, he makes it clear that he regards us as inferior beings. If you need an ego boost, don't get a cat.

Tonight we had dinner guests, all of them unannounced.

That meant that I threw together the meal—a cauliflower-bacon-and-broccoli salad, cold cuts, bread and soy ice cream. It wasn't exactly gourmet fare, but if it had been just Chase and me, we would have made caramel popcorn and eaten ourselves into a stupor in front of the fireplace.

As it was, Mom, Dad, Kim and Wesley all arrived at our front door at once.

When my mother comes to visit, she often brings food. I'm not sure if she thinks she won't get any at my place, or that it will all be raw, organic and unsalted. Tonight she came bearing one of her signature desserts, a frightening confection she calls "dirt cake."

It's a mousselike dessert of cream cheese, whipped topping and vanilla pudding that Mom serves in a flowerpot. She tops the mixture with crumbled chocolate cookies—the dirt—plastic flowers and a host of gummy worms oozing out of the soil. It tickles her to serve it with a child's plastic shovel and watch people's expressions.

"Mom, do you have any idea how many calories are in that disgusting-looking thing?"

"It's not disgusting, it's cute. It was a big hit at my book club."

I popped a gummy worm into my mouth. "It's not very healthy. Think of all the sugar, the preservatives…"

Mom glanced in my hallway mirror and put the back of her hand beneath her chin where the first sign of sagging skin was still in her future.

"Preservatives? Don't take them away from me, darling. I need all the help I can get."

Chapter Five

Monday, March 22

"**W**haddayamean, you want it by Thursday?" Harry roared through his closed office door. I began to count the seconds until he'd roar again. One, two...

"Whitney, get in here!"

Three.

Harry was at his desk, riffling through the stacks of papers that spilled willy-nilly over the edges of the desk and onto the floor.

"Maybe I can find what you're looking for," I suggested tactfully. Harry views paper as having as much relevance to the present day as dinosaur eggs. Armed with his cell phone, BlackBerry, iPod, DVD player, CD player, memory stick, hard drive, external drive, tape recorder, Dictaphone, tablet PC and walkie-talkie, Harry believes paper is obsolete.

That's what I'm for—keeping the obsolete in order and out of his way.

"That contract we signed with Franklin and Terrance? When did we say we'd meet with them to discuss the changes they want?"

"Thursday."

He sagged like a deflated balloon. "That means I can't go to my mother-in-law's place for dinner." The import of his statement sank into his consciousness, and he straightened a little. Then he grinned. "That means I have an actual excuse. I don't have to eat her salt-free tuna casserole or those hockey pucks she calls biscuits."

"I'm so glad you've turned this into a plus so quickly," I murmured.

"Call my wife and tell her what's happened."

"No fair. I'm sick of being the bearer of bad tidings." Harry couldn't go to his mother-in-law's last week, either, and he missed out on a Scandinavian feast of boiled cod, boiled potatoes and white cake—food so pale it would disappear in a snowstorm.

"You're good at it, I'm not. Besides, my wife believes you."

"That's because I always tell the truth."

"Whatever. Listen, I've got to get busy on this. Close the door on your way out." He promptly turned me out. I was as relevant as the three-day-old newspaper lying on the floor beside his desk. Therefore, I was able to stand there and study him, my mercurial, bighearted, Danny DeVito-like boss, without his even noticing my presence.

Harry's aged in the past couple years. Another chin here, an additional roll around his waist there, two more scowl marks on his forehead…but the biggest difference is definitely his hair loss. For over two years, he's managed to look as if he had, if not a full head of hair, at least an energetic and animated one, but now even the curly perms aren't doing the trick. Today he'd been running his fingers across his pate and he'd disturbed the carefully arranged and lacquered spit curls so that they stood on end like exclamation points and question marks hovering above his head.

Quietly I slipped out of his office. Kim, who I'd barely had a chance to talk to all week, caught my arm as I passed her desk. "Let's go out for lunch soon."

"Great. Where do you want to go—"

"Let's do Vietnamese. I've been craving *pho,*" Mitzi chirruped helpfully from behind us.

We spun around to find Mitzi licking her chops.

"Let me guess. You want to eat with us now because Arch won't be home for dinner."

"Podiatry convention," Mitzi said, as if that explained everything. Mitzi often joins us. She never waits for an invitation. Instead, she bestows upon us the privilege of her esteemed presence.

"So Dr. Foot isn't coming home tonight?"

"His name is Archibald Whitman Fraiser the third," Mitzi said primly. "Not 'Dr. Foot' or 'Sole Man.'"

"Right. *Archie.*" I mentally patted myself on the back for my heroic self-control. Not once have I pointed out the ludicrousness of a foot doctor whose name is Arch.

"What is 'fuh,' and why would anyone want to eat it?" Kim asked.

"Beef noodle soup."

"Why didn't you just say so?"

I picked up my sweater and headed for the door, glad that I had soup to anticipate. Last time Mitzi picked the restaurant and recommended the food, we ended up at an Indonesian place. Fortunately, neither of us ordered Mitzi's suggestion, *semur otak,* which, we discovered later, was beef brains sautéed in spiced sauce. More proof that you can't trust someone who doesn't like chocolate.

"Kim, you really need to consider a new wardrobe," Mitzi observed as we walked through the dimly lit restaurant decorated with faux bamboo paper, red brocade and elaborate hand-carved panels. "Preppy is fine, but…"

"Tailored," I blurted out automatically. "Kim likes her clothes tailored." I didn't want Kim and Mitzi to get into it before we'd even been seated. If Mitzi says Kim's clothes are too preppy, then Kim will say Mitzi's are too Barbie, then Mitzi will tell Kim that if she'd ever read a magazine that had some meaning, like *Vogue,* instead of burying her nose in something fluffy like *Newsweek,* she'd know how people dress these days. To that, Kim would reply… Well, it's just better if I stop the conversation before it gets started.

Much to my surprise, Kim turned around, gave Mitzi a munificent, approving smile and said, "Mitzi, for once I think you're right."

Mitzi nearly tripped and fell headfirst into the koi pond. "You agree with me?"

"Yes, I do," Kim said firmly. "Today I think *everyone* is right."

Even Mitzi? What had made Kim's mood turn on a dime? Last I'd talked to her, her and Kurt's negotiations over the baby issue had reached an impasse.

Mitzi regarded Kim suspiciously. Historically, Kim and Mitzi haven't agreed on anything. So far, they haven't even agreed to disagree.

After that, Mitzi couldn't take her eyes off Kim. She observed her warily, as if waiting for the other shoe to drop or to find out what kind of joke Kim was playing on her. I ended up ordering spring rolls and chicken sticks, with three bowls of pho to follow, while Mitzi charily ferreted out clues as to why Kim might concur with her about anything.

Mitzi observed Kim guardedly until the appetizers came. Then she picked up a chicken stick, waved it in the air and demanded, "What's going on with you?"

"Me?" Kim tried to look innocent, but her eyes were sparkling.

Then, as if she was simply too full to hold it in any longer, she blurted, "Kurt and I are going to have a baby!"

Mitzi, who had been drinking from her glass, turned into a human fire hydrant and spewed it across the table.

"Kim, are you kidding me?" I gasped. "For real? Are you sure?"

"It's not exactly what you think, but…" Kim hugged herself with glee.

"How many ways can you be pregnant, silly?" I felt giddy with pleasure.

"I have to tell you what—"

"That's just awful!"

Shocked, we both turned to stare at Mitzi. Her livid face was the color of an eggplant. "Just awful…" she muttered. "Why you?" Then, so softly that I almost missed it, she added, "Why not *me?*"

I was still unsure about what I'd just heard, but Referee Whitney came to the rescue. "Settle down, you two. Kim, you first. I thought Kurt was worried about having another child."

"He was, but we settled that. We're going to adopt!" She glowed incandescently. "I don't know why we didn't consider it initially. I want to love, nurture and raise another child. I want Wesley to have a brother or sister. Adopting is the perfect answer. We won't be rushing into a pregnancy before the doctor gives me the go-ahead, we'll get the baby we all want, and some child will get a loving home. We've been praying about it, and everything is falling into place. Kurt's as excited as I am."

"Adopt? You aren't having one from—" Mitzi pointed to her flat belly "—here?"

"No, but I'm having one from here." Kim put her hand over her heart. Then she scowled. "Why do you think my having a baby is 'awful' anyway? I'm a wonderful mother!"

"It's not that… I'm sure you are… Wesley will grow out of this stage he's in eventually…he's got to improve sometime." Mitzi wasn't doing herself any favors.

Then she surprised us both by bursting into tears.

Mitzi does not cry. Much, I expect, for the same reason that the Statue of Liberty does not cry—she's too hardheaded. Granted, Mitzi can make others cry, but she is traditionally tough as nails. As she says, "crying ruins your makeup." But tonight she threw caution—and a lot of mascara—to the winds.

It took both Kim and me, patting her back, hugging her and murmuring helpless platitudes—and some fervent unspoken prayers—to calm her down.

Finally, over steaming bowls of pho, she started to talk.

"I didn't mean I'm not happy for you, Kim," she mumbled into her broth, "or that you shouldn't have more children. I'm sure Wesley will grow up to be human eventually."

I kicked Kim under the table to stop her from lunging over it to throttle Mitzi.

"But I wanted to be the first one to announce I was going to be having a baby."

I realized that my jaw was hanging somewhere by my kneecaps and shut my gaping mouth. Kim, too, looked dumbstruck. Mitzi and a baby? Those two things went together like, well, like a hairpin and a flashlight, a toenail clipper and a feather boa, a cotton ball and a spare tire. Frankly, I think Mitzi and a baby are the most unlikely combination of all.

"You're going to have a baby?" I choked out. "A *real* one?" I don't know why I said that, except that most everything else about Mitzi is artificial—her nails, her eyelashes…

"Of course a *real* one! At least I thought I could."

Mitzi looked as though she might start to cry again. "Arch and I have been trying to get pregnant for almost two years. Our doctor recommended a fertility expert. He's optimistic, but offers no guarantees."

"So you *will* be having a baby soon!" Kim blurted. "They can help so many infertile couples these days. We'll all pray for you, won't we, Whitney?"

"Of course." I did a double take as I glanced at Mitzi again. She was scowling as if she'd just put her foot in a wad of discarded bubble gum. "Mitzi?"

"You realize what this means, don't you?"

"Not exactly." I never have a clue what anything means to Mitzi.

"If Kim's going to adopt, she won't be gaining a lot

of weight or looking anymore fat and dumpy than she already does."

Mitzi can ruin a compliment like no other living being.

She turned her sharp eyes on me. "That means that you'll have to get pregnant, too, Whitney, *after* Arch and I are expecting."

"I will?" Chase and I hadn't discussed planning a baby around Mitzi's whims. "Why?"

Mitzi rolled her eyes and looked at me as if I were dumb as rock.

"Because if I'm going to grow a stomach like a basketball, there has got to be someone in the office—besides Harry—who is fatter than me!"

Of course. I can't think of a better reason to bring a child into the world than to make Mitzi's waistline look good. I don't know why I didn't think of it myself.

Chapter Six

❧

"Why didn't you tell us you were trying to get pregnant?" Kim demanded. "We could have prayed for you and your health all along."

An uncharacteristic look of uncertainty flickered on Mitzi's features. Mitzi is nothing if not confident—confident to the point of crazy-making, in fact. As Harry says, "Mitzi may be mistaken, but she's never uncertain."

"I thought I'd get pregnant right away, and I wanted to surprise everyone." She eyed Kim speculatively. "Especially those who think I'm an irresponsible bubblehead."

Everyone on Planet Earth, you mean?

"When it didn't happen right away, I thought I'd better wait until that little strip turned color."

I imagined Mitzi with a case of home pregnancy kits, testing, testing and retesting, like Dr. Frankenstein waiting for his monster's finger to twitch.

"We thought it was a fluke, of course. I never fail a test of any kind, so I didn't see how I could fail this one.

But now that weeks have turned into months…" Genuine puzzlement filled her face.

"The doctor says that there are wonderful fertility drugs available."

The expression of distaste on Mitzi's face spoke volumes. Mitzi doesn't like unpleasant or disagreeable things. These include gargling, splinters, hangnails, cleaning out the stuff left over in the kitchen sink and looking at herself in a mirror when she's having her hair colored. Putting a worm on a fish hook or washing squashed bugs off a dirty windshield—even if it is the windshield of her Porsche—is beyond consideration. I'd never get her started on a hair clog in the shower drain or the thought of Mr. Tibble or Scram urping a hair ball, either.

Her aversion to the nastier parts of everyday life is legend around our office. She once tried to get the fire department to come because she'd heard rumors that someone on the first floor had seen a mouse. She refuses to look in garbage cans for fear there might be a browning apple core inside. Then there was the day that Bryan came down with the stomach flu and she sent him home in a taxi with a brown paper grocery sack over his head so he wouldn't breathe on her.

Any sort of test recommended by a fertility specialist no doubt ranked right near hair ball urping with Mitzi. Clearly, Mitzi is motivated to have a child, or she would never consider it.

She reached into her Kate Spade purse and took out a slender metallic silver case, the kind expensive jewelry might come in. She opened the top and tilted the case toward us so that we could see what was inside.

"A thermometer?" Kim and I yelped together.

Mitzi snapped the case shut and put a finger to her lips. "Shh. I don't want the entire world to know about this."

"When did they start selling thermometers in jewelry stores?" Kim wondered aloud.

"Don't be ridiculous. This is the case for my diamond tennis bracelet. You don't think I'd carry a basal thermometer around in the ugly plastic thing it comes in, do you? I have to take my temperature every morning before I get out of bed."

"Then why do you have it in your purse?"

Mitzi looked at Kim as if she had oatmeal for brains. "Because," she said, drawing out every word as if she were talking to a sweet but slow child, "my housekeeper is cleaning my bedroom today. I couldn't just leave it lying around and announce to the world what we're doing, could I?"

"I don't see why not," I said. "It's nothing to be ashamed of." As soon as I said it, I wished I could take back my statement. Maybe Mitzi and Arch, even though they didn't have to, felt shame or embarrassment that they were having trouble getting pregnant. Me and my big mouth. Insert foot, stroll around.

My high-school girlfriend, now the mother of two, had walked in Mitzi's shoes and opened my eyes to the "comforting" things people say to women struggling to become pregnant. "If one more person tells me to relax and that I'll get pregnant right away or to be patient, I think I'll scream," she'd told me. "And the next person says they know exactly how I feel, is going to 'feel' something they didn't expect, like my hand over their mouth."

Needless to say, I got the idea. Minimizing fertility

problems is a knife in the heart to people who want a baby in their arms.

"I've also had my thyroid checked and we've been taking blood tests. If they don't show anything, then…" Mitzi hadn't noticed that I'd checked out of the conversation for a moment. She began throwing around words like follicle-stimulating hormones, ultrasound, hysterosalpingogram, biopsy, and several words that ended in -scopy, and I wondered how any of them would stack up against a discussion of one of Mr. Tibble's hair balls.

Lord, I pray that Mitzi gets pregnant soon. Otherwise, it's going to be a very tense spring and summer at Innova Software. I already have more information about Mitzi and Arch's life than I care to.

For the first time in all the years I've known her, I saw fear flicker in Mitzi's eyes. "But what if…" She left the question unfinished.

Beneath the flawless makeup, the two-hundred-dollar haircut and the designer suit, I saw the real Mitzi—uncertain, afraid, and longing for a child she wasn't sure she'd ever have.

Kim gently laid her hand across Mitzi's. "You can't give up now, when you are just finding the help you need."

"I'm an overachiever. Everyone says so. I should be able to do this on my own."

Overachiever? That's a quality I haven't noticed in Mitzi, at least not around the office.

Still, my heart goes out to her. She's been struggling for two years with the "what-if" of not being able to have a child. That's a pain I, never having been in her position, cannot judge.

Later, back at the office, I still felt rattled by the alien expression of apprehension in Mitzi's eyes.

Betty was at her desk, eating garlic stir-fry out of a white paper box. The odor wafted through the room, and I felt my eyes sting. I hope she finishes her lunch down to the very last snow pea, because if she leaves her leftovers in our refrigerator we're going to need gas masks.

"Did you go out for Chinese?" I picked up the paper from her fortune cookie. "Treasures will come your way from unexpected places. Beware of the dishonest merchant."

It figures—eBay again, even in Betty's fortune cookie.

"Bryan brought it back for me from a Vietnamese restaurant."

"What was that about?" Mitzi came into the break room, chewing on a large dill pickle.

I stared at the pickle. "And what is *that* about?"

"Oh, nothing."

Hah. Mitzi replying to a question by saying "Oh, nothing," is like asking Genghis Khan or Attila the Hun what they're doing, gathering armies and polishing swords and having them innocently say, "Oh, nothing." There's always more than meets the eye.

"You don't like pickles. Aren't you the one who made the waiter take back a burger last week to remove the pickles and replace the meat so you wouldn't have to taste pickle juice?"

"That was last week." She took a determined bite of the gherkin.

"You didn't have a palate transplant, did you?"

She glared at me in sheer annoyance. "If you must know, I'm practicing."

"For what? A pickle derby?"

"For being pregnant."

"Sorry, Mitzi, I don't get it."

"Of course you wouldn't. Whitney, you have no foresight whatsoever. If it weren't for me, you wouldn't even have our girls' night out on your calendar! You should really spend more time planning ahead."

That's what I thought I was doing by leaving girls' night out *off* my calendar. Mitzi always plans it, and sometimes I just don't want to have my body massaged with stones—there are already enough rocks in my head, thank you—to hear a clothing historian lecture on the invention of the girdle, or to attend an in-home brassiere party where we can all be fitted in the privacy of someone's four-foot-by-four-foot bathroom. Kim, Betty and I have gone along with Mitzi's wacko ideas, because we know camaraderie around the office helps foster a teamwork approach, but if she gets us invited to another one of those brassiere parties, I'm outta here.

"And just what are you planning ahead for, might I ask?"

She bestowed on me her "You poor, benighted idiot" look. "For when I'm pregnant, of course! Midnight cravings? Pickles and ice cream? Don't you ever read anything other than software magazines?"

"Let me get this straight. You hate pickles, so you are practicing eating them so that when you get pregnant and have a craving for them, you will be able to tolerate them?"

"Of course. I want the entire pregnancy experience. I have to learn to eat pickles. Eating ice cream will be no problem."

Weird as it all is, I'm impressed. If Mitzi will go to

such lengths for a baby she isn't even pregnant with, I can't imagine what she'll do for one she's able to hold in her arms.

I looked at her, pickle halfway to her mouth.

She glared at me so I couldn't speak. "Don't you dare make fun of me, Whitney. Not only do Americans consume nine pounds of pickles per year per person, but Elvis loved fried pickles!" She turned and stalked off.

Well, if it was okay with Elvis, then it's okay with me.

Monday evening, later, March 22

Chase was in the kitchen when I got home, making himself a tuna fish sandwich. Mr. Tibble and Scram were weaving in and out between his legs like skaters making figure eights on the ice. Scram was meowing at the top of his lungs. He thinks it never hurts to ask for what he wants—especially if it's from one of his favorite food groups. Mr. Tibble normally doesn't stoop to Scram's level and act like a cat. He allows Scram to speak for him and express his displeasure. He also lets Scram steal food off the table and promptly takes it away from him. He does not let Scram go into the litter box first, sleep in his bed or have the one catnip mouse in the house that hasn't been beheaded. For some reason, whenever I think about Mr. Tibble, I'm reminded of Mitzi.

"Hi, honey." I slipped my arms around Chase's warm, taut middle and laid my head against his back. I could feel him breathing, and his innate, irresistible masculinity held me there as firmly as if he were a magnet and I a metal shaving. "How are you feeling today? Stomach better?"

"I feel great. Must have been something I ate."

"There could be something going around. Or maybe you have morning sickness."

He put down the mayonnaise, wiped his hands on a towel and turned around in my arms to kiss me on the forehead.

"You understand, of course, that I can't dignify that with a response."

"Wise choice." I plucked a carrot from the plate he'd prepared for himself.

"There's too much pregnancy conversation in my life. I have more information about what happens when a couple goes to a fertility specialist than I ever wanted to know. Unfortunately, no matter how hard I try to get Mitzi to quit talking, it doesn't work. I'm the little Dutch boy with his finger in the dike. Mitzi is the water and it's hopeless to think I can hold her back."

"Sometimes medicine can be an insane business— the E.R., people coming in on drugs, hallucinating, hyperventilating, bleeding—but it's nothing like your office. Insanity there is considered the norm."

"No one does drugs, but there is definitely a lot of hallucinating going on." And I began to entertain Chase with Mitzi's newest prepregnancy scheme, learning to love the common pickle.

Chapter Seven

Friday, March 26

It wasn't until today that Chase and I had time to sit down together and rehash our week. After dinner we curled up together on the couch, I with a cup of jasmine tea and Chase with espresso.

I only drink espresso when I can dip sugar cube after sugar cube into it, something my one-hundred-pound mother taught me. Since all this baby-nutrition-good-health conversation has started buzzing around the office, I feel guilty even considering a dietary no-no. Mitzi can read in my eyes when I've enjoyed food she's barred herself from having, and she can smell toffee on my breath from forty paces. It can't last forever, of course, because Mitzi loves junk food.

"Since when did Mitzi become such a force of nature?" Chase asked when I told him. "She's always been a climactic upheaval, but recently she's gained momentum."

"She's more serious about this than about anything

I've ever seen, including sending me to Hasty-Date to find a man and shopping for the perfect pair of Prada shoes."

That might have sounded shallow to an outsider, but Chase got my drift. I told him about the basal thermometer and the list of tests Mitzi and Arch were facing.

Chase whistled. "That should give them a pretty clear picture of what's going on."

"Not entirely," I muttered. "No one has even considered what it's going to be like to work with Mitzi while she goes through this. Aphids eat their mates, right? I'm afraid Mitzi will devour us like so many cheese crackers before she'd done. She's had so many mood swings I feel like we're already dizzy."

"It's an emotional time," Chase murmured.

And an emotional Mitzi is quite a sight to behold. Today she was alternately crying tears into her penne pasta salad with artichoke hearts, gorgonzola and pine nuts—nothing as plebian as a cheese sandwich at lunch for Mitzi—and laughing hysterically at the cartoons in the newspaper. Mitzi is becoming a split personality, and we at Innova have been watching her crack. When she got weepy over Blondie and Dagwood, we retreated to the safety of our desks.

"This has to hurt her more than she cares to let on," I told Chase.

Chase suddenly took my face in his hands and kissed me soundly. It was the kind of kiss that, had I been standing, would have made my knees weak. Since Mr. Tibble and Scram were currently sitting on my kneecaps and had made them completely numb, the kiss only blew every sensible thought from my head as I kissed him back.

He stroked my cheeks with the pads of his thumbs and murmured, "You are amazing, Whitney."

"What did I do to deserve that? I want to know so I can do it again."

"You have compassion for Mitzi, even though she drives you crazy. You never dwell on the negative in anyone's personality and always look for their humanity." He grinned at me and, numb though they were, my knees did weaken. "Maybe that's why I feel so fortunate to have you love me."

"I love you because you are impossible not to love," I told him. "Sometimes my heart hurts, I love you so much."

"Hurts? I don't want to hurt you."

"It's a good hurt. It feels as though it might explode with joy." I snuggled into his chest and sighed.

"And?"

"And what?"

"And what was that sigh about? It wasn't the sigh of a totally happy woman, now was it?"

"No fair. You know me too well."

"So spill it. What's not right in your world?"

"It's Kim. She's…" I searched around in my mind for a word, and could only come up with one. "Obsessed."

Chase tucked me closer to himself, a sign that he was ready and willing to listen.

"They are finding adoption complicated and intimidating." I thought back to this morning when, during her coffee break, Kim had filled out a self-assessment quiz meant to help her and Kurt identify their feelings and goals about adoption.

"Whitney," she'd said, her eyes wide, "I assumed we'd adopt a healthy infant and raise him or her as we

did Wesley. I didn't even consider the children with disabilities who are in desperate need of parents." She'd
held out a paper for me to read. "Look."

"Which disabilities in an adoptive child," the sheet
had read, "would you be willing to consider?" The inventory had been nearly a page long, listing everything
from premature and drug-exposed babies to those with
Down syndrome, blindness and a host of family history
issues, such as diabetes, mental disorders and alcohol
addiction. Then it had asked which racial heritages she
and Kurt would consider and whether they had gender
preferences or would think about taking twins.

"How can I decide? If a child needs love—needs
us—then we would take it, wouldn't we?" she'd
lamented. "And what about all those we can't take?
What happens to them?"

"She either wants to bring all the children home with
her or give up on the process entirely, depending on her
mood," I told Chase.

"They're forgetting something important," he commented. "They already have someone who is willing to
direct them, someone who will find the perfect child for
them—if it's His will."

I looked Chase in the baby blues. "You are absolutely
right. God is on their side. He knows if they should
adopt a baby or not. And He also knows who and where
that baby is right now. Perhaps it isn't even born yet."

You knit me together in my mother's womb…
My frame was not hidden from you, when I was
being made in secret… Your eyes beheld my
unformed substance. In your book were written all

the days that were formed for me, when none of
them as yet existed.
Psalms 139:13-16

I, too, sometimes forget God is in charge and try to
tackle the world on my own.

"You're so wise." I brushed my fingers against my
husband's cheek. "Kim and Mitzi are both doing the
'What-ifs'. No wonder they're nervous."

It makes more sense for Mitzi to be nervous.
Although she doesn't seem to mind that Kim and I are
Christians, she doesn't appear interested in joining the
club herself. Just because she and Arch once committed to join a denomination in order to marry in a particular church, that didn't make them Christian anymore
than standing in a kitchen makes one Julia Child.

"Ah, for the good old days." He gathered me into his
arms and nuzzled his nose into my hair. I detected the
faint, crisp smells of shaving lotion and soap.

"What's that supposed to mean?"

"I want to have a baby the old-fashioned way. You
know, homemade, a do-it-yourself endeavor..."

"And if at first you don't succeed, try, try again?"

He grinned, and his even white teeth flashed. "It's a
project I'm willing to commit my life to."

"Like the post office? 'Neither rain, nor hail, nor
sleet will stop...'"

"Something like that. In fact, I think playing post
office is a good place to start."

I didn't even hear Mr. Tibble or Scram complain
when I dumped them off my knees and onto the floor
so that I could get my arms around my husband's neck.

Monday, March 29

On Monday morning, Mitzi dealt out party invitations around the office as if they were Old Maid cards.

"For you, for you, for you…" She paused and gathered herself together before putting one on Bryan's desk. "For you…"

Bryan isn't exactly the life of the party. In fact, he can suck the energy right out of one. If he overhears an argument, he gets nervous and hides in the bathroom until it's over. "What's this?" Kim held hers up to the light to see if the flat vellum envelope contained a bomb.

"Arch and I are having a get-together on Saturday night. There will be appetizers, a buffet by the pool, music, and scads of doctors and their wives there. I thought it might be good to water down the intellectuals with you guys."

Leave it to Mitzi to extend a gracious invitation.

"Suddenly, I think I'm busy," Kim retorted.

"Don't get huffy. You know what I mean. I don't want these people discussing appendectomies and thyroidectomies all evening. You'll be a diversion."

"Like a juggling clown, or someone who does balloon art? You aren't helping your case, Mitzi."

"I'm having the food catered by Ziga's."

Ziga's is a well-known dining spot on Lake Zachary, where Mitzi lives.

"Well, why didn't you say so in the first place? They have the best food I've ever eaten." Kim exchanged a resigned glance with me over Mitzi's head. We're a family; we show up for each other no matter what—especially when food is involved.

*Thursday, April 1, April Fools' Day—Innova's Annual
Day of Celebration*

Forget Presidents' Day, Labor Day and the Fourth of
July. April 1 is my company's day to howl. Quite literally, in fact.

The first thing Harry did when he walked into the
office this morning was to stub his toe on the leg of
Kim's desk and start hopping around as if he was riding
a crazed pogo stick.

"Ouch, ouch, owww…"

Immediately, Kim jumped up to help him, Bryan
headed for the bathroom to get out of the way, and Betty
lunged to the phone to call for help. I, meanwhile, had
the presence of mind to find the man a chair so he could
sit down. But it wasn't until Mitzi sauntered over to
examine the damage to Harry's shoe, that he erupted out
of the chair and yelled, "Gotcha! April Fool!"

We all groaned in unison. How could we have let
Harry get away with the first April Fools' gotcha? There
is, after all, a trophy at stake for the one who tricks the
rest of the office with his or her April Fools' joke. Harry
had, in the first moments of the day, set the standard
high. Now, if one or two of us did hoodwink the others
with our stories, we'd still have to face the play-offs—
a highly competitive game of dominoes, something to
do with Mexican trains or chicken scratches or whatever
Betty dreams up.

It's not like the traveling trophy is so fabulous or
anything. It's actually a spectacularly ugly lamp with the
names of past winners taped to the shade, but such is
the competitive element of our office that everyone takes

pleasure in displaying it in a place of prominence in their homes. Mitzi won it last year and had a small decorative niche installed in her basement family room to show it off.

After a high-level meeting of the minds over the water cooler, we decided to play a group trick on Harry in retaliation for catching us all so early in the day.

While I distracted him with a bogus question about a spurious client, Mitzi sneaked into his office and took his car keys out of the pocket of his jacket and passed them off to Kim, who, on her break, went outside to the parking lot. Harry always parks in the first row of cars, those nearest our building. In fact, if there's no opening when he arrives, he circles the area until someone leaves.

Kim reparked the car in the fifth row and returned to the office unnoticed because Betty was intercepting him with another counterfeit question. Kim handed off the keys to Bryan, who put them back into Harry's pocket and was back at his desk before Betty let Harry return to work.

Then we all sat holding our breath, waiting for lunch-time.

Harry breezed out of his office and called back over his shoulder, "I'll be back at one. I see I've got a luncheon meeting with a client today."

Mitzi smiled and waved at him as he left, never letting on that she had fabricated the luncheon just to get him out of the office and into his car.

Then we all stood at the window and watched.

Harry strode to his parking space and, without even looking at the car, thrust the key into the lock. When it didn't fit, he glanced up and did a double take when he saw that he'd been trying to breach a gleaming black Hummer instead of his charcoal Jeep Cherokee.

He glanced around the parking lot, and then at his key. We hooted with laughter as he tried the key in the lock a second time, as if hoping that upon feeling the familiarity of the key, the Hummer, like Cinderella's coach, would turn back into a pumpkin.

I've got to give it to the man, he's persistent. He stormed up and down the long row of parking places for nearly five minutes before spinning on his heel and marching back toward the building.

When he arrived, we were ready for him.

We greeted him when the office door banged open. "April Fool!"

Harry folded like sails collapsing from a dearth of wind.

"You! You? You…" Then he grinned. "Man, that was good!"

Like sportscasters recapping the game's best plays, we rehashed every moment from Harry arriving at the Hummer to him returning to the office.

And the day only went up—or maybe it was down— from there. Mitzi put a thin layer of Icy Hot on the toilet seat in the ladies' room and nearly drove Betty wild. Bryan, with a piece of thin fabric on his lap, waited until I bent over and then ripped it in half. I immediately clutched my backside and headed for the back room to check out the damage. I also vowed to lose five pounds before his laughter stopped me. I'd been had.

There was a fake spider on Mitzi's keyboard, which stopped all progress in the office for twenty minutes while we talked her down from her chair, and a bloody gash on Kim's knee, which turned out to be ketchup.

I was so exhausted by the end of the day that I went home and fell asleep on the couch and Chase had to carry me to bed.

No fooling.

Friday, April 2

Mitzi was two hours late for work today and came in white as a sheet. Her hair, a never-a-strand-out-of-place do, looked as though she'd combed it with an eggbeater, her jacket was missing a button, and she had a run in her stockings.

"Are you okay?" I hurried to her as she stood propped against the reception desk. "Did you fall?"

She looked at me hazily, as if she recognized my voice but couldn't remember my name. "I've had the most terrible morning."

Kim and I helped her to her desk while Bryan ran for water and Betty fluttered helplessly around us.

When her color started to return, Kim demanded, "What happened to you, anyway?"

"Shh. She probably came from the doctor. She said she had to have some tests this week."

"No tests," Mitzi bleated. "I had my teeth cleaned. The stress was enormous."

The stress of having her teeth cleaned had caused this? I hope I'm nowhere near the delivery room when Mitzi goes into labor.

Chapter Eight

Saturday, April 3

"Do we have to go to this party?" Kim bleated as we neared Mitzi and Arch's neighborhood, an upper-crust outpost where traffic doesn't make noise, children are born with silver spoons in their mouths and crabgrass never grows.

"Do you want a little cheese with your whine?" I asked sweetly. "Or do you want us to drop you off here and let you walk home?"

"You're a hard woman, Whitney."

"You're the one who made me promise that I'd get you here, no matter how often you protested or how many excuses you had."

"I left my vulnerable, defenseless child with a baby-sitter I hardly know, and you made me come anyway!"

"Wesley is as defenseless as a munitions factory, and the babysitter is the girl next door."

Kim grinned slightly. "That's true. Wesley has been

a challenge lately. But he's growing so fast and learning so much. I don't want to miss anything…."

"Kim, he's learned to burp at will. That is not a good reason to stay home and videotape him. Besides, you said yourself that we're here to support Mitzi because she's been under a lot of stress lately."

Kim quieted at that. We at Innova have formed an unspoken club, one that centers on making sure that whoever is having a bad day gets extra support. Even Harry has noticed Mitzi's uncharacteristically weak moments, and once told her to "Go make yourself a cup of tea or something." Meanwhile, Betty Noble, whose sister adopted two children, is showing real tenderness toward Kim.

Bryan, however, is absent from the office more and more, especially from the rooms Mitzi inhabits. I've weighed the idea of setting up a mini workstation in the men's room, so that when he's hiding, he doesn't fall behind in his work. I've also been waiting for the right moment to approach him about his behavior, but so far he's managed to elude me. I've considered calling his girlfriend to see if something is seriously wrong with him. Unfortunately, she can be as vague as he. Talking to Jennilee is like having a conversation with the Cheshire cat as he fades in and out.

I was pleased to see Bryan and Jennilee pull into the driveway of Mitzi's house just ahead us. The house is a huge white wedding cake of a mansion with a colonnade over the walkway that spans the entire front. The portico is huge, with oversized wooden doors that drifted open silently to reveal a tall, gray-haired butler looking down his nose at us as we huddled together like Tin Man,

Dorothy, Lion and Scarecrow on their first visit to the Wizard of Oz.

"I didn't know Mitzi had a butler!" Kim hissed into my ear.

"She doesn't. She hired him for the occasion."

"Rent-a-Jeeves? Really? Cool!"

Chase and Kurt, blissfully unaware of anything other than the fact that there was bound to be great food inside, hurried us past the intimidating butler and into the house. Mitzi drifted across the foyer in a vision of teal chiffon that made her skin look like porcelain and her eyes like jewels.

Sometimes it's difficult to remember this elegant side of Mitzi when she's setting up a security camera in the break room to see who has been stealing her imported designer water out of the refrigerator or calling every office supply store in town to find a pen fat enough so that her fake nails don't click together when she writes.

"You came!" For a moment, Mitzi looked truly delighted. Then she burst that bubble. "I thought you'd never get here. They're replaying a face-lift and tummy tuck in the living room and a gall bladder horror story in the den. Worse yet, Arch and his friends are debating bunion treatments in the living room." She pushed at Chase and Kurt. "Go ask them about the Super Bowl or something. Find out if they think the Yankees or the Red Sox will win."

I patted Chase's arm. "Go on, dear, ask that. I'm sure the answers will be interesting."

He rolled his eyes as he and Kurt walked off, first to the buffet table and then to the big-screen television in the entertainment room, where, no doubt, Mitzi thought someone from the National Hockey League was facing off with the Gophers basketball team. Such is sports in Mitzi's world.

"Nice party."

Mitzi gazed around absently. "Yes, I suppose it is."

Kim took her by the arm. "Now, if you'll just show me where the chocolate is, nobody will get hurt."

"You can't say I've never done anything for you," Mitzi said obliquely, and pointed toward the dining room.

There, Kim and I found the sort of treasure we might have expected at the end of the rainbow. A chocolate fountain, running with the thickest, sweetest chocolate this side of Hershey, Pennsylvania. Around it were piles of fresh fruits, tiny cakes, pretzels, handmade marshmallows, cookies and anything else that could be dipped in chocolate.

Kim rushed right in to spear a bit of pound cake and thrust it into the dark, sweet waves.

"Just pick me up when the party's over," she instructed. "I'll be right here. I don't plan to move for hours."

"I still don't understand what you people see in that stuff." Mitzi spoke as if chocoholics everywhere were a species to be pitied. "Oh, by the way, there's Black Forest Cake, German Chocolate cake and a double Dutch fudge cake on the buffet table."

Kim's eyes glazed over with bliss.

"What's this about, Mitzi?" I hissed. "Chocolate everywhere?"

"What else could I do? I don't want to be tempted to eat the leftovers."

By midparty, Harry and Betty and their spouses had also arrived, making us a little island of software geeks in a world of medicine. We were in Mitzi's vast dining room, packing food into our mouths like chipmunks and debating the merits of key lime pie over chocolate pecan turtle cheesecake, when Mitzi's husband, Arch, strolled in.

Now, Arch, although the kind of man you know is just itching to wash his hands every fifteen minutes, the kind who alphabetizes his socks—Angora, Black, Cashmere, etc.—is a really nice guy. He'd have to be—or else stone deaf—to put up with Mitzi. In fact, he adores her and finds her as entertaining as late-night television. What's more, he has cultivated a blind spot for her foibles and eccentricities, much as we at Innova have had to do. Mitzi is just, well, Mitzi. She employs stealth technology, much like the cloaking device used to hide starships on *Star Trek* reruns, to charm people. Then she blows them out of the sky.

"Sorry I didn't get to you sooner. When those guys start talking ingrown toenails, it can go on for hours." He grinned his toothpasty smile. "Chase, there's a group in the other room talking treatments for football injuries. And one of the docs used to be a physician for World Wrestling Entertainment. Thought you and Kurt might be interested."

For a moment, I'd actually forgotten that my husband, too, was a doctor. I am so grateful he doesn't bring his work home with him. An appendectomy retrospective over dinner is not my idea of a relaxing meal. Of course, Kurt, a WWE fan, led the way out of the room. Then Arch turned to Betty and Harry. "Maybe you'd like to see the new twenty-seven-inch computer screen I purchased for my office." Arch looked—dare I say it?—archly at Betty. "It's great for shopping on eBay."

Before they left the room, he turned to Kim and me. "By the way, Mitzi told me to tell you to meet her by the front stairs. She wants to show you something."

As we made our way past the scowling Jeeves, the string quartet and the cluster of women who were going to need chiropractic treatments after they took the multicarat diamond-crusted jewelry off their necks, Kim whispered. "How did Mitzi get a gem like him?"

"She's pretty and funny and he doesn't have to work in the same office with her?"

"Well, there is that…"

Mitzi swooped down upon us, grabbed my arm and towed me up the curved staircase without explanation. Her flight of stairs hinted not only at antebellum Southern plantations, but also, oddly, at Andy Warhol. The wall along the sweeping white steps is decorated with somebody's ancestors, strangers Mitzi picked up in an antique store, and large bright acrylic paintings of Mitzi and Arch. I don't know how, but the look actually works, even though I keep expecting to see Marilyn Monroe or a large Campbell's soup can in the mix.

The hallways are carpeted a soft yellow, perfect with the white-painted woodwork and florals and landscapes in many shades of green. In each piece is a hint of the same maize color as the walls, like the soft yellow light of the sun. Discreetly placed speakers enveloped us with rain forest music.

"This is beautiful, Mitzi." Kim stared up at the architectural details on the ceiling. "Did you decorate it yourself?"

"With help. That's why I wanted you to come upstairs. I need some decorating advice."

As Mitzi tripped on ahead, Kim and I stared at each other. *Mitzi* asking *us* for advice? Had the world tilted on its axis when we weren't looking? Were we being thrown into an alternate universe where everything was upside down and backward?

Mitzi is the giver of advice, not the taker—advice about clothing, diets, behavior, grooming, nail art, body polishing and any other subject matter she deems worthwhile. No matter how many times we'd tried to stop her, Mitzi is the gift that keeps on giving.

She halted in front of a door so quickly that Kim and I nearly fell on top of her.

"This is it." Drawing a breath as if to steel herself, she opened it and stepped inside.

The only way I can manage to describe what we saw was Toys "R" Us meets Ralph Lauren meets stuffed-animal factory. The walls were streaked with various test colors—pale pinks, blues, yellows, peaches, greens and creams. There were more animals than Noah had on the ark, overflowing a bright red-and-blue playpen. Three cribs lined one wall. The round one with the jungle-print mattress and bumpers and the lion-tiger-and-elephant mobile was my immediate favorite.

"What are you doing? Starting a new business? There's more stuff in here than in Kmart!"

Mitzi's eyes suddenly filled with tears. "I wanted to decorate a room for my baby, and all I've got here is a big mess. No theme, no color palette, no…"

"No baby?" Kim said gently.

Mitzi sat down on a big yellow ball like the one I use

at the gym. "I thought it might encourage me while I'm going through all these tests. I'm beginning to feel like a pincushion and not a person." Her voice trailed away, and she stared in the direction of one of the cribs. "It just reminds me that perhaps I'll never have a baby and this room will be a monument to my failure."

"Failure? Mitzi, don't feel that way."

"How should I feel? Isn't that what women are designed to do? Have babies?" Her eyes glittered. "I know you all think I'm a big goof-off at work, that I'm just there because I'd be bored staying home, but that's not true. I actually…"

I waited for her to say she loved us.

"…am used to you now and it's not so awful."

How *do* we keep our heads from swelling?

"But my body isn't cooperating. Can you even begin to understand how that feels?"

Kim took Mitzi's hand. "I know my issues aren't the same as yours, but my body hasn't always cooperated, either. Depression and breast cancer—I didn't ask for either, but there it is. That doesn't mean that I am only a cancer survivor or a depression-prone female, anymore than you are only an infertile woman. That's a small part of who we are as people, not the sum total of our lives."

Mitzi looked at her doubtfully. "I suppose so." I could see her gaze had cleared. Little lasers were emanating from her eyes. "It's like Whitney before she found Chase. She wasn't a total loser, but it was kind of hard to remember that."

"Wait a minute," I protested, "I—"

But Kim stopped me. "Yeah, just like that. She was never a loser. Not for a minute. And neither are you."

Well, thanks for that. I think.

"Maybe you jumped the gun by trying to set up a nursery when you're still working with the doctors."

A cunning look flickered on Mitzi's face. "I suppose I did, but it usually helps to be ahead of the pack."

"What on earth do you mean by that?"

"Now if you want a nursery as nice as ours, you'll have to copy me, not the other way around."

"You mean this is all about being first?" I took her by the shoulders. "Mitzi, I can assure you that there is no way that you will ever be less than cutting-edge in the style department, so just relax. Get pregnant first, then do the nursery. It will be easier, I'm sure."

I could see her blue mood lifting. "Good idea." Then her eyes began to sparkle. "But I have picked out baby names, and I'm never going to tell you what they are. You'd probably want to copy me."

"No doubt."

As if I had a tendency to run out and do whatever it is Mitzi does. If that were true, right now I'd have blue nail polish on my toenails, enough gloss on my lips to wax the floor at Grand Central Station and an ego the size of South America.

Chapter Nine

Three hours later, Bryan and Jennilee had already left and Betty, Harry and their spouses were saying their goodbyes to Arch. Chase and Kurt were standing in the foyer doing that back-slapping see-ya-later-good-buddy thing that guys sometimes do. Kim's eyebrows rose as she watched this newfound camaraderie Kurt shared with Arch and his friends. Kurt, though outgoing and gregarious around Chase and me, is not always happy in social settings. As Chase says, driving a truck and studying to be an accountant aren't the two most sociable occupations on earth.

Kim could hardly contain herself until we got into the car. "You guys looked like a bunch of fraternity brothers planning your next big get-together. Did I hear someone say they were looking forward to seeing you next weekend?"

"Arch has some really nice friends," Kurt commented blandly.

"Podiatrists? Well, I'm sure they're nice, but…"

"You aren't prejudiced against podiatrists are you?" Chase teased. "How do you feel about internists?"

Kurt ignored the banter. "Several of Arch's friends have a housing repair project planned. They've hired people to do repair work on the homes of single mothers and elderly patients. Now they're preparing to take a weekend, and rather than hire others to do the jobs, they're going to do the work themselves. They not only want to finance the project, they want to experience it."

"So," Chase added, "Kurt, in a fit of goodwill, volunteered our services, too. What are we doing on the weekend of April seventeenth, Whitney?"

"Plumbing and shingling, apparently," I said with a sigh.

"What are we supposed to do while you guys are off having fun with hammers and nails?" Kim inquired.

"That's the best part!" Kurt brightened. "They need women to work, too. I volunteered you and Whitney to be with me and Chase. Isn't that a great idea?"

Chase angled himself on the seat so that I could catch his eyes, which he rolled helplessly, and I knew immediately that he had succumbed to Kurt's enthusiasm with some reservations.

"You volunteered me and Whitney?" Kim squawked. "Without asking us? What are we supposed to do—knit curtains?"

"Arch said there would be plenty of stuff— wallpapering, staining woodwork, that sort of thing. Don't worry, he volunteered Mitzi, too."

A deadly silence fell as we processed that bit of information. Arch is a man with a death wish. Why else would he volunteer Mitzi to help rehabilitate run-down houses in the city?

Kurt added quickly, "He believes it will be good for

her. She's become fixated on getting pregnant, and he thinks getting her mind off it might just do the trick."

This is why podiatrists are not fertility experts.

"Oh, she'll get her mind off it, all right," Kim drawled. "No doubt about that."

Kim is absolutely right. Mitzi will be thinking of a thousand ways to make Arch pay dearly for this.

Monday, April 6

"Put it back!" The words crackled around me like shards of broken glass.

I'd never heard the upper registers of Bryan's voice before. It's impressive that he can squeak that loudly.

Feeling a headache starting in my right eyeball, I turned to him and patiently explained. "I am not going to eat your meatball sandwich, Bryan. I am, however, moving it to get to my salad, which is in the container beneath it. You are going to have to accept, sooner or later, that I am not the Pierogi Bandit, that I like my own meatballs better than the ones your grandmother makes and that, in general, I do not make it a policy to steal food from hungry people."

He slumped onto a stool. "They all say that."

"'They?'"

"Betty, Mitzi, Kim…" He looked so defeated, sitting there with his mushroom-colored eyes, hair and skin, that I pulled up a stool and sat down beside him.

"What's up? Really."

"The food…"

"I know, but there's got to be more. You don't usually get so emotional, even about your grandmother's food. There must be something else going on."

His head jerked up, and he stared at me as if I'd just touched a sore spot in his heart. "Jennilee wants to get married."

Well, knock me over with a feather.

"No kidding? Congratulations!" I studied his facial expression. "Or not?"

Bryan shrugged helplessly. "You know how I am about confrontations. Jennilee is giving me an ultimatum. Either we start talking marriage or she starts looking for someone who can commit."

"You have been dating for two years," I ventured, trying to imagine the timid Jennilee even knowing what an ultimatum was, let alone giving one. "It's not an unrealistic expectation to discuss your future together."

"But it's just so hard to *know!*" Bryan fussed.

"Know what?"

"Whether she really loves me for myself, or if it's all about my looks and charisma."

It took me an entire thirty seconds to get the imps in my mind to quit rolling on the floor of my brain and laughing.

"Oh, Bryan…" I laid a comforting hand on his arm and willed myself not to wonder where Bryan parks the magnetic and alluring part of himself when he comes to work. "I wouldn't worry about that, if I were you. I'm sure Jennilee loves you for who you are as a person and isn't blinded by all your sparkle and glitz."

"No?" He looked hopeful. "Maybe I just worry too much."

"Maybe you do," I agreed. "Take a break. Enjoy your life."

He nodded to himself, like one of those car window

dogs whose head is attached to its body by a wire spring. Bobblehead Bryan. In more ways than one.

Smiling to myself, I sat down at the table, pulled a packet of diet French dressing out of my purse and popped the lid off my delicious salad, the one I'd been looking forward to all morning. I looked into the container, then lifted my head and yelled, "Who ate all my chicken and cherry tomatoes?"

Pierogi Bandit, now you've gone too far. You went and messed with my salad. Consider yourself history.

Thursday, April 8

"But you have to go with me. Arch has patients."

"I have a job. Here. Remember? Some people actually count on us to write and sell software programs. Silly, I know, but—"

"You *have* to go."

At that moment, Harry, the little row of punctuation marks on his head looking more pronounced than usual, wandered by with that glazed look in his eye that he gets when he's in the creative flow.

Mitzi lasered in on his befuddlement. "Doesn't she, Harry?"

"Huh?"

"Whitney. She has to go to my doctor's appointment with me, right?"

Harry stared at me as though he didn't recognize me. "Yeah, sure. Whatever."

She looked at me triumphantly. "See?"

I'd been hijacked in broad daylight, in front of an audience, and no one had lifted a hand to save me.

Mitzi, who is having a series of ultrasound films taken in specific cycles to monitor follicular development—which sounds like something from a program on the rain forest to me—and some blood tests, didn't seem to mind the tests nearly as much as she did the clinic's choice of X-ray wear and cleaning supplies. I don't know what she expects to smell when she goes into a hospital, other than antiseptic odors. I've never known one to smell like Eau de Gucci or White Diamonds.

"Why is it that parking spots open for you like Moses parting the Red Sea?" I asked as she pulled her Porsche into a spot right next to the clinic door. "If I'd been driving, we would have had to park at the tire shop across the street and hike over the interstate."

She looked at me blankly. Parking spots always appear for Mitzi. And jewelry. And good hair days. It's no wonder she's having such a difficult time with this infertility thing. It's the first time Mitzi hasn't immediately gotten what she wanted.

As I sat in the waiting room, reading *Good Housekeeping* from February of 2003, I covertly observed the stream of patients entering and leaving through the front door of the fertility clinic.

A pale, limp woman entered the room. Everybody knows such a woman—bland complexion, mousy hair, hunched shoulders, leaning forward slightly as if she were heading into a brisk wind. Her clothes were clean but wrinkled, as if they'd resided a little too long in the dryer before being rescued, and her sweater was stretched out on one side. This was not surprising, since there was a small child hanging on its hem. The woman shambled along, one hip raised slightly to support the robust blond baby on her hip. She was the most worn-out-looking woman I have ever seen. Even the tongues of her shoes were hanging out, panting for breath.

The nurse at the desk, I soon deduced, was Limp Woman's sister. She kissed the baby, gave the toddler dragging on his mother's sweater a Tootsie Roll and handed the woman a package that she was to deliver to a third family member who was waiting in the car outside.

They tried to carry on a conversation, but the baby stuck its drooly fist in his mother's mouth and the child on her sweater lifted its feet off the floor and dangled from it like a capuchin monkey. Finally the mother shuffled toward the door and disappeared, looking even more stooped than when she'd entered.

I felt exhausted just watching her.

For the sake of truth in advertising, perhaps we should see more tired mothers on the pages of national magazines and fewer rested ones who appear to have, before lunch, sewn up matching outfits for their darlings, cooked a nutritionally balanced gourmet breakfast that included pancakes in the shape of Disney characters, and taught them to speak French.

Maybe, I thought, as I thumbed through the dog-eared magazine, it's a reprieve for Mitzi that she doesn't see all the actualities of motherhood quite yet. The circus will begin when the dawning light of reality starts to shine on Mitzi.

And, speaking of motherhood, I dropped in on my parents after work tonight because Chase's nurse had called to say he'd been held up at the hospital.

Mom, in a pair of leotards and a baggy shirt, was cooking dinner. It's no fair, really. The woman is looking at fifty-five in the rearview mirror, and she doesn't appear old enough to drive a frying pan. There are the occasional crow's feet, of course, and a couple of frown lines in her forehead that I put there when I was a child, but overall, she looks too young to be a grandmother, even without makeup. Maybe she *is* too young to be a grandmother.

"Hi, darling, bring me a bag of chocolate chips from the cupboard? I want to frost this cake."

Obediently, I opened the cupboard and peered inside. Funny, isn't it, how a daughter organizes things in her cupboards exactly the same way her mother does? Soup at eye level in rows—mushroom, tomato, chicken noodle— tuna fish on the same row as the soups, and baking supplies all on one shelf, etc. Sometimes when I see that someone has put a garbage can anywhere other than behind the right-hand door under the kitchen sink, my mind automatically screams, "Wrong! It's just wrong!"

"There aren't any chips in here." I held up an empty bag. Two elderly gray chips rolled onto the counter.

"Oh, that father of yours." Mother looked ready to slap him with her spatula. "He could buy a candy bar when he wants a snack, but no. He has to eat my chocolate chips. He thinks he's getting away with something… Ha!"

"Ha" is right. My dad hasn't fooled my mother in thirty years.

"Now what will you do?"

"What I always do when your father eats all the chocolate chips." She put a finger to her lips. "But you must never tell."

She went to the small cupboard where she kept cough syrup, aspirin and any sort of medication she didn't want a child to reach. She dug in the back and pulled out a flat white box with bright blue lettering.

"Mother, you wouldn't!"

She stared at my horrified expression, then down at the box in her hand—and burst out laughing. "Oh, Whitney, even I'm not that cruel! I hide a can of frosting behind the Ex-Lax so I always have it on hand. Your father never looks in here when he's hungry." She put the laxative back into the cupboard and pulled out a can of fudge frosting.

I sagged with relief. Even though Dad needs to be taught a lesson about eating between meals, Ex-Lax frosting would definitely be overkill.

"You know, dear," Mother said as she greased and coated a pan, "next time you bake, flour your cake pan with a bit of the cake mix itself. Then you won't have that messy white stuff all over the bottom of your cake."

But if I go to a bakery, I don't get messy stuff all over my kitchen.

She handed me the can to open. She's finally quit sending me to the neighbors' to have their hunky bachelor son open anything with a lid. Her theory was that if she sent me over there often enough, and if I looked helpless enough, he'd fall in love with me and ask me to marry him. He opened a thousand bottles over the years, with nary a proposal, much to my mother's disappointment.

Chapter Ten

Too much information! I have heard more about what happens when a couple goes to a fertility specialist than I've ever wanted to know. Unfortunately, no matter how hard I try to get Mitzi to quit talking about her and Arch's exploits, it doesn't work. Today she'd pounced on me the moment I entered the break room to get coffee.

"And the phlebotomist said I had the *smallest* veins he's ever seen. Do you want to see the bruise on my arm? My skin is very delicate, you know. I just can't be poked and prodded like some people. Can you see those tiny little veins? And look at this bruise. Black, blue and red! She put a bandage on it, but, of course I just bled anyway. Why, Arch says…"

Bryan, who was pouring himself a cup of coffee, skittered out of the room.

I handed Mitzi a sheaf of papers, hoping she'd get the

hint, leave the break room and get back to work. "If you'd just file these, I'll…"

"Sometimes I feel like I'm in school, worried about whether I'll pass or fail a test. I never liked that part about school. I'm very sensitive, you know. I don't believe in failure. Why, there was this time in geometry class that…"

I escaped into the office just in time to see Kim at her desk, systematically breaking pencils in half. As she did so, she muttered to herself, "Take that, and that and *that*." She gritted her teeth so tightly that I could hear her molars grinding. Then she picked up one of the broken stubs and rammed the lead tip into the desk so that it shattered and left a large dark graphite smudge where it hit. She smiled with satisfaction, picked up another and did it again.

"Kim…" I approached her warily, much as I might an unfamiliar dog with speckles of foam around its mouth. My eyes went to the corners of her lips—just in case.

She looked up at me, face flushed, eyes darting. "Yes?"

"Is there something you'd like to tell me?"

She thwacked another pencil lead into oblivion. "No. Why would you ask?"

"Oh, just a guess, that's all. Woman's intuition. And the fact that you are pulverizing number two lead pencils just for the fun of it."

"A girl has to have hobbies, doesn't she?" She rammed another pencil into the desk.

"Whatever happened to scrap-booking and golf?"

Through gritted teeth, she muttered, "Get me out of here."

"Noon?"

"No, *now.*"

There are advantages to my position in the company. Normally, I do not exercise these benefits, but when one of my staff is losing her mind—and her writing implements—before my very eyes, I need to act.

"Bryan, will you see that Kim's desk is covered? I want her to come with me for a quick meeting. We'll be back in a half hour, forty-five minutes, max." And before anyone could protest, I hustled the maniacal Kim out of the office.

She was still muttering to herself when I brought her a latte and a chocolate biscotti from the coffee shop. I sat down across from her and waited. Eventually her breathing started to slow and the tenseness in her body began to fade.

"Thank you, Whitney. You may just have saved a life." She swilled down the coffee as if it were ice-cold instead of steaming.

"Yours?"

"No. Mitzi's." She poked the biscotti into the remaining coffee, sloshed it around until it was soft and gobbled that down, too. "And Kurt would never forgive me if I wrestled that woman to the floor and put a gag in her mouth."

"No?" I took a sip of my own java. "But think of the thank-you cards you'd receive from Mitzi's friends and neighbors."

Finally, she smiled. "Poor Mitzi. She doesn't even know what she's doing, does she?"

"Want to talk about it?"

Kim rumpled her hair with her fingers. "Whitney, I'm so ashamed!"

"I would be, too, if I'd wrecked all those pencils. Think of the trees...."

"She makes me crazy, and it's not even her fault."

"For once," I said, still clueless about what we were discussing. If there's trouble in the office, it usually can be traced back to Mitzi. "Care to clue me in as to what we're talking about? Or would you like me to play twenty questions with you?"

Kim looked at me quizzically. "But don't you... No, of course you don't!"

Here we go again. Our own little Tower of Babel. Everybody's talking, and I haven't a clue what any of them are saying.

"I can't believe it, but I'm jealous of Mitzi!"

That's what this is about?

"It's so stupid. She's been talking nonstop about she and Arch getting pregnant, and I'm green with envy. I want to feel a baby growing beneath my heart, to feel it kick and flutter...." Kim, grieving over the loss of that treasured experience, rested her hand just above her diaphragm and looked so wistful that I felt like crying for her.

"She's not sure this will work, Kim. Below all that bluster, Mitzi is terrified that it won't. She's talking about this to convince *herself* she's going to have a child—not you." I crossed my arms over my chest and stared Kim down. "And I think you already know all that. You'll be delighted for Mitzi when she becomes pregnant. There's something else going on with you."

Her eyes welled with unshed tears. "I'm the paper version of Mitzi, and I hate it. She's got to pass all these physical hurdles in order to get her baby, and I have to pass the paper ones. Kurt and I have spent hours filling out forms and gathering documents to compile a dossier and get our adoption started. We've been assigned a social worker. Our home study looks at everything about us, our personal and family backgrounds, how we were raised, our siblings, the significant people in our lives, our marriage and family relationships, our motives for adopting and what we expect for this child. They want to know how we plan to integrate a baby into our family, how we'll parent, our health histories, education and finances. They want references and background clearances to make sure we aren't criminals. They'll know more about us than we know about ourselves!"

"Too bad they don't have that information before babies can be born into all families. We'd probably learn a few things about how to be good parents before the fact, rather than by trial and error. Cars come with owner's manuals, but babies you have to figure out on your own."

Kim smiled wanly. "You're probably right. After filling out some of these forms, I wonder if I'm fit to be a mother to Wesley."

"And he's a smart, healthy, funny, happy little boy. Go figure."

Kim cheered slightly. "We were told that it could take six months or longer to compile everything we need, but we think we can get it done in half the time. Then we have to send it all to China and wait for a referral."

I must have looked surprised.

"We went to a meeting last night with several families with children from China. The moment I walked into the room, I knew it was where we needed to be. There's a child in that country, Whitney, that's meant for us. I feel it in my heart."

Kim scowled. "Yet when Mitzi yammers about all her tests and I think about what it was like to carry Wesley for nine months…" She touched her flat belly.

"You want that, too."

"It's hard to let go of that dream, even though I know adopting is the right thing for us to do. Am I totally selfish, Whitney?" She toyed with the stiff paper the biscotti had come in.

"You and Mitzi aren't in a race to see who gets a baby first. This isn't an Olympic event, you know."

Kim wiped her eyes with a rough paper napkin. "You know how to put things in perspective, don't you?" She snuffled. "Now I really feel stupid."

"I should think so. I'm going to make you explain all those broken pencils to Harry. That will make you feel absolutely ridiculous."

I left the office at five, hoping that Kim would feel better now that she'd destroyed a little office equipment, but I forgot my concern when I heard my stomach growl. Well, maybe not growl, but I did hear a faint purr coming from the direction of my waistband.

Being budget-conscious, hungry and in need of groceries is a triple threat. My logic went like this:

I really hate to spend anymore money on groceries this week. Why I thought it was a smart idea to spend an entire week's grocery money on surf and turf for dinner last Saturday night, I'll never know.

Because I've been feeling guilty about overspending my budget, I've been serving Chase beans ever since to make up for it. Not only is that a gastric disaster, but there are only so many ways to cook beans before one's recipes, one's creativity or one's husband runs out.

But we still need to eat. And I'm starving right now. If I don't put something in my stomach soon, I'll... I'll... I'll what?

I have never been truly, dangerously hungry, not the kind of hungry that demands I eat or risk fainting dead away. I'm usually just mouth hungry. It's my taste buds that are starving, not my body, and they're usually starving for chocolate, chips and dip, pretzels, ice cream, cheesecake, cookies or coconut cream pie.

I will just buy things that are on sale...fruit...vegetables...Beano...whole grains...healthy foods...

Money spent on reasonably priced food that's good for me is a balm and a benefit to my budget and my conscience.

Almost without knowing how I got there, I found myself in the parking lot of one of those huge warehouse stores.

I'm always amazed by these warehouse clubs. They sell everything from ink to olive oil, tires to croissants, and rice in sacks large enough to feed small cities.

I don't know why I go anywhere else, I thought as I pushed a cart as large as a horse trailer down the aisle. I can buy my underwear, my sheets and towels, my beauty products and a garlic-roasted chicken right here, all conveniently under one roof. If I need caviar or a water cooler, here it is.

Well, maybe if I go somewhere else, it's because *they* don't force you to buy eggs three dozen per carton, orange juice in jugs larger than our water heater and enough blue cheese to depress an entire therapy group.

But it's so sensible! So good for the budget! So cheap!

And I, to make matters worse, was *so hungry.*

I tripped down the aisles filling my cart and feeling virtuous. Why, not only was I saving money, but I was on my way to ensuring that Chase had a healthy heart. After all, I had ten pounds of carrots and a sack of flaxseed in my cart. That had to count for something. And we would never again spread germs to our family and friends once I purchased four gallons of antiseptic hand soap and a tank of bleach. And trail mix. Trail mix is definitely nutritious. Can't pass that up!

Then, happily, the little ladies who do the food demonstrations began to set up shop. Samples of pork loin and blue corn chips with pineapple salsa provided sustenance and enough energy to push the cart, which was getting heavier and heavier. And who knew how delicious a combination of carrot and pineapple juice could be? Two bottles for the price of one! Sample sausage rolls. Yum. Baby éclairs. Mangoes straight from the tropics. My mouth was in ecstasy. Caught up in a veritable cyclone of flavors and bargains, I tossed food into my cart the way a farmer loads bales of hay.

By the time I reached the checkout line, my cart was almost as full as that of the woman ahead of me, who told me she had a family of twelve.

Once the checker had scanned all my healthy bargains, told me the amount I owed and called for a paramedic to revive me from sticker shock, they sent me on my way, gamely pushing a flatbed full of food to my car.

Now why, I ask myself, didn't I just acknowledge that a snack would be good, stop at the Dairy Queen, get myself a small cone and save myself four hundred dollars? Not counting, of course, the cost of the 15,000 minutes on the phone cards I grabbed just before I passed out.

Fortunately, Chase had stopped for a pizza. I was too tired to cook and too full from all those samples.

"How many get-togethers did you say we had to have to get rid of this stuff?"

"Two large brunches, a sit-down dinner and a Super Bowl party should do it."

"I'll take some of it to the site while we do those house renovations. Men with hammers tend to get hungry."

I kissed him gratefully. He'd helped me unload the car without comment—okay, without *much* comment—and sat down, rather than fainted, when I showed him the bill.

"You are my dream man, do you know that, Chase?"

"Bad dream?" he teased, tucking me beneath his arm, where I could feel his heart beating.

"You know better than that. Besides, if I'm going to have a nightmare, it's going to come from the office."

Chase whistled when I was done telling him about my morning among the hormonal, hysterical females at Innova.

"And to top it off, Bryan went home sick. I didn't think he could get any paler than he's been recently, but he did."

Bryan's been acting very strangely lately. That's saying a lot, because he's always strange. I'm sure it takes effort to be even more so. Besides Bryan leaping out of closets trying to catch someone stealing his pierogi, and Harry's recurring hairdo, which resembles a series of punctuation marks floating over his head— not a bad visual for his state of mind, really—Betty has been selling Mitzi's shoes on eBay during her lunch hour. Mitzi runs off to take her temperature every half hour, even though the only time it counts is in the morning, and Kim pores over information about adoption. I am the only one holding the office together, and I am running out of masking tape.

Chase, thankfully, is my glue. I'd be completely undone without him.

He massaged my neck, brought me hot chocolate and warm blankets and rubbed my feet. Bliss. Then he held me in his arms and kissed me like there was no tomorrow.

Now if only Mr. Tibble and Scram had not shredded the lovely artificial ficus tree I'd purchased at the warehouse club, life would be perfect.

Chapter Eleven

Thursday, April 15

"I forgive Mitzi for everything," Kim said as she handed me a sheet of paper. "Well, maybe not *everything*, but for a lot."

I put down a spreadsheet that was making my eyes cross and picked up the paper. With Mitzi, there's always plenty to forgive.

"She noticed I was upset yesterday about the adoption paperwork. She handed this to me this morning and suggested that someone should start asking the *kids* for their list of parental qualifications, instead of the other way around."

So whatever Mitzi was typing yesterday had nothing whatsoever to do with Innova. Business as usual.

WHAT A CHILD WANTS IN
AN ADOPTIVE PARENT

Personal and family background:

Children prefer parents who are:

- toy store owners
- circus clowns
- golden retrievers

Required parental abilities:

Parents must be able to:

- fingerpaint
- play with blocks and dolls for hours on end
- reread the same book five thousand times without complaining
- show willingness to eat mud pies on demand.

Motivation to adopt:

- wants entire house decorated with crayon drawings
- prefers stained carpets to clean ones
- desires less sleep, fewer adult conversations and more cuddling

Family environment:

- no furniture or flooring that can be ruined by grapejuice
- bottom drawers in kitchen filled with Tupperware, wooden spoons and small, lightweight pans for banging
- dog(s) available to clean child's face so that child may avoid trauma of washcloth

Physical and health history for adoptive parents:

- squishy enough for cuddling
- fast enough to keep up

· energetic enough to spend entire nights walking
  floor

Education:

· trained and certified in both Dr. Spock and Dr.
  Seuss

Employment:

Parents preferably employed at

· pet store
· Toys "R" Us
· amusement park

I was unable to stop a smile from spreading across
my face. "Good for Mitzi."

"There's more to her than you might first think,"
Kim marveled. "She surprises me all the time."

"It's her unique combination of intelligence, cunning, flightiness, idiocy and fashion savvy. One sees that
so seldom these days."

"Do you think she will be able to get pregnant,
Whitney? It would be dreadful if she couldn't. I, at least,
have Wesley."

Friday, April 16

I watched Mitzi breeze into the office in her usual
flurry. She wore her hair piled high on her head. Three-
inch-long earrings dangled from her lobes, and fake
eyelashes that looked like tarantulas flapped against her
cheeks. Something big must have happened for her to
go all out like that. I glanced at my watch to time her.
Usually, Mitzi can't keep information to herself for
more than two minutes—three, tops.

She sat at her desk looking coy and immediately busied herself with the files I'd left for her.

Something's up. Mitzi never gets right to work. In fact, Mitzi rarely gets to work at all—and never before 10:00 a.m. There's funny business going on.

I sauntered toward her desk to investigate her aberrant behavior. She was humming to herself and happily tending to the files, just like a normal employee. Scary. I'd never seen her act like that before. Normal, I mean.

Kim noticed the same thing and headed for Mitzi's desk from the opposite side of the room.

"Mitzi," I began. "You aren't complaining about anything and you got right to work. Is something wrong? What's—" I sniffed the air "—that *smell?*"

Kim put her hand over her nose and grimaced. "Wherever you got that perfume, you should take it back. It's nasty."

"It's not perfume. It's aromatherapy. There's a difference."

"That's probably true," I admitted. "If I have to smell that aroma all day, I probably *am* going to need therapy."

"What is it?" Kim looked curiously at the source of the odor.

"Betty found some recipes on the Internet. I combined a couple of them, just to make sure I got the full effect. It is cinnamon, clove, onion, garlic, camphor, lavender and lemon."

"The question is, why?"

Mitzi is a master of the pitying look. "Whitney, don't you know anything? It's an alternative therapy. A woman in the adjoining pedicure bay at my salon told

me it really helped her. She got pregnant almost immediately after she began aromatherapy."

So this woman *did* have qualifications for dispens-
ing medical advice…smooth feet.

Lest I become too superior-acting, I have to remember that there may be something to that. Mary washed
Jesus's feet with nard as an unsparing tribute. When I
was a child, the pastor of my church brought a tiny vial
of nard back from his travels in the Himalayas. To this
day, I can remember the warm, fragrant muskiness and
imagine its scent filling the room Christ and his follow-
ers inhabited.

"Mitzi, do you actually think this is going to help?"
Kim wondered. "Smelling like either a perfumery or a
fertilizer factory isn't going to…"

To our amazement, Mitzi's eyes filled with tears.
"I have to try everything, don't I?" she said fiercely.
"Everything."

"Have you prayed, Mitzi?" I asked softly, but she
didn't seem to hear me. Her aroma was so thick it had
probably clogged her ears as it had my olfactory glands.

Harry called me into his office after lunch. His ever-
growing forehead was creased in a series of deep
furrows. He gestured me into a chair, leaned forward
with his elbows on his desk and wove his fingers
together to make a single fist. His gaze burned into my
eyes. "Whitney, you have got to do something about
your staff!"

My staff?

"Excuse me?" Should I be getting excited? Had Harry
just handed Innova to me on a silver platter? Or have we
unintentionally developed one of those parenting/man-

agement styles in which when the children are good they belong to him and when they're bad they belong to me?

My parents used to play that game. "Why is *your* daughter making mud pies on my tool bench?" vs. "That's *my* daughter who hit that home run. She obviously takes after me when I was a boy."

"I know how they are, Harry, but it's not any worse than usual, is it?"

"Mitzi smells like a compost heap, Bryan is weirder than usual, Betty uses every break and her lunch hour to sell shoes on eBay, Kim stares dreamily into space, and you…" He searched for something to say. "Well, you're okay, but that's only one out of five."

There's no use arguing. He's right. The monkeys have taken over the zoo.

"What do you suggest?"

"Tell Mitzi that she has to keep her 'alternative therapies' at home. Yesterday I caught her 'meditating' in my office because it was quiet in here. And make Bryan go to a doctor or something. And talk to Betty and Kim. Tell them you want them to pay attention here at work."

"Right." As if anything I said would help!

But Harry, who thinks I can do anything, looked relieved. "Take care of it, Whitney."

A question burned on the tip of my tongue. "Why do you put up with us, Harry?"

He considered the question a moment before answering. "Because, somehow, in spite of everyone, this office is productive. Flaky as this place looks from the outside, we all know how to come through in a pinch." A smile twitched at the corners of his mouth. "And you know how to protect me from most of the lunacy, that's why."

In a painfully honest admission, Harry added, "Because I like them. I like you. We work well together." Then he scowled. "But feel free to fire them all if you have to."

"I'll take care of it, Harry. Don't worry. Just go back to work."

His sigh of relief filled the room, and before I reached the door, he'd tuned me out completely.

Now what? I wondered. Where to start?

Why couldn't Harry have asked me to do something simple, like make us a Fortune 500 company overnight?

I *love* my job.

Chapter Twelve

Saturday, April 17

"Tell me again whose brilliant idea this was?" Kim growled as she flung herself into the backseat of our car, wearing old jeans and a red-and-black buffalo plaid jacket, a stocking cap and a scowl.

Kurt slid in behind her, wearing a matching jacket and a huge grin. "Don't mind Kim, she'll be fine when she wakes up." He handed her a thermos. "Here, have some more coffee."

I looked at Chase, who, even after a night in the emergency room with patients, looked incredibly handsome in a fleece-lined denim jacket, black jeans and a blue turtleneck that made his eyes look an inky blue. I could have used a few more hours of shut-eye, myself.

We had snapped at each other this morning as we tripped over one another to get ready. Chase has been short-tempered the last couple days. It's stress, I know, but sometimes I lose my patience. He tells his patients how to avoid stress. Doesn't he hear himself talking?

How we got talked into coming with the guys on the first day of their renovation project is beyond me, other than the fact that *Mitzi* had announced that she'd be helping, too. Kim and I were just too curious to stay home. Besides, it's for a first-rate cause.

"The family who lives in this home has five children," Kurt said. "The father had surgery recently and hasn't been able to keep up with the house. It's so leaky that they were warming more air outside the building than in. We've committed to sealing the leaks, repairing the holes in the walls and making the home warm and cozy again."

Chase has always taken James 1:27 seriously. "Religion that is pure and undefiled before God, the Father, is this: to care for the orphans and widows in their distress." Sometimes donating money to a cause isn't enough. He's thrilled about an opportunity to put his hand to a hammer and actually see the difference he's making.

Still, I couldn't imagine what good Kim, Mitzi and I would do. I can learn how to install flashing on a door, seal a draft or insulate a pipe, but Mitzi? Unless the techniques for applying plaster and nail polish are the same, we're in for an interesting time.

"I see the problem," Kim said as we arrived at our destination.

The house, an old white two-story built in the 1940s, was showing its age. Badly hung shutters matched the green roof. The enclosed front porch drooped low on one corner, making the front door hang kittywampus. The house looked sad. It was, just like its family, crying out for some tender loving care.

Arch and several others were standing on the sidewalk, talking to a man on crutches with his foot swathed in bandages. Mitzi was nowhere in sight.

A woman carrying a child on her hip exited the house, followed by four more children, all under the age of ten. Her gaze scanned the crowd and settled on me.

"Are you the wife of one of these doctors?" she asked, awe in her voice. "This is the most wonderful thing you're doing…."

I laid my hand on her arm. "Thanks for accepting their offer to help. My husband is delighted to be doing something tangible and concrete. It's one thing to talk about helping someone, it's quite another to do it."

To my surprise, tears filled her eyes and spilled onto her cheeks. "I didn't know anything like this could happen to us. When my husband lost his job, he didn't expect to have such a hard time finding another. Then, when he had to have surgery…" She looked at me as if she weren't sure she should say what was coming next.

"I finally tried praying, even though I didn't think it would do any good. And now…" She looked at the activity around her in wonderment. A truck had arrived with new storm windows and doors that Chase and Kurt were helping to unload. "Maybe there is a God after all."

"Oh, yes, I'm sure there is."

She looked at me appraisingly. "We haven't seen much of Him around here, but maybe…"

We had definitely come to the right place.

At that moment, Mitzi pulled up and flung open the door of her Porsche.

She does know how to make an entrance. She tottered out of the car wearing designer denim jeans, a pale blue silk blouse and a faux fur jacket. On her head she wore a billed baseball cap.

So this is Mitzi's idea of working clothes. Working a runway, maybe. At least she'd deep-sixed her fake eyelashes.

"Here I am!" she chortled. "Ready, willing and able. What do you want me to do first?"

I was certainly the wrong one to ask about that, considering I had no idea what I was doing here, either.

"How do you like it?" Mitzi spun around so that I could see the rhinestones on the pockets of her jeans.

I bit my tongue so hard I tasted blood but, to my credit, I didn't say what I was actually thinking. Then Kim trudged over in her battered hiking boots and lumberjack attire. The diva and the hired hand, both ready to get their hands dirty.

Arch walked up to us and kissed Mitzi full on the mouth, delighted to see her. She batted her eyelashes at him and gave a Southern belle sort of giggle and a look that asked the question, "How's my big, strong, handsome man?"

Besotted, Arch gazed at her in adoration. Note to self: Start batting eyelashes at Chase.

Kurt and Chase sauntered up beside us to get directions from Arch who was foreman of this operation. Before they left, I, as a test, fluttered my eyelashes in Chase's direction.

He paused to stare at me and grew serious. "Are you okay, honey? If your eyes are bothering you, I think there's some Visine in the car."

Okay, so controlling a man by batting one's eyelashes may be a little harder than it looks.

"We're going to insulate pipes," Arch announced as I willed my eyes to stop twitching. "Maybe you three ladies could empty the bottom cupboards in the kitchen for us. We'll repair windows inside the house, and then we'll have to retouch or repaint those walls. We can use help with that, as well."

"Shall we?" Kim gestured toward the house.

Inside, Mitzi walked up to the kitchen sink and squatted down in front of it to peer into the cupboard. "Ohh. One of you will have to do this."

"I can," I offered. "But why can't you?"

"She keeps onions under here. And potatoes. Do you see the white thing coming out of that one?"

"That's a potato sprout. It just needs to be broken off so that the potato doesn't go soft. I keep my potatoes under the sink, too."

"It looks like a worm. I don't do worms. And onions make my hands smell. I don't do onions."

We quickly discovered that Mitzi did not "do" a lot of things. She refused to kneel because it was hard on the knees of her jeans. She declined to touch cleaning supplies because they were too caustic for her delicate hands. Mitzi also did not scrape paint, caulk cracks or wield a hammer. She declined to lift, bend, stretch or flex. She would not drink coffee that was not made from freshly ground beans, go to the bathroom without piling six layers of toilet paper on the seat or dry her hands on anything but a fresh towel. She did not believe in holding things while someone else worked. Nor did she act as a gofer for anyone. Mitzi is practiced at saying, "Get it yourself."

Three minutes into our cleaning venture, Mitzi broke a fingernail.

When we first heard her scream, I thought she'd shattered her arm. Mitzi latched on to her wrist and did a dance that should have brought rain pouring down upon us. Then she sat down at the table to examine the extent of the damage.

"Oh, look at the poor little thing," she moaned. "Gone, completely gone. And it was so pretty, too—the one they put a rhinestone on. It was art, really, with little gold swirls…."

I bent and picked up the artificial nail from the floor. "It's so thick and heavily lacquered that we could glue it right back on. The guys must have brought along some wood glue…."

She screamed again, this time as if I'd tried to remove her toenails through her mouth.

"Don't even joke about that, Whitney." She stood up. "I'll have to go to the salon and get this taken care of right away."

"Oh, no, you don't," Kim and I said in unison. We each grabbed her by a shoulder and pushed her back into the chair.

"Who knows how many more nails you might break before the day is over? You'd never get a lick of work done here with all that running back and forth to the salon. Stay here, brave the emotional pain, and go later."

She glared at me so icily that I felt my blood start to congeal, but she stayed where she was.

I thought she'd be completely useless for the rest of the day—and she was, workwise.

She did, however, prove to be a remarkably adept cheerleader, manager and chief. From a chair in the middle of the kitchen, Mitzi got us to do everything that

Arch had assigned to the three of us and more. And she didn't even demand a sling for her "bad arm."

"Good job, girls," she crowed as Kim and I sank wearily onto the floor, tired from doing double duty kneeling, scraping, caulking, lifting, bending, stretching and flexing. "Don't you think it would be nice if instead of just touching up the paint on these walls, we repainted the entire kitchen?"

"Right. Nice."

"We can't just change the James family's decor," Kim protested, even though the "decor" was desperately in need of a pick-me-up.

"Sure we can. I asked the lady who lives here what her favorite colors are and if we could paint for her."

"So you didn't come here to work," I said in a moment of clarity. "You came to play interior decorator."

"I work to my strengths," Mitzi said primly. "You should know that by now, Whitney. I do it in the office all the time."

She views avoiding work as a strength. This explains a lot.

"So let's go shopping!"

This, too, was an evil plan on Mitzi's part. While Kim and I trudged around the store like two mountain men shopping for paint and curtains, Mitzi was the best-dressed woman in the place. When Kim and I stopped to look at floor tile, a salesman eyed us warily, as if we had room under our large, dumpy work clothes to shoplift enough flooring for an entire family room. Then Mitzi arrived, and he spent the next twenty minutes discussing the merits and durability of wood versus tile.

Feeling part workhorse, part lackey, Kim and I loaded the car while Mitzi sat behind the wheel, fiddling with the radio.

"Why does this feel so familiar to me?" Kim murmured.

"Because it's just like a day at Innova with Mitzi. We do the work and Mitzi takes the credit."

"It's our own fault, you know. We let her get away with it."

"We not only let her get away with it," I said, resigned to our fate, "we don't even know how to stop her."

"You're her superior. Aren't you supposed to know how?"

"Somehow, despite driving everyone crazy and never seeming to work, she manages to get things done—lots of things. As soon as I figure out how she does it, I'm going to write a book about it, tell her secrets and make a million dollars. Until then…"

"I know, I know. Keep loading."

By the time we got home after the long, long day, my legs were leaden and every fiber of my body ached. Despite that, I felt a glow of satisfaction that I've rarely experienced. Every ache and pain I would have tomorrow was worth it, just to see the expression on the Jameses' faces when they returned home. The delight on our husbands' faces told another side of the story. The satisfaction of digging in and getting dirty, of seeing immediate benefit from their work and getting out of their coats and ties, had had a remarkable effect on their spirits, as well.

The pleasure didn't last long however. Shortly after we got home, I found Chase lying in bed.

"Honey? Are you okay?" Chase is usually the one who has to scrape me up off the floor after a long day.

"Just tired, that's all. You don't have to worry about turning off the lights. I'll be able to sleep with them on...."

He dozed off in midsentence. My Energizer Bunny husband's batteries had run out.

Chapter Thirteen

Saturday, April 24

Never ask a toddler to hold a raw egg.

That is only one of the instructions I would have given Mitzi for the care and handling of Wesley, but apparently Kim forgot.

Mitzi, acting on a continuous string of daft ideas, decided that it would be good for her to spend some time with a child before she had one of her own. I don't disagree with that, but I do think she should have started with something smaller—like a six-pounder. Or at least one with slightly less energy. Wesley exists on a natural, permanent sugar high. She should also have chosen one with fewer creative ideas that run in the direction of mayhem, turmoil, pandemonium, bedlam, destruction and annihilation.

Did I miss anything Wes is good at? Neither would I have chosen a child with such a strong fascination for bathroom plumbing, rodents, reptiles, dish soap and garbage cans. I also would have weeded out a budding Van Gogh armed with his mother's lipstick and access to an oatmeal-colored living-room couch.

I mentioned this to Kim, but she brushed me off, saying I worry too much. She had an evil gleam in her eye when she said she viewed this whole experiment as a wonderful learning tool. Mitzi had the potential to learn a lot, considering the aptitude, skill and capacity of the pint-sized teacher.

Kim and Kurt left at two o'clock for an afternoon at the movies. I, acquainted with Wesley's propensities, chose to stay home and wait for the phone to ring.

Mitzi lasted forty-five minutes—forty minutes longer than I'd expected—before she sent up a smoke signal calling for help.

"Do you want to come with me?" I asked Chase. "It might be fun."

He waved at me from the couch, where he, Mr. Tibble and Scram were tangled together like a bunch of rubber bands. "Go ahead and tell me all about it when you get back."

"You've been hanging out on the couch a lot lately," I commented.

"Just being lazy. Have fun rescuing Mitzi."

I bent to kiss him on the lips and smoothed hair away from his forehead. "You're warm. You'd better shake those two live fur coats you're wearing."

Chase wiggled his leg, and Scram leaped to the floor. Mr. Tibble didn't budge.

"I'll manage these two. You'd better hurry. A lot can happen in five or ten minutes over there."

Ain't that the truth!

As I rang the doorbell, I eyed Mitzi's Porsche in the driveway and entertained myself thinking of Mitzi in a Mom-mobile, a minivan with room for her children, groceries, three dogs and an entire team of little soccer players.

Fortunately, she opened the door before my head exploded from trying to imagine it.

Well, at least *someone* answered the door. Wesley stood there wearing a pair of soggy Spider-Man underpants and a smile.

Evidently little boys are much harder to potty train than little girls. Though the odds are now running in Kim's favor, Wes still has accidents—particularly when he's having too much fun to stop and take care of business.

Mitzi appeared from around the corner, limping on a broken shoe heel and waving a pair of dry SpongeBob SquarePants underwear in her hand.

"You can't just open the door!" Mitzi panted to Wesley. "What will the neighbors think? Here, put these on and we'll find the rest of your clothes."

"I want Spider-Man." Actually, Wesley pronounces it "Piderman."

"Piderman is all in the wash. You have to wear this pair." Mitzi examined the underwear closely. "What *is* this? A sponge?" She sounded horrified. "No wonder you don't want to wear these. Who on earth thought of dressing children in household cleaning equipment?"

Finally, she noticed that I had arrived. "Hi, Whitney. Don't let him escape. I've got to find him something more appropriate to wear. Sponges? What will they put on children's clothes next? Toasters? Mops and brooms?"

Muttering to herself, she hobbled off, a woman on a mission to ban kitchen utensils from boys' underpants.

Wesley took me by the hand and tugged me into the living room or, more aptly, the former living room.

Every toy Wesley owned was piled in the center of the room. A condominium made out of a card table, Kim's good comforter and a series of large boxes sat in one corner. Broken crayons ground into the beige carpet made a lovely contemporary bit of artwork on the floor. A splash of artificial orange-flavored drink was an exclamation point for the Dadaist look of the crayons. Wesley probably could have gotten hundreds of dollars for it at a gallery. Too bad it was all done on wool carpeting instead of canvas.

"Ridiculous!" Mitzi tromped into the room holding an assortment of underwear. "Ponies, puppies, Cat in the Hat, Mickey Mouse, teddy bears, Pluto, Goofy…but not another Spider-Man."

"Piderman. I want Piderman."

"Well, you're just going to have to choose something else."

"Nooooooooo!"

I took the toon underwear and studied it carefully. "Uncle Chase has a tie with Pluto on it. Did you know that, Wes?"

He eyes me appraisingly. "Unca Chase?"

"Yep. And Mickey Mouse socks, too." Chase never takes himself too seriously. No matter how formally he dresses, I can count on a bit of silk in a Donald Duck motif or a money clip shaped like mouse ears in his pocket.

"Unca Chase?"

Sometimes visiting with Wesley is like talking to an echo.

He stomped toward me and took the Pluto-adorned undies. He held them up to Mitzi. "These."

To Mitzi's credit, she didn't lose it. Her fingers didn't twitch and her hands didn't encircle Wesley's neck. Her eyes, however, wore the glazed look of someone who has been knocking her head on a wall and is relieved to have stopped.

"This is harder than I thought." She looked at Wes as if he was a school science fair experiment gone bad.

I sniffed the air. "Is something burning?"

"My pizza!" Mitzi dashed out of the room as Wesley clapped and chortled "Peeza, peeza."

It was only a tiny bit brown on the crust, I assured her, as she studied the charred pizza. That was much better than serving it underdone. Once we sat down at the table, however, Wesley took one look at the table set with paper plates and glasses of apple juice and burst into tears.

"What is it, honey?" I asked.

"Eatinthetent, Mommy says."

"What's 'eatinthetent'?" Mitzi asked. "Some weird language they speak in this household?"

"What did Mommy say, Wes?"

"Eat in the tent," he enunciated carefully. "Mommy says."

"What tent?"

Wesley tore off into the living room, where we found him sitting happily under the card table draped with Kim's comforter. "My tent!"

"Your mother told you that you could eat in there?" Mitzi gasped, appalled.

I was just happy to have deciphered his request so early in the game.

That is how the three of us came to be sitting under the card table, dining off burned pizza on paper plates. It was a squeeze for Mitzi and me. We sat, heads touching the underside of the table, shoulders hunched. Mitzi eyed me like a crabby vulture and glared at me as if this were my fault. Wesley, however, ate two pieces of pizza and dozed off in one of the adjoining boxes— er, rooms—in his makeshift condo.

"How does Kim do it, Whitney?" Mitzi asked after we'd untwisted ourselves and crept out from beneath the table. She rubbed her shoulder and sat down on a chair in the kitchen.

I handed her a cup of tea and opened the sack of cookies Kim always keeps in her secret, known-only-to-us stash.

"She loves it and she loves him. She's a very devoted mother and Wes is a happy, normal little boy."

"With the energy of a nuclear reactor," Mitzi muttered.

I recalled having used that comparison myself.

"Maybe I can't do it," Mitzi murmured. "Maybe the reason I can't get pregnant is that I'd be a terrible mother."

"That's ridiculous and you know it." I shoved the cookies closer to her. She delicately picked the chocolate chips out of them as she ate.

"Then *why?* There's got to be a reason."

"Bodies aren't all perfect." *Especially not in two-piece swimsuits.* "Sometimes they need a little help with something—insulin, thyroid medication…"

"And, in my case, fertility pills. I suppose I should be happy we have options, but it seems so unnatural, so forced. If nature doesn't want me to have a child…"

"Mitzi, you've been improving on nature for as long

as I've known you. Those false eyelashes, fake nails, fake and bake tanning lotions, push-up bras…"

"I do not wear a push-up bra! Usually."

"…electrolysis, dermabrasion, foundation makeup."

"Okay, I get it."

Maybe it was because in her tussles with Wes all her makeup had rubbed off or because, for once, she wasn't done up like a mannequin in an expensive department store, but she looked soft and vulnerable, as genuinely lovely as I'd ever seen her.

"Do you want me to hang around until Kim and Kurt come home?"

Mitzi glanced at the clock on the wall. "How long do you think Wesley will sleep?"

"A couple hours, I'm sure. He plays hard, and he sleeps just as hard."

"Then I'll lie down with him. Kim should be back in an hour or so."

As I got ready to leave, Mitzi went down on her hands and knees and crawled back under the table where Wesley was napping. She lay down next to him, cradled her head in her arm, and before I got to the door, she was asleep.

If I hadn't seen it, I wouldn't have believed it. Mitzi, barefoot and disheveled, her hair a disaster, her lipstick faded, sleeping in a child's make-believe tent with a soft smile on her face and a look of tranquility I normally see only in artistic renderings of Madonna and child.

Chase was still sleeping on the couch when I got home, his forehead damp and Mr. Tibble curled onto his chest. Scram had found his way back onto the couch and was covering Chase's legs like a blanket. Glad he could rest, I tiptoed to the kitchen to make something special for dinner. Chase hasn't been quite himself lately. He needs a little extra tender loving care, and I'm just the one to provide it.

Mr. Tibble here.

Good news. Whitney's other pet—the large, two-footed one—doesn't push me off when I take naps on his chest anymore. It's a very toasty napping place, but his behavior is highly atypical. As a rule, they are both sickeningly animated.

Now if I could just get my pet Whitney and that annoying little pest Scram to settle down, things would be completely under my control at this house. It's a struggle to maintain my dignity in such chaos. I still have difficulty doing so when my pet Whitney insists on pushing me onto my back and scratching my stomach. How humiliating. I wouldn't tolerate it if it didn't feel so good. I had no idea what problems I was taking on when I adopted my human. Someday I should write a book. Dogs drool, Cats rule.

Mr. Tibble, signing off.

I curled up beside Chase and wiggled into the curve of his body. He woke up slowly and began to roll a curl into my hair with his index finger.

"Hi, sweetheart. How were Mitzi and Wes?" He burrowed his nose in the nape of my neck, and I squirmed with pleasure.

"Okay. Mitzi is a trouper. Wesley insisted on eating his lunch in a tent in the living room and Mitzi says that underwear with sponges on it is 'unsuitable for a self-respecting toddler.' When I left, they were both asleep on the floor."

"I hope you don't mind that I'm not even going to ask you how all that came about. Tents, unsuitable underwear, and Mitzi sleeping on the floor? It's too much for the human mind to comprehend."

"You should have seen her. You know how Wesley careens around the house like a billiard ball around a pool table? Naturally he banged his head on the edge of the dining-room table. Mitzi was right there kissing Wesley's 'boo-boo' and cradling him in her arms.

"She's serious about this baby thing, Chase. And, although I can't believe this is coming out of my mouth, I think she'll be a wonderful mother."

He squirmed until he got his arms around me. "She's not the only one."

"We already know Kim's a great mom. A little lenient, but great."

"I know someone else who'll be a great mother, too."

A little frisson of pleasure spread through me. "Anybody I know?"

"As a matter of fact, you do."

"Want to tell me about her? List some of her best qualities."

"Well, for starters, I'm in love with her..."

And then we forgot about the rest of the list.

Chapter Fourteen

"Where was Mitzi yesterday?" Betty asked as we stared into the break room refrigerator at something unsavory that was greening up near her store of bottled water.

"She took a personal day." I poked at the item with the tip of my pencil, and it sank into the green globule's flesh. "Is this an orange?" I speculated.

"Maybe it's a peach," Betty conjectured. "It is pretty fuzzy."

"Your guess is as good as mine." I admit to turning a blind eye to the refrigerator since I've been unable to convince Mitzi that it's her turn to clean it out. I keep thinking that someone, someday, will have had enough and just get the job done. I had very high hopes that the three-week-old egg salad that's been fermenting in the salad crisper would work as a motivator, but everyone has just ignored it. And the old broccoli that, once it turned yellow and began to smell

like a men's locker room, should have driven someone over the edge. Again, no response. It's a funny
place to stage a war, inside a refrigerator, but that's
what this has come to. It's literally and figuratively a
cold war. Tensions are escalating, and no one is
willing to back down.

I even offered a prize for the first person to clean out
the dumb thing—a box of brand-new plastic containers in
every shape and size, the ideal gift for the organized brown
bagger. Not a twitch of interest. I think they're enjoying
this showdown. Far be it from me to ruin their fun.

"What did Mitzi take a personal day for?" Betty
asked when we became bored poking at the Fuzzy
Green Tennis Ball Formerly Known as Fruit.

"I don't know. Harry took the message and left a
note on my desk."

"Mitzi *never* misses work."

Don't I know it? There have been times when I've
longed for a day off from Mitzi, but I never get one.
Even when she's planning a party or a vacation, she's
here. She says it's easier to figure out her guest list and
wardrobe when she's with us. We stir her creative juices.

Ah, for a little dribble of inspired juice on her
actual work!

I poured a cup of coffee to take to my desk and nearly
ran into Mitzi on the way out the door.

"Welcome back. We missed you yesterday." She
drives me crazy when she's here, and I miss her when
she's not. Mitzi is a walking model of the approach/
avoidance conflict.

"I have to talk to you."

"Here I am."

"Not here. Not now. Lunchtime. Usual place. Back booth. Bring Kim."

She sounded as if she'd rented the video of *Mission Impossible*. Or could Mitzi be leaving Innova to work for the CIA? One could only hope.

"Hey, sweetie, what are you up to?"

I pressed my ear closer to the telephone receiver. "Chase?" I still get a rush just hearing his voice. "What are you doing calling this time of day? Don't you have rounds?"

"Just got done. I had a brilliant idea, so I thought I'd call and check it out with you."

"Shoot."

"Why don't we go away this weekend? Just for a little rest and relaxation. I know I've been a pain in the neck sometimes lately. I must be touchy at work, too, because one of the charge nurses recommended a B and B in Wisconsin that she and her husband like. No telephone, no meals to cook, just the two of us. What do you say?"

"When do we leave? If you pick me up here, I can buy a toothbrush along the way."

His warm chuckle tickled my ear. "I'd love to, but I have some patients who might be annoyed if I walked out on them. We can leave on Friday and come home Sunday night. Ask Kim if she'll feed the cats."

"Consider it done. This is a wonderful idea."

"I'm beginning to feel the consequences of the pace I've been keeping. I don't enjoy feeling that I need to apologize for having a short fuse. Spending a couple days romancing my beautiful wife is just what the doctor ordered."

"I'll be happy to help you fill the prescription."

"And pack something sensuous and lacy, will you?"

I smiled to myself all morning, even when Harry had a hissy fit over changes a client demanded and even through Bryan's insistence that Mitzi was trying to drive him insane with insidiously placed typos in the reports she was doing for him. I don't doubt she's capable of that, but it would be hard to prove.

By noon, Mitzi looked as though she were going to erupt from her seat and splatter all over the ceiling. Kim never took her eyes off her, as if holding fast to the adage that a watched pot never boils and afraid that if she blinked, Mitzi might explode like a pressure cooker with a bad seal.

Harry wandered through the office with a frown on his face. He stopped at my desk and took a handful of the candy I keep in a bowl there. "Foraging for lunch, Harry?"

"I've got to take a call over lunch hour. Got anything besides Tootsie Rolls?"

"No, but I can bring something back for you."

He put a ten-dollar bill on my desk and said, "Surprise me. Anything's fine, but not too much garlic and no water chestnuts." He shuddered. "I hate those little white things crunching in my mouth when I least expect them."

"Gotcha." I turned to look at Mitzi to indicate that we could leave. "Ready to go?" Before I blinked twice, she had her jacket on and was standing by the door.

"How come she never moves that fast when *I* ask her to do something?" Harry muttered.

"Because you never ask her to do anything that involves leaving work."

Harry popped a Tootsie Roll into his mouth. "I'll have to remember that." He meandered back into his office and shut the door.

"Walk faster," Mitzi ordered as we headed toward the restaurant. "Don't shuffle, Kim. It's hard on your shoes and it slows you down. Whitney, make her hurry up."

"Hup, two, three, four. Hup, two, three, four…" Kim muttered, like a recalcitrant child.

"Behave, you two. Let's eat here. Mitzi, is this fast enough for you?"

We entered a little noodle joint that serves everything from pad thai to spaghetti and meatballs.

After we'd ordered, Mitzi made a great show of getting settled in the booth. "Well," she blurted, "aren't you going to ask me?"

"Ask you what? Where you lost your mind and how you plan to find it again?"

"No, silly." She folded her hands primly on the table and tilted her head to one side. "Ask me what I did yesterday."

"What did you do yesterday?" Kim asked obediently, intent on opening a packet of sweetener for her tea.

"I went to the doctor. Now ask me what he did." Mitzi squirmed in her seat like Wesley sometimes does when he can't contain his excitement.

Humoring Mitzi is easier than rushing her, so I played along. "What did he do?"

Mitzi whipped a written prescription out of her purse. "Fertility pills! Isn't that wonderful? Now I can get my baby!"

There was so much hope and anticipation in Mitzi's expression that I couldn't help but be touched.

"I can hardly wait to start." She frowned. "If I get pregnant in May, I'm going to look like a beach ball at Christmas. I'll have to plan on wearing something in black or hunter green velvet. I can give up a red dress for one year. But New Year's Eve will be a problem." She eyed us thoughtfully. "I'll have a party at my house. You guys can come. You'll be used to how I look by then."

"Mitzi, you haven't been to the drugstore to fill the prescription yet. Don't you think it's a little early to go shopping?"

I saw that little flicker of fear in her eyes again. "I have to think positively, Whitney. I *have* to."

Giving my blessing to Mitzi's coping mechanisms, no matter how unlike mine they might be, I turned to the menu.

After we'd ordered, Kim and I turned back to Mitzi. "What else did the doctor tell you?"

Mitzi chattered on about the possible, mostly mild, side effects. Then she said the words that made my blood run cold. "He did say I could have some mood swings…hormonal, you know…but I'm optimistic that…"

Mood swings. Mitzi on hormones. I didn't want to go there. The *normal* Mitzi kept us swinging like a family of monkeys. What were we in for now?

By the time I contained the horror show going on in my head, Mitzi was on to other things.

"She'll look like me, I think. My dark hair and oval face. I've always looked good in hot pink, so I think I'll buy a few receiving blankets…."

"How did you decide you were having a girl?" I asked. "And with dark hair, too!"

"Don't be lame, Whitney. What self-respecting baby would want to look like anyone but me?"

Of course. Mitzi would expect nothing less than a carbon copy of her lovely little self.

Thursday, April 29

The mood swings started even before Mitzi began taking the pills. This morning I found her in the ladies' restroom, leaning over the sink so close that her nose touched the mirror. She twisted her head from side to side with the compact mirror in her hand, examining her face from every possible angle.

"What are you looking for? We're supposed to be having an office meeting. Harry sent me on a search-and-rescue mission to find you."

"I certainly can't go back into the office now." Mitzi's breath fogged the mirror in front of her.

"Why not?"

"Something terrible has happened."

I moved closer. "What?"

"Look! See for yourself." She jabbed an index finger toward her eye.

"Have you got something in your eye? Does it hurt?"

"Not in it, by it. It's Royal Gorge!"

I squinted to see what she was looking at. There wasn't much where she pointed, other than a heavy fringe of mascara. "What?"

"Crow's feet," she screeched. "Wrinkles. Oh, Whitney, I'm getting *old.*"

"Hardly. I can't even see what you're complaining about."

"Then you need glasses. They aren't wrinkles, they're canyons! This is dreadful."

"All I see is a couple smile lines, Mitzi."

"So you *do* see it." She sat down on one of the plastic chairs by the long countertop. "Maybe I'm too old to have a baby. Maybe…" Her roller coaster certainly travels downhill quickly. It's going to be a long, long summer.

Kim and I discussed Mitzi's crow's foot—there may have been one foot, there certainly weren't several— over a pizza.

"Americans hate getting older." Kim sprinkled dried red peppers over her pizza. "Baby boomers like your parents are planning to live longer and with better health than any generation before them. I predict that someday every boomer in America will have a lift, nip or tuck."

I tried to imagine my mother or father going that route. My father scowls at his belly occasionally, when his belt is buckled in the last notch. Mother eyeballs herself from the side with her makeup mirror, checking for sags. Neither seems interested in surgical solutions.

"And those magazines! They use children as models and make grown women believe we need to look like that. Wesley's babysitter actually complains about the way she looks in her jeans, at size four."

She stared morosely into her slice of supreme pizza with extra cheese. "What will be left for us when we're forty, Whit? And what about—" she shuddered "—fifty? Will it be all downhill from there?"

I burst out laughing. "Kim, at forty we'll just be getting *started,* not winding down!"

She looked at me doubtfully, as if my aging brain had already taken a turn for the worse.

"The way I see it, at fifty we're finally getting ready to roll." I took another piece of pizza before Kim ate it all. "Look at it this way. The first twenty-two years of our lives, we're kids. We're in school and college, worried about our grades and our social status. Then people start to marry and have children of their own, which ties them up for another eighteen. And there's college to pay for, too. It's between forty and fifty that we rediscover who we are and do the work we want to do. That's the kind of woman that's going to spend the next thirty years learning, contributing, inventing, creating…"

Speaking of creating, I'd like to do a little of my own. Baby fever is catching.

Chapter Fifteen

Friday, April 30

Mr. Tibble here.

My pet is doing something of which I do not approve. She has put the dreaded "suitcase" on her bed. This is a bad sign. It indicates she is planning to run away from home. Who knows what kind of mischief she will get into without me? She doesn't allow me to prowl at night, therefore I have deduced that it is a bad and dangerous pastime.

I cannot let her go. I will lie inside the lidded box until she gives up trying to fill it. It is padded and smells good. Meanwhile, I have assigned my other annoying pet to sleep on the fresh laundry. He is too small and weak-minded to be effective at guarding the suitcase. We cannot let her get away.

Even though I hide it well with aloofness and total independence, I am fond of my pet and do not like to have her out of my sight. I will also use my telepathic abilities—those I use to instruct her when it is time to feed and pet me—to make her rethink this decision.

If my pet tries to remove me from this box, I will use my claws to hang on. I will snag things if necessary. I know she hates that, but desperate times call for desperate measures.

Mr. Tibble, signing off.

"I cannot tell you how wonderful this feels." I leaned back and closed my eyes as we sped down I-94 toward Wisconsin. "I'm running away from home and all my responsibilities."

"Mr. Tibble acted as if you were running away from *him*," Chase said. "I haven't heard such caterwauling since he batted the door shut on Scram's tail."

"He loves me. He doesn't want to be away from me."

"He's like me, then." Chase put his hand over mine as it rested in my lap. "I'm ready for a couple days off. I think I could sleep a week."

"Don't be disappointed, my dear—" I put his hand to my cheek "—but I have other plans for you."

"Promise?" Chase's smile widened.

The bed-and-breakfast was a quaint, colorful Victorian with gables, a turret and a large wraparound porch that cried out for lemonade, sugar cookies and rocking chairs. Actually, the chairs were already there. What the porch needed most was me and my husband, cuddling on the porch swing.

"Welcome to Delight!" A plump, rosy-cheeked woman greeted us wearing a—believe it or not—red-and-white-check gingham apron. She looked so wholesome and cozy that she could have just come from milking Elsie the Cow and having tea with Mrs. Butterworth.

"This is delightful," I agreed.

"Of course it is, it's Delight," she said amiably.

"Yes, it is. Very." I agreed again. Chase listened to the strange conversation with a faint smile on his face.

"No, really, it *is* Delight," the woman assured me.

And who's on first?

"This is the Delight Bed-and-Breakfast, named for the family who built the home and founded the town in 1895, Marvin and Hilda Delight. Would you like to walk around outside before we go in? The tulips and daffodils are at their peak. Or are you ready to get settled?"

We voted on settling first.

I watched Chase tote my luggage up the stairs to the front door, wondering why I cannot pack lightly for a two-night stay.

It's the decision-making process and the lack of information that stump me every time. Will it be warm or cool? Sunny? Windy? And the most important question of all—will I feel fat or thin? Will we eat out or eat in? Fancy or plain? Gourmet or burgers on the run? And what will we do? Hike? Shop? Go for a bicycle ride? I like to be prepared. Therefore, I pack as though I'm setting out on the Iditarod with a team of huskies—in case it's unseasonably cold—and something sheer and sleeveless—in case it's unexpectedly hot—and a little something for every weather system in between.

And then there's my *mood*. Romantic—of course; playful—I might need my tennis racket; ambitious—hiking boots; or lazy—something in velour with a loose waistband. I have a large range of emotions, so, like the Boy Scout I never was, I have to be prepared.

And reading material? I stockpile books to read on vacation. One would think that sooner or later I'd realize that I *never* read while I'm on vacation. My eyes are busy at work all week. I read in the evening at home. I devour newspapers and even sometimes skim Chase's medical magazines. The last thing I want to do when I'm away is read. Still, I toss a couple books in the suitcase "just in case." One of my New Year's resolutions—I should know better than to make them by now, but I never learn that, either—was to read the classics, those books that everyone who is well educated talks about. I, too, want to make great literary conversation at parties.

"Tolstoy's *Anna Karenina* really struck a chord with me," I'll say, or, "*Crime and Punishment* by Dostoyevsky wasn't nearly as hard to read as everyone says."

Yeah. Whatever.

As I worried about the condition of Chase's back and imagined his complete collapse under the weight of heavy reading, I made a decision. Next time I want to bring the classics with me on a two-day trip, I'm bringing the "Gettysburg Address."

And I can't forget the oils, scrubs, rubs, moisturizers, lotions, potions, makeup, hair dryer—just in case they don't provide one—curling iron, hot rollers, hair spray…all despite the fact that Chase says he loves my glowing natural look and that I'm perfect just as I am. Have I bought into the beauty myth or what?

To help out, I carried Chase's bag. This contained a shaving kit, toothbrush, two sets of extra underwear, a pair of jeans and two comfortable shirts. I could carry it up the stairs dangling it from my index finger.

The man is a saint. He wrestled my bags to the room without a whimper. He put them on suitcase stands and then returned to the hall, where I was still visiting with Mrs. Bump—yes, Bump!—our hostess. When she'd bustled away to change the potpourri somewhere or check the sheets that were air-drying on the clothesline, Chase bent over, scooped me up and—be still my heart—carried me over the threshold. I was speechless—a novel experience for *moi*.

If our room wasn't a centerfold pinup from *Victorian* magazine, it should have been. The walls were a pale blue slate, and from the windows hung velvet draperies that would have made Scarlett O'Hara drool with envy. The woodwork was maple, as was the bed—a vast sea of white, slate and soft pink lace, linens and pillows, the kind of bed a person could get lost in and not be found until morning. Fortunately, Chase and I have the instinct of bats flying in the night for finding one another. No problem there.

I spun around to hug Chase and noticed for the first time the fire burning in the fireplace. A tiny table and two chairs sat before it. On the table was a teapot tucked snugly into its cozy. On a three-tiered tray were brownies, petit fours, miniature cream puffs and fresh raspberries in chocolate cups shaped like swans.

I bolted for Chase to hug him, but veered off when I saw the two-person whirlpool tucked into the corner behind another plethora of ruffles and lace. One edge of the tub was rimmed with scented bubble bath and bath oils. There were pillows to use behind our heads, and there was a jar of rose petals waiting to be spread across the water.

"Chase, this simply could not be more perfect." *I love this man.* "You have outdone yourself this time. I am absolutely blown away by this."

He took me in his arms and buried his nose in the dark mass of my hair. "Anything for you, Whitney, you know that. I love you so much." His voice caught as he spoke. His incredible blue eyes grew a little misty, as did mine.

We took a nap after devouring the tea, and it was nearly five o'clock when I awoke. Chase was sprawled on the bed, one arm thrown up by his head, the other rising and falling slowly as it rested on his belly. His hair was tousled, and he reminded me of a little boy.

I slipped out of bed, leaving him to rest while I went to the windows. Delight sits on several acres of oak, maple, pine and fruit trees. Mrs. Bump and company had strategically placed wrought iron benches and swings around the house. A curving trail led from bench to swing to fountain. One could meander at leisure or sit and read or sketch anywhere on the property.

Despite this pastoral setting, the B and B is only a few minutes' walk from downtown, as I discovered when I asked to see brochures or pamphlets on what there might be to do in the area. That is, *if* we even wanted to leave our room.

"There are a dozen little shops within walking distance," Mrs. Bump said as she efficiently dusted a display of old china. "Full of lovely little things you don't need. That's why people enjoy coming here. There's nothing practical or sensible or even familiar. Delight and the surrounding area are a little world of their own."

"I love it. What do people usually do when they visit Delight?"

"There are nice trails, if you enjoy walking. Sometimes in the evening I play the piano and we sing. There is a local string quartet that practices in the parlor. They're very good. We have music most evenings from seven until nine. There's a reading room in the tower which is quite comfy. If it's cool, I build a fire in the grate. It's also a wonderful spot to watch the sun rise and set. There's a salt lick at the edge of the property, so deer come by for a visit. It's such fun when the fawns are born, to watch them follow their mothers."

Delight is definitely delightful—bordering on bliss, even.

"There is a well-known quilt shop in town," Mrs. Bump continued placidly. "If you are a quilter, you could lose yourself there for hours."

"I might, but I'm not sure my husband would be up for it. Where do you recommend we eat dinner tonight?"

After she handed me a list of restaurants and pointed out two of her personal favorites, I took the information back to our room.

Chase was awake and looking warm, rumpled and very desirable as he leaned back on the mound of pillows he'd piled behind him on the bed. He was reading from the same list Mrs. Bump had given to me.

"Hey, darlin', are you as hungry as I am?"

"Starved."

"Getting away is good for the appetite."

We ate at a tiny Italian restaurant where the owner was also the chef and his wife acted as hostess and waitress. They both bussed dishes on the side.

After much laughter and enough pasta to feed a small village, Chase and I shared tiramisu and drank espresso in tiny cups.

"Can this get anymore perfect?" I purred, feeling like Mr. Tibble after he'd eaten a can of tuna. "Everything that's been concerning me at home has simply vanished—Kim and Kurt's adoption woes, Mitzi and her desire to get pregnant, the office..."

Chase put a finger to my lips. "Leave it where it was, Whitney. This is about us."

"And what about us?" I intertwined my fingers with his.

"The two of us are perfect together."

He studied me so intently that I finally began to squirm. "Chase?"

"I was just wondering what you'd look like with a baby in your arms. I think it's time our family of two became three."

My response surprised even me. An emptiness I hadn't known existed in me filled as if warm, soothing liquid were flowing into a hole in my heart.

With all this fuss and flutter going on with Kim and Mitzi, I'd made my own feelings about having a baby secondary. Someone, I'd told myself, had to hold those two together. Besides, what would Harry do at Innova if all three of us were pregnant and giving birth at the same time? But now all the minor doubts and questions were washed away by this warm, nurturing sensation in my heart.

"Three," I told Chase, "is my new favorite number."

Chapter Sixteen

Saturday, May 1

Wouldn't you know it? I finally have a day to sleep in, and I'm wide-awake.

Not that I mind. I like mornings and I particularly like watching my husband sleep because he's so relaxed and peaceful. I haven't seen him that way much in recent weeks, not with his schedule at the clinic and the hospital. Determined to get the most out of every minute, I took a shower, dried my hair and slipped into one of the fuzzy white terry robes provided by the B and B.

Mrs. Bump—or one of the little Bumps—had placed a carafe of coffee and a copy of *USA Today* outside our door.

When I'd read the paper, breakfast was still an hour away. Chase was sleeping soundly so I decided to take a morning prayer walk. I slid into a pair of jeans, a T-shirt and a thick hooded sweatshirt and slipped out of our room.

Grabbing a granola bar as I went by the dining room

buffet, I headed for the walking path and started down the rock path, feeling a little like Dorothy on her way to Oz.

"Good morning, Lord. This is an amazing day. Thank You for Your creation and all that is in it. I've been thinking about Mitzi and Kim a lot this morning. They both want to be mothers so much. Could You help Kim and Kurt through this adoption process and find the perfect child for them? You know where that child is, Lord. I ask that finding him or her be made simple for them.

"And Mitzi…we've talked about Mitzi before. She's wacko, but I can't help loving her anyway. Bless her and, if it is Your will, I pray that she will have that child she dreams about.

"We're a pretty funny bunch, Kim, Mitzi and I, all focused on having children to love. You know what's best and I leave it all in Your divine hands. Your will be done."

Then I put in a good word for my parents. I also brought up Harry, Betty and Bryan at the office, who are not Christians but are not averse to it, either, and for Chase.

"He's been tired a lot lately, Lord. He's working too hard. He is an amazing doctor, but it can't be easy, seeing patient after patient, being steady and comforting when people are upset or frightened. I know the responsibility of making wise decisions for these people weighs on him day after day. Take care of him, will You?"

By the time God and I were done chatting—and it really is like chatting for me, a conversation with a beloved friend—it was time to go back to the B and B for breakfast.

Easier said than done.

Intent on prayer, I hadn't watched where I was going. The path I'd followed had somehow disappeared without my noticing it. I stood in a thin stand of paper birch trees in the middle of nowhere, with no idea how I'd gotten there.

First things first. I checked my pocket to make sure my granola bar had not fallen out on the trek. I imagined myself parceling it out, oat by oat, to my frail, famished body as I wandered aimlessly in the woods of Wisconsin. Then, to fortify myself, I opened it and gobbled it down.

So much for preventing myself from starving to death.

Wishing for a cup of Mrs. Bump's strong black coffee, I decided to follow my footsteps backward in the soft earth. Quickly the way became stony and my footprints disappeared. As I paused again, a squirrel descended from the branches of a tree to study me as he hung vertically on the bark, his tail flicking and his nose twitching. The insides of his ears were white and his eyes were alert. His entire body quivered with interest— surely it couldn't be fear. I was shivering with that.

I do not like being lost. When I was five, I ran away from my mother in a shopping mall. While she looked at purses, I decided to visit a toy store we'd passed earlier. I was fine for a while, investigating an indoor pond filled with pennies, peering into garbage cans and staring at the mannequins in store windows. I discovered a dollar bill on the floor, sat down by it and waited patiently to see if anyone would pick it up. When no one came, I claimed it for myself, thinking that with cash, I could do some serious shopping in the toy store. Unfortunately, the toy store had disappeared. I couldn't find it anywhere. In fact, nothing looked familiar, and suddenly shopping for purses didn't seem like such a bad idea after all.

Worse yet, I had no idea where I'd left my mother. The indoor shopping mall had grown since I left her. It seemed gigantic. There were stairs and escalators everywhere. As the vivid, pulsating colors and deafening chatter whirled around me, I began to feel as though I'd just come off a Tilt-A-Whirl. I wanted to throw up.

Even now, in my thirties, I had that same panicky little-girl feeling. Back then, I'd resolved the problem by bursting into tears and wetting my pants. A mall security guard had found me, bought me ice cream and paged my mother, who, in minutes, had come dashing hysterically toward me, tears streaming down her face.

She'd taken me home, changed me into dry undies and sent me to bed to think about what a naughty thing I'd done by wandering off. I remember cuddling into the cocoon of my bed, believing it was the best place on earth. And I'd sucked my thumb and fallen asleep.

Frankly, I felt like crying, wetting my pants and sucking my thumb today, too, but it just didn't seem practical anymore. I am a capable, responsible, smart individual, I reminded myself. I am resourceful. I have a master's degree. I can do the *New York Times* crossword puzzle in one sitting, and without a dictionary. I can make a soufflé that does not fall before it gets to the table. I have made croissants from scratch, knitted a sweater and made a replica of the Eiffel Tower in Tinkertoy pieces.

"I can do this," I muttered as I surveyed the landscape. "This is easy. Just remember what you went past on the way out here."

Engaged as I'd been in prayer, I hadn't really looked. This was obviously the time for a little more prayer.

I petitioned for help in finding the way home, protection from coyotes, bears and moose stampedes and anything else I thought could happen in the wilderness. I prayed especially for a calm head.

And fast feet.

I do know that the sun rises in the east, and that it had been at my back as I'd walked, so I turned to face the sun and headed in that direction. If I didn't find the B and B, at least I'd eventually reach the Atlantic Ocean.

A sudden rustle and a flapping sound caught my attention. Off to my right, staring at me as hard as I was staring at him, was an enormous wild turkey. He craned his neck upward until his beady little eyes appeared to pop out of his featherless head, on either side of a long brown stick of a neck. He made a sound that made my insides sink.

Fortunately—or unfortunately—I have a wellspring of knowledge about the wild turkey. My mind flew back to the report on wild turkeys for which I had received an A plus in fifth grade, and I scanned my memory banks for information.

Turkeys come down from their roosts at daybreak, so it made perfect sense that we had crossed paths. *A reason to stay in bed late from now on.* Young toms often act aggressively in mating season, which is—gulp—in May.

I'd probably stumbled onto some sort of turkey dating scene and there were a dozen young, hormonally active males preening for cute young hens that might cross their paths. My long-ago report had also said that tom turkeys like to fight among themselves for domination of the flock and sometimes don't differentiate between their turkey brothers and children or people too frail to run away from them.

Tom—we went quickly to a first-name basis—eyed me speculatively, plumped his chest and let his wings fall toward the earth. He was flaunting his best qualities for me, in the hope I'd think him a worthy mate. Showing off, just like any other man.

I spun into action, stamped my feet, flapped my arms and yelled, "Go away! Bad turkey, bad turkey!" Not optimum verbiage, but in the heat of the moment it would have to do. Then I started to run.

Screaming, flapping and stomping, I didn't see Chase until we collided.

He grabbed my shoulders and gave me a little shake as I yelled "Bad turkey!" into his face. My wings—er, arms—dropped to my sides.

"You saved me!" I flung my arms around him and clung to him with a desperation matched only by the passengers on the deck of the *Titanic*.

He cuddled me close, patted my back and asked, "From what?"

I turned to point out King Turkey Kong, but there was nothing there. "He was attacking me!" I babbled. "A turkey! I was lost in the woods and thought I'd never find my way out. I ate my only granola bar. I could have starved to death or been eaten alive."

"Whitney, this land belongs to the Delight B and B," he said, patiently and with far too much amusement in his voice. "If you'd walked to the back of the property, you would have seen a potato chip factory and a warehouse that stores pumps and equipment for swimming pools."

Oh.

So I wasn't so far out in the wilderness after all.

Steps from potato chips and swimming pools? How humiliating.

"Mrs. Bump has breakfast ready. I came to tell you to come in."

"Good," I said brightly, eager to be far away from the site of my humiliation. "I'm starved. Let's go." Tonight I'd be dreaming of big red turkey wattles and a tom streaking out of a tree to peck my eyes out.

"The turkeys have scared other guests," Mrs. Bump said with a chuckle as she put a platter of French toast and bacon on the table. "I keep forgetting to remind people that they are out there. Most people like them, of course, and enjoy watching them from the tower room."

I bobbed my head and kept my mouth shut. Nothing I could say would redeem me, and everything I had said so far had made Chase roar with laughter. He hadn't been there to see the fierceness of that gobbler or feel the first pangs of starvation pierce his belly. He hadn't experienced the fear of having his eyes pecked out, had to rebuff a turkey doing a mating dance or... Never mind. There's no way to put a good spin on the fact that I'd gotten lost and scared of a turkey on the grounds of a B and B, only yards from a potato chip factory. I'd made a fool of myself. It wasn't the first time, but it was one of the most memorable.

"More juice? Fresh squeezed. Or a muffin? Some fruit compote?"

Chase and I shook our heads as best we could with food stuffed all the way from stomach to esophagus. Mrs. Bump had gone all out with lit candles, fruit, a heaping tray of muffins and pastries, French toast dipped in batter and deep-fried, homemade maple syrup, strong black coffee made from freshly ground beans, whole cream for the coffee…and then she'd brought out dessert.

Dessert for breakfast? This is a concept I can get my head around.

"I like something sweet at the end of a meal. Most of my guests find they enjoy it, too. Lemon bar? Oatmeal cookie?"

After breakfast, we dragged ourselves upstairs to our room and lay on our backs on the bed, groaning.

"I'll never eat that much again."

"I feel like I'm going to explode and splatter on the ceiling."

"I tell my patients not to overeat, and now look at me." Chase moaned.

I peeked at him out of the corner of my eye. He looked great. "There *was* that wonderful-looking toffee muffin I didn't get to taste…."

He rolled over and began to tickle me. "You are incorrigible, darling."

There was a positive in this. I had a pair of pants with an elastic waistband packed in my suitcase. I could try a toffee muffin at breakfast tomorrow.

We both fell asleep, and it was nearly 11:00 a.m. when I awoke. Chase had a pillow over his head to block out the light. I changed into my elastic-waisted pants and a lightweight pink sweater and pink slip-ons that Mitzi had forced me to buy last time we went shopping.

Then I gave Chase a gentle poke. "Want to come with me? I thought I'd go shopping."

He snuffled and waved his hand at me. I took that to mean I should go alone.

I managed to negotiate my way through the kite shop, the perfumery, the candle shop and a frame-and-print store before I got caught in a funky little dress shop.

What to buy? A hand-painted T-shirt with rhinestones? A broom skirt in luscious faux suede? Gauchos? The leather beaded belt with tie closures, or the handbag decorated with coins? I held back until I had a meltdown in the children's clothing store. Mobiles of zoo animals and teddy bears hung from the ceiling. Lullabies played on the sound system in the background, and the entire place smelled like talcum powder. I was hooked.

"Can I help you?" I turned to see the clerk, a woman of about my age, with a roly-poly baby on her hip. The little girl was bald as a billiard ball, but wore a little pink headband sporting a satin bow that matched her pink-and-white ruffled dress and pinafore. When she saw me, she started to kick her bootie-clad feet and held her arms out to me.

"May I?"

"Hold her? Sure. She usually doesn't take to customers like this."

I took the soft, cuddly bundle into my arms. "She's heavier than she looks."

"Wet diaper," her mother said practically. "I was on my way to change her."

That didn't deter me. I was immediately and irrevocably in love.

"Do you have children?" the woman asked. "What ages are they? I can help you look for sizes. We just got a new shipment in, and there are some adorable things in the back."

"No kids…yet."

She gave me a sympathetic look. "Someday?"

"I hope so." The baby laid her head on my chest, and my heart felt as though it might burst.

Chase caught up with me in the quilt shop.

"There you are. Mrs. Bump thought I might find you here." He put his arms around my middle and gave me a squeeze. "Sorry I slept so long. It felt great, though. I'm a new man."

"What if I told you I liked the old one?"

"Oh, he's in here, too. Don't worry. Did you find anything to buy?"

"I did, but I resisted." I decided to tell Chase about the baby later. I still hadn't processed for myself the overwhelming strength of my emotion.

"I found us a place to go tonight. There's a place within walking distance with great food, live music and—" he paused and grinned "—booths with curtains, in case we want to be alone."

And we do. We definitely do.

Chapter Seventeen

The stars seemed closer here than they did in the city. As we walked home after dinner, I felt I could have reached up and plucked one from its blue velvet bed. Involuntarily, I shivered.

"Need my coat?" Chase pulled off his jacket and threw it across my shoulders. It was warm from his body heat and infused with the scent of his shaving lotion.

He hugged me to him as we walked. "Do you see the Big Dipper?"

"There?" I pointed to the seven bright stars that formed a small pot with a long handle in the sky.

"And the North Star?"

I drew a line through the two stars at the front bowl of the dipper and followed it as it pointed to Polaris. "And God hung them there. Incredible."

"Everything God does is incredible. That's why some people have such a hard time believing in Him."

"Because He's beyond imagining?"

"It's easier to limit Him, to keep Him in a box with

our preconceived notions. His vastness becomes more manageable for us when we don't try to comprehend all He is." Chase moved his arm, as if to encompass both us and the sky. "It's less difficult to look closer to home for answers than to imagine that this—and humanity—are divine creations."

"For me, it's more risky to believe a patchwork of ever-changing scientific explanations as to why things are than it is to see and acknowledge the divinity in front of my eyes," I murmured. "But I've met Him personally, and you know what happens then."

Chase placed a gentle kiss on the top of my head and held me closer, confirming that where God is concerned, we are on the same page.

We returned to the house, and on the way up the stairs to our room, we heard a loud thump coming from the nether parts of the mansion. Chase and I stared at each other in alarm. "It sounds like someone fell."

"Or something heavy toppled."

Another thump echoed through the house, and Chase and I raced down the stairs toward the sounds, which, as we neared the back of the house, were increasing. *Thunk, thunk, thunk.*

"It sounds like someone is dragging a dead body down a flight of stairs," I blurted, my active imagination, primed by this morning's turkey episode, going into overdrive. "Maybe one of the guests hit Mrs. Bump over the head and is trying to hide her body."

"Whit, you have got to quit watching cop shows on television. And no more mysteries, either. Come on, I think it's coming from in here."

We burst into the kitchen, a rescue team of two. The

lights were on, and at the far end of the room was a door open to the basement.

I imagined Mrs. Bump lying broken and unconscious at the bottom of the stairs, an evil-looking man with a kitchen knife standing over her, all of Delight's silverware stashed in a pillowcase at his feet. Then she appeared, flushed and puffing, at the top of the stairs.

I screamed.

"Oh, dear, I didn't mean to wake you folks." Mrs. Bump, now in blue jeans and a maroon hooded sweatshirt that didn't fit her Victorian persona at all, dusted off her hands. "Sorry if I made noise."

"We thought you might have fallen," Chase explained. "I'm a doctor, and…"

"Well, bless your hearts." She beamed at us. "I'm just fine. I went shopping tonight for things for the B and B. Then a friend and I went to a movie and I was just getting my Jeep unloaded now."

"Jeep?" Where was the pleasant Victorian lady that had greeted us on Friday? She'd been overtaken by a plump baby boomer with rosy cheeks and a Grand Cherokee.

"Do you need help?" Chase asked. A large bag of sugar and some boxes still sat by the back door.

"No, I've taken the biggest pieces downstairs already. I have cold storage and a bit of a cellar down there. I buy flour in fifty-pound bags. You must have heard me dragging it down the steps. It makes quite a racket. I should have waited until morning."

"No problem. Just as long as you're okay," Chase said. "We'll return to our room, then."

"Thanks so much. My church starts at eight, if you'd like to go."

My heart wasn't pounding so hard and my imagination was no longer in overdrive when we reached our room. In fact, I'd reconciled myself to the fact that there really are things that go Bump in Delight.

Sunday, May 2

After service with Mrs. Bump in her small country church, where the singing was enthusiastic if out of tune, the sermon passionate if rambling and the friendliness overwhelming, she fed us a banquet of baked eggs and sausage, pastries, homemade applesauce and an assortment of cookies that would rival any bakery's.

With a series of hugs and grateful goodbyes, she sent us out the door with a bag of cookies for the road and admonitions to come back soon.

"I feel as though I've been gone an entire week," I said as we drove out of town. "What a wonderful break."

"I could have stayed there a month—or two," Chase said agreeably.

That was surprising. Chase has never been good at vacations. A part of his mind, no matter where he is or what he's doing, is always with his patients.

Monday, May 3

Nothing, unfortunately, had changed at the office while I was gone.

Kim couldn't quit talking about the adoption process, and Mitzi told anyone who would listen about the trials and tribulations of taking fertility pills. Bryan smiled and nodded at Mitzi with almost doglike devotion as she jabbered on. Of course, he was wearing earplugs and hadn't heard a word she was saying.

Harry called me into his office at three o'clock. His eyes were wild and the row of hairy question marks on his head was once again erect.

"You have got to make those two quit talking about fertility and adoption. It's scaring our clients."

"Harry, we rarely have clients in our part of the office. And despite the impossibility of it all, they get their work done. We're in great shape. You could go out and get a few more customers." I eyed him speculatively. "Are you sure it's not *you* who's getting scared?"

He sagged into his chair. "What am I going to do, Whitney, if these women go out on maternity leave at the same time?"

Now was not the time to mention that Chase and I had talked about my getting pregnant, as well. "It could be a problem," I ventured.

"Well, it's a problem I can't have. I've got too many other things on my mind." He looked at me, his eyes aglitter. "I want you to find a solution. It's your new assignment. This office can't fold in on itself over a baby or two. You figure it out."

Having divested himself of all responsibility for whatever happened at the office over the next few months, he drew a satisfied sigh and shooed me out of the room.

Thursday, May 6

"Do you want sprinkles or chopped peanuts on this thing?" I called from the kitchen, where I was concocting an ice-cream extravaganza for Kim. Kurt and Chase were out of town, and Kim and Wesley had appeared on my doorstep with pajamas in hand and offered to "keep me company" for the night.

That translates as "We're lonesome." Wesley was already zonked out on the guest room bed, where Kim would join him after we'd finished gorging on ice cream and popcorn.

"When is Kurt coming home?" I plucked off one of the many maraschino cherries I'd put on the ice cream and popped it into my mouth.

"Not until Saturday morning."

"Does this mean you and Wesley will appear on my front step tomorrow night, too?"

"No. We're going to stay overnight at Kurt's mother's place. She likes it when we do that, because she can get her 'full Wesley fix.'"

It doesn't take much to get full of Wesley these days, but I didn't say that to Kim. The more she and Kurt fuss and stew over this adoption process, the more attention Wesley demands. It's as if he already knows that once this still-on-paper child arrives, he'll be deposed from his throne and forced to act like a normal child with a younger sibling, that his kingdom will be overthrown by someone wearing Onesies.

"We're trusting Him for the right thing to happen, but I don't see…" Kim stirred her ice cream into a muddy mess. "Every way we turn there's a roadblock. Someone needs more information, another paper…"

I methodically ate another cherry. "Sounds like you don't trust Him all that much, then."

She sighed and sagged into the chair. "It is Psalms 128: 3 and 4 that's really getting to me."

> Your wife will be like a fruitful vine within your house; your children will be like olive shoots around your table. Thus shall the man be blessed who fears the Lord.

I'd wondered when that might come up.

"Silly, isn't it? Especially since we have Wesley. But I still feel like such a failure."

I felt an unaccustomed flair of impatience. "You, you, you."

Kim looked at me sharply. "What's that supposed to mean?"

"*You* are depriving your husband of a child. *You* are the 'unfruitful vine' who isn't putting any little 'olive shoots' around the table. *You* are failing Kurt. I thought you said this was about waiting on God, but it sounds a lot more like it's all about you."

Her face flushed and she slapped her spoon on the table and shoved the ice cream out of reach. "I hate it when you do that, Whitney."

"Do what?"

"Hit the nail on the head." She ran her fingers through her hair. "You're right. 'I' this and 'me' that…" She looked at me thoughtfully. "When all the time it should be *Thy* will be done."

We sat quietly for a long time. So long, in fact, that Mr. Tibble decided we had perished and jumped onto the table to finish our ice cream.

As I was shooing him away, I added, "It's Mitzi who's the challenge, not you. If she goes on another hormonal rant tomorrow…"

Kim nodded wearily. "The woman exhausts me."

Friday, May 7

And exhaust she did.

Mitzi entered the office like a sailing yacht that had just won the America's Cup, head held high, prow aimed purposefully toward her desk, a "don't-mess-with-me" look in her eyes. She appeared particularly tense and on the edge today, like a high-tension wire humming with electricity.

"Cute outfit, Mitzi," Betty commented on her way by. "Love the short jacket."

"Don't mock me," Mitzi snapped.

Betty blinked, stupefied, and Bryan headed for the men's room.

"I wasn't mocking. I meant it."

"Well, then, thank you." Mitzi walked behind her desk and began to furiously dust the seat of her chair. "Who sat here? There are cookie crumbs all over the seat. How does anyone expect me to get any work done in a pigsty?"

Betty rolled her eyes, and Kim and I exchanged glances.

"If I recall correctly, yesterday you found a box of old Girl Scout cookies in your freezer and brought it to work."

"Are you accusing me of being messy, Whitney? I'll have you know…"

I stood up and crossed the room. With as much

sweetness as I could muster, I said, "Would you come with me to the break room, Mitzi? I have something I'd like to talk to you about."

"I have obligations here at work, Whitney. I don't see why I should have to trot around the office after you all day." But she followed me anyway.

Once we were alone, I looked straight into her eyes. "What is going on? You're acting like a porcupine with a grudge this morning."

"Nothing's going on. Don't be silly." Then her eyes filled with tears and she sat down abruptly on a nearby stool. "Oh, Whitney, I feel like I'm having the worst case of PMS that ever was! I bit Arch's head off this morning, yelled at my cleaning lady because she didn't scrub behind the kitchen appliances and ran over the garbage can because it was in my way."

"Hormones?"

"Apparently they don't agree with me."

Or anyone else.

"You've got to pull yourself together. If you're going to be on these pills for a while, you'll have to manage your emotions."

"How?"

"I don't know, but we'll have to think of something."

"Just pretend Mitzi is PMS-ing," I advised Kim and Betty while Mitzi was out of the room. "She's suffering hormone fluctuations. Perfectly normal. You know how to handle that."

"What do you think PMS stands for, Whitney—Pyschotic Mood Swings?" Kim demanded.

"I know what it stands for to me if Mitzi keeps

acting this way," Betty muttered under her breath. "Pass My Shotgun."

Okay, so suggesting the others humor Mitzi through this didn't work out so well. If Betty means what she says, PMS will take on an entirely new meaning.

Potential Murder Suspect.

Chapter Eighteen

Sunday, May 16, Mother's Day

A truly pathetic group gathered at my house today.

I don't know why I thought having Kim and Kurt, Mitzi and Arch and my parents for dinner would cheer anyone up.

Kim and Kurt are stalled in the adoption process. It's out of their hands and they're playing the waiting game. Kim has never been good at waiting for anything, and she's doubly bad at this.

Mitzi is still on a hormonal Tilt-A-Whirl, and Arch, bless his heart, thinks she's "cute as a button" in her frenzied state. The man is either a saint or an idiot—or maybe he truly enjoys being a knight in shining armor who continually rescues his damsel from distress. The more weepy, helpless and annoying Mitzi is, the more Arch pampers and adores her.

"My brave little wife," he croons. "Everything is going to be okay." Then he looks up at the rest of us and says, "You have to understand how much stress my darling is under."

We all stared, our eyeballs hanging out of our heads in amazement. Doesn't he realize how much stress *we* are under, just being around her?

Not only has Mitzi tried aromatherapy—which she finally gave up when Harry told her she smelled like a three-bean salad—and meditation, she has experimented with a half-dozen naturopathic remedies, including pressure acupuncture.

All the while I keep saying, "Pray, Mitzi, pray."

"Doesn't the Bible say, 'God helps those who help themselves'?" she asked sourly.

"That was Benjamin Franklin, Mitzi, not God. Actually, God *does* like to help us, but He wants us to ask for it."

"Why?"

"He doesn't want to be like the stamp machine in the post office, spitting out help and having no one acknowledge His presence."

"He's very persnickety sometimes, isn't He?"

"'I am a jealous God,' He says," I murmured.

"What does that mean, exactly?"

"He wants us to recognize that without Him we are nothing. He doesn't want work, money or material things to become more important to us than He is."

Mitzi didn't respond but she wore a thoughtful expression. It was better than nothing. Until Mitzi started praying for herself, I was willing to do it for her.

I used to view women who acted helpless and needy with disdain, but now I see that it has its useful qualities. Arch cooked her burger, dished up her plate and brought it to her with a glass of lemonade. He found a pillow to put behind her back, and arranged the footstool to show off her feet to their best advantage. She rewarded him with loving looks and a wan brush of her hand across his cheek and called him "my dearest darling sugar pie."

It's taken a while for Kim and me to admit to one another that we're not really annoyed with Mitzi and Arch. We're jealous. Today, while Arch played footman to Mitzi, Chase, Kurt and my father watched car races on television and reenacted them with Wesley and his miniature cars on the living room floor. They were blissfully unaware that they were in trouble with us for not being knights of the Round Table. Neither did they know when Kim and I came to our senses and forgave them—all during the space of an afternoon.

My mother, whose big day it actually was, spent her time in the kitchen working out the intricacies of her new cappuccino machine and carrying her experiments out to the deck to have us taste them, making us not only pathetic but also overcaffeinated.

Tuesday, June 1

The past few weeks have passed quietly. Chase works and sleeps, works and sleeps. The office is quiet, as long as no one pokes at Mitzi. She reminds me of a beehive with all sorts of touchy little things buzzing around inside. But, like a wasp's nest, if she isn't prodded—that is, if we don't look at her crosswise, talk to her too early in the morning, criticize anything she does or suggest that she could work a little harder—she's fine.

I'm watching programs on Animal Planet regularly to further develop my management style. There's so much to be learned from nature. Sometimes, instead of thinking of Mitzi as a wasp's nest, I imagine her as a sleeping alligator or a snapping turtle. Don't mess with them, keep your hands away from their mouths, and you'll be fine.

Something good is happening in our spiritual life, Chase's and mine, since we've discussed starting a family. It's heavy-duty stuff to think of bringing a new life into the world. It's not all about cute babies, new high chairs and decorating a nursery, but about a life that didn't exist before and never would but for our decision to create it.

Life is everlasting, which means that our child will be here for the long term, eternity, time without end. There is nothing else I can do in this life that will last forever except love God.

My mother insists I think about this too much. She says that if we're meant to have children, we'll have them. And if not, she suggests another cat. That's the best motivation of all for having a child. I couldn't live with another creature like Mr. Tibble or Scram.

They have started sitting in my kitchen sink when I'm not home. There is a small drip in the faucet that Chase can't seem to fix, and they laze there, catching drops of water on their tongues. Chase thinks it's funny, but I have to sanitize the entire area before I can start supper.

And then there's that little issue of their discovering soap operas on television. We've had to start putting the television remote in the silverware drawer so they can't get at it. Otherwise they watch TV all afternoon. I've secretly observed them. They have favorites, and switch from NBC to ABC to CBS depending on what show is on. At first I thought it was an accident, but they follow a pattern. Then Mr. Tibble puts his paw on the power button and turns it off to make it appear that he and Scram have had nothing to do all day but feel abandoned by their humans. Later, Chase lies on the couch, pushing harder and harder on the remote control buttons and wondering why the batteries get weak so quickly.

Fools. These cats take us for fools.

Scram isn't smart enough to have figured this out on his own, and would have been content to watch my plants grow, but Mr. Tibble is a genius. Sometimes he stares at me so intently that he scares me. I can't help but wonder what he's thinking.

Mr. Tibble here.

I hate to say it, but Whitney's other pet, the two-footed one, is getting on my nerves. He's been hogging the sofa at night for weeks now. How can I get my daily twenty hours of sleep if he's got the couch? The other one—Scram—is ridiculously poor company. How they expect me to enjoy something whose only two hobbies are shedding and chasing his tail is beyond me. No scholarly stimulation, no thought-provoking conversations, not even an incentive to hypothesize on the mysteries of life. It's hard being an intellectual trapped by such plebian surroundings and low-brow activities. I do trust that Hope and Bo never leave *Days of Our Lives*. That would be the last straw.

Mr. Tibble, signing off.

Wednesday, June 2

Mom stopped over with an armful of photo albums.

"Isn't that cute?" My mother pointed to a photo taken of me with a full diaper drooping somewhere between my calves. I was also topless, barefoot and obviously howling at the top of my lungs.

That, it appears, is a recurring theme in my baby pictures. Other themes include photos of me with food outside my mouth instead of in it, ridiculous outfits pulled together from my mother's closet—her bra and pearls and Dad's work boots, for example—and me with every four-footed thing that ever crossed my path.

My mother, an aspiring Anne Geddes, took pictures of me as an infant in a flowerpot, a flower bed and a flour sack. She recorded every time I sucked on my fingers, put on a hat or a ballerina costume. She managed to snap a shot every time I pouted, therein making a pictorial record of my lower lip jutting outward like a Ubangi woman in the making.

Most unfortunate of all, there were several baby pictures of me looking like a small Winston Churchill. So much for that old Bing Crosby song "You Must Have Been A Beautiful Baby." I'm keeping these photos under wraps. If Chase ever sees them, he may decide it would be a good idea if we never reproduced.

"Did you ever get a *good* photo of me, Mom?"

"What do you mean? These are all good." She beamed deliriously at a photo of me digging in the garden, round little backside to the camera. "This was the day your dad bought you a new pail and shovel. You were the cutest child ever born."

Talk about being blinded by love!

Mother looked at me, her eyes sparkling. "Whitney, I was so head over heels in love with you from the moment you were born that I thought I'd burst. There you were, all goopy and wet, howling like a banshee, your dark hair curled to your head—a very *large* head, I might add—and I knew immediately that you were perfect. If I hadn't believed in God before then, I would have from that moment on. Birth is a miracle, an absolute miracle. You are our miracle."

"Oh, Mom…"

"Oh, Whitney…"

We did one of those mushy hugs that we do sometimes when we're overcome with emotion.

"So that's how it is to be a mother."

"I didn't say that." Mom looked aghast. "I said that's how it is to give birth. Motherhood is a different thing entirely. Motherhood is being in the trenches—changing diapers, trying to get prunes into a moving target, driving a minivan full of eight-year-olds to soccer practice, sewing a ladybug costume at three in the morning, making cupcakes for a hundred Girl Scouts…*that's* motherhood."

"Whoa. You're making me tired just talking about it."

"Oh, you will be tired. But it's worth it."

Chapter Nineteen

Harry's birthday is a big deal around our office. We like birthdays. Or, more specifically, we like birthday *cake*.

He's a real softy, where his birthday is concerned. Harry likes to reminisce about his childhood, eat chocolate fudge cake with chocolate icing and chocolate ice cream and open presents. Sometimes he gets a little misty-eyed recollecting the past. This year he's especially maudlin. I have a hunch it has to do with his balding pate. Harry has looked the same ever since I've known him—ageless. He could be forty or sixty. No one knows for sure, and no one ever asks, but the hair thing is getting him down. He's finally succumbed to a comb-over, and he isn't happy. Next thing on the agenda for him is the monk's tonsure, like the dust ruffle on my bed—nothing on top, but a decorative fringe beneath.

That's probably the reason Harry got three hats for his birthday—a billed baseball cap from me, a Stetson that Betty purchased on eBay and a shower cap and back-scrubbing brush from Bryan. Mitzi, of course, forged her own path in the gift department—and not a very tactful path, at that.

She gave him a piece of torture chamber equipment for tightening his abs. It frightens me a little to think that Harry actually has abs to tighten. People aren't usually born without them, so that must mean he does have muscles somewhere under that soft pillow of flab he carries. Not a pretty visual.

His gifts didn't cheer him up much this year, and I regretted not buying him my first impulse, a box of Godiva chocolates.

Then I recalled the box of truffles that Chase had given me two weeks earlier and made me take to the office so he wouldn't be tempted to eat them. He's obviously more worried about his own waistline than mine. I'd hidden the box well, because the Pierogi Bandit is still striking occasionally, even though Bryan seldom brings them anymore.

The chocolate was in the one place where no one would ever find it, a wide-bottomed file in my desk labeled Things To Do. Nobody would look there in a million years.

I slipped out of the break room, found the chocolate and added it to the birthday party foods we'd already assembled. Betty had brought cucumber sandwiches, Kim had provided chips and dip, Bryan's offering was M&M's and I'd purchased the cake. Mitzi, as usual, had donated a tin of caviar and some tasteless crisp bread to serve it on. Also as usual, no one would eat it, and she and Arch would finish it off at home while they watched videos of *Extreme Makeover,* Mitzi's favorite show.

We made small talk as we drank pink lemonade out of Dixie cups and, because we didn't have enough forks, ate with our fingers.

"Have you set goals for this year yet, Harry?" Mitzi asked as she spread fish eggs on cardboard toast.

Harry looked at her with bulging eyes. "Goals?"

"I always make birthday pledges. This year my birthday pledge is to use my elliptical trainer, even if it does make me perspire."

Mitzi doesn't believe in sweating. She ranks it right up there with other undesirable bodily responses, like drooling and twitching, to be done only when one is completely helpless to do otherwise.

She slid a piece of birthday cake onto her plate and nibbled at the frosting. "Arch's birthday pledge is to do a triathlon."

It's difficult not to hyperventilate just thinking about it. Jumping into a lake, swimming into the middle where it's a zillion feet deep, flailing back to shore, leaping on a bike with a seat the width of dental floss and then running a race isn't my cup of tea. Jumping into bed and dreaming of swimming, biking and running is plenty for me.

"I tried kickboxing," Betty offered helpfully. "It's supposed to be very good for you."

"Is that when you dislocated your hip?"

"No. That was when I fell off my bike in spinning class."

Is it any wonder I'm afraid of exercise?

"You still work out with Bernard, don't you, Whitney?" Mitzi asked as she dug into my box of candy.

My trainer is the only reason I'm as fit as I am. I'm afraid to quit going to him, for fear he'll hunt me down and drag me back to his studio by my hair. It's easier just to keep going than it is to have the cousin of the Incredible Hulk stalking me.

The gym really isn't all that bad. Lest I be thought of as a completely fitness-averse person, I always point out that my sports club makes great protein shakes. I prefer the Macho Smoothie—six kinds of fruit, protein powder and something that's white and quivers, maybe tofu, or a spare internal organ.

"Anybody want another piece of cake?" Mitzi inquired. "I think I will. It's very good, Whitney."

She took a bite, closed her eyes and rolled it around on her tongue. "Very nice. I'll order this next time Arch and I have a party."

I watched her with a growing sense of disorientation. Something was out of kilter. I looked around the table, trying to puzzle out what it might be. Harry was wearing my baseball cap and eating M&M's. Betty and Kim were debating the merits of regular paper plates versus reinforced ones while Bryan arranged M&M's by color. Mitzi was eating cake—*chocolate* cake.

"Mitzi, what are you doing?" I asked in astonishment.

She looked at me innocently and glanced down at the table. "I'm eating Harry's birthday cake. What else?"

"Mitzi, the cake is chocolate. You hate chocolate."

"I certainly do…." Her voice trailed away.

Everyone stared at Mitzi, whose finger was suspended in midair, a glob of chocolate frosting halfway to her lips.

She looked at her finger, puzzled, as if it held a great mystery of life. "I don't get it. Chocolate is disgusting."

Then she lifted the finger to her mouth and licked the

frosting with as much delicacy as Mr. Tibble might display when sampling a bit of tuna. "But it isn't. It tastes good." Then she asked the question we were all asking ourselves. "Why?"

"You should have seen her, Chase, gobbling up chocolate cake and truffles like there was no tomorrow."

We were seated on the floor across from each other, huddled over the Scrabble board on the coffee table. Mr. Tibble was curled into a boneless ball, just out of reach.

I'm a people pleaser, the kind who bends over backward to make sure that everyone is happy and that I am well liked. I allow others ahead of me in line at a buffet and then discover that, by the time I get there, the chicken legs and the fruit salad have run out. I keep the peace. I share my Hershey bar. I let someone else have the last peanut butter cup in the bowl.

I also agree to more than my share of chores. "Let Whitney do it. Busy people always get things done." "Everyone else has turned us down, let's ask Whitney." And "Whitney isn't here, so we'll appoint her chairman of the committee."

Cats don't allow that to happen. They won't even come to supper when you call them. A cat would never stoop so low as to be on a committee.

We've been tricked into believing that they are domesticated creatures, but nothing could be further from the truth. At any moment, Mr. Tibble could stage a mutiny, shred every curtain and cushion in the house and choose the life of a feral cat. I see it in his eyes, the disdain, the icy regard, the haughtiness. He plans to the inch how far away he must lie down from me so that I must be the one to move to pet him. If I've been on a trip—our romantic B and B escape, for one—when I return I can count on him to refuse to sleep on our bed and to spend the next night howling just outside our bedroom door as punishment for abandoning him.

I laid out my tiles to spell F-E-L-I-N-E.

But back to Mitzi. "She was as shocked as the rest of us, Chase. I could tell by the look on her face."

He looked amused but not surprised. "If she's on fertility meds her hormones are changing. She may have an altered sense of taste and smell or…" He set out F-I-N-I-C-K-Y. "Thirty-eight points."

"So that's what it is?" I asked, still stuck on Mitzi's weird behavior. "C-R-A-Z-Y. Fifteen points."

"It could be something nutritionally based, too. A-V-O-C-A-D-O. Twenty-six points."

This isn't a game, it's a rout. I laid out M-O-T-H-E-R-L-Y. "Twenty points, plus I used up all my tiles."

"For example," Chase continued as he trounced me with S-Q-U-A-S-H, "pregnant women often crave pickles because they're salty and their body is low in sodium. Also, their taste buds usually have a heightened acuity." He looked at the board with satisfaction. "Forty-two points."

But Mitzi isn't… Of course not. Not yet.

M-A-D-N-E-S-S. Twenty-two points.

Tuesday, June 9

At noon today, Mitzi opened her Gucci lunch box and began to lay out her lunch of leftover poached salmon, three stalks of cold asparagus, a whole wheat dinner roll with a pat of butter and two Ziploc bags of chocolate candy.

"What are you doing?"

"Eating, of course. What does it look like?" Mitzi sipped on her bottle of Evian and daintily picked up an asparagus spear.

"I thought you were hung up on nutrition these days."

"And your point is?"

"That's hardly a balanced diet." I pointed at the generous bags of candy.

"It most certainly is. Haven't you ever studied nutrition?" Mitzi calmly picked up her fork to point at the salmon and then at the asparagus. "Protein and veggie." She skewered the dinner roll. "Grain and fat. And fruit."

"I get the protein," I agreed, "and even the dinner roll. But *fruit?*"

She looked at me wearily, as if beleaguered by my idiocy. "Chocolate-covered raisins and chocolate-covered cherries. Whitney, don't you know *anything?*"

Saturday, June 12

It must have been something we ate.

Instead of going to Kim and Kurt's to have dinner and watch another video on China, Chase and I lay around the living room, wondering which of us would throw up next.

As a doctor, Chase is exposed to everything, but he rarely catches anything. I, on the other hand, can pick up any flu virus within a twenty-five-mile radius.

"Want to watch a video?"

"What do we have?"

"*Titanic, Castaway* and *The Perfect Storm.*"

"Too much rolling water. We'd get seasick."

"Want a ginger ale?"

"We finished it."

"Saltines?"

"All gone."

"Maybe we could just move into the bathroom and play checkers on the tile floor."

"Chess?"

"You've got it."

Of course, neither of us had the energy to stand up and move, which precluded any sort of competition. Instead, we lounged where we were until I recalled seeing a bottle of Pepto-Bismol in the bathroom cupboard.

"I'm going to run for supplies," I announced, and rolled off the love seat onto the floor. "If I'm not back in three hours, come and find me."

Chase lifted a hand and waved me off.

It felt good to move. Being curled in a fetal position is fine for a fetus, but when one is five foot seven, it gets a little old.

As I went by the laundry room, I threw in a load of clothes and folded a few towels before continuing on my mission.

I was positive I'd seen Pepto-Bismol somewhere, but obviously it wasn't our medicine cabinet. There was, however, a box in the top back corner that I'd nearly forgotten about. I lifted it down gently and stared at the label. It was a home pregnancy test I'd purchased once and never used.

"Out of date," I muttered, and threw it into the trash.

Chapter Twenty

Wednesday, June 16

Office meeting—9:00 a.m. promptly. No stragglers. Harry's rules.

I squeezed my arms tightly across my chest and willed Betty and Bryan to arrive. Harry likes these meeting to be as quick and efficient as possible.

Personally, I could barely put two sentences together today, so it would be impossible to follow Harry's scattershot method of running a meeting. Besides that, Mitzi is up to something. I can always tell.

If she doesn't give you her opinion, it's there to read on her face. She came to work looking like Mr. Tibble with cream on his whiskers, complacent and utterly self-satisfied. When Mitzi is cheerful, it usually means trouble for us. Not only do we have to listen to stories about the source of her joy—"Arch said it was the biggest diamond the jeweler had ever sold…" or "…then they asked if I'd ever considered modeling…"—but we also have to sit at rapt attention and murmur "amazing" or "congratulations" every few minutes until she dismisses us, her captive audience.

"Come on, come on, come on!" Harry bellowed, shooing the others into the room as if they were wayward sheep.

"Now that I've got you all here," Harry began, "and before we get to what I have, do any of you have anything to report?"

"The building custodian said the elevators will be out between 1:00 and 4:00 p.m." Betty announced. "Please use the stairs."

Harry nodded vaguely. "Anybody else?"

Bryan gave details on the status of our new computer system, and Kim turned in the budget she'd been working on. Then Harry turned to Mitzi and me.

"Do either of you have anything to say?"

I stared at the agenda I'd prepared and watched the words blur before my eyes. Unbidden, something unstoppable bubbled up inside me and escaped my lips.

"I think I'm pregnant."

If that old pregnancy test is accurate. Maybe I shouldn't have dug it out of the garbage last night, but I couldn't help myself.

I paused and blinked as my words echoed in the room. *Echoed?*

Mitzi had repeated my words.

I turned to gawk at Mitzi, who was gawking at me. "I think *I* might be pregnant," she said.

"No, I said *I* might be…"

"You? Not you. Me."

Kim uttered a piercing shriek that called dogs from

all parts of the city. Bryan's eyes bugged out of his head, and Betty started to clap furiously.

"This is wonderful!" Kim threw her arms around me. "Both of you! But are you *sure?*"

"I didn't mean to say anything…" I blathered, amazed at the size of my mouth and the lack of a filter on my brain. "It just spilled out. The test wasn't new…. The expiration date had passed…. Chase says he thinks it was all right, and he should know. I'm going in today to—"

"No fair!" Mitzi howled. "I wanted to be first to tell. I didn't think we'd both be—"

Harry, who'd been sitting in his chair looking stupefied, jumped to his feet and roared, "Both of you? Two at once?" He bounced on the soles of his small feet, and what little hair he had stood straight off his head. "Not now, not with the deadline for the Kelsey and Klanger project only ten months away! I need you here!"

"This," Kim observed with a huge smile on her face, "is like an avalanche that's already started rolling down the hill, Harry. Kelsey and Klanger Project or not, there's no way you're going to stop nature now."

Needless to say, the rest of the day was shot.

Harry walked around pulling on his few fragile curls. Betty began giving advice from the birth of her son nearly thirty years ago, and Bryan, ever-predictable Bryan, went into avoidance mode and clamped his hands over his ears every time someone said the words *pregnancy, hormone* or *birth.* Kim just sat at her desk with a huge, stupid grin on her face.

Fortunately, Mitzi decided not to spend her time pouting about the fact that I had announced my news first, and we got directly to the good stuff.

"It was the chocolate cake that tipped me off," she said giddily. "Even as a child, I spit the chocolate chips out of cookies. But there I was, having my second piece of this delicious concoction—and M&Ms—and not even thinking for a moment that I don't like them." She dug into her purse and pulled out a candy bar. "Look, a Snickers!"

Proof positive. Mitzi is definitely pregnant. Or taste-bud-damaged. Or has been replaced by another alien from her home planet.

Then the uncertainty set in. *What if I'm not pregnant after all?*

I should never have said anything until I knew for sure. The test was past the expiration date. Perhaps pregnancy tests are made to self-destruct if not used by the proper time. Was Chase wrong to think it would still be accurate?

Why didn't I keep my big mouth shut? I felt like banging my head against my desk. I might just have done so, if it wouldn't have attracted attention. Impulsive fool, blurting out that I'm pregnant that way! Now I'm one of those people my mother talks about, the excited woman who announces her twenty-four-hour-old pregnancy in June, saying she's expecting a baby in February. How embarrassing.

But it's impossible not to be excited. My thirty-third birthday isn't far off. If Chase and I are going to start a family, we shouldn't wait much longer. Hmm… Now *that* makes me sound desperate.

Which is more pathetic? An overly enthusiastic big mouth or a woman desperate and grasping at hope? At least Mitzi had had a doctor confirm her news. And she's eating chocolate. What would suggest that I could be in the same condition, other than a questionable test? Nothing! Nada. Not a thing.

Except that pickle incident. Maybe it *was* a little odd that Chase came home last week and found me dipping pickles in fudge ice-cream topping. Did that count?

"How cam'st thou in this pickle?" Bill Shakespeare once wrote. He was obviously talking about me.

After work I stopped by Chase's office to take a fresh—as in not expired—test and wait in his office for the results.

Chase sat with me as I twitched and squirmed.

"What's taking so long?"

For once, he wasn't patient, either. Potential fatherhood can do that to a guy. Finally he jumped to his feet and went in search of the lab report.

When he returned carrying my chart, his face was a studied blank. He looked very aloof and professional in his white coat with his stethoscope looping out of his pocket. My heart sank.

I rose partially from my chair before dropping back into it again. "Chase?"

"Good news, Mrs. Andrews." His blank eyes began to sparkle. "You have passed your test. You will be promoted to the next grade—motherhood."

A wash of emotion overtook me as I launched myself out of the chair and into his arms.

I felt Chase bury his face in my hair. He was trembling.

I lifted my face to his. "Honey? Are you okay?"

"I've never been so okay in my life, Whitney." He crushed his lips to mine. "We're having a baby."

"Oh, Chase, we've got to get busy. We've got less than eight months to get ready. The nursery…"

He laughed and stopped me with a kiss. "I'm almost done for the day. Two more patients. Wait for me?"

"You've got it."

I sat in the waiting room, trying not to explode, tapping one foot and then the other. Finally I stood up and began to pace. The emotions rioting within me were legion. Excitement, I'd expected. Delight, ecstasy, exhilaration, anticipation? Of course. Gratitude? Without a doubt.

But fear, trepidation and alarm? I hadn't realized how scary the idea of becoming a parent could be.

A young mother exited an examining room carrying a squalling baby. The more she attempted to soothe it, the louder it wailed. Its tiny red face was distorted with fury and indignation.

Oh, Lord, what have I gotten myself into now?

Well, whatever it is, there's no turning back.

When Chase had finished with his last patient, I could finally do what every maternal cell in my body was screaming for me to do—go shopping!

I felt as giddy as a girl on a first date as we walked hand in hand down the long corridors of the Mall of America.

"Let's go in here." Chase tugged on my hand and pulled me into a specialty children's store populated with tiny ducks, soft bunnies and sofas and chairs no higher than my kneecaps.

I fingered a blanket that was soft as cashmere. "I want to buy something."

"We don't know if we're having a boy or a girl."

"Then we will buy green or yellow. Or peach."

Chase scowled. "No son of mine will wear peach."

Oooh. Macho Dad. Cute.

He picked up a soft white blanket. "How about this?"

"White? Are you sure? Babies have a lot of…excretions…you know."

"A baptismal blanket. Something special *he* can pass down to his children." His eyes burned into mine. "Our grandchildren."

"I'm sure *she* will like that. But don't give her children yet. She isn't even old enough to date."

"Enjoy it. As long as that baby is hanging out in your womb, at least you'll know where it is at night."

Ewww. Had Chase and I thought this through thoroughly enough?

Then I punched him on the arm. "Whattdayamean, 'grandchildren'? Don't rush me. I want to enjoy every single moment of this."

"Okay. Enjoy this." He pulled me close and kissed me, right there, between bibs and receiving blankets.

Thursday, June 17

At five o'clock I began to wonder where Chase was, and by seven-thirty I was worried. He's never late without calling. As I dialed the number of the hospital, I heard his car pull into the driveway.

"Where were you—?" I began, bursting with thoughts about our baby that I wanted to share, but when I saw the expression on his features, I stopped cold. "Chase? What's wrong?"

He shrugged out of his suit coat and dropped it over the back of a chair. Without speaking, he took me in his arms and laid his cheek against my hair. A tremor shuddered through him.

"Honey?" I pulled away to look him in the face.

"Give me a minute, will you?" He pulled out a kitchen chair and sank into it heavily. "It's been a rough day."

Silently, I poured him a cup of coffee and waited.

He bowed his head to knead the muscles at the back of his neck until he winced. Finally he looked up.

"Sorry about that. Thanks for the coffee."

I pulled out a chair across from him. "What's happened?"

"I lost a patient this afternoon," he said softly. "It was totally unexpected. If I'd had any idea…"

Chase doesn't usually bring his work home to me. What happens at the hospital stays there. He's a stickler for confidentiality, so the fact that he was even speaking of this was unusual.

"What happened?"

"That's the crazy thing," he murmured absently. "He came in for a follow-up on a broken arm. He'd had X-rays and everything looked fine. Then he told me he'd been having some unusual pain in the arm and up into the shoulder and asked if that was normal.

"It isn't, really—not with a break like his—so I suggested we investigate a little further. He was too young to be much of a candidate for heart trouble, but I never let shoulder pain go unexamined. We joked around a little. He told me that his oldest boy had just learned to ride without training wheels and that had given him a few breathless moments. Then I sent him down for an EKG just as a precaution, never thinking…"

Chase looked up, and for the briefest moment his guard was down and the wells of pain behind his eyes seared my heart. "He coded during the EKG, and we couldn't get him back. Massive heart failure. Here one minute and gone the next. None of us had a clue, least of all me, his *doctor.*"

I wanted to speak, but no words came. The grief I read in Chase's eyes wasn't going to be allayed by sympathetic but helpless words or empty assurances.

"It was unbelievable, Whitney, bizarre. There we were, joking about 'the big one' and within a half hour..."

"You did the right thing," I ventured. "You sent him for an EKG."

"Sure it was the right thing, but it didn't help. I've been racking my brain, trying to think of anything I missed that might have tipped me off, any signs—shortness of breath, sweating, even poor coloring—but there was nothing." Chase sounded bewildered. "He literally just dropped dead."

"I am so sorry." How shallow the words sounded in response to so deep a pain.

"So much was going on that at first I didn't realize that his wife and children were in the waiting room. They'd come with him because they were on their way to a baseball game."

My stomach lurched. "Wife and children?"

Chase looked at me, his eyes brimming with misery. "He was thirty-five years old, with two children and another on the way."

I laid my hand protectively across my still-flat belly. *Another on the way.* What must that poor woman be thinking? Feeling?

What would I have done if he hadn't come home tonight? If he'd been the one taken? What would I want to say to him when I no longer could? What would I have regretted?

There are no moments in life that we can take for granted, not one.

Chapter Twenty-One

Friday, June 25

We'd planned to tell my parents about the baby last night, but neither Chase nor I could muster the energy. We'd spent a good deal of time in prayer and gone to bed early, neither of us feeling much like celebrating.

Tonight, then, I was pleased to see my mother appear at our door with a German chocolate cake with pecan and coconut frosting, an armful of catalogs and my father.

My father gets dragged to a lot of things. The only things he absolutely refuses to attend anymore are rummage sales. He says that rummage sales "diminish his manhood." Maybe it has something to do with the fact that if my mother finds a piece of clothing she likes, she insists on draping it across Dad so she can see how it looks.

After more than thirty-five years of marriage, Mom is as energetic and full of life as she was at twenty, he tells me in a tone somewhere between awe and dismay. He'd hoped they'd grow old together, but so far he's the only one willing to age. Of course, living with my mother would make any man grow old quickly. The odds are stacked against him. When he looks at her, however, it's with a tender, indulgent sort of gaze that tells me how much he's still in love with her.

Mom, who can read me like a book, studied me with an appraising eye. "You look terrible. What's happened?"

I was taken off guard, and the story of Chase's patient just came pouring out.

"He was so young," I blubbered. "What's she going to do? I barely slept last night. I can't get it out of my mind."

Mom considered me for a moment. "You have a tender heart, Whitney, but I've never seen you quite this emotional. It's as if you were…"

Then she changed her mind about saying more and, with a flourish, spread her catalogs across my dining-room table. "Look at this."

My jaw dropped as I saw pages and pages of maternity clothes, baby supplies and strollers. "How did you know?"

She eyed me suspiciously. "Know what?"

"That Chase and I are going to have a baby? We just found out. We were going to tell you, but then Chase had this happen at the hospital…"

"So *that's* why everything I've looked at for the last month has had a baby in it. I sensed that something about you was different." Her face lit with delight. "Now it all makes sense!"

"You've suspected I was pregnant for a month?"

"Mother's intuition," she said modestly. "Congratulations, darling. I'm elated for you!"

"What about all that stuff you told me about your being too young to be a grandmother? I thought it might bother you. You *have* been introducing me as your younger sister for some time now."

She looked at me mysteriously and blinked slowly. Her smile was serene and wisely maternal. "Darling, I'll sing it from the rooftops when you and Chase have a baby. And as for my being a grandmother, people won't believe it. And if they do, I'll tell them I adopted you when I was a teenager.

"I think it is glorious, Whitney. It's about time." Then, more to herself than to me, she muttered, "And babies need aunties, too, you know." She turned back to the catalogs. "Which bumper pads do you like? I'm partial to Peter Rabbit."

When we returned to the kitchen, it was apparent that Chase had told my father the good news. Dad jumped to his feet and gathered me into a large, warm bear hug. As I burrowed my nose in his chest, I could smell the same aftershave that he'd worn every day when I was a child. Old Spice. If there is a more comforting fragrance on the planet, I don't know about it. When I smell it, I'm transported. I'm five years old again and sitting in his lap.

He took me by the shoulders and studied me as he had so many times over the years. "My baby is having a baby." I heard his voice breaking. "Praise God."

At that moment, Mr. Tibble came marching through the room, his tail held high in the air. Scram, like a court jester to the king, followed, occasionally standing on his hind legs to bat at Mr. Tibble's majestic tail.

I dropped into a leather chair and patted my lap. "Come here, guys." As Mr. Tibble jumped into my lap, my mother let out an unearthly scream.

"Noooooooo!"

Mr. Tibble, who is no dummy, headed for the hills.

Scram, who *is* a dummy, froze in place, every wisp of fur on his body erect. Then, realizing that his leader had abandoned ship, he took off, yowling for Mr. Tibble.

"Mother, you nearly scared the cats to death!"

My mother, red-faced, pointed at the doorway through which the cats had disappeared. "You can't touch them. Not now. Not anymore."

"Excuse me?"

"Have you given up reading women's magazines, Whitney? Cats and pregnant women just don't mix. Toxoplasmosis."

You mean I'm *already* a negligent mother?

Chase cleared his throat. "Don't worry. We'll make sure the cats are healthy. They live indoors. It's unlikely they've come into contact with the parasite."

My mother didn't buy it. "I don't want anything to jeopardize my grandchild's health. No cats."

I shot Chase a pleading look. If mother got it into her head that the cats were dangerous, she'd kidnap them and not bring them back for months.

"I'll take care of the cats," Chase assured my mother. "We'll have them tested, and I'll clean the litter box. It's not only cats that carry this, you know. You can get it from unwashed fruits and vegetables."

Mother's ears perked up. "Vegetables? You can get it from vegetables?"

Oh, spare me. Now she'll patrol my vegetable bin. Being pregnant is already thornier than I thought it would be.

Mr. Tibble here.

Whitney's Momma Cat, the one she calls

"Mom," is very annoying. She screeched like an owl and flapped her wings at us today. I don't care for the cold, calculating way she stares at me. I do not trust her. I must be on guard. She has a predatory look which makes me believe that Scram and I are in danger.

I, of course, am much larger—and more magnificent, if I do say so myself—than that idiot Scram. Maybe if I fed him to her she would leave me alone. A brilliant idea, really. It would solve two problems at once. Momma Cat would be full and Scram would be history. I would have Whitney all to myself again.

Next time the screeching one arrives, I must entice Scram into the same room with her and see what happens. Oh, this will be fun.

Mr. Tibble, ruthlessly signing off.

Monday, June 21

Innova's break room has turned into Baby Info central.

Betty spends her evenings shopping for baby items on eBay and brings new batches of printouts for us to examine every morning.

I had no idea babies were so complicated. Silly me, I thought you fed and burped them, diapered, rocked and loved them, and that was enough. Of course, that was before marketing, technology and consumer awareness.

Betty thrust a color photocopy of a little criblike bed under my nose. "Mitzi is getting one of these. You should, too."

Of course, I thought, since I'm trying so hard to be a Mitzi clone.

At that moment, Mitzi breezed into the office wearing maternity clothes, a weird pink blouse with a huge pink bow at the neck and black Capri pants. She looked like a rerun of Lucille Ball pregnant with little Ricky. Talk about rushing things.

"It's very cool, like a little apartment for your baby," she announced.

"Isn't a week old a little young to have your own apartment? My parents said I couldn't move out until I was eighteen." Actually, my father told me I couldn't move out until I was thirty, but for once I didn't follow his advice.

Mitzi tripped toward me carrying her ever-present carton of milk. If nothing else, her baby will have bones of steel from all the calcium she's pumping in there. She pointed at the picture with a hot-pink fingernail. "It's a bedside crib that attaches to your bed with fasteners. You never have to get out of bed to take care of the baby. No stumbling around in the dark looking for the bassinet! Isn't it clever?"

"What if you *want* to get out of bed and that thing has you trapped?"

"Crawl over your husband, of course. He'll go right back to sleep. They always do."

"Or you could have this." Betty handed me a picture of a tiny boxlike bassinet plopped in the middle of a large mattress. "The baby sleeps between you in its own little bed. Isn't that cute?"

"Between the two of us? No wonder Kim says a new baby is a great form of birth control."

"Well, what *are* you looking for then?" Betty asked impatiently.

"Exodus 2, actually."

Betty and Mitzi stared at me as if I were missing some brain cells. Fortunately, Kim wandered in at just the right time to quote the familiar verse.

"'Now a man from the house of Levi went and married a Levite woman. The woman conceived and bore a son; and when she saw that he was a fine baby, she hid him three months. When she could hide him no longer she got a papyrus basket for him, and plastered it with bitumen and pitch; she put the child in it and placed it among the reeds on the bank of the river.'"

"That's what you want for your baby? A basket covered with tar?"

"I doubt you'll find that on eBay," Mitzi muttered.

"I want a Moses basket, silly. The kind that has handles and is woven with palm or wicker, like the one his mother put him in and hid among the reeds on the river."

"Now why'd she do a thing like that?" Harry asked as he walked through the office for a fresh cup of coffee.

"Because the pharaoh of Egypt had ordered that every Hebrew boy be killed, thrown into the Nile."

"Well, that's rotten!"

"The pharaoh's daughter found the baby Moses in the basket and adopted him."

"All's well that ends well," Harry said philosophically, and wandered out of the room again. Harry's not much of a history buff. To him, 1984 is the Dark Ages.

"A baby outgrows a basket pretty quickly," Mitzi observed between slugs of milk. "You'd better get both."

This baby has already run up a huge shopping bill,

and I've known about it for five days. I already feel I've been remiss in not having set up a college fund.

"And," Betty said triumphantly, "wait until you see the breast pumps I found for you!"

At that, Bryan, who had been minding his own business and quietly eating a cup of applesauce, stood up and left the room.

I'd had no idea he could move that fast.

Sunday, June 27

"You're looking like you lost your best friend," I commented to Chase as he sat on the deck, staring at a vacant bird feeder.

He turned to look at me, his eyes serious. "The funeral is Monday."

"Oh." I knelt in front of him and took his hands.

"I'm still shocked. I've been over everything a dozen times, and I know there was nothing I would do differently were that patient to come into my office again. There were no warning signs." He stared at me with a disconcerting look in his eyes. "It could happen to any of us." Chase snapped his fingers, and I jumped. "Just like that."

"Please don't brood about this. We'll continue to pray for his family, but it isn't going to help to replay that afternoon in your mind." Even as I said it, I knew that it was impossible for Chase to turn off those images in his head.

"He was thirty-five, Whitney. *Thirty-five.*"

Chase is also thirty-five and no doubt he had brushed up against his mortality when his patient died. It didn't surprise me that he was brooding.

Chapter Twenty-Two

Tuesday, June 29

The flu must be going around.

"Have you seen Bryan?" I asked.

Betty looked up from her desk. "He went back to get a cup of coffee and hasn't returned."

I spun on my heel and headed for the break room. To the right of the door was the compact counter on which the coffee machine sat. The vertical folding door closing off the shelves that held coffee cans, filters and cups was not entirely closed and the toe of a shiny black shoe protruded from the opening. I pulled the door back to find Bryan angled against the shelving, his face a ghastly white.

"Bryan?"

His eyes bulged from his eye sockets like a bullfrog's, and I noticed a bit of ashy gray around his pinched lips. He was clutching the small garbage can we keep next to the coffee machine and making small fishy motions with his lips.

"Do you need help?"

Before I could finish, he bolted past me, green-faced, cheeks puffing, the garbage can tucked into his arms like a football in the hands of a running back protecting the pigskin. All I could do for him was pray he'd make it to the men's restroom in time.

When Bryan came skulking back into the room, the garbage can dangling precariously from his fingertips, some color had returned to his face, but it didn't look any healthier than the green hue he'd had when he ran out. His cheeks were red and splotchy and his eyes were watering.

"What on earth is wrong with—"

Mitzi took a bite of the pickle she was practicing on, and the crunch resonated throughout the room.

Bryan whimpered, spun around and headed again for the bathroom, once again clinging to his garbage can.

"That boy is weird," Mitzi concluded airily.

It takes one to know one.

"I hope no one else catches it," I commented to Kim.

"Wesley picked up something at day care a couple weeks ago, and it only lasted twenty-four hours," she assured me. "Neither Kurt or I got it."

"Good. You'll need all the energy you can get, because I'm planning to start cracking the whip around here. We need to work fast."

"Where's the fire?"

I patted my stomach. "Here. We can't leave Harry in a bind when we run off to have babies. I've moved some project deadlines ahead so that they're finished before early February, when Mitzi's baby and mine are due."

"We're hoping and praying to be in China to collect

our new baby, too," Kim murmured. "What *are* we going to do about work? Betty and Bryan can't keep this office afloat without us. Mitzi we might not miss, but…"

"And just exactly what is that supposed to mean?" Mitzi entered on a cloud of Baby Touch perfume. Mitzi is going for a mother-and-baby theme these days. It's disconcerting to have her come into the office looking like Donna Reed one day and Bart Simpson's mother the next.

"Ignore her," I said. "She thinks she's being funny."

"Oh. Ha, ha."

"We're discussing what will happen if everyone goes out on maternity leave at the same time."

"You could move the office to my house," Mitzi suggested airily. "There's plenty of room there. Then I wouldn't have to leave home."

"Somehow I don't think Harry would go for that."

"Well, you can't say I didn't invite you." Mitzi flitted out again, a life-size Tinkerbell, off to spread confusion along with her fairy dust.

"She's got the space," Kim said. "I want the sunroom with the wicker furniture and the fountain as my office. If you can't move Mitzi to the mountain, move the mountain to Mitzi."

"Think about it, Kim, moving Innova to Mitzi's house is more like moving Shadrach, Meshach and Abednego into the lion's den."

Wednesday, June 30

"More pot stickers?" I shoved the plate toward Mitzi, who was downing sweet-and-sour pork as if it was popcorn.

"Order more egg rolls, will you?" Mitzi dipped another fatty, deep-fried bit of pork into a neon-orange sweet-and-sour sauce. "Or maybe just some more shrimp fried rice. And ask for a handful of fortune cookies, please."

Kim grimaced as we watched Mitzi eat enough for ten starving Chinese children.

"This is so good that I can hardly stand it," Mitzi purred. "Whitney, aren't you hungry?"

"I filled up on the cashew chicken and the beef and broccoli, thanks."

Kim glanced at her watch. "We've only got twenty minutes until we have to be back at the office."

Mitzi waved down a waiter. "Will you put these in those cute little boxes you have? And add extra rice and a few packets of soy sauce, please?"

"This did taste good," I admitted. "I've been craving Chinese food for three days."

Mitzi looked up from the fortune cookies she was disemboweling. "If you crave Chinese food, I wonder what pregnant Chinese women crave?"

Tacos, maybe?

Mitzi happily settled down to read and eat her fortune cookies.

"You don't believe in those things, do you?" Kim asked.

Mitzi looked hurt, as if Kim had questioned her intelligence. "Of course not, but sometimes they offer wise advice." She picked up one of the tiny bits of paper and read, "'A woman who wishes to be to be equal to a man lacks ambition.'" She looked up proudly. "See?"

Kim plucked a fortune out of Mitzi's pile and read it aloud. "'You are fond of Chinese food.'"

Mitzi nodded solemnly. "It's true, isn't it?"

"We're in a Chinese restaurant, Mitzi, why wouldn't we be fond of Chinese food?"

"Try another one." Mitzi pushed the pile of unread papers toward Kim, who took one reluctantly.

"'Beware of offensive odors coming from strange people.'" Kim rolled her eyes, "Excellent suggestion, don't you think?"

"Now you, Whitney," Mitzi insisted.

The only written advice I take comes from scripture, but I humored her. I picked one that looked promising and read aloud. "'Never wear your best dress to a taffy pull.'"

Hmm. "Maybe you are right, Mitzi. That's very sound advice, and I plan to follow it."

Fortune cookies are like so many other dead-end bunny trails people follow trying to find wisdom and happiness—pointless, useless or even, sometimes, harmful. If people would only look to God first for their insights, we'd all save a lot of time and energy. And calories.

"Once I had a cookie that said, 'Do not eat your fried rice cold,'" Mitzi said. "I ate lukewarm fried rice at that very restaurant before I opened the cookie."

"And?" Kim said wearily.

"I got food poisoning from it. I should have opened the cookie first."

Fervently wishing I hadn't had rice for lunch, I gathered the leftover boxes so that our little group could go back to work.

* * *

Estrogen and maternal vibes emanate from our office in clouds these days. They travel like sound waves through space. Everyone who comes within ten feet of Innova's door senses that something unusual is going on inside. We've become a hatchery with everyone sitting on an egg. It could be the Shh. Baby's Sleeping sign on the office door that gives it away or the fact that Mitzi has supplied the waiting room with books like *Name the Baby* and *Creative Baby Names for the Twenty-first Century.*

I don't appreciate this trend toward making up baby names. I don't care if my child shares a name with others. Why would anyone want to name their sweet little baby Mabrinina, Chelsetta or Zigfroid? There are babies named after garden tools—Spade, for example—and weather—like Stormie and Raine. Whatever happened to Susan, Dick and Jane?

Unfortunately, Chase and I don't share the same opinions about names. That's a bridge I'm dreading having to cross when we finally come to it.

Harry and Bryan walk around us as though we're bombs with faulty timers that will explode unexpectedly at any minute. I'm not unstable—in a TNT or nitroglycerin sort of way—but I understand their concern about Mitzi. Most days she's totally unhinged.

She's currently researching baby names by country. This week it's Ireland. Although she says she already has favorite names, she feels obliged to continue to do research. She compiles lists of names she likes and then gives them to Kim and me with the order that we cannot choose our babies' names from the list. This week we aren't allowed to name our babies Alana, Aislinn,

Brianna, Bridget, Cathleen, Cara, Claire, Colleen, Dierdra, Shauna or Turlach.

Who knows? By the time Mitzi is done, maybe Mabrinina, Zigfroid, Spade and Raine will be the only names left to choose.

"Want to go out for dinner?" I waved a hand in front of Chase's face as he sat on the couch staring at a mind-numbing reality program on television.

"I'm not very hungry."

"You're never hungry anymore." I moved toward him and slipped my arms around him. Thinner, much thinner.

"I had a late lunch at the hospital."

"Cafeteria food?"

"Tortilla chips and salsa and a couple sodas."

"You've got to be kidding me." I sat down beside him, and he pulled me close to tuck me into the curve of his arm.

"Would I kid you, the mother of my child? I also had a bag of peanuts and some salt-and-vinegar potato chips."

"That doesn't sound like you, Mr. Eat-Your-Vegetables-and-Keep-Your-Cholesterol-Down."

"I didn't have much time today, and frankly, all that junk sounded kind of good. Craving salt, I guess."

I looked at him out of the corner of my eye. Junk food sounding good to the man who thinks Brussels sprouts are as delicious as gumdrops?

"Chase, you sound like the pregnant one instead of me."

"Maybe you're rubbing off on me." He pulled me closer. "I like it."

I was about to say something but Chase started nibbling kisses along the curve of my neck.

Conversation could wait.

Saturday, July 3

Chase, Kurt and Arch were off visiting one of the homes they'd repaired today.

"I'm stopping by Mitzi's today," I told Kim. "She ordered some Belgian chocolates that she says are 'to die for' and wants me to come over and try them. Do you want to come along?"

"You're going to see Mitzi on a Saturday? Five days a week isn't sufficient? Haven't you suffered enough?" Kim sounded appalled.

"Weren't you listening to me? *Belgian chocolate!*"

"I thought you were eating for two, a healthy diet for a healthy baby and all that. You said you didn't want to end up looking like a beached beluga."

"The Swiss eat twenty-two pounds of chocolate a year and have a very low obesity rate."

"Any other ways you'd like to justify this chocolate binge you're about to go on?"

"Chocolate has fewer milligrams of caffeine than coffee, and I skipped coffee this morning." I glared at her. "You know how I am without my coffee."

"Okay, I'll go," she said hurriedly. "There's always something weird happening at Mitzi's. It will be more interesting than sitting at home in Wesley's homemade tent, which has, by the way, now engulfed our entire living room."

"Good. I'll pick you up." I hung up before she could change her mind.

We rang the doorbell at Mitzi's home. "Somewhere My Love" chimed through the cavernous house several times before anyone answered. As the last notes died away, Mitzi flung open the door.

"Come in," she mumbled from beneath a face mask. She wore rubber gloves, a large white coat—obviously one of Arch's from the clinic—and a pair of rain boots. I've always thought the image of Dr. Frankenstein is scary, but this was much, much worse.

"What on earth are you doing? Inventing a cure for the common cold or taking out someone's gall bladder?"

"I'm petting the cats."

She led us into the family room, a spacious high-beamed area. Although Tiger Woods had dibs on the walls in a series of posters of impressive golf swings, Mitzi had managed to put her touch on everything, even this masculine space. The cabinets holding video tapes were stocked with things that were pure Mitzi—buns, abs and pecs of steel, Jane Fonda during her feel-the-burn years, *30 Minutes to Thinner Everything,* Shirley Temple movies and Disney stuff starring Kurt Russell in his pre-Goldie Hawn days. She also had a bank of plants to rival Sherwood Forest in the corner of the room where the light was best.

Mitzi's cats, two squash-faced, pompous Persians named Fiona and Pauline—actually, its name is PawLeen, which Mitzi thinks is hysterically clever—were seated like reigning monarchs in the middle of a large beige leather couch. Fiona had draped herself across an oversize pink pillow to best show off her rhinestone collar, while PawLeen was cleaning the spaces between her toes with a delicate pink tongue.

Mitzi has managed to create duplicates of herself in the animal kingdom. Amazing. The idea gives me pause…paws? Are Mr. Tibble and Scram like me? If so, I'm arrogant, finicky, standoffish—Mr. Tibble—and overly enthusiastic about idiotic things and not too bright—Scram. I don't think I want to go there.

Kim put Wesley, who'd slept on the way over to recharge his batteries, onto the floor. Naturally, he went directly for the cats. Mitzi, moving faster than I knew she could, scooped him into her arms.

"My cook is here this morning, and she's making cookies. Petit fours, actually, but you won't know the difference. Want one?"

"Cookies," Wesley gargled in a perfect imitation of Cookie Monster. "Cookies!"

Mitzi plodded to the kitchen, her rain boots making sticky rubber sounds on the floor, and came back momentarily.

"Cook says she loves children," Mitzi said doubtfully. "We'll see."

"Now will you tell us what you're doing in that ridiculous outfit?"

"I told you, I'm petting the cats."

"Then how do you dress to feed the fish? Scuba gear and cowboy boots?"

"It's your fault. If you hadn't told me about toxoplasmosis, I wouldn't have to be so careful."

"I thought Arch had the animals checked and they're fine."

"He did."

"You aren't cleaning their litter box, are you?"

Mitzi looked at me, horrified, as if the thought had never even occurred to her.

"Then you don't have anything to worry about. You

can pet your cats without putting on a fire-retardant suit and galoshes."

"One just can't be too careful with new life," Mitzi said importantly, and for once, I agreed with her.

Chapter Twenty-Three

"Why didn't you tell me how good chocolate is?" Mitzi asked accusingly as she handed us large boxes of imported candy. "I might have started eating it years ago."

There's no use pointing out to Mitzi that she never listens to us and, even if she had, she wouldn't have believed us, anyway.

She took off her hazmat suit, and we joined Wesley in the kitchen for snacks. Wesley had attached himself to the cook's leg, afraid to let go, for fear he might miss a crumb of something delicious falling to the floor.

Mitzi is the only person I know who actually owns a copper espresso machine like those in gourmet coffee shops. And she knows how to work it.

"You aren't wearing maternity clothes today," I pointed out. "What gives?"

"Arch said if I started wearing them now, I'd be sick of them by February. He's right, of course, but it's rather exciting to have an excuse to buy a brand-new wardrobe.

I got carried away." She frowned. "My waistband is tight already, and I keep telling him so, but he says it's too early. Of course, he is a podiatrist…."

"Mitzi, you buy a new wardrobe every season. You don't need an excuse."

She frowned. "Whitney, you aren't going to wear ugly maternity clothes, are you?"

"Not intentionally." *Not with you on duty as my own personal fashion police.*

"We need to shop for you. There are some atrocious things out there, and I don't want you to get involved with them. We'll have to set a date soon."

Ever since Mitzi decided to be my friend, I've had to put up with her good intentions. The road to my insanity is paved with Mitzi's good intentions.

We were lulled into a dangerous sense of complacency by the chocolate, the whir of the espresso machine and the sun shining through the windows. We were no better than Fiona and PawLeen, who lay on their little window shelves with their eyes closed, ignoring a bevy of birds pecking at the bird feeder outside. Not even a canary could entice them—or us—to move.

"I'm ready for this baby. I just wish I didn't have to wait seven months to have a child in my life."

Kim and I bobbed our heads in lazy agreement. Three perfect mothers-in-waiting…

"Kim?"

"Hmm?" She licked a daub of milk chocolate on her fingertip.

"Where's Wesley?"

We all turned to the cook, who was standing over the kitchen sink, humming. Wesley was no longer attached to her calf.

"Carla, where's the little boy?" Since the day Mitzi babysat for Kim, she's been taking Wesley's prodigious power for creating chaos more seriously.

"I don't know. I didn't think I had to watch him once the three of you came in. Was I supposed to?"

How long had we been sitting here, engaged in idle chatter, leaving the creative and destructive Wesley to his own devices?

"My child!" Kim squawked.

"My house!" Mitzi groaned.

We bolted to our feet and ran into the other room to fan out in a search, but there was no need. Wesley had not wandered far. He was still in the family room, only feet from the kitchen, entertaining himself quietly with Mitzi's indoor garden.

He, in a systematic botanical undertaking, was checking the roots of all Mitzi's houseplants. He was doing so with a scientist's care. Each of the plants lay uprooted on the floor in a line on Mitzi's hand-tied Turkish rug. Violets, dwarf citrus trees, coleus, jade, even a prayer plant—none had been spared. He'd meticulously knocked all the dirt off the roots to investigate them more fully. He had also dumped the dirt in a tidy pile—as tidy as dirt can get—and was currently playing a game with two of Mitzi's Lalique figurines, running them up and down the side of the mound of soil, making humming sounds as if the collectibles were on dirt bikes.

"Are any of these plants poisonous?" Kim bleated. She turned to Wes. "Did you take a bite out of any of these?"

He looked at her with disdain, as if to say, "Are you serious? What kind of a fool do you think I am?"

She grabbed my arm. "Do we need to take him to a doctor?"

I kneeled over the dead and dying bodies. "I don't see anything that looks like it's been chewed on. Should we open Wesley's mouth and look for signs of plant life?"

Mitzi, frozen into a statuelike position, stared at the mayhem. "My plants…my figurines…my…" And then she fainted dead away.

However, she fainted conveniently onto a large over-stuffed chair and ottoman, which broke her fall. Mitzi even faints well. She looked like a beautiful broken doll draped delicately across the butter-colored, button-tufted chair.

"Does anyone use smelling salts anymore?" I asked as we stared down at Mitzi.

"I have no idea."

"If not, how do we revive her?"

I ran to the kitchen to see what the cook might suggest and found a bottle of vinegar on the counter. It would have to do. I splashed a large amount on a dish towel and returned to wave it under Mitzi's nose.

Good choice. She was immediately awake and furious.

Fortunately, Kim is accustomed to picking up after her son, and she already had the pots refilled and was frantically sticking plants back into the soil.

"Get that out of my face!" Mitzi cried, and brushed me out of her way. "My figurines, my rug, my hard-wood floor…"

"Have you got a vacuum cleaner? Give us a few minutes, and you won't even know what happened."

"How would I know where the vacuum cleaner is? I don't clean!"

Welcome once again to Mitzi's world.

Wesley, still clinging to a graceful signed statue of a crystal polar bear, finally noticed the agitated adults around him. He looked from his mother to me, and then at Mitzi, who was now sitting upright on the ottoman, tears on her cheeks. Unexpectedly, he bolted toward Mitzi and scrambled into her lap.

"Don't cry," he crooned, putting the polar bear beside her and taking her cheeks in his filthy little hands. "It's okay. Don't cry."

Which, of course, made Mitzi wrap her arms around his sturdy little body and cry all the harder.

Mitzi is definitely ready for children. She forgave Wesley for the havoc he'd created, called a cleaning service and served us all more chocolate to fortify our nerves.

That was all, of course, after a loud and lengthy rant to Kim about how she, Mitzi, would *never* let her children misbehave. Ever. Under any circumstances. Because her child will be perfect. Flawless. Obedient. Discerning. Brilliant. Angelic.

Famous last words. As far as I can tell, every time a mother says, "My child will never do that," the child will commit the act under discussion as soon as is humanly possible. If Mitzi doesn't quit yapping about her fault-less offspring, she is likely to doom herself to raising a mob of unruly hooligans who will make Wesley look downright boring.

Sunday, July 4

The Fourth of July will go down in history as the day Mitzi discovered that pregnant women shouldn't eat sushi.

I didn't intend to go to a party today. Chase, the cats and I were planning an Elvis movie retrospective with homemade caramel corn and lemonade, to be followed by traditional July Fourth fare—burgers, corn on the cob, watermelon and brownies.

We were already through with *Roustabout* and *Love Me Tender* and deep into *Blue Hawaii* when the phone rang.

"Should I answer it?" I inquired lazily from my part of the tangle of bodies on the couch. Arms, legs, paws and tails, we made a cozy little family knot propped up by pillows and fortified with disgustingly unhealthy and delicious snacks.

"Are you curious?"

Chase knows me too well. I talk big about letting the answering machine pick up, but, truth be told, I'm too snoopy to carry through. I unwrapped his arm from around my waist and reached for the receiver.

"Whitney, what are you doing?"

"Hello, Mom. Nice to hear your voice, too."

"When are you leaving?"

"For what?"

"Kim's party, of course."

Kim, as apology for the flower demolition derby we'd attended yesterday at Mitzi's, had invited us, my parents and who knows who else to a picnic at her house where Mitzi and Arch would be guests of honor.

I looked longingly at the pile of tapes I'd scoured video

stores to find—*Girls, Girls, Girls, Jailhouse Rock* and that old classic *Wild in the Country*. "We've made other plans."

"You two aren't watching old movies again, are you? Who was it last time? Audrey Hepburn?"

"You've got to admit, we've got taste. Food, old movies and cats are the best antidote Chase and I have found for a crazy-making week at work."

"I was at Fong, Fong and Wong today. I'm bringing goodies."

Fong, Fong and Wong is a little deli/sushi bar/tea shop near my parents' home. My parents are good friends of the Fongs and the Wongs, so they get the best of everything. Even I have been known to abandon Elvis for one of Mr. Wong's egg rolls.

Chase dozed off while I was talking, the remote on Pause.

"I think I've seen enough of Kim and Mitzi already this weekend. You go in my place."

"I'm going in my own place, dear. I'll tell them you'll be late. Chase looked tired the last time we saw you two. Take a nap before you come." And then her cell phone went dead.

We arrived at the party just in time to hear Mitzi demand, "What do you mean I can't eat sushi?" We walked onto the deck in time to see her hand trembling over a colorful tray. "It's a staple in every diet!"

"Not mine," Kurt muttered.

"Don't eat it, Mitzi." My mother, just as she had with my cats, freaked out as she saw Mitzi going for a bit of raw tuna. "It's bad for pregnant women."

Mitzi turned to Chase. "Tell your mother-in-law she's wrong. Fish is healthy."

"Not the raw stuff, I'm afraid. There may be parasites in uncooked fish. You don't want a tapeworm sharing your body with your baby."

"Tapeworm? As in...?" She made little pinching motions with her fingers.

"Victorian women used to swallow them in order to be thin," Chase said bluntly, "Bad idea even when you aren't pregnant."

Green is not Mitzi's best color. Especially when it's her face. But she didn't touch the sushi platter for the rest of the day.

"How's Chase doing?" Kim asked as we sat by the pool with our feet in the water. "Kurt said he's been down over a patient of his."

I nodded gloomily. Earlier I'd overheard Chase and the other men on the patio outside the kitchen door. They were discussing heart attacks.

"No kidding? Just like that?"

"Who'd have thought...at that age..."

"Two kids, and one on the way? That's terrible."

"It just goes to show that you can't take any day for granted."

The death of that young man was still weighing heavy on Chase's mind.

Chapter Twenty-Four

Wednesday, July 21

Harry came storming out of his office, looking as frustrated as he had when the electricity had gone off in the building. Harry without electricity is like a day without sunshine, Bert without Ernie, yin without yang and, most aptly, dark without light. He doesn't know what to do with himself without electricity pumping through the veins of this complex. He does everything online—reads the newspaper, downloads the crossword puzzle, makes overseas calls, orders groceries, does his shopping for clothing, gifts and furniture. He plays chess and even bought his dog over the Internet.

Harry hasn't used paper for anything in years, except to train the new Yorkie. Needless to say, he was upset then, and he was just as upset today.

"You have to do something about Bryan."

There's little I'm able to do about anyone in this

office. If I could actually fix things around here, I would have fixed Mitzi long ago.

"And what do you propose I do with him?" Should I get him out of those repulsive lavender dress shirts Jennilee keeps buying him because it's her favorite color? Or make him quit threatening to lift fingerprints off the refrigerator if any of his food is stolen again? Hardly. Harry doesn't notice things like that. I doubt he even knows what color shirt *he* has on.

"He's in the men's restroom constantly. Now his laptop is set up in there. What'd we buy a desk for, if he isn't going to use it?"

"You know how Bryan is, Harry. He's always been skittish."

"Skittish is one thing, bonkers is another."

"Is he getting his work done?"

"Yes, but I don't see how."

"Could he be..." I cleared my throat. How does one ask such a delicate question? "Unwell?"

Harry rolled his eyes. "Far as I can tell, nobody's 'well' in this office. Just do something about it, Whitney."

Once again, the buck stops here.

Harry's right. Kim's jumpy as a kangaroo mouse over this adoption thing, Mitzi is a certifiable lunatic, I'm feeling queasy in the mornings, and Betty is a relapsed eBay addict. Why should Bryan be sane?

Betty inundates all of us with baby things she thinks we should buy, from lamps that look like balloons to balloons that look like giraffes to giraffes that look like lamps.

Queasy, Jumpy, Nutty and Obsessed. I'll just add Bryan to the list of names that didn't make Snow White's short list—Wacky.

I picked up the telephone and called Chase.

"Hi, sweetheart." His low, delighted tone gave me a thrill of pleasure. "To what do I owe this pleasure?"

"I have a delicate question I thought perhaps you could answer."

"Okay. Shoot."

Making sure no one could overhear me, I told him about my concern for Bryan. "If he's really sick, I can't ignore it. As a friend, I have to say something. If he's just barmy, he fits right in around here. What should I do?"

Chase was quiet for a long time, considering. "Weight loss, unusual behavior, poor coloring, nervousness, a lot of time spent in the restroom, maybe an upset stomach…that could be a lot of things." He hesitated again.

"Chase?"

"This sounds crazy, but it's possible that Bryan has Couvades syndrome."

"Is it serious?" I repented of all the flippant thoughts I'd ever had about Bryan.

"It's sympathetic pregnancy, the male counterpart to pregnancy. Sometimes men suffer symptoms for which there are no physiological explanations, such as indigestion, increased or decreased appetite, headaches or mood swings. The word *couvades* is derived from the French word *couver,* which means 'to hatch.' In some cultures it's actually an intentional ritual. It generally resolves upon the birth of the baby."

"You mean you think that Bryan has *morning sickness?*"

"It is normally found in men whose wives are pregnant, but…"

"Bryan isn't even married!"

"No, but he's obviously very sensitive to his coworkers. There are two pregnant women in your office, and one who talks about adoption nonstop. Maybe, just maybe…"

"And what am I supposed to do about that?" I wailed.

Kim looked up curiously, but I made a face at her and waved her back to her work.

"You and Bryan have known each other a long time. Ask him if he's feeling okay. If he hesitates, tell him he's welcome to talk to me. Maybe Jennilee has noticed these changes, too."

"Okay," I said hesitantly. "I'd better think a little more about this."

His voice lowered. "I love you, darling. How about a date later?"

"Deal," I said absently. I hung up and stared blankly at my computer screen. Now what?

Poor Harry. Instead of having three people expecting babies in his office, he has four!

Scheduling our work hours around this is going to be more complicated than I ever imagined. Let's hope Bryan delivers first.

Friday, July 23

Mitzi hummed as we walked down the street to a café to get a bite of lunch. I've never seen her in such high spirits as she's been in recently.

"Isn't it *fun?*" she chortled happily.

"What's fun?" Kim, frustrated by the slow turning of the adoption wheels, sometimes gets a little tetchy about Mitzi's enthusiasm.

"I got a cartful of maternity catalogs and baby magazines yesterday. I'm going through every one to pick out what I want. I can't buy anything yet, of course. I still have five weeks until my amniocentesis test. Once I know for sure if I'm having a boy or a girl—look out, Mall of America!"

I said nothing until we were seated at the café and had placed our orders. Even lunch has become weird. Kim ordered a club sandwich. I ordered a chicken breast, a side of cabbage—which I don't much like—and fruit. Mitzi ordered chips and salsa and a double, double chocolate fudge dessert. While I'm striving for healthy, Mitzi is giving in to every food craving she's ever had. There are artichoke hearts, sardines, fig bars and guava juice in the refrigerator at the office right now that prove my point.

"So you hope to find out the sex of your baby?"

"Of course. How else can I decorate properly? I thought of doing yellow and green and something with doggies and kitties, but that's silly in this day and age, when I can find out if I'm having a boy or a girl." Mitzi looked up from her chips. "Aren't you planning to find out? They are recommending it for everyone these days."

"Chase and I want to be surprised."

"Aren't you curious?"

"It isn't a long wait, only a few months. I'll have years to decorate. Mitzi," I began cautiously, "what will happen if you have the amnio and discover something you don't like?"

"I'll like either a boy or a girl, silly. Why do you even ask… Oh." The meaning of my questions dawned on her. "You mean, what if there's something *wrong* with the baby?"

She stared down at her plate for a long moment. When she looked up, her eyes were flashing. "Why do you do this to me, Whitney? I was all excited about the test, and now... So you really aren't planning to have the test?"

"I'm happy to take what I get, babywise."

"So am I!" she responded indignantly. Then she paused. "So why am I doing this if all I want is to pick color swatches for the nursery?" She glared at me ferociously. "Whitney, you've got to stop it."

"Stop what?"

"Stop making me think! You ask me questions that drive me crazy."

"Good."

She didn't speak to me all the way back to the office.

Tonight I asked Chase what he thought about my conversation with Mitzi as we lounged together outside on the deck chairs and looked at the stars. He put his hands behind his head and gazed upward.

"Amniocentesis is useful. If a woman is having a repeat Caesarean, it's important to establish dates on the pregnancy. The LS ratio predicts respiratory maturity in infants—"

I cut him off before we could get too deep into doctor jargon. "But what about using it just to discover if you're having a boy or a girl or if the child has genetic defects? That wouldn't change anything for us," I hesitated. "Would it?"

"Of course not. We'll love the child we get."

I got up from my seat and curled against him on his lounge chair. "For me, double-checking on what the Maker of the universe is creating in me seems a pretty audacious thing to do." I rested my hand on my belly.

God is in charge. He created hummingbirds, sunlight and rain. I don't need to do a quality check before the bundle arrives.

"Some people, even if they plan to carry a pregnancy to term, feel the need to know that everything is all right. Or, if it isn't, they believe the knowledge will give them time to prepare," Chase pointed out.

"I realize that. It's not my place to judge. I haven't walked in Mitzi's Jimmy Choo footwear. I just want her to think this through, that's all."

"You're a good friend to her, Whit. In spite of all her crazy-making and her annoying habits, you've really been there for her." He looked at me with such love in his eyes that I felt emotion clutching at my throat.

What wonderful thing did I ever do to deserve him?

Chapter Twenty-Five

Saturday, July 24

"**I**'m mad at you."

I held the telephone receiver away from my ear and looked at it in surprise. That's not usually the kind of wake-up call I get on Saturday morning.

"Hello, Mitzi. Nice to talk to you, too."

"Arch says to tell Chase that the guys are going to meet at our house this morning to talk about their next project. He's supposed to call Kurt, too."

"I'll give him the message. Now do you want to explain your greeting?"

"You scrambled my brain, and I resent it."

I refuse to take responsibility for Mitzi's brain-scrambling. It's been a long time in coming, and it started way before I knew her. One can't get that scrambled overnight.

"Do you want to come to my house and talk about it while the guys are meeting over there?"

"I don't know. I'm *really* mad at you."

"Pick up Kim. I'll put the coffeepot on."

They appeared at my doorstep, Mitzi and Kim—sans Wesley—promptly at ten o'clock. Kim was carrying a white box from the bakery, and Mitzi held a bag full of chocolate doughnut holes. She requires chocolate by her bed now, to soothe her to sleep at night and as a morning pick-me-up. Chase has suggested, tongue in cheek, that she may need a chocolate intravenous drip before delivery.

Kim caught my eye as Mitzi tramped past me with barely a "hello." Mitzi is a very small-framed person, but she can stomp like a lumberjack.

"What did you do?" Kim whispered.

"I have no idea. That's why I invited you over, to find out. The suspense is killing me."

By the time we got to the kitchen, Mitzi was arranging bakery goods on a plate. She slammed my cupboard door shut after finding three mugs. Then she slapped the mugs on the table and splashed coffee into them. She was right. She was very angry.

I sat back and waited for her to heap burning coals upon my head.

"I did not sleep last night because of you." She narrowed her eyes and glared at me. "And I always sleep at night."

"Sorry. What did I do?"

"Don't play Little Miss Innocent with me! You know perfectly well what you did!"

Kim's head was swinging back and forth as the verbal tennis match unfolded before her.

"I really don't know. It would help if you told

me." Why do I put up with this? I wonder. As a high-maintenance friend, Mitzi has reached the top of the charts.

"All that talk about whether or not I should have amniocentesis to find out my baby's sex. Now I don't feel like doing it anymore, and the nursery draperies won't be in until spring! I can't order them until I know what color they should be."

Kim played absently with the napkin she'd pleated into a paper fan. "When I was pregnant with Wesley, most of my pregnant friends were having it done. Many of them wanted the reassurance that their babies were healthy and normal, with no genetic problems. But even if I did find that something was amiss with my baby, I knew I'd still carry it to term and love it and raise it."

"I want to know," Mitzi said, "but I wouldn't do anything about it if the news were bad. This baby is *mine* no matter what!

"You Christians drive me crazy," Mitzi muttered. "Until I met you guys, I always thought that Christians were fanatics, but sometimes you actually make sense."

Thanks. I think.

Then, without any warning, Mitzi clamped her hand over her mouth, turned an unlovely shade of green and headed for the bathroom.

Morning sickness. Just like Bryan.

Chase and I were eating crackers in bed, watching the late news and discussing the conversation we'd had that morning. He indulges me in all my quirks—saltines in bed, foot rubs, banana bread with orange marmalade—a relatively new whim—and watching old John Wayne

Westerns, which, while not as fun as watching Elvis, pleases me no end.

"Sounds like Kim said it all," he commented.

"I do understand Mitzi, though. It's hard to get my head around the fact that this isn't just my baby or your baby," I mused. I'd brought the peanut butter with me to bed, and I was scraping it onto the crackers with a butter knife. If I don't weigh a ton by the time this pregnancy is over, it will be a marvel. I'm already wearing Chase's boxers to be comfortable. A vision of loveliness, if there ever was one.

"What do you mean?"

"This baby isn't our possession, but its own little being. He or she won't exist to make us proud or to feel good about ourselves. Ultimately, this child will have to answer to God, just like the rest of us."

"It's entirely different when you think about it that way, isn't it?" Chase put his arm around me. "That the child in your womb, once it is born, is an eternal being. Talk about starting something you can't stop! No matter how many years he or she is on earth, that child will now exist for eternity—either with God or without Him."

"With Him," I said immediately. "I'm already praying about that. I want our children to know Him personally, like we do."

"That's what God wants, too." He put a finger under my chin and tipped my face toward his. "God is good, Whit. Look at us."

Friday, July 30

"Where's Mitzi?" Harry came out of his office at 11:00 a.m. "I've got something I want her to work on."

Kim and I exchanged glances. Bryan dipped lower in his seat.

"Mitzi didn't come in today."

"What do you mean, 'didn't come in'? She always comes in, even when we don't want her to." Harry plopped a file on her desk and went back to his office. "Tell her to get it done as quickly as possible."

"Where do you think she is?" Kim asked after Harry had closed his door. "He's right, you know. Mitzi is always here."

"I called her house, her cell phone, her car and her hairdresser. She's nowhere to be found." I kept my voice light, but I had to admit to being worried. Mitzi is nothing if not dependable. She enjoys making us miserable here at work.

"You don't think she's sick, do you?"

"Maybe she's shopping for maternity clothes," Betty suggested.

"Or getting a manicure and pedicure," Kim postulated.

"Eating her way through a Godiva chocolate shop?" Bryan hypothesized.

At four-thirty, about the time I was wrapping up for the day, my phone rang.

"Whitney?"

"Mitzi? Where have you been? I was thinking of coming by the house to check on you…."

"Will you? Right now? Can you bring Kim?"

"Sure," I stammered.

"Hurry, Whitney. I really need you." She gave a teary little hiccup and dropped the receiver back into its cradle.

Kim was watching me.

"She wants us to come over. She says she needs us."

"Needs us? What, like Swiss cheese needs holes?"

"She sounded genuinely upset."

"I'll tell Kurt to feed Wesley." She grabbed her purse off her desk. "Let's go."

Mitzi must have been watching for us, because as soon as we got out of the car she came to the door. I wondered who it was at first, the petite, dark-haired, makeup-free, barefooted woman in intentionally tattered designer jeans and a man's white T-shirt.

Her eyes were large in her face, and dark rings smudged beneath them. Her lips were rosy, even without lipstick, but her mouth was tremulous, as if she could cry at any moment. Mitzi is a lot of things, but this was a side of her I'd never seen before—as fragile as a brown and brittle leaf in late fall. She looked as though if I touched her, she might crumble into a hundred little pieces.

Today, the irrepressible, indomitable Mitzi was a faint shadow of her usual self.

She opened her mouth to say something and abruptly closed it again.

"Let's go inside," I suggested as I took her arm and guided her into the vast foyer of her house as though she were a porcelain doll.

She stumbled a little as I led her toward the large sunlit kitchen at the back of the house. Mitzi's kitchen, although she hates to cook, would make a professional chef's mouth water. Commercial-grade refrigerator and stove, two sinks, two dishwashers, warming ovens, a microwave-convection oven, gleaming carving knives, granite countertops. And all Mitzi ever admits to making is an occasional smoothie. Talk about overkill.

Kim found mugs and heated water in the microwave

for tea while I scoured the cupboards for chocolate. It wasn't hard to find. An entire pantry was stocked with the stuff. The paradox didn't escape me. Mitzi, who for years has been trying to make me fat by tempting me with chocolate éclairs, is now a more serious chocoholic than I am.

The irony is *delicious.*

She allowed Kim and me to stir sugar into her tea and toss a napkin across her lap.

It crossed my mind that I should call Arch at the clinic, but I decided to wait until I heard what was troubling Mitzi. He's a podiatrist, after all, and her husband. For impartial, clear-eyed medical advice, I need Chase.

"Now what?" Kim whispered to me. "She's hanging on to that mug as if it's a life raft and staring into the bottom of the cup like a treasure map was drawn there. What do we do?"

I took a stool and pulled it close to the counter across from Mitzi. "Do you want to talk about it? Kim and I are both good listeners."

She looked up from the cup, and her eyes were brimming with unshed tears.

Chapter Twenty-Six

"Something terrible happened, and it has to do with my babies!"

"Is something wrong with your pregnancy? Talk to us, Mitzi, tell us what's going on."

With a sigh that seemed to come from somewhere near the soles of her feet, Mitzi straightened.

"We went to the doctor yesterday. It was my scheduled appointment, and I wanted to ask him why I was...you know...so big already."

So the early maternity clothes and loose blouses she'd been wearing hadn't been purely recreational after all.

"I know I'm small and wear things rather snug, but I didn't dream that I'd outgrow my clothes so quickly. The doctor said he thought we should check it out, so he ordered an ultrasound. We could get in right away, so when it was finished, Arch and I went back to his office for a report. He had an odd look on his face, like he was surprised or puzzled. That's when he dropped the bomb and told me about the babies."

"Babies?" She'd made that slip of the tongue earlier, too.

"As in more than one?" Kim ventured incredulously.

Mitzi nodded forlornly and held up the right index, middle and ring fingers of her right hand.

"*Three* babies?" Kim gasped. "You're having *three* babies?"

"The doctor told you that you and Arch were having triplets?"

Mitzi bobbed her head miserably. "At first I thought he was kidding. Me—three babies? How ridiculous is that? I'm not sure I know how to take care of one, but with Arch's help I can muddle through. But three! It's absurd!"

Mitzi plus three. That just doesn't add up in my addled brain. Mind-boggling.

Then her chin came up. "But I can do anything I set my mind to. I got you married off, didn't I, Whitney?"

Well, not exactly.

"Plus, I straightened out the Innova office and got things organized there."

No, not really.

"And I did major work on that house the guys were refurbishing. I even held a hammer!"

Held it? Yes. Swing it? No.

"So I should be able to manage three babies." Her eyes narrowed slyly. "And I have you two to help me."

I glimpsed the look on Kim's face. The only way *we'd* sign on as nannies was if Mitzi forged our signatures.

"That's why I can't imagine the doctor suggesting what he did. It's awful. Just appalling." Tears leaked from her eyes and down her cheeks.

"What did he say to you?"

"He told me that I was a petite woman and that it could be a problem for me to carry and deliver three babies." Mitzi's face grew even paler. "He said that because fertility treatments often cause multiple births, occasionally they consider what he called 'planned reduction.' He wanted to know if that was something I'd want to reflect on."

"Reduce the number of babies you are carrying? Not…" My mind refused to go any further.

"I didn't even know they did that!" Mitzi wailed. "I've been sick all day just thinking about it!"

Then, as Mitzi always does, she rallied.

"I have to admit I don't like the idea of being fat. I know you're used to it, Whitney, so it will be easy for you, but…"

At any other time, I would have taken issue with that statement.

"…now I realize that there is *nothing* more important than whatever is going on in here." She put her palm across her stomach. "And I think everybody should know that life is precious. Why would I give up a child for my convenience? What's wrong with people these days, anyway?"

A wave of sadness engulfed me. What indeed?

Saturday, August 21

I have lost my mind. I hope I'll feel better without it.

When my mother was pregnant with me, she said she had a compelling desire to clean her house, put things in order and prepare for the time when her baby would arrive. She calls it nesting.

I've always told her that nesting is for the birds and that people simply don't do that anymore. Yet lately

I've been having these weird compulsive urges to do things I've never enjoyed all that much before, like washing windows, cleaning the stove, scrubbing air vents and cleaning the little holes in the dryer filter with a toothpick.

God gave all his creatures the instinct to prepare for and nurture new babies. Without that impulse, birds wouldn't build nests, and then what? Robin's eggs all over the patio furniture? I don't think so. It's a great design, God's, but I, as a twenty-first-century woman, never thought I'd turn broody, too.

I've been dreaming about having every part of our house clean and picked up at the same time. That, of course, is impossible. While I'm cleaning the kitchen, Chase is showering, shaving and sending splashes of water all around the bathroom. We've had fights—or, as Chase calls them, "spirited conversations"—about it.

I tell him to use a towel to wipe up when he's done in the sink. "Why waste a towel and make more work for you in the laundry?" he says.

"You're not saving me work!" I reply. "It's harder to scrub a sink and clean a mirror than it is to wash a towel."

Whatever. He doesn't listen. I wonder, does a tree falling in the forest still make noise?

The laundry is never completely done, because Chase and I always have some of it on our backs. Meals must be cooked, even though I've spent hours cleaning the top of the stove. I'm currently on a "No Fry" campaign to keep splatters off my cooktop. I also have been following Chase around the house with a paper towel, just in case he decides to wash his hands or get a drink of water and doesn't wipe out the sink. He's been patient, but he did say that he's getting sick of TV dinners—the tidiest meal you can make—you can even throw away the dishes.

"What are you doing now?" Chase asked.

"Soaking the knobs from the kitchen cupboards in soap while I wax the fronts. Who knows how long it's been since those knobs and screws were disinfected? I did the insides of the cupboards yesterday, so I thought I'd get the outsides done today."

"Whitney, you washed every dish, spoon, fork and mixing bowl in the house with bleach!"

"Hardly. I put a splash in the dishwater to just to make sure they got sanitized."

"Why don't you just use the dishwasher?"

"We need to take it apart. The drain must be horrible. Can you imagine what's been collecting in there? We can do it tonight, instead of watching a movie."

"Just the kind of romantic evening I envisioned," Chase groaned.

"Let's not start another debate. It feels romantic to me." I stopped waxing long enough to put my arms around his neck. "The two of us preparing for our baby is sweet."

"It will all be dirty again by the time the baby gets here."

"Not if I can help it. Mother cleaned until she went into labor, and even on the way to the hospital. Dad said that while he was driving she tidied the dashboard of the car with Q-tips and a soft cloth."

"That's what I have to look forward to?"

"Think of it, a perfectly ordered house with no germs and dust. By the way, we need a new mattress for our bed. Pillows, too. Do you realize how many dust mites and dead skin cells a mattress collects?"

"I think of nothing else," he said resignedly.

"I also started packing another box for the Salvation Army."

"What are you giving away this time?" He rocked a little on his feet, as if he were bracing himself.

"I thought we should get new bedding and towels. I'm sure I'll nurse the baby in our bedroom, and I want it just right."

"What's wrong with the old towels? Can't you wash them in bleach, too?"

"That wouldn't matter. They still wouldn't match the new wallpaper."

He swallowed hard. "Wallpaper?"

"I tore down the old stuff while you were out. And have you any idea how dirty our light fixtures were? Disgusting!"

Being pregnant brings out strange things in a person. Oddly, the strangest things have been drawn out of Bryan.

He didn't take it well at first when I suggested that he might have Couvades syndrome and that his troubles could be sympathy pains for Mitzi and me. In fact, he agreed to go to a doctor to prove me wrong.

The physician said it was the first case he'd ever seen where the suffering fellow wasn't the husband of a pregnant woman. His only explanation was that Bryan's sympathy pains had developed because of our close proximity at work. The doctor asked if he could study Bryan further, but Bryan declined. I'm glad. We have enough trouble around here without being written up in *The American Journal of Medicine.*

Chapter Twenty-Seven

Thursday, September 30

How one's sole form of entertainment for an entire month can be throwing up is beyond me. Yet that and cleaning are all I've done, except for showing up at Innova disguised as an employee. Fortunately, I'm good at my job and I can practically do it in my sleep. Or, in this case, engulfed in waves of nausea that rival a rough sea.

The nesting compulsion is still almost as great as my gag reflex. I've gone through three pair of rubber gloves this month. I noticed one day while I was showering that my nice clean tile grout had developed a dingy cast. Shame on me. I'd been neglecting those little lines between the tiles. And once I started cleaning the grout and found out how well Chase's toothbrush worked for the job, I couldn't stop. The same domino effect occurred in our living room.

All I wanted to do was paint the walls a soft sage color that would make me feel serene and maternal.

Although sage goes with everything, it took several quarts of paint and many test patches on the wall before I found the perfect shade. And once the walls were painted and I'd begun to rehang my curtains, I noticed how dusty they were.

After the *new* curtains were hung, it became very clear to me that the living-room chairs and ottoman needed a face-lift. That, of course, meant new furniture and, inevitably, new accessories. This, naturally, made me realize how drab our foyer had become. And the boring eggshell color on the walls down the hall? Disgusting! Chase finally stopped me when I suggested that we rearrange the furniture in the bathroom.

I still think the stool would have looked lovely on that other wall....

I've been worried about Chase. He's looking as peaked as Bryan these days, and I don't know what's brewing. It scares me sometimes. We have both been feeling very mortal ever since Chase told me about the patient he lost.

Mitzi rolled into the office carrying a box of éclairs and a purse the size of Georgia. Kim and I, like rats following the Pied Piper to their doom, trailed her into the break room to get the first two éclairs.

She plopped her purse on the table, and a remote control tumbled out of the bag.

"When did you start carrying the remote control to your television in your purse?"

"Arch has the week off," she said, as if that explained everything. "And he's supposed to be doing my honey-do list at the house, putting the cribs together, finishing the stenciling on the walls while I'm out so I don't smell the paint, little things like that."

"And the remote control fits in where?"

"The only thing Arch likes less than a honey-do list is watching television without the remote. Not being able to channel surf takes all the fun out of it for him. So, with the remote here and him there, I can count on everything being done when I get home."

Smart Mitzi. Nasty Mitzi. Devious Mitzi. Mental note: Remember to see if it works on Chase.

At four o'clock, Bryan stopped in front of my desk, trembling with righteous indignation, and announced, "I quit. My food is gone again, and I can't take it anymore. Jennilee made me stuffed mushroom caps and little smokies in barbecue sauce, and they've disappeared. Do you know how much I love stuffed mushrooms?"

Bryan has the most peculiar taste in food I've ever seen. Yesterday it was pickled pigs' feet from the deli down the street. Last week it was a tuna fish sandwich made with horseradish and green grapes.

"I'm sorry to hear about your mushrooms, Bryan, but I'd like you to reconsider."

I'll bet nothing like this ever happens to Donald Trump.

Then Harry came out of his office and meandered over to my desk.

"Whitney, do you have a toothpick? I got something stuck between my teeth, gristle from those little sausages. They weren't bad otherwise, though. Does anybody have dental floss?"

"Harry, did you eat the mushrooms that were in the refrigerator today?"

"Yeah. Not bad. Who made 'em?"

"Jennilee did. They were Bryan's lunch."

Harry turned to look at Bryan with surprise. "No

kidding? I'm sorry. I thought that whoever has been
bringing snacks brought those, too. You should put your
name on your stuff, so I know not to eat it. Otherwise,
the refrigerator and the stuff on the counters are fair
game, right? Sorry I ate your sausages. Next time put
your name on stuff, please." And he disappeared back
into HarryLand, where life is easy and personal contact
is minimal.

Bryan's mouth opened and closed, but nothing came
out. Finally he managed to gargle, "Now what do I do?"
he bleated at this unexpected turn of events.

"You have two choices," I offered. "You can quit, as
planned. Or you can start bringing food in well-marked
containers. So are you going to quit or not?"

He sagged like a deflated balloon. "Not." He turned
away, and as he walked off, I heard him mutter, "Harry.
Why didn't I ever think of Harry?"

Mostly, dear Bryan, because you thought all men
could be trusted.

Case closed.

Friday, October 1

"Want to go to Kim and Kurt's tonight?" I asked.

Chase, who'd just come in from the garage, shook his
head. "I don't think so." He crossed the kitchen and
pulled me backward against his chest so he could lay
his palm on my belly. "I'd like to stay home with you
and mini-you. I don't want anything more exciting than
giving the cats a fresh catnip mouse."

"Tough day? You've had a lot of them lately."

"I'm strong, don't you know that?" He spun me

around and kissed me full on the mouth. He tasted like peppermint.

I smacked my lips. "Are you hiding candy in your pockets?" My sweet tooth these days is the size of the fiberglass tooth on display on the roof of the dental clinic I pass on my way to work. Four feet wide by six feet high.

He appeared puzzled momentarily, but then he laughed. "Not candy, antacid. Want some?" He pulled a packet of antacids from his pocket.

"Stomach upset again?"

"Just a little. No problem."

"Maybe you're getting ulcers. You should take an extra day off work to stay home and play with me." I grabbed his hand and pulled him toward the couch. My favorite place in the world is in Chase's arms. Even though he's been on edge lately, nestled against that warm, wide chest, with his chin resting on the top of my head, is my idea of bliss.

"But you'd be at work. Would Harry let you stay home just to make me happy?"

"Speaking of staying home, Harry's begun to panic. We're racing to finish all the projects we can, and I've enticed someone from an affiliate office to fill in, but Harry wants us."

"Because you're all so witty, intelligent and charming?" Chase asked with a chuckle.

"No, because we're so slow, thickheaded and idiotic that he can control us like puppets and make us do his bidding. He'll never find people like that again."

"I knew you were special." Chase rubbed his hand over my arm. If I'd been Mr. Tibble, I'd have started to purr.

"Besides, much as we fuss and complain, we all have

great jobs. Harry is a good employer. He pays well, he's generous and fair." Now that he's quit eating Bryan's lunches, that is.

"He expects me to figure out how three of us can acquire babies at the same time and still keep the office running."

"Would you like to stay home with our baby, Whitney? You don't have to work if you don't want to, you know."

"I know." I laughed ruefully. "Believe it or not, I'd miss the zoo if I weren't there every day. I wish there were a way to be two places at once."

"A common mother's complaint." He kissed the top of my head. "Just know that I'm behind you, honey."

"Then perhaps this is a good time to discuss baby names."

"I told you, I like Benjamin Franklin Andrews. It was my great-grandfather's name. A good, sturdy, reliable moniker."

"And what do you plan to name it if it's a girl? Betsy Ross Andrews? Or should we just do a presidential theme? George Washington Andrews, Abraham Lincoln Andrews and Theodore Roosevelt Andrews?"

Chase thought about it for a moment. Then he nodded. "Ben, Betsy, George, Abe and Ted. Sounds good to me."

Grrrrrrr.

I've been thinking about the at-home mom versus the working mom lately. I got caught in the cross fire at a baby shower last week. I expected to witness a knock-down, drag-out fight between two women defending their stay-at-home-go-to-work positions.

It sounded to me as if each was a little envious of the

other. As a working-away-from-the-house mom, I would wish for more time with my child. As a stay-at-home, I'd probably yearn for more creative outlets.

All I can do is ask Him to show me what He wants for me and be obedient either way.

The cats jumped onto the couch, entwined themselves in our tangle of arms and legs and purred softly until they both dozed off.

We both nodded off for a few minutes before I remembered Kim.

"Chase?"

"Hmm…?"

"I'd better call Kim and tell her we're not coming. If we don't go over there tonight, I'd like to spend some time with her tomorrow, if that's acceptable with you."

"I've got to do rounds at the hospital tomorrow morning. Go ahead. Is something wrong?"

"Cheerful and upbeat as she tries to be, she's struggling again."

"She's getting a baby, too," he reminded me.

"It doesn't feel real to her yet."

It's getting more and more real to me all the time, even though I still feel like a waif when I stand next to Mitzi. She's growing by leaps and bounds. Those babies of hers are going to weigh fifteen pounds each, by the look of her.

"Maybe you could take Kim shopping or something," Chase suggested.

How can I help loving a man who encourages me to go shopping?

"The only thing I need is maternity clothes. I'm not sure that would help."

"How about shoes? Your feet haven't changed sizes, have they?"

If they have, I'm not admitting it.

"Great idea, Chase. I'll call her right…"

Then I thought about how cozy I felt and how I'd have to disrupt Chase and the cats if I got up right then. "I'll call her later."

Chapter Twenty-Eight

After our nap and dinner, Chase went to the foyer and came back to the dining room table with his briefcase.

"What have you got? Theater tickets?"

"I stopped by our attorney's office today to get the questionnaires we need to write our wills." He laid the stuff on the table. "I thought we could work on that tonight."

That's about as far from theater tickets as you can get.

"Wills?" It's prudent and necessary to do these sorts of things, but frankly, it gives me the heebie-jeebies, as if we're trying to hurry the inevitable by sticking our hands in the air and saying, "My will's done, I'm ready to go, pick me, pick me!"

I also despise talking to life insurance salesmen. They are so cheerful about what your children are going to do with your money after you're gone. I'd like to think the kids will be having fun with us all along and not be waiting for the time when they can finally buy new cars.

I know where I'm going for eternity, and I'm

not worried about that, but I do hate the preliminary paperwork.

"With a baby on the way, we should get our wishes down on paper."

"But what's yours is mine and what's mine is yours."

"We do have to name a guardian for the baby, just in case. I thought Kim and Kurt would be a good choice. And we *are* already named as Wesley's guardians."

"This is not my idea of a fun Friday-night date, Chase. Maybe we should go have the roots of our teeth planed or pierce our noses instead."

"It won't take long. Now let me read this power-of-attorney and health-directive information to you."

Chase isn't usually so persistent, but tonight he was determined to get this done.

I went along with it, because it's the prudent thing to do, and because Chase was so unwavering in his determination to get it completed. But why sooner rather than later?

After he'd fallen asleep, I felt restless and uncomfortable, like the princess with the pea beneath her mattress. I sat up, curled my arms as far around my knees as I could get them and watched Chase sleep.

A little shiver of apprehension slid down my spine as I watched my soul mate, my husband, my gift from God. For the second time in not so many weeks, I realized I couldn't imagine my world without him.

Saturday, October 2

Mitzi can smell a shopping trip a mile away.

Kim and I were already at the Mall of America—in

the Food Court getting sustenance for the day, where else?—when my cell phone rang.

"Are you shopping without me?" Mitzi demanded imperiously.

"Ah…could be. Right now, we're eating Cinnabon and drinking coffee."

"Well, stay there. I'm on my way."

"Do you have shopping to do, too?" Mitzi practically lives at the mall in her spare time.

"I always have shopping to do, but that's not why I'm coming. Whitney, If you're going to buy maternity clothes, you need an expert with you or you'll likely come home with one of those dreadful pink pup tents with the big bow in back and puffy little sleeves."

"Thanks for the confidence in my taste in clothing."

"You know what I mean. I want you to look elegant while you're pregnant—like me."

Actually, Mitzi is not looking all that elegant. Instead, she looks bulging and lumpy, as if she's storing basketballs under her shirt. Or maybe she resembles a boa constrictor with its large lunch lodged in a big lump in the middle of its body. Yesterday, when Mitzi turned around near my desk, her stomach sent my pencil holder flying. By the time she gets to term, she'll have to push a grocery cart just to support her stomach.

"I'm already in my car. I'll be there in twenty minutes. Don't buy anything until I get there." And her phone went dead.

"I can never decide if it would be easier to have Mitzi as a friend or enemy," I said to Kim. "She's not an easy keeper either way."

Kim smiled faintly. "You love her and you know it."

I suppose I do, but it's a conflicted relationship.

"Do you want to tell me what's bugging you?" I asked bluntly. Kim and I never dance around each other's feelings. We've been together too long for that.

She played nervously with the straw in her soda.

"It must be juicy. Spill it."

"The doctor has suggested I increase my antidepressant medication. The red tape and hurry-up-and-wait process seems endless. Sometimes I feel so hopeless that I wonder if we'll ever get a baby.

"Kurt and I are going to a support group tonight. I hope it helps, but…" She looked at me miserably. "I hate to admit it, but my real problem is jealousy. I'm still finding out for myself what Proverbs 14:30 means.

"'A relaxed attitude lengthens life; jealousy rots it away.'" She exhaled a deep sigh. "I'm rotting away, Whit. Jealousy is like poison. I'm happy for you, and yet it's just killing me not to be pregnant right along with you."

"What if the baby you are meant to have isn't born yet? God knows. Or maybe He's uncrossing wires and running interference for you with all the administrative snarls that could occur. Sure, *you're* ready, but is the child?"

Kim tilted her head thoughtfully. "Good point. I hadn't thought about it that way. It makes all the difference, doesn't it, to remember to lie back and rely on Him."

"*All* the difference."

"Come on, you lazy couch potatoes, let's go shopping!" Mitzi's battle cry rang out across the Food Court. Everyone looked up to stare as she trotted across the expanse, dodging tables as she came.

These days, Mitzi really is something to stare at. She's the walking epitome of "If you've got it, flaunt it."

As is the current style, she does nothing to hide the roundness of her belly. Today she wore snug black leggings, a black knit sweater that clung to the mound of her belly and enough jewelry to make Queen Elizabeth jealous. She looked like a bowling ball with bling.

She plopped herself down in the free chair at our table, helped herself to a bite of my breakfast, sipped Kim's coffee and pulled out her shopping list.

"Make yourself at home, Mitzi," Kim said drily.

"Thanks, I will." She pulled Kim's plate toward her and polished off the cinnamon roll Kim had been eating. "I don't know what's wrong with me these days, but I'm always hungry."

"You're eating for four. No wonder."

She rubbed her stomach thoughtfully. "I can't seem to get my head around the idea yet. It's easy enough to buy three cribs or three high chairs, but to think of little people in them?" She sighed. "Well, I suppose I'll believe it soon enough."

The idea of Mitzi with three children is almost impossible to get my head around, too.

Sometimes I don't feel pregnant. I feel fat, nauseous and moody, of course, but I've been guilty of that without being with child. Yet here I am, the perfect little baby factory. How God figured all this out is beyond imagining. Every day I am more in awe of His divine plan.

Mitzi had turned back to her list.

Or rather, *my* list.

"You need new shoes, Whitney, with lower heels. You don't want to get varicose veins. Arch says you should be sure that they aren't too snug. Swelling and all that."

"You consulted your husband about *my* feet?"

"He's a podiatrist, isn't he?" She continued along the single track of her mind. "I've found some lovely maternity underwear I want to show you, and I know every maternity section in the mall. Kim, while Whitney is getting all these sensible things, I think you should buy some high heels and something lacy. No sense in all of us looking like grandmothers in hideous lace-up shoes and undies with enough fabric to reupholster a Volkswagen. Besides, I can see it's been getting you down, all this baby talk. Maybe you should buy something for your baby to cheer you up."

Kim stared at Mitzi wide-eyed. "How did you know?"

Mitzi craned her neck and tapped her temple with her index finger. "I'm very intuitive when I choose to be. Come on, let's get going."

Just when you think she doesn't have a brain in her head...

It took less than forty-five minutes of shopping for me to start whining.

"Why are all these clothes so snug?" I pulled on the hem of a T-shirt Mitzi insisted would be "adorable" with a pair of maternity jeans.

"One, because you're pregnant and you're growing the waistline of a sumo wrestler. Two, it's the style. Be proud you're pregnant. Show it off." Mitzi slung another shirt at me.

"Whatever happened to modesty?" I complained. "When my mother was pregnant with me, she wore these plaid shirts with turtleneck sweaters underneath, and long, flowing dresses. I've seen pictures—"

"And how did she look in them?"

In the photos, she looked squat, chubby and lumpy,

with the telltale bulge not all that well hidden despite the ugly clothing.

Dressing room mirrors are evil. They are made by the same company that makes mirrors for carnival fun houses. How else can I explain the weird shape I see every time I look in one? According to my reflection in these mirrors, I have developed the round midsection of Tweedledum or Tweedledee in *Alice in Wonderland*.

Not only that, these mirrors magnify cellulite, hair follicles and pores to twenty times their normal size. They can rip away hope and shred self-acceptance to ribbons with one quick pirouette in front of them.

"Mitzi, don't bring me anymore clothes. Get me out of here. I'll confess to anything, you've broken my spirit. Puh-leeze…"

"Don't be a wimp, Whitney. I'm not letting you stop until you find something you like."

"Then find me something suitable to my age. Chase won't be seen with me if I wear a skimpy T-shirt with 'Baby' and a rhinestone arrow pointing to my stomach."

She went off muttering something like "Such a prude," but returned with a white hankie tunic with beautiful lace trim and a cropped khaki vest that flattered my figure and didn't make me look trapped in the seventies. I was elated. After trying on only seventy-three outfits, I'd found one I liked!

And so it went. Mitzi would make sure I found something, then she'd turn to Kim and prod her into the fun.

By lunchtime, Mitzi had nixed several items of clothing, including a horizontal-striped tieback shirt and gauchos, a linen blazer that managed to make me look simultaneously like a small building and an unmade bed, and a tie-dyed green T-shirt in which I resembled a glob of floating seaweed.

To satisfy my particular brand of cravings at lunch, I ordered nachos covered with a poisonously orange "cheese-type food product" and a root beer float. Oh, yes, and a side order of steamed broccoli from the Chinese place. Mitzi had a submarine sandwich with tuna fish, jalapeño peppers, fried onions and mustard that she washed down with a mango and peach health smoothie containing lecithin, ginko biloba and chocolate sprinkles.

Kim had a burger.

No wonder she's depressed, I thought as I dipped my broccoli in my fast-congealing blaze-orange cheese. She doesn't eat anything fun.

"I think," Mitzi announced imperiously, "I am going to have to do something about the state of fashion in the maternity world."

"What's that supposed to mean?" Kim asked.

"I will design my own. I'll start with fashions for the 'multiple' mother, those of us who have more…"

"Girth?" I suggested sweetly.

She glared at me and went on. "…substance. Who needs the pick-me-up of attractive clothes more than us?"

For the rest of the afternoon, she regaled us with what *she* would do if *she* were designing clothes.

By the time we headed for the car, I'd overdosed on shopping and I knew I'd hate myself in the morning, but Mitzi had one more stop to make.

She wanted to look at diaper bags. *Designer* diaper bags. The baby equivalent of the mink-covered toilet seat. Nice, I suppose, but totally, clearly, unnecessary. It's a fever, this baby business.

"Five hundred dollars for a diaper bag?" Kim squealed. "You could give layettes to a hundred babies in an orphanage overseas for that."

"But look at these lovely grommets down the sides. It's very attractive." Mitzi pointed out the merits of the hulking leather bag as if she were on the shopping channel. "And it has a leather key ring, as well as little pockets for baby bottles. What more could you want? It's waterproof…." Seeing she wasn't making any headway with us, she added, "And you could use it for your laptop when the baby grows up!"

Kim held out her hand. "I'll make a deal with you, Mitzi. Give me four hundred and fifty dollars, buy a nice plastic diaper bag somewhere and I'll make sure that a hundred layettes are sent to our church mission."

Mitzi huffed and puffed and put the bag back on the shelf. "See if I show you the stroller I found that's made to look like a Mercedes!"

To her credit, Mitzi did give Kim five hundred dollars for layettes. I hope she finds something that suits her taste in diaper bags in the discount store.

Chapter Twenty-Nine

❧

Chase found me on the couch with my feet up, a cold compress on my head and Mr. Tibble sleeping soundly next to me.

"Too much shopping, I see." He glanced at the bags still piled by the front door.

"Marines, Navy SEALS and SWAT teams aren't trained well enough to keep up with Mitzi in a mall," I muttered from beneath my ice pack. "I don't know why I think *I* am."

"I know what you mean. I'm whipped, too." He sank down in the chair across from me.

"Anything wrong?"

"I'm just tired a lot lately." He grinned a boyish grin. "Maybe I have Couvades like Bryan. It would make much more sense for me than him. You go shopping, I get tired. Hardly seems fair, does it? By the way, how's Bryan doing? Do you think he needs prenatal vitamins or anything?"

"Don't change the subject with me, buddy. If you aren't feeling well, you're the one who needs to see a doctor."

"Whitney, I am a doctor. Don't you think I'd know if something were wrong with me?"

I looked at him doubtfully. Though he's casual about his own health, he treats me like a Fabergé egg. I would trust Chase with my life. Whether or not I trust him with his own is an entirely different matter.

Maybe he does have Couvades syndrome. Chase with a sympathetic pregnancy—wouldn't that be ironic?

Monday, October 12

Mitzi breezed into the office carrying a large portfolio and flung it onto the break room table.

"What's that?" Bryan asked. If it was more work for him, he'd probably head for the hills, or at least the men's bathroom, where he could hide out until she found someone else to do her dirty work.

"My designs."

"Designs on what?" Bryan is not trusting where Mitzi is concerned.

"No, just designs. Maternity clothes."

"You mean you actually did it?" Kim gasped. "How awesome!"

"Of course I am," Mitzi responded modestly. "Arch says that all the time. Want to have a look?"

She flung open the portfolio with great flair, to show us vast pages of pregnant women in their fourteenth month of pregnancy.

Bryan whistled. Kim's mouth worked, but nothing came out. I managed a "Wow."

"Aren't they great?" Mitzi burbled.

"Great with child," Kim murmured.

When I looked beyond the bellies to the fashions, however, I had to agree with Mitzi. "They are breathtaking." Ball gowns, tea-length dresses, flirty tops and lacy nightclothes—just the kinds of things Mitzi would wear.

"I decided to design what I'd want, and see if anyone else would be interested in it. Stunning, aren't they?"

"I didn't know you could draw. You're very artistic."

"Oh, that's not me. I can't draw." She waved her hand dismissively. "But my cleaning lady is a wonder. I told her what I wanted, and she did it. If someone buys these— and I don't see why they wouldn't—we'll split the profit. I made her sign a contract, of course, saying that even if she becomes rich and famous she still has to keep cleaning my house. Good help is hard to find, you know."

"So you're actually going through with this?" Kim inquired.

"Of course." Mitzi preened a little. "I have an entre-preneurial streak, you know. If I decide to stay home after the babies are born, I'll have something to do."

"Stay home?" Harry, who'd come through the door to the break room, looked stricken. "Not come back?" He spun and faced me. "Not you, too, Whitney?"

"We're just gabbing, Harry. No one has màde that decision, least of all me."

He turned to Mitzi. "And you?"

"I'll have to work here at least part-time. All my friends are here. It wouldn't be good for my mental health to quit entirely. Even Arch says so."

I can imagine. Coming home to Mitzi after a day with three crying babies and no social contact would be downright scary. All her friends are here, and that's true for all of us.

"Well," Harry said as he shifted uneasily from one foot to the other, "if you can think of some way to keep us together…"

I could have kissed him on the top of his strange little combed-over head.

Tuesday, October 27

Betty has started having packages delivered to the office, and I don't mean just a few. The UPS man has become her best friend and the FedEx guy salivates at the sight of her. She's gone over the edge ordering baby items for the three of us—whether we want them or not. For Betty, the thrill of the chase motivates her—finding the ideal item online for the cheapest price imaginable. For her, it's all about the hunt. Then she presents us with the bills.

We are considering an intervention.

Monday, November 1

Mitzi has found something new to worry about.

She came to work this morning looking very much like a large fall pumpkin with legs, in an orange sweater decorated with falling leaves. Cheery as her outfit might have been, she was not.

"This is terrible!" She plopped into her chair so heavily I expected the earth to tremble. Mitzi is no lightweight anymore. "I hadn't even considered it until I saw it happen on a television show."

"What's that?" Kim twiddled her fingers as she gazed at Mitzi.

We've abandoned Harry's strange hairdo and we're watching Mitzi grow instead. I received an amaryllis plant for Christmas once, and it grew so quickly as it sat in the sunlight, I actually saw it jerk, tremble and stretch upward. Mitzi's like that. If I watch her long enough, she swells before my eyes.

"This woman had twins and… Oh, what a mess it would be… She had one before midnight and one after, so they didn't have the same birthday! Isn't that awful?"

"What's the problem?" Kim sounded puzzled. "If they are healthy, that's what counts."

Mitzi sent her a withering glance. "Of course it counts. But what about birthday parties?"

"What about them?"

"We'd have to have them on consecutive days. If little Jennifer is born on Tuesday at 11:59 p.m. and Jodi and Jessica are born at 12:01 a.m., they have separate birthdays!" She put her hand to her head theatrically. "This could be a social nightmare!"

To me, a social nightmare is like the time the arm of my one-piece jumpsuit fell into the toilet and I spent the evening in the restaurant bathroom drying it off under the hand dryer. Another social nightmare is coming out of the bathroom at a dinner party with the hem of my slip caught in the waistband of my panty hose. Compared to that, double birthdays aren't even a blip on the social-suicide radar screen.

"Can't they share a party?" I asked. "They would have to if they were all born on the same day."

"It wouldn't be the same. It's not like they are a big lump of children. They'll have their own distinct personalities."

"Let's just hope none of them get yours," Kim muttered under her breath.

"I heard that," Mitzi retorted, and kept on talking. "The logistics are going to be terrible. I can see it now. Three separate playdates, three wardrobes, three—"

"They can all play at my house," Kim offered, "with the other new babies and Wesley. And buy them the same outfits. If you can't tell them apart, write their names on their heads, like Bryan does on the shells of his hard-boiled eggs."

Bad idea. For one thing, we don't want Wesley teaching any of the new little ones his tricks. He's potty trained, but Wesley has the aim of a nearsighted mole on a windy night. Desperate, Kim has painted a big red X inside the toilet bowl for target practice. There are a lot of things we don't want Wes to teach these new little ones. He doesn't have the nickname Destructo Baby for nothing.

For a moment, Mitzi looked as if she might actually consider Kim's offer, but then she shook her head. "If I go into labor late in the evening, I'll just have to refuse to push until after midnight," she concluded. "That will do it."

"I don't know, Mitzi. It's pretty easy to keep out one person pushing on a door, but three's a crowd. I'm not sure you'll have any choice about keeping those babies under wraps until it's convenient for you."

"Well," she said her in most impressive Scarlett O'Hara impression to date, "I'll just have to think about it tomorrow."

Saturday, November 20

"Whit? It's Kurt."

"I'm surprised to hear you on the phone so early on

a Saturday morning. Don't you usually spend Saturday morning in a toons-and-cold-cereal extravaganza so that Kim can get something done around the house?"

He chuckled a little. "I'm calling from my cell phone. We're doing fast food and Playland today. Kim didn't just want us out of the way, she wanted us out of the house entirely."

"Trouble?"

"Mitzi's babies and yours are less than three months from being born, and we haven't heard anything from the adoption agency."

I rubbed my growing belly. I've quit teasing Mitzi about her size. The Goodyear blimp has no business pointing a finger at an orca. Chase thinks my new walk is cute. Of course, *he* likes ducks.

"Maybe we could do something tonight, to get her out of the house. She likes to go bowling."

"Ah…sure. Why not?" My heart sank.

Bowling? Could he think of a more ungainly thing for a blossoming pregnant woman to do? But Kim needs us, and that, I suppose, is cause enough to make a fool of myself. I've certainly done it for less.

Chapter Thirty

Bowling has never been one of my favorite sports.

Perhaps it's because I was emotionally damaged by a bowling ball on my eighth birthday. I forgot to let go of the ball as I threw it down the lane and sent myself sprawling along behind it, landing both myself and the ball in the gutter. I did not outgrow the nickname "Gutter Girl" until my parents moved and I was fortunate enough to end up in another school district.

Then again, it might have been because of a ninth-grade Sunday-school class outing. I was just beginning to notice that boys were not of my species and was rather interested in ensnaring one—for scientific purposes only, of course. Unfortunately, the one I snared was knocked unconscious by the ball when it flew out of my hand on the backswing. Not only did he never want to date me, he flinched every time he saw me in the school hallway for the next three years.

I tried it again as an adult, without much better luck. Fortunately, I did not injure anyone else, but I did lose my toenail some weeks after I dropped my ball on my foot.

Needless to say, I didn't anticipate the evening with great enthusiasm, even though Kim, who bowls a two hundred seven on a regular basis, was quite cheered by the prospect. Chase, too. He wants to see if my back-swing and release are enhanced or exacerbated by having to get around my growing backside and belly.

My husband has taken great satisfaction in observ-ing me through all the stages, peccadilloes and delights of my blossoming pregnancy. Sometimes he gets way too much enjoyment watching me trying to squeeze my puffy feet into my shoes or my growing middle into one of the clothing samples Mitzi sends my way.

She and her cleaning lady are designing up a storm. Mitzi has models made and tries them out on me. She likes to "see how it flows."

Unfortunately, not everything she designs is meant to flow. Chase had way too much fun over a spandex and cotton pullover I got caught in with the shirt half on and half off, my hands and arms trapped in the air as if I was a bank teller in the middle of a robbery. I had to stand in the middle of the bedroom and yell for help until he rescued me, and he took his sweet time doing so, too. It's the first time I've ever seen Chase laugh until he had tears in his eyes.

I'm so glad I could share such a special moment with him—*not.*

"Thanks, Whitney," Kim said to me as we picked out shoes, hoping to find a pair that wasn't harboring athlete's foot or plantar warts. Chase assures me that the disinfectant and deodorizer they use make all my worrying pointless, but I don't like sharing my shoes with anyone, and especially not with a woman named Gladys, who was using her shoe as an ashtray when we came in.

"Thanks for what?"

"I know bowling isn't your idea of a good time, but you came for me. I appreciate it."

"What are friends for?"

"You're the best."

"Boys against the girls?" Chase asked cheerily.

"No," Kim blurted, much too quickly. "You take her."

"Me? Why do I have to take her? Kurt, you can be her partner."

"Why me? I came with Kim, can't I have her?"

Even my husband doesn't want me on his team when it comes to bowling.

I, however, had the last laugh. Pregnancy did what humiliation, lessons and countless hours of jeering had not. It made me into a bowler.

Looking back, I'm speculating that my posture had something to do with it. Being required to be erect and sure-footed, so as not to lose my center of balance, forced me to bend my knees and acquire heretofore nonexistent arm and wrist action. Frankly, I blew them all out of the water—she said modestly!

I even won coupons for free games and a twenty-five-pound turkey that, because of the imminent arrival of Thanksgiving, was tonight's high prize. Meat as a bowling prize is something new to me, but apparently it's very popular at Stardust Lanes.

"I haven't laughed so much in ages," Kim chortled later at a greasy spoon near the bowling alley. She slurped on her shake and dragged a French fry through the ketchup on her plate. "Lately, all I've felt is helpless."

"Isn't there anything you can do?"

"The nursery is ready. We've been reading Chinese history and trying to learn some words to help us once we get there. We've purchased a compact camcorder and a new camera for the trip. I've put my luggage together. I purchased a backpack to use as a diaper bag and filled it with diaper rash cream, sunblock, insect repellent, rice cereal, diapers, wipes, toilet paper, a baby book, formula powder…"

"You're more ready than I am then." Suddenly I felt like a real slacker. While I'd been watching my navel disappear, Kim had been figuring out what she actually needed to do when her baby arrived.

Chapter Thirty-One

Thursday, November 25, Thanksgiving Day

Lord, You are awesome! Forgive me for forgetting to say "Thank You" as often as I should. I usually come to You with a litany of "I want" or "I need" or "Please help," when praise should be the first thing from my lips. Thank You for being the net beneath my high-wire act, my soft place to fall. Thank You for loving me.

"Hey, darling, anything I can do to help?" Chase came up from behind me, put his arms around my round, ample midsection and laid his cheek on my hair. "You smell great."

"New shower gel. Lavender."

"I was thinking sage, thyme and a hint of onion."

"Has the smell of turkey stuffing always had this effect on you?"

"Not until today." He turned me around, kissed me and licked his lips. "Umm. And butter."

"How's the table situation?" In our most daring entertaining event to date, not only were my parents coming for dinner, but also the entire office staff and their spouses.

I hadn't planned for that to happen, but when Harry came out of his office with a long face and told me that his daughter had had to cancel her trip home and that he and his wife would be alone on Turkey Day, an invitation to our house had just slipped out. Harry and my father get along famously. They both tell dreadfully corny jokes, worry about their hairlines and think I'm the best thing since sliced bread. Harry's wife and my mom are pals, too. Having to live with Harry and my dad provides them with enough war stories to commiserate for hours on end.

It was only then, when the invitation was out of my mouth, that I noticed Betty and Bryan looking longingly in my direction. "What are you guys doing for Thanksgiving?" I asked, hoping they'd had their family plans arranged months in advance.

"My grandmother is flying to Indiana to see my aunt and her family," Bryan said sadly. "Everyone is going their separate ways this year."

"My husband's mother in Nebraska is ill, so he's going to spend a week with her and help her around the house," Betty added. "It made sense that he go the week of Thanksgiving, so he wouldn't have to take off so many days of work."

"So you'll both be alone?"

"At least I'll have Jennilee," Bryan said.

Never one to leave someone out at a party, I blurted, "Then come to my house!"

I have got to get a muzzle—and use it.

Next thing I know, Mitzi is telling me that their

Thanksgiving guests' travel plans have fallen through and Kim is hinting that my turkey gravy is the smoothest and tastiest in three states and I've invited the whole crew.

Even now, as I peel my millionth potato, I can't believe I did it. I'm a glutton for punishment. Five days a week obviously isn't enough for me with these people. I've become addicted to the unhinged madness and folly they provide in my life.

Fortunately, Chase loves them, too, or it would have been much harder convincing him he had to find seating for twelve at our dining room table.

"I set the table," he said, "and I will accept a reward later for actually ironing the tablecloth before I put the plates down."

"You are a gem, darling." I lifted my hand to caress his cheek and pulled it away, startled. "You're all clammy. Don't you feel well?"

"Fine. Aren't you the one who asked me to…" and he listed all the things that had kept him occupied since 7:00 a.m.

"Then go take a shower. I'll pop this into the oven and be in to get ready, too." I love listening to Chase sing in the shower while I put on my makeup. It's just one of those married things of which I'll never tire.

Mr. Tibble and Scram, having smelled the scent of turkey while it was still frozen solid in the bag, have been making royal nuisances of themselves. Mr. Tibble has sat motionless since daybreak, watching me wash and truss the big bird and send it into the oven. His tail flickers, right, left, right, left, like a metronome as he waits for an opportunity to pounce on the biggest catch of his life.

Scram, ever vocal, has meowed off and on for hours. He sounds like a suffering infant when he cries. If our baby goes on and on like this, Chase and I will both be walking around with tufts of toilet paper sprouting from our ears like explosions of excessive ear hair. Oh, yes, motherhood is going to be a glamorous thing, I can see it all now.

In my closet, I pawed unhappily through my maternity clothes. I've come to depend on Mitzi and her housekeeper to provide me with their experiments, but they have been in a green-brown-and khaki camouflage fabric stage recently, so my newest maternity garb from them makes me look like an army tank. Maybe there will be younger mothers for whom this will work, but after thirty, one should not try to present oneself as a Humvee out for a ride on the open road.

Then, feeling guilty for my lack of gratitude, I tried to think of something for which I am profoundly thankful. It came to me right away.

In the shape I am in, I am deeply grateful that I can still see my feet.

I was tempted to simply cut a hole in the center of a bedsheet and wear it as a dress, but cheered considerably when I remembered that no matter how ungainly and large and pregnant I look, I am a mere sylph compared to Mitzi.

Mitzi hasn't seen her feet in weeks. Her kneecaps are a pure mystery to her, as well. I know this for a fact, because she admitted as much the day she called me in a panic, asking me how she was supposed to shave her legs when she could no longer reach them.

"My arms aren't long enough!" she wailed. "I can't reach over my stomach to shave my legs unless I attach the razor to the end of a yardstick!"

None of my suggestions helped. When she put her leg on the edge of the tub, all she could see was her ankle. When she held her leg out to one side, she saw it, but the three babies convened a quick committee meeting and decided that their mother was no longer going to be allowed to turn at the waist. Fastidious Mitzi of the high heels and the perfectly turned ankles has now resorted to Birkenstock sandals and jeans to cover her hairy legs. She's turning into a regular granola lover and will next be marching to save the tufted three-toed albino needle-nosed wood mouse.

I decided on a peachy blouse with high ruffles at the neck and a hemline with the circumference of a parachute, and a pair of brown slacks. Even though I know I look like a large poisonous mushroom, Chase always tells me I'm beautiful, and I choose to believe him. Living in a delusional fantasy has its merits.

The guests all came at once, and they were bearing gifts. Harry carried a cornucopia full of fresh fruit. Betty bore a lemon meringue pie, and Bryan and his girlfriend presented me with a huge bouquet of fall flowers. Kim and Kurt came with a sound-asleep Wesley—a gift in itself—and a huge tray of freshly baked buns. Mom and Dad brought up the rear with even more pies— pumpkin, mincemeat and cherry.

Mitzi and Arch pulled into the driveway, and I surreptitiously watched as Arch pried Mitzi out of the passenger seat. Arch got red in the face as he held Mitzi's hands and pulled. They rocked back and forth together, Mitzi perched on the edge of the car seat, her feet dangling toward the ground, until she had enough momentum to launch herself upright. Arch staggered back as he caught her, but managed to keep his footing.

Once he had Mitzi balanced on her feet, he reached back into the car and pulled out the largest box of Godiva chocolates I have ever seen. Mitzi's craving for chocolate has grown right along with the rest of her, and if she doesn't watch it, each of those babies will emerge with a Snickers bar in one hand and a Milky Way in the other.

"We're here!" she chirruped proudly as she teetered toward the door.

We did air kisses from about four feet apart—as close as we can get together, given the size of our stomachs—and toddled into the house to a friendly chorus of "Sixteen Tons."

Rather than have Mitzi sit down in the living room and risk not being able to get her up again, I called everyone to the table. Mitzi immediately rearranged my seating chart, demanding that Arch sit on her right—to do her bidding more quickly—Kim on her left—to take up the slack while Arch was off doing said bidding—and Chase, because he's the best-looking guy in the house, across from her, where she could look at him.

Once we were seated, Chase, who normally says grace at our house, looked around at the guests and inquired, "Would someone like to say the prayer before we eat?"

To everyone's amazement, Mitzi waved her hand in the air. "I will."

I held my breath as she began, wondering what would come out of her mouth.

"Lord," she began, "I don't know You very well, but Whitney does, and she says You are for real and that

You're nice. Whitney never lies, so I believe her. I just want to say thanks for everything—the babies, Whitney's, Kim's baby to come, and my threesome. I was afraid I'd never even have one baby, so if You had anything to do with this, good job. Thanks for our husbands and families and all they are doing. Thanks especially for Arch. He hurt his back pulling me out of the car the other day, so maybe You could take care of that for him, okay? And keep Harry calm. He's worried what's going to happen to the office, but he's being pretty decent about it so far, so don't let him get cranky.

"Whitney's food looks really good. She always prays 'give us this day our daily bread,' so thanks for however You got it here. Like I said, I don't know You very well, but from what I hear, You are a great guy.

"Thanks and all that. Amen."

Everyone found their voices at the same moment. "Amen!"

I looked at Chase, and he pulled a handkerchief out of his back pocket and slid it to me under the table. Our fingers met, and he squeezed my hand. Quietly I wiped a tear from my eye.

Harry and Bryan ate an inhuman amount of stuffing and yams, Mitzi nibbled on Godiva crèmes between courses, and Mr. Tibble and Scram lurked under the dining-room table like the mangy scavengers they are. All in all, it was a very successful meal.

After dinner, the men retreated immediately to the living room, where they jockeyed for position in the easy chairs and on the couch and were all sleeping with their mouths open—except for Chase, who is a lovely sleeper—within twenty minutes of leaving the table.

Mother, Betty, Jennilee and Harry's wife insisted on doing the dishes so that "the pregnant ones" could rest. Kim is an honorary "pregnant one."

We sat at the table with what was left of the pies and made sure that the remaining edges were properly and evenly cut. We sculpted them like I do when I'm trying to straighten a row of brownies. Just slice off a sliver here, another there, and pretty soon you have nothing left.

Suddenly Mitzi snapped her fingers. "I almost forgot to tell you, Whitney, I'll need a couple days off next week."

"Are you going to another convention with Arch?"

"No. We're going on a *babymoon*."

"A babymoon?" Kim echoed. "What's that?"

"A honeymoon for expectant parents, a last time to get away before the baby arrives. It's the new thing. Isn't it a great idea?"

A babymoon. What will the travel industry think of next?

"You're kidding, right?" Kim asked.

"Not at all. We're going to a spa. I've booked beauty treatments for me and tennis lessons for Arch. Breakfast in bed, nearby five-star restaurants, and shopping— what could be better?" Mitzi's eyes gleamed. "And it will be very romantic, too. We can hardly wait. The airplane tickets are purchased, and I've already packed."

Most people ask for the time off before they buy the plane tickets, but that logic would fly right over Mitzi's head. Besides, a spa and a romantic weekend with Chase didn't sound too bad to me, either.

"What do you pack for a babymoon?" Kim inquired, still trying to process the concept.

"Sweats for the spa, dinner dresses for the evening, and chocolate."

"Chocolate?"

"Sure," she responded with sublime Mitzi logic. "If the plane goes down, I want the taste of chocolate on my lips."

Chapter Thirty-Two

"I could use a vacation." I sighed and imagined myself under a palm tree. Unfortunately, I also pictured myself propped on a chaise lounge in a maternity swimsuit and floppy straw hat.

Frankly, right now I'd be happy with a fake ficus tree in a nice hotel somewhere. "No fair that you should have all the fun, Mitzi."

Mitzi eyed me and then Kim. "You're both looking a little pathetic right now. Maybe a few days off would help."

"Thanks, Mitzi. You sure know how to boost a girl's spirits."

"When was the last time either of you did any traveling?"

"I went to Iowa for a family picnic in September," Kim offered. "We stayed in a tent and didn't bathe for three days."

"Lovely." Mitzi's turned up her nose in disgust. "Whitney?"

I thought hard. Apart from that weekend in Wisconsin, Chase and I have been working like fiends. "I looked up Switzerland one day on Google. The photos were lovely."

"Refusing to bathe and looking at pictures on the Internet do not a vacation make," Mitzi intoned.

Kim brightened. "I had electrolysis done on my upper lip. I relaxed then."

"While someone shot electric shocks into your hair follicles? That does not count as a vacation."

"It's not like Kurt and I don't do anything. We go to movies all the time. Did you see *Titanic?*"

"In 1997."

"That long ago? Really?"

"Point taken, Mitzi, but it's not always so easy to get away. Kim has Wesley, and I…"

My mind went to the piles of unironed shirts in my laundry room from my good-housewife period, when I announced that I could do Chase's shirts just as well as the laundry. I recalled the piles of stuff and boxes we'd moved out of the spare bedroom to make room for baby, and how they filled up the third stall of our garage, forcing Chase to leave our lawn mower and snowblower outside. As my thoughts ricocheted to the list of things I wanted to finish before the baby came, I saw myself unable to leave home until sometime in 2030.

"Frankly, Mitzi, it's easier to deploy the National Guard to Timbuktu than it is to get Wesley ready for a weekend away from us. Clothes, toys, vitamins, bedtime instructions…"

"They're supposed to be *portable* at this age, Kim. You're just making it too difficult," Mitzi scolded. "I don't know why you think everything is so hard."

I smiled nastily to myself. Just wait, Mitzi, until you have three babies to haul around every time you want to go somewhere. You don't know the meaning of *hard* yet. Soon you'll be able to define *impossible*.

Feeling a little guilty for my uncharitable thoughts, I put in a good word for Mitzi's point of view. "An overnight wouldn't be so bad, Kim. Maybe Mitzi and I could each watch Wesley for a night, and you and Kurt could have a weekend away."

The expression on Mitzi's face told me that suggestion was going to fly like a lead balloon. Mitzi's idea of "helping" is limited to telling people what to do, not actually implementing it.

Kim brightened. "We could go camping."

I shuddered, remembering family camping trips from my childhood.

It was genetically impossible for my parents to remember everything they needed to make a camping trip, if not pleasant, at least tolerable. It was usually something important that they forgot—cots, coolers, bug spray, maps. Once they forgot my sleeping bag, and I had to sleep with my mother in hers. She was suffering from a sinus malady at the time, and snored and snorted like a cross between a diesel engine and a crazed bull. Although my mother weighs barely a hundred pounds soaking wet, she commands a large presence—particularly in a sleeping bag. It was like sleeping with a Great Dane in a twin bed. I was eight years old when we left on that camping trip. I was twenty by the time we finally got home again. First thing I did when I got out of the car was run into the bathroom and check for gray hairs.

Then Mitzi dropped another bombshell.

"By the way, I've had an offer to do some designs for a manufacturer of maternity clothes. They loved my ideas for mothers of multiples."

It shouldn't have surprised me. Mitzi really shows talent in that area. Although I grouse about being her guinea pig, I enjoy the things she's asked me to wear. Except, of course, for that diaphanous peach-and-white number that made me look like a Creamsicle on steroids, and the stiff khaki-and-green dress that made me resemble a very large, slightly rotted cantaloupe.

"Does this mean you're going to leave Innova?" Kim asked.

Mitzi looked at us in amazement. "Quit? I couldn't quit. You guys would be lost without me!"

Not *lost* exactly...

"So what are you going to do?"

"Just what I'm doing now. My cleaning lady is delighted with the extra money."

"And you?"

Mitzi frowned. "At first I thought I'd take the money and run, but I guess I've been hanging around you guys too long.

"For the time being, the money will go to a program to teach teenage unwed mothers how to parent. Maybe later I'll find something else to donate it to. You're always tithing at church, Whitney. I figure if *you* can do it, then I certainly can, too."

Now this is the kind of one-upmanship I can live with.

"What a wonderful idea."

Mitzi batted her eyelashes and said demurely, "I know."

After she and the others left, Kim and I marveled at what was happening in Mitzi's life.

"This is a God thing," Kim kept repeating. "Definitely a God thing."

I believe that, too. I've been praying for her for a long time. Once Mitzi really puts her—currently considerable—weight down on God's side, it's going to be amazing.

I walked Kim and Kurt to the door, while Chase went ahead with Wesley and chased him around the yard to run off a little steam before putting him in his car seat. Kim joined their game, but Kurt grabbed my arm and held me back.

"Whitney, I'd like to ask you something."

"Sure. Anything." I couldn't take my eyes off Chase and Wesley. Chase will be such a wonderful father.

"Is Chase okay?"

"More than okay, as far as I'm concerned. Why?"

"He's just a little off his game, that's all. As long as I've known him, Chase has had boundless energy. He's turned me down the last few times I've asked him to play racquetball."

I laid a hand on Kurt's arm. "He is absolutely swamped. He's been covering for another doctor, and putting up with the pregnant and persnickety me. Wouldn't you be tired, too?"

Kurt looked at my ballooning form and chuckled. "When you put it that way…"

As they drove away, I rubbed my hand across my belly and vowed to work at easing the pressure on Chase. Maybe a babymoon would be a good idea after all.

Saturday, December 11

DANGER: BABY SHOWER:
KNOWN TO CAUSE GROWN WOMEN TO
REGRESS TO EMBARASSING INFANTILE STATE!
ENTER AT YOUR OWN RISK.

That's what it should have said on the door to Betty's home. Women were perched on every available chair and surface in Betty's living room, all sucking candy pacifiers and trying to make origami diapers out of stiff white paper.

Those present are, in their other lives, doctors, lawyers, corporate executives, sensible human beings. Yet, brought together for a baby shower, they began to vie for stupid prizes and willingly model old maternity clothes in order to win a case of squash baby food in the Worst Maternity Outfit contest.

Betty, bless her generous heart, had insisted on giving us a three-way baby shower. We tried to talk her out of it. Purchasing gifts for three mothers-to-be is bad enough, but when you throw in Mitzi's triplet factor, that's a lot of gifts to buy. But Betty insisted. She'd gone all out with a Baby Brunch theme, which sounded rather gross to me. What's the entrée? Babies Benedict?

She put my mother in charge of choosing the games we would play. What would a shower be without games? Pleasant, probably.

My mother loves games. When I was a child, she was the one always begging to play Chutes and Ladders, not me. I outgrew it almost immediately, but had to humor my mother by playing it with her until I was nearly seven years old.

After unscrambling words such as dtaebesrfe, yattele, and cijprolet gintimov—breastfeed, layette and projectile vomiting—we were on to that old standby, Guess How Fat This Woman Is. As Mitzi and I—Kim bowed out due to a normal waistline—stood in the middle of the room to be eyeballed, the women unrolled balls of string and cut lengths to the size they thought our waists might be.

"Well, that couldn't be anymore humiliating," I whispered to Kim. Several of the guests guessed Mitzi to be approximately the same distance around the equator as me. Until now, I've considered myself lithe and willowy compared to Mitzi, who will soon be rolling her stomach around in a wheelbarrow.

"No? It's good for Mitzi's ego, though."

"Mitzi does not need her ego stroked. It's already as big as her stomach."

"Touchy, touchy," Kim chided. "I know you don't like shower games very well, but your mother says the next one is going to be great fun."

Oh, yes. Great fun.

My mother appeared from the kitchen carrying a tray full of label-free baby-food jars. "The point of this game is to identify what type of food this is by simply looking at it. The one who gets the most right wins."

"How will we find out what they are?" Jennilee asked with excitement.

My mother's face glowed. "Our moms-to-be will taste the food in the jars and tell us!"

I swallowed thickly. The baby has been acting as a gatekeeper for the food I eat lately. If he/she doesn't like it, he/she just pushes it right back out. And now I'm being forced to eat liquefied vegetables that I don't even enjoy in their original forms.

The orange family is well represented in baby food—carrots, squash, peaches, sweet potatoes—as is the beige family—bananas, tapioca, turkey, apple sauce and pear. The jars of prunes and plums looked downright frisky compared to the rest. What's more, I can see why this is a challenging game. To win, one must have intimate knowledge of the differences between smashed apples and pulverized pears—not common knowledge in today's corporate world.

Chapter Thirty-Three

If Americans eat ten pounds of chocolate per person annually, then, judging by the amount that Mitzi and I have eaten in the past few months, there is a small town somewhere in Kansas that didn't get its quota this year.

Even today, as Kim and I made Christmas candy—fudge, chocolate peanut clusters, pretzels dipped in chocolate, truffles—I couldn't keep my hands off the sweets.

"What am I going to do when this baby is born and my weight doesn't change?" I asked as I licked a mixing spoon before putting it into the dishwasher.

"Don't be silly. You haven't gained that much weight, Whitney."

"No? You aren't the one who's worried that the doorways in this house have shrunk. Chase has started calling me his 'Little Bonbon' because I'm round and full of chocolate."

I love that man. The more rotund I get, the more beautiful he tells me I am.

There are advantages to being pregnant, of course. Those prenatal vitamins have made my hair long, thick and luxurious. My fingernails are so strong that I can use them as can openers. My skin glows, and my mother and Chase say I'm the most beautiful pregnant woman on the planet. Who am I to argue? I'd rather believe them than my mirror.

"Have you got big plans for Christmas?" Kim asked. "I haven't heard you talk about it much."

"Not this year. It's too easy to lose the point of Christmas in the hubbub. We're giving gifts to charities in the names of our family and friends, and planning on lots of time spent in church and with people we love. I'm looking forward to it."

"I agree. We've purchased a few toys for Wesley, but other than that, we're planning on things being simple. We'll need the money when we go to China. That will be gift enough."

"Have you heard anything lately?"

Kim shook her head. "Our dossier has been sent. Now we wait until the Chinese government gives us a referral. Right now it's 'hurry up and wait.'"

I studied her face for signs of strain. "How are you guys holding up?"

"Romans 8:25.

   "If we look forward to something we don't have yet, we must wait patiently and confidently."

"And Hebrews 10:35?

"Do not throw away this confident trust in the Lord, no matter what happens. Remember the great reward it brings you!"

"I feel I'm in a gestation period myself," Kim murmured. "Pregnant with anticipation. It's been hard watching you and Mitzi, but I know we're doing the right thing. I don't need the experience of giving birth to know I'm going to be a great mother to this child." She smiled. "I wish I had a due date, though. I'd like to know that I won't have to wait longer than the rest of you to get my baby."

"I feel like I've already been pregnant eleven or twelve months," I said with a sigh. "Why should you be any different?"

"This place smells great," Chase commented as he walked through the door. "Delicious." He kissed me tenderly. "Like you."

"I've got good news and bad news. Which do you want first?"

His lips tipped in an amused smile. "The good news, of course."

"I have a great dessert planned—samples of everything Kim and I made today."

"And the bad news?"

"I didn't have time to cook, and you get to choose between a chicken pot pie or a peanut butter and jelly sandwich for dinner."

"Let's go with the chicken pot pie. I have some papers we have to fill out while they're baking." He reached for his briefcase, pulled out a few papers and spread them on the table. "The lawyer asked for a little more information before he can finish our wills. I know you wanted more time to think about this, but we need to decide who to name as guardian for our baby. Just in case—"

"What is *with* you?" I was surprised at the anger in my voice, and more amazed still at the illogical frisson of fear I felt. "You keep bringing this up, and it's beginning to creep me out!"

"Be logical, Whitney," he said with a spark of exasperation. "If we get this done, then we won't have to think about it anymore."

"I don't think about it anyway. I don't like thinking about it." Even though he's right, his persistence annoys me. I know it's irrational, but I *am* pregnant. Who says I have to be rational every minute of the day?

My mother and dad say the secret of a happy marriage is never to go to bed on an argument. "Kiss and make up," Mom insists. "You'll sleep much better."

Although we definitely kissed, we went to bed with something unresolved hanging between us.

Monday, December 20

If in doubt, clean it out.
If it's torn, send it round the Horn.
If it's broken, don't keep it as a token.
If it's…

I am a compulsive cleaning machine. I thought the nesting instinct would pass, but it's like an infection raging out of control. I can't help myself.

The baby's room has been sterilized, sanitized, deodorized and disinfected. Chase says he's done surgery in messier places than our nursery. I've sewed curtains, made quilts, cross-stitched and needlepointed pictures for the walls. According to Chase, the only thing I haven't done is rewire the room for the new lighting, and that's already on my to-do list.

This nesting thing is dangerous. I've raged at Chase for splashing water in the bathroom sink, forced him to fold the end of the toilet paper roll in a little V as they do in fancy hotels and made him fold his dirty towels before he throws them into the laundry basket. He's very sweet about everything, but he's notified me that if within six weeks after this baby is born I have not calmed down and quit bleaching his shirts, he will have me sent to some lovely place with bars on the windows and maid service.

Frankly, that sounds pretty good, because I have no idea how to stop myself from cleaning every vent in our house with Q-tips and dental floss.

Tuesday, December 21

Even doing last-minute Christmas shopping with the girls didn't lift me from the strange mood I've been in since my disconcerting conversation with Chase. I'd filled out the forms as he'd asked, with much emotion and crying on my part. Maybe I've blown this all out of proportion. Chase is a responsible man. Why wouldn't he want everything in order? It's no doubt my hormones acting up.

What else should I expect while I'm pregnant? Mitzi, for example, is a walking hormone right now.

Technically, tonight she was a *riding* hormone. Rather than depend on Kim and me to keep her from losing her center of balance and pitching into a rack of

Christmas tree ornaments or a display of the kitschy paste jewelry that always pops up at Christmastime, she'd signed out one of those little riding carts, making our shopping trip into a mix of motocross, soapbox derby and raid on the television shopping channel.

Mitzi's aggressive tendencies hovered near the surface as she nearly clipped a fellow ambling along chatting on his cell phone. If she'd had a horn, she would have honked it.

Not quite shopped out after dinner, we wandered in the mall. Mostly Mitzi and I just put our faces to the windows of the shops and drooled over normal-sized clothing.

"What if I'm this way forever?" Mitzi asked mournfully, looking down at her monstrous circumference. "What if I'm so stretched out that my skin hangs around my knees after the babies are born? These things happen, you know. What if—"

"Quit awfulizing, Mitzi. Bodies bounce back. You'll look great in no time."

Then I looked at her, really looked at her.

She's still beautiful, of course, but she does look like someone who's joined the circus as "Globe Girl, Big as Life, Big as Earth."

She rubbed the small of her back with her hands. "The doctor says I should anticipate going on bed rest soon."

Ouch. Harry's going to love that. I've already lined up temps for the office. Each will work for three months. That should carry us over the maternity leaves nicely, but he's still in denial about the fact that Kim, Mitzi and I aren't going to be showing up for work every day. I've suggested that I start interviewing full-time replace-ments just in case one of us decides to stay home permanently, but he insists that unless one of us demands to quit, we'll make do for the time being.

I'm chalking this all up to feeling twenty-nine months pregnant, but my anxiety level is very high. I know God is with me and will get me through what's coming next, but the edginess still comes and goes.

I've got to buy my mother a really nice Christmas gift. Until now, I had no idea how much she went through for me.

Mr. Tibble here.

Something is dreadfully wrong with my pet.

She is cranky. Sometimes I expect her to hiss and spit. She's not declawed, but has so far not tried to gouge me in the nose like that idiot Scram. I've had to teach him painful—painful for him, that is, but vaguely enjoyable for me—lessons about respect and deference. My lineage stems from the lion, the king of the jungle. His heritage is plebeian. Some days I suspect that he is merely a mutant rat. I have no solid proof, but I did see my pet feed him cheese once, and he ate it. Blech.

Her mate is not acting like himself, either. He is acting more like a cat, and sleeping longer hours every day.

This worry is disturbing my rest. Yesterday I was only able to sleep sixteen hours. These creatures and sleep deprivation will be the death of me yet. Next time I get a pet, I will choose birds.

Yum.

Mr. Tibble, signing off.

Chapter Thirty-Four

Friday, December 24

They shall name him Emmanuel, which means, "God is with us."

I love Christmas.

Christmas Eve for my family is a time of anticipation, of bringing to full awareness the enormity of the events surrounding Christ's birth. *God* is with us. God *is* with us. God is *with* us. God is with *us*. Any way you say it, it is astonishing, magnificent and miraculous.

Mom and Dad came to our place after five-o'clock services at church.

Dad always reads the Christmas story with great drama and tears in his eyes.

While they were there, the time came for her to deliver her child. And she gave birth to her firstborn son and wrapped him in bands of cloth, and laid him in a manger, because there was no place for them in the inn.

When I was young, we shared Christmas with

numerous aunts, uncles and cousins. With the encouragement of our mothers, who thought we should have a more experiential celebration, we decked ourselves out in bathrobes, sheets and dish towels to create a pageant of the Christmas story. I, for some reason, always ended up as Joseph, the one who, apart from leading the donkey—usually my father—was relegated to the background.

My cousin Louise, a spoiled and demanding child, was always Mary. Frankly, those are the only times I ever saw Louise sweet, docile and tender—a brief relief for the entire family during our amateur productions. She is now a partner in a large law firm in Chicago and is aggressive, obnoxious, insufferable and confrontational for a living.

Louise's little brother Randy, because he was the youngest, did his stint as Jesus until he outgrew Louise's lap. His last Christmas as the infant Jesus, Randy's arms and legs nearly reached the floor as he lay back in Louise's arms. Recalling it now, I realize what a vulnerable position Randy put himself in for the sake of the pageant. I'll bet Mary never dropped Jesus, but Louise landed Randy on his head more than once.

The Christmas spirit overtook me even then, and I couldn't find it in my heart to be jealous of any of them—Mary, the shepherds, the wise men, and especially not the angel who announced Christ's birth. One year he fell off the back of the couch during his big proclamation and broke his arm.

The next year, our angel was earthbound.

Tonight, there was no reenactment, but the sweet memories resurfaced nonetheless.

Christmas Eve dinner has always been a bit of an adventure in my family. When we'd visit my aunts' and uncles' homes, I could count on meatballs, mashed potatoes and gravy, and perhaps even ham. My grandparents on my father's side were an entirely different story. Grandma, a Scandinavian who still sounds as though she's just vacated a Viking ship, insists that Christmas Eve is meant for lutefisk and lefse and, on the odd occasion, oyster stew.

Now, anyone who knows anything about lutefisk knows that it is the famously revered food of the Scandinavian countries of Norway, Denmark and Sweden and their adopted state, Minnesota. People from these parts of the world have developed an emotional attachment to lutefisk that cannot be explained. For my grandmother, not serving lutefisk on Christmas Eve—"Just a taste, dear"—is tantamount to showing outright disrespect to her mother country.

Lutefisk is disquieting for the uninitiated. First, most sane people do not realize that whitefish soaked in lye is edible. Yes, lye, the stuff of drain cleaner. Some people, once they have eaten lutefisk, still say it is not edible. Just don't tell that to my grandmother.

Grandma's traditional meal includes lutefisk (boiled), potatoes (boiled) and green peas (also boiled). Scandinavians are fond of beige and gray foods. Though not many realize this, one *can* actually cook the green off a pea. I was taught to mash this combination together on my plate while watching for one of the bazillion bones in the fish, sprinkle it with salt and pepper and flood it with melted butter. I've never really minded this meal. Of course, if I poured enough melted butter on an overshoe, I'd probably like that, too.

Texture is a big deal with lutefisk. It is a *jellied* fish, so its texture can range from the firm quality of grape jelly with pectin to the consistency of applesauce. I'm always wary of gray applesauce. I take a whiff first. If it's fishy, rather than fruity, I put it back.

But tonight, Grandma is in Florida, cooking lutefisk for her friends in her retirement village, and we're having lasagna.

Chase came into the kitchen and buried his nose in my hair as I arranged crudités in a crystal dish. "How's my love?"

I turned to face him and bumped him with my belly. I bump everything with my belly these days. Fortunately, I don't do much damage with mine. Mitzi can turn around and knock people over like bowling pins with hers.

"I've got a little something I'd like you to open." He took a small flat box from his pocket and laid it on the counter.

"Don't you want to do it later, when we exchange gifts?"

"I want you to have this now. Go ahead, open it."

He looked down at me with such a loving expression that I felt my chest tighten. The baby fluttered and kicked inside me as if he/she sensed Chase's love, too. He treats me as if I'm as fragile and beautiful as a hummingbird these days. His tenderness overwhelms me sometimes. I raised my hand to his cheek and stroked it.

"Aren't you curious?" He prodded. "Open the package."

I lifted the lid of a jeweler's box. Inside, on a bed of

navy velvet, rested a gold pendant with three individual diamonds separated by several smaller diamonds in a channel setting.

"Chase, it's spectacular." My voice sounded strangely breathless to my ears.

"Pick it up and look at the back."

I lifted the treasure out of the box and turned it over in my hand. There were two more diamonds on the back, separating three engraved words—*Past, Present, Future.*

"I saw it and thought of us, Whitney, of what we've shared and what we have to look forward to. I had to buy it for you."

"It's the most beautiful thing ever." I handed it to him and lifted the thick blanket of my hair so he could put it around my neck. Then I touched it lightly, hardly believing this beautiful thing was mine. "I had no idea…."

"It represents our past, our present and our future." He gently placed his hand on my stomach, and I felt the baby move, as if attracted to the warmth of his hand. "We have so much to look forward to, the three of us."

So very, very much.

"Lord, thank You for this food, this family and this opportunity to share this meal. You're all we can think of tonight as we remember how You came to earth in human form to save us from ourselves and our sin. May our lives honor You. Thank You, Lord, for the baby in the manger who saved us all."

My father looked up from his prayerful pose and winked at me, just as he has every Christmas Eve since I was a child. "Now let's eat. We have another birthday party to go to later, you know." We return to church for the midnight candlelight service. After all, what's a birthday party without candles?

"I wonder if your grandmother has poisoned anyone with that lutefisk of hers yet," Mom said as she dished up seconds of lasagna. "The woman should come with a health warning stamped on her forehead."

"A little lutefisk never hurt anyone," Dad said, in a weak attempt to defend his mother. "I ate it every year, and look at me."

"Exactly my point," Mother muttered.

"If lutefisk is so great, why do you eat it so seldom? Grandma never cooked it more than once or twice a year. If it's that delicious, shouldn't you eat it at least once a week?"

Both Mom and Dad looked a little green at the idea, and Chase, who had first been introduced to lutefisk when he met me, turned a lot green and disappeared into our bedroom and likely into the bathroom beyond.

When I brought dessert, a baked Alaska, from the kitchen, he still hadn't returned to the table.

"Did Chase go outside?"

"No. He hasn't come out of your bedroom. Want me to go check on him?" Dad offered.

"No. You guys have done enough harm already. If we hadn't gotten into this lutefisk conversation, we'd all feel a lot better right now."

But when Chase hadn't returned by the time I'd cut the dessert, I decided to look for him myself.

Smiling, I touched my fingers to my throat and felt the warm, smooth gold and diamond necklace against my throat. My sweet, sweet man...

"Honey, dessert is ready," I called at the bedroom door. "Are you coming? I made fresh coffee, too. Hurry up, will you? Now that Mom's seen my necklace, she's itching to open her present from Dad. Dad's looking a little nervous. I hope he learned his lesson last year and didn't buy her something like a pressure washer again."

The silence in our darkened bedroom was deafening.

"Chase?" I hurried into the bathroom. Empty. Where on earth had he gone?

Outside, probably, and Dad had just missed seeing him. But when I turned to head for the garage, I saw Chase lying on our bed.

"Honey, I…" As I neared him, I realized that his hair was dark with sweat and his shirt…his damp shirt was plastered to his body. I reached out and touched his cheek. Clammy.

"Chase?" I took his face in my hands. Something was very, very wrong.

"Whit," he whispered through gritted teeth, "I think you'd better get me to the hospital."

I didn't have time to be afraid. I lumbered into the living room. "Mom, Dad, Chase is sick. I'm going to call an ambulance."

"Should I drive him? Maybe that would be faster." But after one look at Chase, Dad shook his head. "Get on the phone, Whitney."

In what seemed like hours but was, in fact, less than five minutes, the ambulance pulled up, its lights cutting sharp swaths in the darkness of the night.

Dad let them into the house, and I, who hadn't left Chase's side, moved out of the way so the crew could work. Chase, his voice weak, mumbled something to them that I couldn't hear. When they moved him from the bed to the gurney, he gave a sharp cry of pain that sliced through me like a knife.

I gasped and sat down heavily—the only way I can sit down these days. One of the EMTs glanced at me and then looked at my father. "Maybe you'd better bring her with you in the car to the hospital. We'll have someone look at her, too. She's not ready to go into labor yet."

Instinctively, I clutched the dome of my belly. The baby was flailing around in there like an Olympic speed swimmer out for the gold. "Shh," I whispered, rubbing my hand across my abdomen as I might across a baby's back. "Shh."

Then the room commenced to tip and whirl, and I hoped Chase wouldn't fall off the gurney when the floor and the ceiling changed places. I must have blacked out for a moment. When I came to, Mr. Tibble, who had been sitting on the bed with Chase, began to yowl, a keening sound that sent shivers down my spine.

For once, on the ride to the hospital, I didn't hear my mother tell my father to slow down. I gazed dully at the lighted houses as we sped by and remembered that we'd left every light in our house on when we made our exit. The coffeepot was on, the dessert was melting on the dining-room table, and for the life of me, I couldn't remember if I'd turned off the oven after I browned the meringue on the baked Alaska.

When I mumbled as much to my mother, she took out her cell phone. "I'm going to call Kim. They're home tonight, aren't they?"

She and Kurt were scheduled to be at our house for dinner tomorrow. Tonight they'd planned to spend alone with Wesley, reading him the Christmas story and wrapping gifts for their new baby. Wesley has accepted the idea of a new baby, in theory at least. Kim is trying to embed the concept in his mind that once this child arrives, it is here to stay, not to be traded in for a bike with training wheels or a big-boy bed that looks like a race car.

New baby. Mine lurched and reeled inside my belly.

What if Chase dies? What if he leaves the two of us here alone?

The baby, as if it had read my mind, thrust some little appendage into my side with such force that it took my breath away.

The hospital looks entirely different when your husband is a patient, rather than an attending physician. The halls are longer, the lights are brighter and the antiseptic smell is more pungent. An E.R. isn't a high-tech wonder, it's a chamber of horrors, filled with equipment Dr. Frankenstein would have given his—or somebody's—eyeteeth to own.

The on-call physician was Martin Steele, a doctor Chase says is "one of the best in the business."

He took one look at me hovering by Chase and frowned. "Do you need a wheelchair, Whitney?"

Hysterical laughter bubbled through my lips. "Of course not! I'm fine. This baby isn't due for six weeks yet. It's Chase I'm worried— Oh!" Whitney or Chase Junior has the kick of an ornery mule on a bad day in the pasture. I imagined permanent footprints marking the inside of my womb.

"Sit down, Whitney. I'll take a look at Chase and call for someone in obstetrics to check you out."

"This baby is not being born today," I said, teeth gritted. "I want to know what's wrong with my husband."

"Whit?" Chase's voice was soft, but I heard him immediately.

I moved to put my ear closer to his mouth.

"Don't make me worry anymore than I already am. Sit down and behave yourself. Dr. Steele will take care of me. You need to tend to our baby." Then he grimaced, and a shudder spread thorough him. "Please."

"I will, honey, I will…." I promised, begging him with every fiber of my being to be okay.

And then the gurney began to move and he was spirited away into the bowels of the hospital without me.

Chapter Thirty-Five

Kim and Kurt arrived just after midnight. My parents offered to sit in the car with the sleeping Wesley while they came inside.

Tears flowed silently down my cheeks when I saw Kim come around the corner to find me.

"What's happening?"

"Oh, Kim, he's in so much pain…. They're running tests right now. They won't let me stay with him because my blood pressure spikes when I am. Dr. Steele told me he'd talk to me as soon as he knew something, but he's never come back." I clutched at her hand. "What if Chase dies?"

"Surely it isn't that serious, Whitney." But a flicker of fear crossed her features. "Is it?"

Kim reached for my hands as I wrung them over the plumpest part of my belly. "Your parents said that Chase was fine, and then all of a sudden he was in the other room, writhing on the bed. Has he complained about not feeling well?"

"Nothing I can think of…" Then my mind began to replay all the recent times when Chase had slept too long or refused to eat.

"He's been so attentive to me, and I've been so wrapped up in this pregnancy, that I didn't take notice." I told Kim about the times I'd found him on the couch warm and feverish. "But he always said he was fine…"

"So this isn't the first time he's been ill?"

Tears welled in my eyes. "If I'd been a decent wife, I would have paid more attention—"

"Stop that." Kim splashed figurative cold water on my distraught emotions. "You're pregnant, growing an entirely new person in there." She pointed to my rotund middle. "And your husband is a doctor. If anyone should have noticed he was sick, it was Chase."

Physician, heal yourself. That advice hadn't worked in this case.

Kurt came in to say that Wesley and my father were sawing logs in the car and my mother had taken them home to put them to bed. I nodded dumbly, already having convinced myself that I would spend the rest of my life sitting in a miserable plastic chair with arms so snug that they held my belly in place like a bad girdle.

Then Dr. Steele strode through a pair of double doors and headed for me.

"Whitney, we're taking Chase into surgery. His appendix has burst."

"Appendicitis?" I echoed stupidly. "But he's never said anything…"

"From the examination and what he's told me, I think he's been suffering from chronic appendicitis."

"'Chronic?' You mean he's had it a long time?"

"Some patients have an atypical clinical course of re-current inflammation in the appendix, something you may have heard referred to as a 'grumbling appendix.' The symptoms vary from patient to patient. It flares and settles down again, so there aren't specific clinical characteristics that might aid in a diagnosis. I under-stand why Chase didn't realize what it was. His episodes resolved spontaneously in a day or two.

"We don't see chronic appendicitis often. As far as I can tell, he's been diagnosing himself with indigestion or possible gallstones. Since it was chronic, it actually could have been either."

"Or Couvades syndrome?" Kim murmured.

Dr. Steele looked at my stomach and smiled faintly. "I suppose that's a possibility, too. Doctors are some-times the worst patients. They pay more attention to their patients than they do to themselves."

He should have told me!

If I weren't so frightened, I'd be furious with him for not telling me he'd felt ill. Now, I thought illogically, I'll have to wait until he gets well to be angry with him.

If he gets well.

"Could he have done something sooner?"

Dr. Steele's eyes darkened. "It would have been better if treatment hadn't been delayed." He looked at me with compassion that made me want to cry. "I'm sorry I don't have better news for you." He glanced at the clock. "I'd better go."

He looked me in the eye. "I need to be straight with you, Whitney, he's a very sick man. I don't know how long surgery will last, and you are in no condition to sit in a hospital waiting room all night. The nurse I sent out to take your blood pressure says your ankles are swelling."

I looked down at my feet in surprise. They were thick and looked like lumps of blistered skin. I hadn't even noticed.

"I'm not leaving my husband." *I'll stay here until I pop, if necessary.*

Dr. Steele sighed. "I thought you might say that. There are a few rooms available for those of us on call to use to get some shut-eye. Chase will never forgive me if I leave you sitting in a chair all night." He faced Kim. "Will you be staying?"

"As long as necessary."

"Okay. I'll have a nurse show you where to go."

"I'm not leaving Chase."

"You won't be. There's a phone in the room. I'll have someone call or stop by to tell you how the surgery is progressing. You won't be any farther away from him there than you would be sitting here. You need to put your feet up." His voice grew stern. "No argument. I'm not afraid of you, young lady, but I do *not* want to have to answer to Chase as to why I didn't take care of his wife."

He waved, and a nurse hurried over. He gave her instructions before turning back to Kim and me. "I've got to get into surgery. Ms. Benson will show you where to go. Whitney, feet up. Hear me?"

I nodded weakly, feeling like a child banished from the festivities. "But Chase…"

"We'll do everything we can for him. He's in good hands." And he turned and was gone.

Good hands. Everything we can for him. That wasn't

what I wanted to hear. I wanted Dr. Steele to say, "He'll be fine. Everything will work out."

But he hadn't. No guarantees.

The sleeping room was as cramped as the waiting room, but it had two beds, a recliner, a telephone and a small television set. I promptly lay down on the bed to get some relief for my aching back and realized how tired I really was. My bones ached. My skin ached. My aches ached.

Kim covered me with a blanket and brought me an extra pillow to shove under my abdomen so that I could rest on my side.

"Sleep if you can. I'll be awake to talk to the nurse or pick up the phone."

"How can I sleep with Chase in the operating room? He might be—" I stopped, unwilling to say aloud what I was thinking.

"I know you're scared, Whit, but you've got to pull yourself together. This baby…"

"Kim, Chase has been bugging me for weeks to get our wills written."

That got her attention.

"He's been absolutely obsessive about it. I dragged my feet, but he got it done in spite of me. He said it was 'just good sense' to plan ahead. Maybe he knew something I didn't. Perhaps he had a premonition…"

I tried to rise, but Kim pushed me back onto the bed.

"He's a sensible, responsible man getting ready to become a first-time father. Kurt did the same thing before Wesley was born. I told him to quit fretting about actuarial tables and life expectancies, because it upset me. When it was finally done, though, he settled down. Chase is like Kurt. He wants to take care of his family."

Tears leaked down my cheeks. Why hadn't I been more in tune with him? Guilt reared its ugly head and moved into my head and heart, taking up residence right next to my fear.

"What am I going to do, Kim?"

"Trust the doctors, for one thing. And trust God, for another."

Kim picked up her large shoulder bag and pulled a Bible out of its depths. "I make it a policy never to go to the hospital without one of these."

I felt an unfamiliar bleakness overtaking both hope and faith, a terrifying, empty resignation as to what the next few hours would bring.

Where are You, God?

"I read Jeremiah a lot after my surgery," Kim continued. "'Oh, Lord, You alone can heal me, You alone can save. My praises are for You alone!'

"I find it comforting to think that the One we depend on to save us from our sins is the same One who can heal us. If I'm counting on the Lord to get me to heaven, then I can certainly count on Him for everything else, right?"

Some of the knots binding my heart loosened a little.

I will give you back your health and heal your wounds, says the Lord.

"Make it so for Chase, make it so."

The minutes passed like hours.

It was worse, I decided, to lie down than it was to stand and pace. I walked the length of the small room dozens of times before Kim sent me out into the hall, where I could stride out, instead of suffering more mincing footsteps in the crowded room.

Finally, when my legs throbbed, I sat down in the

battered Lay-Z-Boy and ratcheted my feet up to keep them from swelling even further.

"Let me help you." Kim bent to pull off my shoes.

"Wait. My feet are too swollen. If you take them off now, I'll never get them back on."

"You can wear my shoes. My feet are bigger than yours."

"Then what about you?"

"I'll have your mother bring more from home. I talked to her on the phone while you were in the hall. Everything is fine there. She wanted to come back to the hospital, but I told her to wait until later. Chase is going to be here a few days, so we need to spread out our man—and woman—power so someone is here all the time."

My head snapped up. "Do you think he's so ill that we don't dare leave?"

"No. I think *you* are so stubborn that you won't leave the hospital, and someone has to be here to watch you."

"What's going on in there, Kim? It's been hours."

"No, it hasn't. It just seems like hours. Why don't you try to sleep? I'll wake you if anyone comes by."

"Would you be able to sleep if it were Kurt in the operating room?"

"Of course not." She smiled faintly. "But I thought the suggestion was worth a try."

We visited the vending machines, read large-print *Reader's Digest*s and played twenty questions. Still no word.

Kim rubbed my back, massaged my feet and helped me clean my purse. No word.

"Where is Dr. Steele?" I wailed. "He said he'd be back—"

At that moment, there was a knock on the door and a young nurse entered.

"Chase?" I rocked forward to rise from the chair.

"Dr. Steele called to say that they are still in surgery. He'll be out when he can."

I grabbed the woman by the front of her jacket. "That's all?"

"I'm sorry, Mrs. Andrews, that's what he said, nothing more."

Kim pried me off her and nudged me toward the bed. "Lie down, Whitney. You're going crazy. You've got to get some rest. When Chase does come out of surgery, you don't want to be the one going in. You've got to take care of yourself, for him and for the baby."

"What if he dies in there, Kim? It's taking too long, and you know it."

"Don't jump to conclusions."

"I can't believe Chase did this!" An unexpected avalanche of anger swept down on me. "He *knows* how important he is to me and how much I need him. How dare he…"

There I was, building up a head of fury toward a man lying on an operating table. Fear and logic do not cohabitate.

I glanced frantically around the room, looking for something to distract me. If I started to cry now, I doubted I could stop. I would weep until even my poor baby's watery home went dry. My gaze fell on a calendar with a photo of a majestic bald eagle soaring across a bright blue sky. The bird's wingspan was enormous, and his eyes were bright, sharp as pinpricks as he dominated the sky. All strength and wild beauty, the eagle soared effortlessly above the earth.

As I stared at him, so magnificent and strong, I recalled a verse from Psalms. *He will shield you with His wings. He will shelter you with His feathers. His faithful promises are your armor and protection. Do not be afraid of the terrors of the night, nor for the dangers of the day, nor dread the plague that stalks in darkness, nor the disaster that strikes at midday.*

In other words, "Don't worry, Whitney, I've got it covered."

Chapter Thirty-Six

I finally slept, and when I opened my eyes I saw Dr. Steele's imposing frame in the doorway.

"Chase…" I struggled out of bed, wondering why, just when my body was most disobliging and otherwise engaged, I needed it most to cooperate.

"He's out of surgery and in intensive care, Whitney. You won't be able to see him quite yet."

"But he's alive?"

Something flickered in Steele's eyes, but he said calmly, "Yes."

"What can you tell us?" Kim, fortunately, was as clearheaded as I was fuzzy.

"Frankly, it was a messy business. Secondary peritonitis. This occurs when there's a spillage of bacteria into the peritoneum. Now that we've removed the source of the infection and identified the microorganism, we can treat him with the proper medication."

"Peritonitis? That's very serious, isn't it?"

"It is potentially life threatening, but Chase is on

antibiotics to control the infection. We've begun an IV to restore hydration and have him on morphine to reduce the pain."

The room began to swim, and I felt myself spiraling downward in an eddy of panic. Dr. Steele caught me when my knees buckled.

"I'll get a nurse." But before he could pull away, I grabbed his arm.

"I'm okay. Just the shock…" I fixed my eyes on his, and it was excruciating to see my own concern mirrored there. "What are his chances?"

"He's a strong man, Whitney. His immune system is not compromised. He's athletic, has a good heart and is a nonsmoker. All that is in his favor."

"That doesn't answer my question."

Dr. Steele sighed and pulled the one straight-backed chair in the room toward me. He straddled it and rested his arms on its back to face me.

"Chase would want me to be honest with you. I know how much he loves you, and how he admires your strength and courage, so I'll be blunt. I can't give you a prognosis right now. Given a little time, we'll be able to see how he responds. I'm hoping that we get the infection under control and that the worst will be past."

"And if not?" I had to ask the hard questions.

Dr. Steele considered a moment before speaking. "There are several complications that can arise. We haven't seen any of them yet, and may not, but I think Chase would want you to know what we're facing."

Because I'm courageous, right? As courageous as the Cowardly Lion on the way to Oz.

"The first danger is sepsis. It's the body's response

to infection going into overdrive, and causes a cascade of events that lead to widespread inflammation."

"And if it does?" I noticed that behind the doctor, Kim had sunk onto the second bed and was ghastly pale.

"It can cause multiple organ failure. Of course, I'm not saying that's going to happen...."

"But it could?"

Do not fear the terrors of the night nor fear the dangers of the day.

"If there is considerable spread of the infection, we may also see abnormal blood clotting," Dr. Steele said doggedly, "or lung infection."

"His lungs?" Kim blurted. "But I thought he had appendicitis."

"Respiratory distress syndrome. The infection can travel through the entire body."

"But you've got him on medication," she said.

"We are counting on that to work."

"Why wouldn't it?" The baby in my womb was cartwheeling with anxiety, a mirror image of my own distress.

"Listen, Whitney, you don't need to—"

"I do *need.* I *need* to know what I'm facing. I *need* to know my husband's condition. I *need* to know what to expect. This is my life, too, you know."

Don't leave me, Chase.

"Some forms of peritonitis don't respond well to treatment," Dr. Steele said resignedly. "But like I said—"

"You said you don't know."

"I've given you a worst-case scenario, Whitney. We're doing everything in our power not to let it get that far."

"You aren't making any promises, though, are you?"

He shook his head. "You know as well as I do that medicine doesn't always lend itself to promises."

Saturday, December 25, Christmas Day

Christmas Day. Instead of embodying hope and joy, it felt draped with hopelessness and despair. The jolly Christmas music playing on the small radio in my room irritated my jangling nerves. Finally I smothered the sounds with a pillow and Kim hurried to wrench the plug from the wall.

I had dozed off and on during the night, and dreamed there was a battle going on, a tug-of-war with Chase as a human rope. Two figures, one light and one dark, alternately yanked and tugged at him until I thought he would rip in half. When I couldn't bear to watch this hideous game any longer, I moved toward him, but no matter how far or fast I ran, I couldn't reach him. Then the dark figure wrenched Chase from the light figure's grasp, and they tumbled together into a dark chasm and disappeared from sight as if Chase were a star being drawn into a black hole.

I woke up screaming, frightening both Kim and myself, and this morning I rose with a sense of an empty darkness within me the likes of which I've never before experienced.

I have no peace.

There's a growing void within me, like a gaping, cavernous maw. It was the dream that started it. Chase being pulled toward life and toward death, God and Satan, good and evil. In the dream, Chase disappeared into the darkness.

The empty space within me is where God had resided. *Had* resided. *Past tense.* I lay on the bed, taking inventory of my body and feelings. Then I prayed. But my prayers seemed to dissipate into thin air, as if I'd spoken but no one was there to listen.

"Kim?" I sat up.

"I'm here. Did you have another bad dream?"

"I can't find him."

"Who?"

"God. I feel nothing. He's not here."

She looked at me as if I'd lost my mind.

I told her about the dream and how, when the dark figure wrenched Chase away from the light, something had been wrenched from me, as well. "I can't feel Him, Kim."

"You're just overtired and emotionally exhausted. God didn't go anywhere. He promised, remember? Besides, you don't have to 'feel' Him in order for Him to be present." Then the verse about God always being with us rolled off her tongue.

I stared at her in a kind of disbelieving haze. That's it? That's all? A handy verse that's supposed to fill the void in my heart? It's like saying, "Sure God is here, now snap out of it."

A hot wave of shame passed over me as I recalled the times I'd come up with pat, easy answers for people who were hurting.

"Turn it over to God," I'd say. "He's there for you."

"Keep praying."

"Look toward Him."

"He cares."

The words had rolled so easily from my lips, I

realized, because it was not me who was in pain, who was desperate or afraid.

But now it *is* me.

"Oh, these Christians," I once heard someone say. "They have an answer for everything, and it's always God."

I squeezed my eyes shut and sent a volley of desperate prayers heavenward, but I might as well have been talking to the wall.

Where are You, Lord?

"Whitney, are you okay? You look like you just lost your best friend. Of course you didn't, because that would be me." Kim handed me a cup of coffee in a foam cup from the cafeteria.

My earthly best friend, yes. It was the heavenly one who had vanished.

Had I made God the easy answer to everyone's troubles, including my own? Or had I begun to take Him for granted, assuming He would pop up like a jack-in-the-box whenever I called for Him?

Or maybe He doesn't exist, and never did.

If a spiritual abyss exists, I am in it.

Kim couldn't understand what was happening to me, and I didn't know how to tell her. What would I say? "My husband is dying and God ran out on me, and I'm not sure He ever really existed at all. Bummer, huh?"

I stared out the window at the bleak grayness of the day. Even the sky was mourning.

The news from intensive care had been choppy at best. *The antibiotics seem to be taking hold. No, you can't see him yet. Chase is resting. We'll let you know if something changes.*

I felt so distant from everyone around me, as if my baby and I were in a bubble, orbiting alone in another dimension, locked away from everything, thinking only of what was happening in the intensive care unit.

Kurt had gone home to care for Wesley, and my parents had returned to the hospital. Kim diligently ran for food I didn't eat and coffee I couldn't drink. She refused to leave my side. Helplessness was written on their faces, and I was powerless to ease their pain. I felt like apologizing for being so much trouble, but knew it would only insult them. I felt so useless.

There's peace in exhaustion, I discovered. Sooner or later, it forces one to cave in to its seductive snare. I didn't so much sleep as pass out from exhaustion.

I awoke about noon, with a start that produced a chain of reactions in the room. My mother jumped to her feet to peer down at me. Kim hurried to my side.

"Whit? Are you feeling better?"

"Have you heard anything about Chase?"

"Dr. Steele called to say that when you woke up, you could go into Chase's room for five minutes."

I scrabbled to a sitting position. "Why didn't you wake me right away?"

"We thought you needed the rest."

"What if he'd died? What if I hadn't been there? Anything could happen…." I'm not an angry person, but an unexpected fury blew so hot in me that it could have incinerated me. "Don't *ever* make a decision like that for me again!"

Kim and my mother exchanged glances, but said nothing.

"I'm sorry," I raked my fingers through my hair. "I'm just so frightened…."

"It's okay, Whit. Really. Comb your hair, and we'll take you down to ICU."

I rose and lumbered to the sink.

The face that looked back at me from the mirror was haggard and drawn. If I'd had the energy, I might have cackled, just to see if a broomstick would appear. "I can't let Chase see me like this. I'll scare him to death…." Not funny.

Kim held out a washcloth. "Wash your face. I've got lipstick in my purse. You're fine. We'll go when you're ready."

Outside the door to our room sat a wheelchair. My mother took the handles and said, "Sit. I'm driving."

"Are you kidding? I don't need a wheelchair. I can walk on my own two feet—" Unfortunately, my knees chose that moment to buckle and make a liar out of me. "Okay, I'll ride, but just this once."

The intensive care unit is a remarkably noisy place, considering that everyone there is terribly ill. Monitors beep, nurses converse, people move about. How is anyone supposed to heal in such chaos? But when I reached Chase's room, I realized that although the clatter and busyness might bother me, he was oblivious to it. And to everything else.

It seemed like weeks instead of hours since I'd seen him. The golden tones of his skin were ashen now, and he, who always slept with a soft smile on his face, looked bleak even in repose. There were wires and hoses I couldn't identify, although I recognized the cardiac monitor, the IV stands and the blood pressure monitor. An oxygen tube ran into his nostrils.

Kim pushed me closer to the bed. "I'll be outside."

I put my hand out to touch his arm. His skin was warm to my touch. I ran my fingers along the soft golden hair on his forearm and ached at the thought that he didn't even know me.

Then the cardiac monitor noted a slight increase in his pulse rate. Somehow he had sensed it was me.

"Chase, it's Whitney." I struggled to keep my voice natural and light and hoped against hope that he could hear me. "You've given me a bad scare, and I want you to stop it. You've got to snap out of this now. We still have things to do to get ready for the baby. You haven't even put the crib together yet.

"It's not many weeks away now, so you'll have to re-cuperate fast. I need you to take care of me, you know, not the other way around. I've heard giving birth isn't all that fun, sort of like trying to pass a basketball through a... Well, you get my drift. Not that I'll have any stories that will trump yours..."

I kept talking softly until Kim returned to tap me on the shoulder. "Five minutes are up, honey."

I turned back to Chase. "I'll be back later, darling. I love you so very, very much."

And before I could say more, Kim took the handles of the chair and pulled me out of the room.

"Oh, Kim, he looks awful!" I blurted as soon as the doors to ICU closed behind us.

"But he heard you. I'm sure he did. He knows you're there for him. If prayer and a cheering section can make a difference, then he'll be well in no time at all."

Prayer and a cheering section. I'm glad someone's praying, because right now, with this barrenness within me, I don't know how to get God's ear.

Lord, if I'm the one who moved and not You, then help me find my way back.

I touched the necklace Chase had given me only hours before, felt the smoothness of the diamonds and recalled the engraving on the back. Past-Present-Future.

Did Chase and I even have a future?

Chapter Thirty-Seven

Speaking of cheering sections, mine was waiting for me in the hall outside the ICU waiting room. A pitiful group, as cheerleaders go, but beautiful to my eyes.

Kurt had returned, and with him he'd brought Mitzi and Arch; Bryan, looking pale as a ghost, but stoic; Betty, who still had one pink sponge roller in her hair that she'd forgotten to remove; and Harry and his wife, who were holding hands and looking nearly as bewildered as I felt. That, as it was now nearing midnight, Kurt had awoken them all from sound sleep was apparent from their state of dishevelment.

Even Mitzi wasn't perfect. She was wearing one pink high-heeled slipper trimmed in marabou and another just like it in blue. She's gained at least sixty pounds in the past few months, and carries it all out front, like a misplaced hump on a camel.

Harry was the first to break out of the pack.

"Listen, kid, I'm so sorry to hear about Chase. We got here as soon as we could. Is there anything we can do?"

I answered the only way I could. I burst into tears and blubbered all over Harry's shirt.

He patted me ineffectually on the back and did some kind of clucking sound in his throat that was meant to soothe me. It was so sweet and he was trying so hard to help that it only made me cry harder. Betty handed me tissue after tissue from a box on the table. They felt like sandpaper against my skin. Bryan, looking olive-green around the gills in the poor hospital lighting, gave me a weak thumbs-up.

They gathered close to put their arms around me and each other, and together we shuffled like some multi-headed creature from the hall into the waiting room. There was a blessing in their nearness, their touch.

After some moments, our hydralike clump broke apart, leaving only Mitzi clinging to me. It is not easy for two women expecting four babies and each less than six weeks from delivery to hug at all, but we managed. I felt someone kick me in the side and wasn't sure if it was my baby or one of Mitzi's.

Then Mitzi attempted to reassure me, Mitzi-style.

"I'd be scared spitless if I were you." She reduced my emotions into one concise statement. "Dry-as-a-bone spitless."

"I am, Mitzi. Believe me, I am." Too much of Mitzi's comforting is a dangerous thing.

"Well, at least you've got something going for you." She snapped the gum in her mouth.

"I do?" I couldn't think of a thing that was going my way.

"God, of course. You're always talking to Him. He has influence. Ask Him to do something about this."

The smile I gave her was tremulous. "About that…"

"What?" She squinted at me suspiciously.

"I don't feel Him here, Mitzi, and I don't know where He's gone. I've tried to pray, but…" I felt the desperation building in my voice. "I haven't been able to find Him."

Mitzi put her hands on her newly ample hips. "You misplaced *God?*" Her expression was incredulous. "*Not* a good idea, Whitney. Especially now." She gave me a disgusted glare. "And you are usually so organized, too!"

Somehow, the idea of my having the power to misplace God, as if He was a hairbrush or a set of car keys, struck me as funny. Had I squeezed my heavenly Father into a box so small that I could forget where I put Him? And here stood Mitzi to remind me that God isn't easy to lose.

I am with you always.

Who am I to think that just because *I* don't feel Him, He's gone? That's pretty egotistical on my part.

Through my tears, I started to sputter with laughter.

Everyone in the waiting room stared at me as though they were watching me crack and slide, bit by bit, into the pit of insanity.

Only Mitzi understood what was going on. She patted me on the back. "There, there," she assured me. "You'll feel much better when you get over yourself."

Now that's the pot calling the kettle black, but she's right. God is like the sun on a cloudy day. No matter how it might look from my vantage point, He's always there. The clouds may get in the way so I can't see the light of the sun, but that doesn't mean it isn't there, right where it always is, shining, dependable, sure.

God's here. I didn't misplace Him. I don't have that kind of clout.

Instead, I had allowed storms and clouds to block my vision, and told myself that because I couldn't see Him, He wasn't there. He's proven Himself to me over and over, and yet, in the darkness, I can't remember His light.

If I need to see God to believe in Him, I don't have much faith. If I believe in Him without demanding that I see Him first, that's real faith. I have come to a fork in the road, and I have to decide. I choose faith.

Lord, faith is believing without seeing. I choose, by faith, to believe in You.

A weight lifted from my shoulders.

"That's better." Mitzi mopped at my face with one of those dreadful tissues. She peered curiously into my eyes. "Did you find Him again?"

"You know, Mitzi, I believe I did, thanks to you."

She looked pleased and surprised. "No kidding? *Me?*"

I was tempted to remind her that this was not something she should put on her résumé, but held my tongue.

"So God used *me?*" She was rolling something around in her mind—what, I would never attempt to predict.

"Yes, He just might have." I took her hand. "You reminded me that He's not easy to misplace. He's huge, immovable, immutable and God."

Mitzi looked impressed. "I did all that?"

"God did it through you."

She looked down at her huge stomach. "He's working a lot of things in me lately, isn't He?"

"I'd say so." Where was she going with this?

"Very cool. I've been thinking. Now that I'm going

to be a mother, I should probably get to know Him a little better."

I was suddenly breathless. Here, in the most terrifying, horrifying moments of my life, with my husband near death, was a prayer being answered. "I…I think it's a wonderful idea, Mitzi."

She wrinkled her brow, deep in thought. "Yeah, I think so, too. You'll have to give me the details. I always thought there was some kind of big holy club you guys belonged to, and there were membership rules, but it's not like that, is it?"

"We're all welcome to join His club."

"It will be easier now, too." Mitzi looked very pleased at the thought. "Now that He's already used me to get to you. Now I know He wants me. I'm like everyone else, you know. I like to be where I'm wanted."

Just like the rest of us.

Everyone was still staring at us, two elephantine mamas in the center of the room, when Dr. Steele walked in. All eyes went to him. Fatigue marked every line of his body.

Then he smiled. A faint, weary smile, but a smile, nonetheless.

"Things aren't spiraling downward out of control anymore, Whitney. I think we'll be able to stabilize him. He's not out of the woods, but if the antibiotics take hold, he's got a chance." He looked at me and then at Mitzi, two pregnant pachyderms desperately clinging to one another. "*Now* I want you to go home and go to bed, Whitney. There's nothing you can do here."

"I won't leave my husband—"

"Then go to bed here, but get off your feet. *Doctor's orders.*"

* * *

I awoke sometime during the night to the smell of leftover turkey and dressing. Kim was holding a plate of food under my nose.

"Chase?"

"No worse, maybe a hair better."

I ate the food Kim put in front of me, drank two large glasses of milk and went back to sleep.

Sunday, December 26

This time I awoke to sausage and French toast.

"What time is it?"

"About one o'clock in the afternoon. I would have brought you lunch, but I thought you might like breakfast first."

"How is that possible? I couldn't have slept that long."

"But you did. Dr. Steele is delighted, I might add. Both you and Chase rested well."

"How could I sleep without even getting up to check on Chase? How is he? I've got to get to him…."

"The nurse will come when it's time for you to see him. It's pretty busy in his room most of the time."

My heart sank. "Is he worse?"

"No, praise God, he's not."

"Better then?"

"Dr. Steele said something about his white count going in the right direction. That's all I know."

Finally, the tide has turned.

Sunday, December 27

Mr. Tibble here,

My pet Whitney has not been home to see me in days. Scram thinks she's abandoned us. He, however, is prone to panic attacks. I can't count on his opinion about anything important.

Fortunately, others have been by to feed us. My favorite is the one Whitney calls "Dad." He opened three cans of food for us this afternoon. That little glutton Scram ate until his stomach dragged on the ground, and then fell asleep on the floor in the sun. He is so uncouth that it is embarrassing. I, on the other hand, am very couth. I have to provide all the class for this joint.

I miss Whitney—the way she scratches behind my ears and at the base of my tail, the silly way she wraps me up in a blanket and dances me around the house, how she talks to me and tells me her troubles. I'm a very good listener. Everything she says to me, I keep completely confidential. I wish she'd come back. I'd listen to her for hours. I hate to admit it, and I would never tell another living soul, but I'm lonesome.

Mr. Tibble, signing off.

Chapter Thirty-Eight

Thursday, December 30

Weeping may linger for the night, but joy comes in the morning.

I've been hanging on to that verse like a shipwrecked sailor to a plank in the ocean.

Day and night are meaningless here, in the artificially lighted hallways, and the cafeteria deep in the basement of the hospital and behind the curtained windows of Chase's room. Dr. Steele made arrangements for me to continue to sleep in the windowless but adequate room I've been in since Chase came into the hospital five days ago.

Five long, terrifying, endless days.

I'm only able to see Chase sporadically. He sleeps a lot, and visits to ICU are limited. Most of what I've done is wait and pray.

God and I have been discussing my shameful lack of faith at the height of Chase's crisis. It is stunning to me how quickly the solid roots of my faith were undermined by doubt and fear. I've learned that God is a lot more willing to forgive me than I am to forgive myself.

The baby and I have gotten to know each other well during these hours spent together with no other distractions. I know what time it gets restless and begins to roll like a log in a lumberjack competition. I feel it stretch, and can occasionally see a little hand or foot pressing under my skin. It likes to be up at night when I'm trying to sleep and to sleep during the day when I'm awake, an omen of sleeping patterns to come. Baby reads me like a book and mirrors my emotions with remarkable accuracy. When I'm agitated, we're both agitated. When I'm composed, the baby is calm.

And I'm most calm when I'm at Chase's side.

"Hey, darling, it's Whitney and company, here to visit." I approached Chase's bed cautiously, avoiding the machines and wires that are everywhere, looping around stands and tables and over the head of his bed.

He opened his eyes, and a faint smile tipped the corners of his lips. "Hey," he murmured, and weakly lifted his hand. That's my signal to move closer, so that he can put his hand on my ever-enlarging stomach. The baby, smart already, seems to know when and where to kick—right beneath Chase's outstretched palm. Chase smiled and closed his eyes again.

He's terribly weak, and sleeps most of the day, but he's alive. That's all that matters.

Dr. Steele walked into the room studying Chase's chart. It has grown uncomfortably thick in the past week.

"Hi, Whitney. Glad you're here. You are better medicine for this guy than anything I have to give him."

I looked at the tangle of wires and monitors. "You have some pretty powerful remedies. Are you sure?"

Steele smiled at me. "For this part of the recovery, yes."

When he was done examining Chase, Dr. Steele beckoned me out into the hall.

"How do you think he's doing, Whitney?"

"He still scares me. He's weak as a kitten." Scram could take him on—and win.

"It's to be expected." The doctor looked at me appraisingly. "We almost lost him, you know."

I shivered, and the baby grew restless within me. I know that all too well.

"It will be a slow recovery process. I expect to move him out of intensive care soon, but he's going to be in the hospital for a while yet."

"Whatever it takes. I'm getting rather used to the food and lodging here myself. You really need to do something about the coffee in the waiting rooms, though. Talk about toxic waste."

"Yes, well—" Dr. Steele frowned "—that's something else I want to talk to you about. You are in the countdown to your own delivery. When's your baby due? Early February?"

"I feel as if I've been pregnant so long that it's a permanent condition."

"You've been under a lot of stress. I've worried more than once this week that we'd have Chase in ICU and you in the delivery room. I don't want you staying here at the hospital 24/7 anymore. It's too hard on you."

"It's harder on me to be apart from Chase."

"That was true this past week, but now it's time we start taking care of you."

"I don't want better care. I'm fine. I just want to be with Chase."

"You can be with him during the day, but no more staying here at night. You need a break from the hospital and a bed with a mattress that feels like it's been stuffed with coconuts."

I couldn't help but smile. "So you've used that bed a time or two yourself."

"I mean it, Whitney. Visit Chase, but rest at home."

"But—"

"Not 'buts' about it. I'll tell Chase it's my decision, and he, at least, will thank me for it." Dr. Steele glanced at his wristwatch. "Now I'd better get going. Call me the bad guy if you must, but sleep in your own bed tonight."

When I returned to Chase's room, the head of his bed was rolled up and a nurse was trying to cajole him into drinking some juice. He's lost almost fifteen pounds in the past few days, but it only makes his features more sculpted. After an ordeal like his, I'd look like a ship-wreck, and yet he's more handsome than ever. Is there no justice? Apparently not.

"Do you want me to take over?" I offered.

As I held the juice glass to his lips, Chase studied me. "What's wrong?" His blue eyes sliced through me like an X-ray.

"I see the illness didn't damage your perceptiveness," I said grumpily. "Dr. Steele told me I shouldn't stay at the hospital twenty-four hours a day anymore. I want to be near you at night, but…"

"Good." His voice was soft but firm.

"*Et tu, Brute?* Are you all ganging up on me?"

Because of the weakness in his voice, I had to lean

close to Chase to hear him. "Whit, I don't want you to deliver early. That's what Steele is worried about. Take care of yourself, will you?"

Returning home after so many days away was a strange experience. Although Mom and Dad had taken down the Christmas tree, cleaned the refrigerator and put fresh sheets on the bed, when I walked in the door the first thing I saw in my mind's eye was Chase, lying on the bed, writhing in agony.

Thankfully, Kim followed me into the house to put my things on the kitchen table. She opened the refrigerator to peer inside. "Mitzi and I went grocery shopping so you wouldn't come home to empty cupboards. Want a soda, or some carrot sticks?"

"What? No chocolate? Is Mitzi sick?"

"I think she's healthy as ever. Come and look."

Inside my refrigerator was a chocolate cheesecake drizzled with fudge and a large jar of chocolate ice-cream topping.

"I hope she isn't eating as much chocolate as she was earlier," Kim said bluntly. "Now Mitzi could stand to lose a few pounds."

Last time she'd come to the hospital, my father had escorted her in and out, afraid that if he didn't, she'd roll down the steps like a beach ball. Mitzi, of course, didn't worry at all. She says she's been doing double duty at the mall to build her strength.

Mr. Tibble here.

Oh, rapturous joy! Oh, wonderful delight! My heart leaps with gladness. I am the lion in the Serengeti, the King of Beasts. My belly is full of wondrous sweet meat and my place in the household has been restored. Never again will I take my gifts for granted or disdain their origins. I roll in the silky depths of my luxurious retreat, the bed of my repose. I stretch my body to its full capacity and relish in the perfect workings of my bones. I will dine on caviar and be showered with rose petals. Even my underling will benefit from my munificent spirit. I dance on the air, leaping from mountain peak to mountain peak in an elegant ballet. My body, like my spirit, soars. I am whole again, no longer ripped asunder from the most tender, most vulnerable part of my being. My heart sings. I croon love songs night and day. I am replenished. I am loved. All is well, all is well. Mr. Tibble, signing off.

P.S. My pet is home. She has fed me all my favorite treats and scratched my belly as we lay together on her bed. She has not even scolded me for jumping on her furniture or serenading her in the night. I didn't realize how much I would miss her. I am happy again, but I must never let her know how much I care. Aloofness, independence and disdain, that's my game. I think I will see if she will scratch my tummy just a little more, however, before I start ignoring her.

Chapter Thirty-Nine

All Mitzi's worrying about what she'd wear for New Year's Eve turned out to be wasted energy. Instead of throwing a party, she was the centerpiece at one.

"I don't want you to stay here tonight," Chase said. "That's no way to start the New Year. Go out and have some fun. You are invited to Mitzi and Arch's place, aren't you?"

"Mitzi wasn't at work Thursday or Friday. Maybe it's all off. Besides, I want to be with you. Last week I almost lost you—" The words stuck in my throat.

He took my hand in his. "All the more reason to go out and have some fun." His lopsided grin was reassuring. The old Chase is coming back.

"I don't want to leave you, even for a minute. They are too precious to waste."

"Then don't waste them by watching me sleep. Go with Kim and Kurt to Mitzi's, and tell me about it in the morning." He tipped his head. "It would make me happy, Whitney. Go. Please?" He passed his hands over his eyes. "I'm tired, honey. Let me sleep. Go have some fun."

"I'll go, but under protest."

He nodded, and I noticed his eyes were already drooping.

"And I refuse to have fun without you. So there."

Perhaps I wouldn't have fun even if I'd wanted to, I realized, when Arch met Kim, Kurt and me at the door to explain what had happened.

Harry and everyone else from the office were already standing in the foyer Mitzi had decorated with Sherwood Forest. There were more evergreen trees in her foyer than in a three-block radius from the house. Each was decorated in sparkly white snow, crystal icicles and iridescent snowflake ornaments. Rotating lights turned the trees from green to red to yellow to blue, much like the lighting on those retro aluminum trees that all my loft-living friends are crazy over. Amazing. A Christmas disco, right in Mitzi's entry.

"She went to the doctor today," Arch said apologetically, "and he said that she has to be on bed rest until the babies arrive. She told him she'd go to bed tomorrow, after New Year's Eve, but he wouldn't hear of it. She's upstairs right now…."

"It's fine, Arch," Harry said. "Don't worry about it. Those babies are more important than a New Year's Eve party."

"No, that's not it. Mitzi still wants to go on with the party."

"Nonsense," Harry blustered. "We'll go out. There

must be somewhere that isn't completely booked this evening. We'll find a place…."

Right. Maybe at Krispy Kreme or White Castle. They don't usually fill up on New Year's Eve.

"But the food is here, and she hired a harpist."

A *harpist?* Leave it to Mitzi.

"But how can you manage a party with Mitzi in bed?" Betty blurted.

"I've moved things upstairs. We'll have the party in our bedroom."

Fortunately, Mitzi's bedroom is not like my bedroom, which is nicely full with a bed, two nightstands, a chest of drawers and a chair. Mitzi's bedroom is a stadium, and she's head cheerleader.

Arch led us upstairs, where the lilting sounds of "Oh, Tannenbaum" hung in the air. For this occasion, their bedroom's double doors had been flung wide to reveal the vast space—the size of some apartments—and the pièce de résistance, Mitzi, sitting in the middle of a king-size bed, propped up with pillows and wearing a red velvet maternity dress that, with stakes and supports, would have made a lovely tent. Even Mitzi, with her designs for mothers of multiples, has been taxed creatively trying to figure out ways to look lovely with an eighty-five-inch waist.

"Welcome, welcome! Happy New Year!" She greeted us from the bed, "I'm so glad you could come. Appetizers, anyone?"

And for the rest of the evening, we almost forgot that we were partying in someone's bedroom, with a bed-bound hostess who insisted on bossing everyone around, pointing and giving directions by waving a paste-jewel-bedecked wand left over from a Halloween party she'd once attended as Glinda, Good Witch of the North.

"Your hair looks great," I commented as I sat at the foot of Mitzi's bed and ate antipasto, jumbo shrimp and chocolate-dipped strawberries.

"I had it done before I went to the doctor." She scowled. "I can't believe he sent me to bed. I feel fine."

"Maybe he doesn't want you to hurry the babies along. All the weight can't be easy on your legs, either."

"My legs are fabulous," Mitzi retorted testily. "At least they were the last time I saw them." She sighed. "I miss my feet. I haven't seen them in so long that, once the babies are born, I'm afraid I might not recognize them."

"This motherhood thing is tougher than it looks, isn't it?"

"At least I don't have to worry about Arch's health. How's Chase?"

"Better. Dr. Steele warned us it would take time to get back to normal. Chase is a stubborn man, though. He's not going to be satisfied until he's back to his old self."

At that moment, Harry came up to us with a plate of food piled high with meatballs, cheese cubes and potato chips. "So, when do you think you'll be back to work, Mitzi?"

We both stared at him, the picture of denial, eating meatballs off a toothpick.

"Harry, have you actually *looked* at Mitzi lately?" I asked.

He eyed her. "She's hard to miss."

"Do you think a woman in her condition will be ready to go back to work anytime in the near future?"

Harry stared at her longingly, obviously trying to

think of some way he could reduce Mitzi to a more manageable size. "No…"

At that moment, Kim scrabbled onto the foot of Mitzi's bed with me. It's a good thing petite Mitzi has a penchant for oversize furniture. "I have the best news to tell you! I was going to wait until midnight and make it the first official announcement of the new year, but I can't wait any longer."

She clapped her hands together and radiated happiness that I could virtually feel three feet away. "Kurt and I got the word. We're heading for China next week! The information about our baby, a little girl, came today.

"They sent photos," Kim babbled. "She's so incredibly beautiful. You just won't believe it. Her mouth is a perfect pink bow, and…" Tears began to roll down her cheeks. "I'm already in love."

Our squeals of delight drew everyone else to the bed.

We managed a group hug, Kim, Mitzi and I. Not easy, considering it now involves seven people. I'm really going to like it when my arms are long enough to reach past my abdomen again.

"How long will you be gone?" Betty asked.

"A month, maybe. We don't know for sure. We'll bring her home as soon as we can, but the wheels of government turn slowly."

"A month?" Harry whimpered, but we ignored him.

"Tell us more," Betty demanded. "We want to hear everything."

Everyone else gathered around Kim, but Harry grabbed me by the sleeve and pulled me into a corner, his expression distraught. "You know what this means, don't you? You can't have your baby until Kim returns from China. A temp can handle Mitzi's work, but you're irreplaceable! Just plan to put the baby on hold till Kim gets back."

"Harry." I laid my hands on the large shelf I've grown. "Babies don't work that way. You can't put them on hold. If Kim is back in a month, we should be okay, but if my baby comes early…"

He paled.

Poor Harry. He hates reality.

"It can't come early!"

"You're talking to the wrong person." I pointed to my belly. "Tell it to the one who's in charge of that. Talk to the tummy, Harry. Talk to the tummy."

Harry moped off like a little boy who couldn't get his own way, but the rest of the celebration went into full swing at Kim's news. At midnight, Mitzi decreed that we would all wear party hats and blow on noisemakers. Her New Year's hat was shaped like a crown and decorated with glitter that shed all over her bed. How fitting.

"Happy New Year?" Harry sputtered as the din died away. "How can it be, when everyone is abandoning ship?"

"The Innova ship will keep sailing, Harry. I'm covering the arrangements. I'll get you a new crew."

"I don't want a new crew. I want you," he said, pouting. "I want the old, weird crew that I already have."

Wednesday, January 5

I said goodbye to Kim and Kurt at the airport and watched their plane taxi down the runway and lift into the sky. It's hard to imagine that when they return, they will be new parents to an adorable baby girl. Kurt's sister Elaine was at the airport, too. She's the lucky one who inherited Wesley for the month his parents will be gone.

I might have taken him to my place if I weren't pregnant and didn't have a very weak husband at home demanding much of my time.

"Bye-bye, Wes, darling. Come see Auntie Whitney soon, okay?"

Wesley, who was entranced by a toy airplane Kim had purchased for him in the gift shop, looked up at me. "Go to your house now?"

"Not now. Later. When Uncle Chase feels better, okay?"

"Unca Chase sick?"

"He has been, sweetie, but he's feeling better now."

I tipped my head upward. *Thanks.*

"Did you give them a proper send-off?" Chase was sitting up when I arrived at the house. The cats have been hanging on him like moss on a tree since he's come home from the hospital, but he never shoos them away.

He has a new appreciation for every living thing, he says, including the antic pair trying to swallow the fringe on the blanket throw on his lap.

I have a new appreciation, too. I take nothing for granted—especially not Chase.

"Kim was giddy, and Kurt couldn't quit smiling. Even Wesley didn't act up when they left."

"A good sign."

"He still doesn't get what's going on. He talks about his new baby in the same tone he discusses his new Duplo set."

"I imagine the baby will upset his world slightly more than the Duplo's," Chase said drily.

"Speaking of 'upsets,' how are you feeling this afternoon?"

"Like I've been run over by a street sweeper, thank you very much." He gave a frustrated little sound. "I'm going to have much more compassion for my patients after this."

"You've always been compassionate."

"Not nearly enough." He reached for my hand. "I thought I was a goner, Whit."

I swallowed the tears that threatened. "I know."

"Life takes on new meaning when you think you might be at the end of it. For one thing, it turns your priority list on its head."

We've had several conversations like this as Chase has processed what happened to him. To his credit, he hasn't taken a "Why me?" attitude about his illness. Instead, he's trying to find the good in what transpired.

"For one thing," he said, a grin breaking across his face, "I decided to hire someone to do the yard work this year—and someone to paint the basement, too. I'm not wasting anymore time on things that don't involve you, our family, friends, my patients or God. It's the relationships that count, not things.

"And I will never again leave my feelings for people unspoken." His inky blue eyes bored into mine. "I love you, Whitney. I'll try to show you that for the rest of our lives, but I doubt you'll ever really know how much."

He laid his hand on my abdomen, and our baby decided to do a head-butt into his hand. "I love you, too, little one. Don't be jealous."

Chapter Forty

Wednesday, January 26

If it's not one sort of crisis, it's another.

Bryan, who has been gaining weight right along with Mitzi and me, has otherwise settled down on the pregnancy front. He did, however, come to work this morning looking as though he'd caught his head in a blender. His hair was mussed and he had at least a dozen nicks from shaving. His shirt was misbuttoned so that there was one buttonhole hanging loose at the neck, and his tie was draped around his collar as if he'd forgotten to knot it.

The new temp taking Mitzi's place is a girl named Lisa. She doesn't say too much, but she's always observing the goings-on in the office. When Mitzi returns, Lisa will probably leave, quit her job, write a book about us and make a million bucks. It would have to be fiction, of course, because nobody in his right mind would believe what goes on in our office is anything but fiction.

I also have floaters coming in to pick up the slack in the office. I think Innova will be just fine.

"Something wrong?" I inquired of Bryan as I observed Lisa out of the corner of one eye.

"How much weight do pregnant women usually gain?" Bryan asked.

"I can't answer that. I don't believe anyone has admitted their true poundage outside a doctor's office, and physicians are sworn to confidentiality. Why?"

"Jennilee says that if I don't quite gaining weight I'll never fit into a tuxedo."

Lisa's eyebrows disappeared into her hairline.

We have got to get these babies delivered soon—if not for our own sakes, for Bryan's.

"Tuxedo? Are you going to a wedding?"

"Mine." He sounded so despondent that the word didn't quite register at first.

"Yours? As in your very own wedding?"

"That's the one." Prisoners on death row have sounded happier.

"Congratulations! I'm so happy for you. I'll tell Kim next time she calls. That's great news." I studied his expression. "Isn't it?"

"I don't know what's going to happen to me if I get married, Whitney. What if we get pregnant? I don't think I can handle another pregnancy right now. A guy can't take too many pregnancies in a row, you know. It's not healthy."

Lisa's jaw slackened, and her fingers slowed on the computer keys.

"Second pregnancies are usually easier than the first, they say, Bryan. I'm sure you won't have nearly as much morning sickness the second time around."

"Could you ask Chase about it for me? Jennilee wants kids right away, and I don't know if I'm up to it."

"Sure. If the doctor gives you the go-ahead, when's the wedding?"

"Sometime in May."

"Cool. I'll see what Chase has to say about your pregnancy. Let me know if there's anything I can help you with for the wedding."

Lisa's mouth fell open, and her hands dropped into her lap.

I'll have to talk to her later. She's never going to get any work done around here if she spends her time eavesdropping.

"I talked to Kim today. Everything is going really well," I told Chase over dinner. "Today they toured with some other families who have come to pick up their children. They went to the Great Wall and Tiananmen Square. They're spending a lot of time with the baby and say she is 'perfect.'"

"When will they be back?"

"She didn't say. When all the paperwork is done, I suppose."

He looked at my astounding shape, all bulges and protruding parts. "Think you can last that long?"

Harry checks on me every day, asking if I've felt any pains or if I need to go to the hospital. The relief on his face when I say "no" is palpable. If I can only hold off until Kim gets back, we may not have to close the office or check Harry into an institution. Otherwise, it's iffy. Business has been good—too good—for a place as short staffed as ours.

I've been racking my brain but I haven't come up with a way to keep everyone happy about our work situation. That's like putting toothpaste back in the tube once it's been squeezed out—messy and nigh on impossible.

Mitzi called today. She's got way too much time on her hands.

"Whitney, have you hired your doula yet?"

"No. I don't even know what a doula is."

"A birthing coach, of course. It's very popular right now. All the stars have one. It's the in thing."

"Nose rings are in, too, Mitzi. I'm not getting one of those, either."

"It's not like that. Women who help other women through labor and delivery have been around forever."

"Why didn't you say that was what you were talking about in the first place?"

"You don't ever read any of those women's magazines I send you, do you? Otherwise you'd know all this. By the way, how's work?"

"Bryan is feeling bloated, the temps are dropping like flies, Harry's having a nervous breakdown. Otherwise, things are great. Oh, yes, and Kim called. They should be home soon."

"Maybe she will make it back in time to save Harry's sanity."

"It will be touch and go." I sighed. "I'm not sure I enjoy being indispensable."

"Well, I certainly know about *that*. In my experience, it's a burden."

There's no way I'm going to ask Mitzi who had ever labeled her "indispensable" in the workplace.

"I'll be in to see you all tomorrow," she said brightly. "I have a doctor's appointment, and Arch said he'd drive me by the office to see you."

"No more bed rest?"

"Yes, but he said it wouldn't hurt if I took a few minutes to say hello. I'll be wearing a new dress I designed. You'll love it."

"Hey, baby, what's new?" Chase greeted me cheerfully when I arrived home from work. He's caught up on reading his medical journals, read all the books he had piled by our bed and even—under duress—put our photos in albums. Recuperation is wearing on him, and he's getting restless. It's a good sign, but Dr. Steele says he isn't ready to return to work quite yet.

"I wish I could send you to work in my place. My feet are killing me."

He gave me a once-over. "Looks like the baby is dropping. Maybe you'll deliver early."

I snuggled against him on the couch. "I've resigned myself to the fact that I'll be pregnant forever. I've come to grips with waddling through life. Don't offer me any false hope. By the way, Mitzi's coming by the office tomorrow afternoon. She has a doctor's appointment at four o'clock."

"So do I." Chase smiled into my eyes. "I'm hoping for permission to do something other than be a couch potato and a scratching post for the cats."

"I'll come home and pick you up."

"Nah, you might miss Mitzi. I'll take a cab."

"Then I'll give you a ride home."

"Great. I'll be in my office." He warded off my

protest. "I won't be working. I am strong enough to read my mail, however. Take your time."

Thursday, January 27

Mitzi appeared at our office on her own two feet and dressed in a black-and-white polka-dot muumuu.

"That's a moo-moo? Looks more like a Holstein to me." Harry has been cranky ever since Mitzi and Kim have been absent from the office. It hasn't helped that the stress has caused more of his hair to fall out. The poor guy must spend twenty minutes a day artfully arranging the hairs on his head for maximum coverage. I jabbed him in the side to keep him quiet.

"You're walking under your own steam! That's great."

"Arch said I could, just this once. Besides, the wheelchair is very tight."

So this is what our little group of Innova mamas has come to. Outgrowing wheelchairs, zipping off to the Orient to pick up a beautiful China doll, and me, permanently pregnant me.

"You look fabulous, Mitzi," I told her, and I meant it. Her eyes glisten with happiness, and she radiates joy. Between God and these babies, Mitzi is a changed woman. After they're born, all we can do is hope and pray she doesn't change back.

Harry disappeared into his office, and Bryan and Lisa took off for a meeting with a prospective client. That left Arch, Mitzi, Betty and me alone in the office.

I was showing her the changes we'd made to the break room when Mitzi suddenly froze. Her head came up, and her hands went to the sides of her dress.

"We finally replaced the coffeemaker when Harry dropped the pot on the floor and broke it. It was so old, the man at the store said I'd have to look in an antique shop to find another like it…. Mitzi, what is it?"

"I…I don't know." Her eyes darted from side to side, and she pulled at her dress. Then she screamed. "What's going on?"

Arch grabbed for her and eased her into a chair. "Where does it hurt, honey?"

"Nowhere."

"Then what is it?"

I cleared my throat. "Arch, I think Mitzi's water may just have broken."

He looked wide-eyed at me, and then at the telltale dampness around them. "Honey, she's right. We're going to have our babies today!"

"Babies? Now?" Even with all these months to get used to the idea, Mitzi sounded shocked that it might actually happen.

"Are you feeling any contractions?"

"No. Just a little backache, that's all."

"We'd better get you to the hospital, honey. It's time."

So Mitzi did the most efficient and prudent thing a mother in labor could do. She fainted. Arch and I tried to rouse her so she could get to the car under her own steam, but she refused to be roused.

She came to in the ambulance on the way to the hospital.

"What's that awful noise?" she mumbled irritably when she awoke.

"The siren. We're almost to the hospital." Arch

looked worse than Mitzi. He had begged me to ride to the hospital with them.

"Why didn't you just drive me there?" Mitzi demanded.

I let Arch tell her that she'd been too heavy to carry to the car.

"This is ridiculous. I don't need to be on a stretcher, tearing down the freeway at a hundred miles an hour. Honestly, Arch, you are just too— Ow!" Her eyes got big. "Owww!"

Arch glanced at his watch. "Tell me when the next contraction starts and I'll time you. We'll see how far apart they are."

"I'm not going to have anymore. The babies will do better if they're not born for another week or two. Owww…"

"Good luck, Mitzi. Stopping contractions is like trying to stop the tide."

"Maybe if I held my breath…" She puffed out her cheeks like a chipmunk.

I counted to ten. Mitzi let out a scream that curdled milk in every dairy case within two miles. *"Noooo…"*

By the time we got to the hospital, the distinguished and elegant Dr. Jekyll side of Mitzi's personality had been fully replaced by the despicable Mr. Hyde.

Chapter Forty-One

As she was rolled into the emergency room, Mitzi had another contraction and emitted a scream the likes of which I've never heard except on large roller coasters. Her wail crescendoed and trailed off, masterful, operatic and terrifying to the other young mother who was being admitted at the same time. "If that's what I'm in for, get me out of here, I've changed my mind," her face said.

I leaned toward the woman. "Don't worry, she's always this dramatic. You should see her with a toothache."

While Arch was filling out forms, Mitzi was insisting to whoever would listen, "I'm dying, you know, and none of you are paying any attention. After I'm gone, my husband will sue this hospital. Won't you, Arch? *Owww...*"

At least the contractions distracted her from her legal machinations and reminded her that she wasn't dead yet.

She reached out and clutched my arm with such force I thought it might snap. "You're my friend, you believe me, don't you, Whitney?"

"I believe…"

I was going to say, "I believe you think you're dying, but it's not likely," but I didn't get that out before Mitzi grasped it as if it was her last hope.

"I knew you would. I want *you* to come into the birthing room with me. I need someone who *believes* me at my side." She glared at the nurse until the woman took a step backward.

"I'll be there with you, honey," Arch assured her. "And you aren't dying, you're just in labor."

Now *that* was the wrong thing to say.

"'Just in labor'? Is that like 'just' having bamboo stuck under my fingernails?" She gave him a glare that could freeze water. "This is all your fault and I'm not speaking to you anymore."

I pictured Mitzi and Arch cooing over each other the last time I'd seen them together. How quickly they forget.

"Now, honey…"

The nurse moved to Mitzi's wheelchair and started toward a birthing room.

"Whitney, *you* come with me," Mitzi ordered.

"Me? You've got Arch and your doula…."

She turned to glower at her husband. "You *did* call her, didn't you?"

For the first time, Arch looked worried. "I…uh… forgot."

"How can she help me give birth if she doesn't know I'm doing it? Go call her. Whitney, come with me."

I must have hesitated, because she added, "Now."

We set off down the hall, with me swept helplessly along in Mitzi's torrent.

"How do I look? Is my makeup smudged? There's a compact in my purse. Owww."

And so it went for the next hour. Mitzi alternated between vocalizations and worrying about her hair, her makeup and the ugly hospital gown the nurse and Arch had forced her to wear.

Then Arch made another fatherly faux pas that almost got him kicked out of the room. He started to take pictures.

At first, Mitzi, absorbed in a contraction and paying no attention to anyone in the outside world, didn't realize what he was doing. By the time she saw him, he already had enough blackmail photos to last a lifetime— Mitzi with her eyes shut and her mouth wide open, Mitzi stuffing her arm into her mouth, Mitzi stuffing *my* arm into her mouth, Mitzi's belly rising above the bed like Mt. Rainier over Seattle. Arch, of course, was blissfully unaware that he was committing marital suicide.

"What do you think you're doing? Put that thing down. I don't want anyone seeing me like... *Owww...*"

"It's okay, honey. You're doing great." He took one hand off the camera and stroked her hair. "You are doing just fine. The nurse says you're moving right along."

"Don't touch my hair." Mitzi's tone was low and dangerous, like that of a suspicious Rottweiler.

"Don't be silly, honey. You love it when I stroke your hair."

"Don't touch my hair."

I can't believe how oblivious men can be. Arch still didn't get it.

Then Mitzi bared her fangs.

"Don't touch my hair!"

Arch stepped back, puzzled.

"Women get a little sensitive sometimes, Arch." I said. "This is one of them. Apparently it bothers Mitzi when you pat her hair."

"At least you understand me, Whitney. Arch, you are no help at all," Mitzi said through gritted teeth.

He looked baffled. "But hair is a dead protein, Mitzi. It doesn't have any feeling. I can't see why…"

Don't go there, Arch. Quit being a doctor. Keep quiet. You're in big enough trouble as it is.

Mitzi was about to attack when, much to everyone's relief, a competent-looking woman with short gray hair breezed into the room. The tension leaked from Arch's body, and I saw his lips form the words *Thank you.* His reprieve had arrived.

"Hi, Mitzi," the woman said pleasantly. "I see you got started without me. How are you doing? What can I get you?"

The atmosphere in the room changed instantaneously. The thunderstorm abated, and the sun came out.

"I'm Ellen," the woman said by way of introduction as she busied herself rearranging Mitzi's pillows. "I'm Mitzi's doula and birthing coach. Looks like you've been doing a fabulous job here, but now I can give you a break. Arch, you look a little pale. Would coffee help? By the way, if you think you need reinforcements, I could introduce you to my friend, another doula. Her name is Molly Cassidy. Her client's baby came so fast that she's available." Ellen glanced at Mitzi. "You know, just in case."

In case Mitzi's even harder to handle than they imagined, I presume.

Now that she was here, I could squirm out of Mitzi's

grasp. I was happy to hand Mitzi off into such capable hands. Arch appeared overjoyed to hand Mitzi off to anyone at all.

"I'll check on you later," I told Mitzi before I left the room. "I'll be praying for you."

Mitzi looked at me with genuine consternation in her eyes. "Do you think I'm dying, Whitney? I never expected it to be like this."

"Mitzi, you are fabulous. I know this is harder than having your teeth cleaned, but you did live through that."

Her expression cleared. "I did, didn't I? I hate having my teeth cleaned. Owww…"

By the time I walked from the hospital to Chase's office in the adjoining clinic, my back ached and my legs felt watery. The baby was pounding on my insides as if I'd handed it a sledgehammer.

When I reach his office, I staggered in and slumped into the closest chair.

He looked up from his desk and smiled at me. The angles of his face are sharper now, and the absence of his golden tan makes his eyes seem even bluer.

"You look good sitting there," I commented, "where you belong."

"It feels good, Whit, to be on this side of the desk. I don't want to spend anymore time being a patient, if I can help it."

"Are you tired?"

"A little." He studied me. "You, however, look exhausted."

"I should be. I've been in a birthing room helping Mitzi through labor."

"What?" He nearly bolted out of his chair.

"She went into labor while she was at the office. Arch insisted I go with them in the ambulance, so my car is still at Innova."

"What made you call an ambulance?"

"We couldn't carry her. The woman weighs a ton, and she was out cold."

I related the whole story, and it was all he could do not to laugh out loud. "Arch ranks somewhere lower than dirt right now, but the doula she hired is amazing. Maybe I should consider someone like her. What do you think?"

"Will you let me take pictures of you in labor?"

"Not on your life."

"Touch your hair?"

"The jury is still out."

"Then maybe you'd better hire one for me. If I can't stay busy, I may need her more than you."

I moved close and stroked his cheek with the back of my hand. "Want to get a bite to eat? Maybe I can ask Harry or Bryan to give us a ride. It will take them a little time to get here."

"Cafeteria food? That's the only thing I haven't missed while I've been away. Let's go."

I stirred my straw in the dregs of a strawberry shake and watched the people at the tables around us. "I wonder how Mitzi is doing."

"We can check on her before our ride gets here. I'm surprised you caught both Harry and Bryan working late."

"Neither of them goes home much before eight or nine these days. The office has exploded with business while Mitzi and I are just plain exploding."

When I was born, Mom said the doctor wasn't all that happy to have Dad in the delivery room. Now entire families visit the lucky lady in labor, as casually as if she were demonstrating the best way to fold a veggie wrap or entertaining them with magic tricks.

Chase rapped on the door of her room, and when Arch answered, he invited us in to see the show.

"She's doing great," Arch said. "We're hoping the babies will be born naturally. The doc says they're all good-sized, and he thinks their lungs will be fully developed. Amazing, isn't it? Mitzi was born to give birth. No complications, and bringing them in close to term. What a girl."

He sounded like a sportscaster praising a quarterback or a winning racehorse.

By the look of her, though Arch might be willing, Mitzi didn't appear ready to do this again any time soon.

She'd forgotten all about her hairdo. Her dark hair was plastered to her skull, her makeup had disappeared, and she was chewing on ice chips like a beaver in a hurry to shore up a dam. While her eyes rolled in her head, her doula calmly rubbed her back and told her what a good job she was doing.

I took Chase's hand. "She's busy. We'll stop back later. Besides, this is too close for comfort. Maybe I don't want to know everything that happens in labor. It will spoil the surprise."

Chase clapped Arch on the back and I waved at Mitzi and gave her a thumbs-up. She either smiled or snarled, I'm not sure which.

My cell phone rang in the elevator.

"Hey, Whit, it's Harry. Bryan and I are in the lobby."

"We're on our way down. Why did Bryan come with you?"

"I didn't dare leave him at the office alone. Once he heard Mitzi was in labor, he fell apart. I thought that if I brought him along with me, he wouldn't pass out and hit his head on a desk or something."

"You could check him in," I offered. "I think there are some rooms open in obstetrics."

"Ha, ha. Very funny." Then Harry's phone clattered to the floor and I heard him yell, "Don't you dare faint, Bryan. I'll fire you if you faint!"

"Oh, dear. I think Bryan's giving birth in the lobby."

"That will draw a crowd," Chase said with a chuckle. "I'm sure glad I'm well enough to be here to enjoy this."

"When you married me, you married into a bunch of loonies, didn't you?"

He pulled me toward him. "I love loonies. Don't you know that by now?"

When we reached the main floor, Bryan was sitting in a lobby chair, panting. Harry was sitting by him, fanning him with a five-year-old hunting magazine.

"Pull yourself together, man. You aren't the one having the baby!"

Bryan didn't look convinced.

"Mitzi is doing beautifully," I assured him. "You'd be proud of her." No need to alarm him with details. "Thanks for coming to get us. I need to get home and put my feet up. My back is killing me. Oh!"

My knees nearly collapsed under me. Chase, Bryan and Harry all reached out to catch me. Even Bryan forgot his own troubles for a minute as the three of them eased me into a chair.

"I must have put my back out," I assured them. "Strange. I've never had anything like this happen before." I rubbed my lower back to ease the pain, but it didn't relieve it much. "Maybe an ice pack would help. Or heat. Which is it, Chase?"

My husband stared at me strangely. "Whit, are these pains steady, or are they coming and going?"

"Coming and going, I guess. I haven't been paying much attention. Why?"

"You may be having back labor, honey."

"Labor? I'm not due for three weeks yet. Don't be silly." Then a cramp wrapped itself from my spine to my belly button. I panted until it passed. "Or maybe you're right."

Bryan whimpered and tipped sideways in his chair.

At that moment, Dr. Steele strode through the hospital lobby and headed directly for Chase. "What are you doing here? You should be home resting." Then he looked at me as another cramp rippled through me. "Oh. So that's why you're here. Have you called a nurse?"

"It just started," Chase said, "but it seems to be moving fast. I'll find a wheelchair…."

"Oh, no, you don't. You need to be in one, not pushing it. You look exhausted. Frankly, you *all* look exhausted."

Dr. Steele was right. I don't know who looked as though he needed attention more, Chase or Bryan.

"I'll push you in a wheelchair, Chase," I offered. "I'm fine, really."

Now four pairs of eyes glared at me. "Okay, I'd love a ride."

Dr. Steele called a nurse to take me upstairs. Then he

forced Chase to sit in a wheelchair, as well, and took the helm of that one himself, leaving Harry to push Bryan's chair after us as Bryan moaned and clutched his stomach.

Chapter Forty-Two

Giving birth is one of those things that sounds good in theory and can be remembered fondly in retrospect but cannot be enjoyed while it is taking place. Under the best of circumstances—dim lights, soft music and a tranquil environment—it might be pleasant enough…if one enjoys being ripped part by semis pulling in opposite directions. But mine weren't the best of circumstances.

By the luck of the draw, I was assigned the birthing room next to Mitzi's and had to put up with her alternating invectives and endearments toward Arch as her labor progressed. Not only that, I could hear Bryan's whimpers and moans as Harry walked him back and forth in the hallway to keep him from curling into a fetal position on the tile outside my door.

Dr. Steele knocked on my door and stepped inside. "Sorry to bother you, but I have a suggestion I'd like you to consider. Chase isn't ready for any marathons yet. To give him a break, I'd like you to meet Molly Cassidy. She's a doula. Would you mind if I asked her to assist you? She can run for ice chips and rub your back, Whitney, so Chase can sit down if he feels the need."

Chase opened his mouth to refuse, but I beat him to the punch. "I think it's a great idea. That way, I won't have to spend energy worrying that Chase is doing too much."

Dr. Steele beamed approvingly at me. He stepped into the hall and came back with a pretty red-haired woman.

"Hello, I'm Molly Cassidy." She shook my hand, and I felt comforted. Here was someone who knew the ropes of this baby-birthing thing. I liked her immediately.

Then my entire cheering squad arrived to join the fun. Harry's wife brought Betty with her. My parents broke away from a dinner party to come and greet their new grandchild, who was, unfortunately, hanging on to one of my ribs and refusing to come out. Jennilee arrived to help Harry with Bryan. By the time everyone arrived, the only ones missing were Kim and Kurt and Chase's cousin Adam and his wife, Cassia, who surely would have been there if they hadn't been on a plane to Africa.

"Whatever happened to completely *un*natural delivery? Drugs? Painkillers? Unconsciousness and 'wake me up when it's over?'" I hissed to Chase as he held my hand and timed the contractions, which were quickly building up steam.

"You wanted a natural birth, honey. This is it."

Molly chuckled sympathetically and managed to find that muscle in my back that desperately needed massaging. "Look at it this way. Women have been doing this for centuries. It's the most natural of acts."

"I had no idea," I panted. "When I think of nature, I think of flowers budding and soft rain. I'm going to write a letter to the nature channel and complain about false advertising as soon as I get home."

"You forgot about volcanic eruptions and flesh-eating plants, that's all," Chase said. "You always look at the bright side of life. Lots of pregnant women forget that 'natural' and 'easy' are not always the same thing."

He stood up and offered me some ice chips. I'd been begging for an iced cappuccino for an hour, but no one had paid any attention.

"Chase," I gasped between contractions that were less than two minutes apart, "I want to take this opportunity to tell you how much I love you and to ask you to ignore anything I might say later as these contractions get stronger. I mean, you can still live in our house and everything."

He laughed and kissed my forehead. "Don't worry. I won't take it personally. I've got Arch as a role model. He's been holding up pretty well, considering that so far Mitzi had fired him as her husband, banished him from her life and asked for a firing squad."

I was pulled into another contraction then, one harder and longer than before. Chase glanced at the fetal monitor and whistled. "Your seismographic readings are getting stronger, honey. I think something may be happening."

"*You* think?" I panted frantically. "You should try being me."

I felt like a pastry tube being squeezed dry, but didn't have the breath to say it.

"I think we're making progress," Molly announced brightly. "We should have new baby Adams pretty soon."

For some reason, that surprised me. "We will? Soon?"

Molly smiled and started moving things around in the room, making way for the carts and trays and people who would be arriving. Soon my room, which had appeared to be a small suite in a decent hotel, would become a regular emergency room.

A knock on the door drew Chase away. When he came back, he was shaking his head. "Bryan heard Mitzi's first baby cry, and he passed out. He hit his head on the lunch cart an aide was pushing by and cracked open his head. They're wheeling him off somewhere to sew him up."

"Mitzi's first baby?"

Chase picked up my hand and held it to his lips. "A little boy."

"And the others?"

"Still coming." He grinned wickedly at me. "If you hurry, maybe you could beat her."

I opened my mouth to tell him what a ridiculous idea that was, but a crushing pressure around my midsection took my breath away.

Chase's eyes widened. "Hey, I was just kidding, honey."

"A couple more like that and we'll be meeting our newest citizen," a calm voice said from behind me.

"Hey, doc," Chase said. "Welcome to the party."

"Quite a party it is." A kindly looking man in his sixties with twinkling eyes above his face mask came into view. "How are you, Whitney?"

"Busy." It's hard to talk while I'm gritting my teeth, I discovered, grateful to see that my physician had arrived. Things were getting a little out of hand, as far as I was concerned.

"I see that." He glanced at the monitor. "Looks like something should be happening here soon…"

I was gripped in a cataclysmic spasm that knocked everything out of my head but the pain itself. I clutched Chase's hand and wondered if it was possible for me to break his bones if I squeezed too hard. He didn't even flinch. As the pain subsided, I heard Dr. Johnson's calm voice. "I think we're going to let you push pretty soon, Whitney. I'll tell you when."

Push? Push what?

Oh, push *that*...

Friday, January 28

"She's perfect, isn't she, Chase?" I stared at the pink-and-white bundle in my arms. I couldn't get enough of that sweet, tiny face. It was after midnight, but I had no desire to sleep.

"Couldn't be more so." He sat at the foot of my bed with such a loving expression on his features that it made me want to weep.

The baby, all six pounds two ounces of her, squirmed, stretched and wrinkled her face into a funny little grimace. I watched in fascination, now able to pick out those parts that had been kicking and punching at me from the inside these past few months.

"How can people not people believe in God?" I murmured. "Especially after seeing this."

"I haven't figured that out," Chase admitted. "My job is to work with the human body, and every day I am amazed at its intricacies and complexities, its ability to heal itself and to adapt. To think that *this*—" and he reached out to touch Miriam Joy "—was all unplanned and not an act of the divine is beyond me."

Miriam—the name is the Hebrew form of Mary—was the sister of Moses and Aaron. In scripture she had her ups and downs, and she had the funkiest babysitting job in all of history, but God loved her. The joy part speaks for itself.

"And Mitzi has this times three."

Chase chuckled. "I've never seen a more stunned set of parents than those two were when the nurses handed them all three little boys. Arch looked as though he'd had a door slammed in his face, and Mitzi held one in each arm and tears ran down her cheeks until the babies' blankets grew wet. It was quite a sight."

"I'm surprised. I thought she might have had a hard time accepting all boys. She desperately wanted a girl, you know."

I could almost hear her yelling at Arch, "But I *asked* for girls!"

Shopping Queen meets *Monday Night Football.* I could see the problems already. Frogs in their pockets. Runny noses wiped on the sleeves of small designer rugby shirts. Three against one.

Mitzi named the babies Ethan, Andrew and Oliver.

"By the way," Chase commented as he stroked Miriam's downy head, "I overheard Mitzi tell Arch that she would be picking out the boys' wives. Miriam and Kurt and Kim's baby are already prime candidates. If you don't want Mitzi to be Miriam's mother-in-law, you'd better start campaigning against the idea early."

Already the trauma of motherhood has begun. Mistakenly I'd thought I'd have a few years before I had to worry about boyfriends.

"I suppose I'd better go home, feed the cats and let

you rest." He yawned and stretched. "Harry drove your car to the hospital so I could drive it home."

"How's Bryan?"

"Other than a headache from knocking himself out on the food cart, he's fine. No more pains or nausea. I think he's going to recover from the births a lot more quickly than you and Mitzi."

He took our sleeping baby from my arms and laid her in the bassinet beside my bed. "And now it's your turn to sleep."

I lay awake long after he left, remembering the gentleness of his lips against mine and giving praise for the cluster of miracles I had received.

Friday, January 28

My first surprise of the day arrived before breakfast, when Kim and Kurt walked into my room.

"What are you doing here? Aren't you supposed to be in China?"

"I didn't want to tell you we'd be home today, because I wanted to surprise you," Kim said. "But you went ahead and surprised me more." She bent over the bassinet and stared at the baby who had—impossibly—grown more beautiful overnight. "She's you all over again, Whitney. She's amazing."

"Mitzi has a surprise for you, too."

"So I heard. Arch was at the coffee machine down the hall. He's a happy man." Kim's brow furrowed. "But he looks awful."

"If you'd gone through labor and the delivery of three babies with Mitzi, how do you think you'd look?"

Kurt shuddered. Kim and I both burst out laughing.

"Where's your baby?"

"We've got Kurt's sister and Wesley in the car with her. She's perfect, Whit. Just perfect. In fact, her name is Jiao, which means 'beautiful' in Chinese."

Tears filled Kim's eyes. "God kept his promise from Isaiah, Whitney. 'Do not be afraid, for I am with you. I will bring your children from the east and gather you from the west.'"

God is good. He's *very* good.

"What does Wesley think of the new addition?"

"He's interested, but holding back his final judgment. He would probably have liked a puppy better."

Kim came to my bed and closed her arms around me, resting her cheek on the top of my head. "Can you believe it, Whit? All our prayers were answered, each in a different way."

I hugged her back. "Bryan's, too. Even with a mild concussion, he's feeling much better."

"Concussion?"

"During labor."

"His or yours?"

"Both, sort of."

Kim grinned and rubbed her hands through her already tousled hair. "It's good to be home."

Saturday, January 31

Mr. Tibble here.

Now she's gone and done it. She's brought home a new kitten. At least I think it's a kitten. It's hairless except for some dark brown fuzz on top of its head. Big, too. It's nearly my size already but not nearly as coordinated. It can't even walk! The thing has a meow like a Siamese. Very grating on the nerves, I might add. Fortunately, they don't let it cry long.

She holds it like she used to hold me. Thankfully, her other pet Chase takes it away from her occasionally so she can play with me.

I think I'll have to bide my time and see how this new cat works out. Maybe she won't like it and will give it away. That's fine with me. More kibble for the rest of us.

Mr. Tibble, signing off.

My mother has completely forgotten about being my older sister and embraced being a grandmother. In fact, she's embraced it so much that I'm having a hard time getting her to go home to my father.

"What do you think the baby should call me? I went online and looked up all the names children call their grandmothers. Gamma, Nana, Mumsy, Gammie, Mee-Maw? Bamma, Mim, Gram?"

"How about Grandma?" The baby isn't tiring me out at all. My other relatives, however, are killing me.

"I really like 'Nana,' don't you?"

"Okay, Nana it is."

"But Mumsy sounds very British, don't you think?"

"Very."

"You're not helping much, dear."

If I were to pick out a name for Mom, I'd choose the

Greek name for grandmother, Ya-Ya. As much as I expect my mother to spoil the baby, Miriam is never going to hear the words *no-no* anyway.

Chapter Forty-Three

Friday, February 11

Miriam and I went to the Innova offices today for a visit. Harry called to say that he was implementing a "brilliant" idea and he wanted Mitzi and me to see what he'd done.

When I got to the office, Mitzi and crew were already there. Her triple stroller, piled high with blankets, toys and clothes was parked just outside the office. She's changed since the babies came. Gone are the heavy makeup, the perfect hair and the designer suits. Her dark hair is usually in a ponytail, lip gloss is her full makeup regime, and jeans are her fashion statement. My kind of girl.

Kim, who is holding down the fort along with Betty and Bryan, met me at the door.

"You're looking relaxed," I told her. "Did you find someone you can trust to watch Jiao?"

Kim smiled complacently. "You could say that."

Most of our conversations these days revolve around

good child care and the stay-at-home/go-to-work debate. I'm surprised at how much I resist the idea of
leaving the baby during the day, even though my mother
is always offering to babysit and has remodeled her
entire house to look like a preschool. I'm just beginning
to realize the power of the mothering instinct and the
deepness of my need to be with my baby. But what
about Harry?

"So what's this new thing Harry has done?" I asked.
"You've been keeping pretty mum about it."

I walked into what had been Innova. It looked as
though a bomb had gone off. The ceiling was open,
Sheetrock was stacked against the walls, and all the
wiring was hanging in loopy strings over our heads.
"What happened?"

"Harry leased the offices next to ours." Kim pointed
to floor plans spread across a desk. "Innova is expand-
ing. When we're done remodeling, we'll each have our
own office. They'll run along three sides of the space,
all facing an open area in the center. There will be a re-
ceptionist's desk there, and space for temps as we need
them. Harry says the business has grown so much that
he has to expand."

"Then what's going to be here?" I pointed to an un-
designated room running the entire width of the space.

"That's the nursery."

"The what?"

"Nursery. It's going to be soundproof. We'll be able
to work and be available for our kids at the same time.
The babies can come to work with us. Harry's also
decided that we can set our own hours. I can work
5:00 a.m. until 1:00 p.m. or noon until eight at night. He

even agreed to job-sharing. Our babies never need to be without a parent on hand. Cool, huh?"

At that moment, Mitzi, Betty and Bryan emerged from the back room, each carrying one of her babies.

"Isn't it great?" Mitzi burbled. "Harry says that a lot of companies provide day care, so he doesn't see why he shouldn't. He's also setting up so that we can work at home when we can't come in."

My relief was so great that it shocked me. It was the best of both worlds. I had the sudden urge to give my little boss a huge squeeze. "Where is he?"

"He'll be back in a minute," Betty said. "I've got treats in the back room."

Betty had laid out a feast of our favorite foods—brownies, lemon bars, cheesecake and chocolate chip cookies. "Help yourself."

"I'll have a lemon bar, please," Mitzi said.

"No brownies?"

She wrinkled her nose. "Ever since I had the babies, I haven't had a taste for chocolate. It's kind of gross, really. I can't imagine why I ever liked it. Hormones, maybe."

"Well, I still like it." I chewed on a brownie and looked around. "I can't believe Harry did this. He's made this into a perfect working environment for young moms. I had no idea he was so full of surprises."

Bryan snickered, and Betty put her hand to her mouth. "You haven't seen all of them yet."

The main door to the office opened and closed, and I recognized Harry's footsteps on the tile. He made a dramatic entrance and stood in the doorway, framed like a postcard, his hair swirling from his head in a curly cloud.

Huh?

He walked in, jaunty pride in his step, and I stared at the bush of curls on the top of his suddenly hirsute head. He wore a glorious curly mop that put all his previous Chia Pet looks to shame. A wig! Harry is hairy again!

I'm on the last page of this journal. It's full now, and I'll have to buy a new one. There's going to be lots to tell as Miriam, Jiao, Ethan, Andrew and Oliver grow. And there will always be things I want to say about Chase—how much I love him and how much I feel loved *by* him.

Mr. Tibble is crazy about my journals, too. He lies on them when I'm not around, as if he can actually *think* his own entries onto the pages. But the most important things I want to write about are God and His faithfulness. Miriam may read my journals one day. If she does, I want her to know about my faith in God and my love for her and for her father. That, after all, is what it's all about.

Whitney, signing off.

* * * * *

QUESTIONS FOR DISCUSSION

1. Whitney manages to maintain friendships with sometimes-difficult people. Do you have them in your life? How do you handle them? What's Whitney's secret?

2. It is said that in order to have friends, you must be a friend. Do you have friends as close to you as Kim and Mitzi are to Whitney? What is the most precious thing about them? How do you make and keep such friends?

3. When Chase is in the hospital, Whitney says that she can't find God. She even wonders if He really exists. Have you experienced this dark night of the soul? If so, what was it that brought you through it? What did you learn about God in the process? What did you learn about yourself?

4. Has one of your loved ones ever faced a serious illness? How did you cope?

5. There is a currently significant debate about stay-at-home mothers vs. working mothers. What are your feelings about this topic? Is Harry's solution for his employees a good one?

6. If you have ever been pregnant, what is the funniest thing that happened to you during this time?

7. How would you feel about having a birthing coach?

8. Whitney delights in her relationship with God, and many of her prayers are much like conversing with an old friend. She consults him and talks with Him all day long. How do you relate to Whitney's connection with God? What is yours?

9. Would you ever consider an overseas adoption as Kim did? Why or why not?
10. Mitzi will have her hands full raising triplet boys. What advice would you give her?

—

Turn the page for a sneak preview of
SLEEPING BEAUTY
by Judy Baer,
available in October 2007 from Love Inspired.

I felt pulled up from a groggy fog, my head swimming and my legs heavy, and stared in horror at the clock on the bedside table. 8:00 a.m.! I must have dozed off again after I dressed for my interview and now, instead of being early, I would be lucky to be only a few minutes late. Not a good start for a job interview.

I scrambled up, grabbed my purse and briefcase and went to the hotel door where I was met with the obstacle course I'd built for myself the night before. I'm a sleepwalker, and I hadn't wanted to chance a nighttime stroll before my big interview. With strength born of frantic dismay, I hurled aside the suitcase, the chair, the garbage can and whatever else I'd managed to stack into the heap in front of the door. If I lost this job because I'd managed to blockade myself into my hotel room and couldn't get out....

The clatter I'd made should have awakened the dead, to say nothing of the people in the rooms on either side of or across from me, but perhaps they, unlike me, were already at their appointments.

I flung open the door and hesitated. It seemed to me that the hotel was cleverly built to resemble honeycombs, which left me confused. Just what I needed right now, a labyrinth to navigate. Willing myself not to scream in frustration, I walked to the left, trying to retrace my steps of the evening before. Where was an early-morning maid when I really needed one? If I'd *wanted* to sleep in today, at least three would have knocked on my door by now, singing out, "Maid service." But when I absolutely had to be up, the place was silent as a tomb. The only sound was a spill of fresh ice tumbling somewhere inside the ice machine down the hall.

Ice machine. That was it. It was not far from the elevators. I headed toward the low grumble of the machine.

I moved quickly, my heart thumping hard, my briefcase clutched to my chest. If I couldn't make it to headquarters on time, how would they ever trust me to get to important appointments or meet significant clients? Seeing my job promotion slipping away into the ether, I finally found the ice machine. I was so nervous that my mouth felt like sawdust. There wouldn't be time to stop at a coffee cart for something to drink, so impulsively I plunged my hand into the ice bin, plucked out a cube and popped it into my mouth. At least now my tongue would not stick to the roof of my mouth as I was meeting the CEO of my company.

Now where was that elevator again?

I turned and ran full force into a wall.

A warm, not unpleasantly hard wall, but a wall nonetheless. I pushed at it, but it wouldn't move. I tried to step around it, and it stepped with me. I attempted to shoulder it out of my way with no success. Finally, I made a fist and tried to punch my way past and elicited a small "Uh" from it. As I drew my elbow back and curled my hand into a tighter fist, the wall grabbed my wrist. No matter how hard I wrestled, its grip was implacable. Trapped! Just like something out of an Edgar Allen Poe story! No matter which way I moved, the wall was in front of me.

Terrified, I did the only thing I knew to do, I opened my mouth to scream.

Suddenly a hand clapped over my mouth, and I felt myself being propelled along the hallway so quickly that my feet barely touched the ground. I was being kidnapped! Immediately, my mind went to some of the terrible things that would no doubt happen to me. My poor parents. They'd probably never know what became of me. And Darla! She would feel so responsible. What would my company think? They'd flown me here to offer me a significantly higher position in the firm. Would they believe I'd run off? My reputation would be ruined. Of course, what's a good reputation if I'm spirited away and kept prisoner in some madman's basement?

I began to pray Psalm 5:11. *Help me! You are the only One who can get me out of this! Let the elevator door open and a janitor or a maid find us. You are my Protector. Spread protection over me that, like David, I may rejoice in You....*

Right where I was, I dropped to my knees and prayed.

And that was where I was when I began to wake up, on my knees in one of the small meeting rooms the hotel provided, praying out loud as the incredibly handsome man I'd seen in the restaurant last night sat in the chair across from me, a cup of coffee in one hand, calmly watching me as if he dealt with frantic, maniacal sleepwalkers every day.

My hands were wet from the now-melted ice cubes, and I realized that I was not dressed for the day in my business suit at all but still in my sheep-and-cloud pajamas. What I'd thought was my briefcase was actually my makeup kit. I'd squeezed it so hard that the cap had come off my toothpaste and was oozing out the top like mint-green glue. The clock on the wall said 3:00 a.m.

Well, God had protected me, all right. He'd protected me from running into the street and being hit by a cab. He had not protected me, however, from profound humiliation and intense mortification, the likes of which— even in all my years of sleepwalking and waking in odd situations—I'd never before experienced.

Instead of looking shocked and horrified, however, the gentleman—whose white shirt, even at 3:00 a.m. was completely unwrinkled and crisp—looked mildly interested and not the least surprised by the raving mess he'd found eating cubes out of a hotel ice machine.

"Are you waking up?" he inquired calmly, gently.

I groaned and rocked forward on my knees to bury my face in my hands. All I wanted to do was to disappear into the carpet. "Yes. Just check me into an institution now. If it walks like a duck and it quacks like a duck, it must be a duck. If it walks like a psycho and yammers like a psycho, it must be a psycho. I am so embarrassed that I want to die."

"No need for that. I understand." He stood up and offered me his hands. I scrambled to my feet and was momentarily glad that my flannel jammies were the least revealing items in my entire wardrobe. I stumbled close to him as I rose and caught a whiff of some delicious, elegant shaving lotion.

His eyes, dark and astute, were also kind. I felt compassion from his every pore. Both amazed and startled by his unusual response, I allowed him to lead me to a sofa and settle me in one corner. He pulled up a chair and sat across from me.

If possible, he was even better-looking up close. Firm jawline, intelligent eyes, finely shaped mouth, a high forehead over which dark hair feathered. Then he smiled, and I thought my heart might leap out of my body through my throat—not the kind of man I (or any woman) would choose as a witness to her embarrassment.

Too late. I should have crawled under the rug when I was down on my knees.

"I am s-so s-sorry," I stammered. "I'm sure you think I'm certifiable and should be locked up immediately, but I'm not, really. It's just that I'm…"

"Suffer from parasomnia? You obviously have a REM sleep disorder of some sort. Sleepwalking is nothing to be ashamed of. Granted, it's embarrassing, but hardly within your control."

"You know about…me?" Relief sprang within me, relief that someone understood. I was also hopeful. I had not sent this Adonis of a man off screaming for help and demanding the demented woman wandering the hallways be hauled away.

"Not you in particular, but I recognize your behavior. Many people with parasomnia have nocturnal dramas such as yours—or much worse."

"Worse?"

"Oh, yes. I've been involved in more than one court case explaining how perfectly sane and rational people can begin to exhibit aggressive dream enactments. Murders, even."

"Who are you, anyway?" I was beginning to feel I'd awakened from one dream only to find myself in another.

"I'm sorry, I didn't introduce myself." He smiled at me in a way that activated every nerve fiber in my body. "Dr. David Grant. I'm a neurologist and administrator of a new institute for brain research and sleep disorders."

Institute, institution. Brain disorders. The perfect guy for me.

"Do you always wander the halls of hotels at 3:00 a.m. rescuing sleepwalkers?"

He laughed, a pleasant rumble deep in his chest. When he smiled, his expression dissolved into smile lines around his eyes. "Purely accidental. I've been overseas, and my inner time clock isn't working properly. After the restaurant closed, I found an all-night coffee shop. I'm a people watcher, so it was good entertainment."

"The restaurant…." I mumbled.

"Yes. I noticed you there with your friend."

"You did?" I hoped he hadn't overheard us behaving like silly school girls. Wait until I tell Darla I met this man of our dreams! And that I met him in my sheep-and-cloud pajamas…eating ice out of a machine… clutching my makeup kit…falling on my knees to pray….

Coming to my senses, I vowed that I would never, *ever,* tell this to Darla or any other living soul. No matter how much fun my friends would have at my expense, I would take this Suze the Sleepwalker story to my grave.

Vanessa Del Fabbro

Set against the dynamic patchwork of South Africa,
The Road to Home is an inspiring story of love,
courage and everyday miracles.

The Road to Home

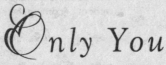

From award-winning author

ROBIN LEE HATCHER

After a lifetime of putting herself last, Shayla Vincent
is finally on the right track. The rustic cabin her aunt left
her is perfect for Shayla's goal of starting her writing career
and spreading His word!

But she hasn't anticpated her feelings for her neighbor
Ian O'Connell, a rugged rancher bringing up his two nieces.
Will she finally put herself first, or will her growing affection
for Ian and his girls place her dreams in jeopardy?

Love Inspired®

Celebrate Love Inspired's 10th anniversary
with top authors and great stories all year long!

A Tiny Blessings Tale

Loving families and needy children continue to
come together to fulfill God's greatest plans!

Look for these six new *Tiny Blessings* stories!

FOR HER SON'S LOVE BY KATHRYN SPRINGER
July 2007

MISSIONARY DADDY BY LINDA GOODNIGHT
August 2007

A MOMMY IN MIND BY ARLENE JAMES
September 2007

LITTLE MISS MATCHMAKER BY DANA CORBIT
October 2007

GIVING THANKS FOR BABY BY TERRI REED
November 2007

A HOLIDAY TO REMEMBER
BY JILLIAN HART
December 2007

Steeple
Hill®

Available wherever you buy books.

RE~~QUEST~~

2 FRE~~E~~
PLUS~~~~
FRE~~E~~
MYST~~~~

YES! Please send me 2 FREE Love Inspired® novels and my 2 FREE mystery gifts. After receiving them, if I don't wish to receive any more books, I can return the shipping statement marked "cancel." If I don't cancel, I will receive 4 brand-new novels every month and be billed just $3.99 per book in the U.S., or $4.74 per book in Canada, plus 25¢ shipping and handling per book and applicable taxes, if any*. That's a savings of 20% off the cover price! I understand that accepting the 2 free books and gifts places me under no obligation to buy anything. I can always return a shipment and cancel at any time. Even if I never buy another book from Steeple Hill, the two free books and gifts are mine to keep forever.

113 IDN EF26 313 IDN EF27

Name	(PLEASE PRINT)	
Address		Apt. #
City	State/Prov.	Zip/Postal Code

Signature (if under 18, a parent or guardian must sign)

Order online at www.LoveInspiredBooks.com

Or mail to Steeple Hill Reader Service™:

IN U.S.A.: P.O. Box 1867, Buffalo, NY 14240-1867
IN CANADA: P.O. Box 609, Fort Erie, Ontario L2A 5X3

Not valid to current Love Inspired subscribers.

Want to try two free books from another series?
Call 1-800-873-8635 or visit www.morefreebooks.com

* Terms and prices subject to change without notice. NY residents add applicable sales tax. Canadian residents will be charged applicable provincial taxes and GST. This offer is limited to one order per household. All orders subject to approval. Credit or debit balances in a customer's account(s) may be offset by any other outstanding balance owed by or to the customer. Please allow 4 to 6 weeks for delivery.

Your Privacy: Steeple Hill is committed to protecting your privacy. Our Privacy Policy is available online at www.eHarlequin.com or upon request from the Reader Service. From time to time we make our lists of customers available to reputable firms who may have a product or service of interest to you. If you would prefer we not share your name and address, please check here. ☐

LIREG07